Effigies of Faith

Book X of The Quietus of Fate

By Brian C. Kershner

ISBN: 1-942082-19-3
ISBN-13: 978-1-942082-19-4

Acknowledgements

As the years pass, and I continue to work on the books in the *Quietus of Fate* series, I reflect back on where everything started and how I have gotten to this point. I'm (more rapidly than I would like to admit) approaching thirty years of work on this series, and while the end of it is in view, the path to that ending still remains uncertain.

Many of these characters were created years ago, some decades ago, and one of the challenges in writing is the idea that your ideas will morph and change outside of your control once they are released into the world. So for example, a certain emperor that appears in these novels who is narcissistic, power-mad, and a misogynist might find himself compared to a certain world leader in real-life. Now as the author I can safely say that in no way did I draw inspiration from that world leader in my creation of Kaitain Lorien, nor has he been shaped by events that have transpired since his creation. Kaitain was written as a counter-point, a mortal with the idea of power that thirsted for more, as compared to other villains that had real power. It's another play on perception versus reality.

But once the books are published and Kaitain is released into the world, the reader determines parallels. And that is partially my fault as the author, because my intention was for my characters to not be rigid but to be flexible and relatable at the need and view of the reader. So as a matter of disclaimer, I will say this. Characters and events in this book, while they may mirror real people in any time period the reader may read these books, I assure you that those parallels are absolutely coincidental.

B.K.

Table of Contents

Chapter 72

Chapter 73

Chapter 74

Chapter 75

Forces of sin and rank desolation,
Born from violence and depredation,
Crawled from the pit of their own damnation,
Their aim destruction and domination.

They rose, like ancient enemies from forgotten tombs,
Unnatural powers at their fingertips,
Turning innocents to monsters on the promise of boons,
Unwitting fuel for the coming apocalypse.

And so the Dark Gods marched,
Only death and devastation left in their wake,
The proud fertile lands of the Creator's love besmirched,
The faithful left to quail and quake.

Until one man stood with the grace of the Creator,
Answering the call of the faithful clarion,
He struck down the vile Dark God's commander,
The Creator's chosen champion Terrik 'Godslayer' Lorien.

> *- The Verses of The Word*
> *From the High Priestess of the*
> *Church of the Creator*

Prologue

Aberrations of Symmetry

Year Four of the Just Emperor Kaitain "Dragonsbane" Lorien,
Creator's Calendar Year 1871

The Plains of Steam had quieted since the massive battle, and the soldiers of the Army of Fire had taken to burying their dead. Though she was being held in custody, because Kiara Aren was a former acolyte of the Church of the Creator, her abilities in the realm of healing were needed. She had been released from her bonds despite her objections and forced into service by a lieutenant who refused to give his name. Jillian would be left alone in one of the tents, still stewing over the loss of Jacqueline and Angelina. From the time they were together after their capture, Jillian had not said a word, and if she had reacted in any way other than to just sit in silence and pain then Kiara had not been privy to it. During her rounds around the camp, Kiara had seen the Amethyst Knight, Tolon Morr stalking around the camp looking for information. A few moments ago, she had seen him push his way into the tent of the leader of the detachment of the Army of Fire; a man whom Kiara had learned was named Arin Chandara. There was something about that name that struck a chord within Kiara, but she couldn't quite place her finger on where she had heard the name before. One thing she did know, and it had nothing to do with the particulars of the man, officers on the level of General Chandara wouldn't like anyone barging in on them, regardless of whether they were members of the Knights of the Flashing Blade or not. Finally Kiara had been able to make her way over to Blade, and though the guards surrounding him had objected, they finally were convinced to allow her to ensure that the prisoner was not wounded. When Kiara knelt beside Blade, he didn't look up immediately, but finally when she placed one of her soft small hands on his cheek to examine a nasty gash that ran from under his right eye across his cheek, he lifted his eyes and found hers. As if it pained him to do so, Blade forced a small smile.

"I guess healers are needed no matter what side they're on," the older man said gruffly.

Kiara smiled softly and reached into her bag for a clean rag and began to tend to his wound.

"There were a lot hurt, not just by the soldiers from Thorigald, but also by the dragons. Lots of collateral damage, and they'll take all of the help they can to make sure that they don't lose more lives than have already been sacrificed."

Blade blew out a long breath, and let his eyes fall back to the ground.

"The only truth of war, my little healer, is that people die. I've been fighting wars longer than you've been an idea in the mind of the Creator, and I can tell you from experience, that most of the men you've patched back together today will end up with a sword in their belly soon enough."

Kiara stopped dabbing at the wound on Blade's face. He could feel her eyes on him, and he could feel the strength and pain in her stare. Finally he looked up and met her bloodshot eyes, knowing the pain that would be inside her from the loss of her fellow dragon hunters, pain that she was trying to work through by healing others.

"But you have to do what you can to make a difference; because those men who survive will be greater for your healing then they ever would have been dying here in this sweltering wasteland."

Kiara's lips parted in to a small, weak smile, and she continued her ministrations. Blade felt a little bad lying to the girl. If things continued going the way they were, nothing that any of them were doing would make much of a difference. Everyone on this world was going to die, and those deaths wouldn't mean any more than the deaths of all the people who were left on Onea when it tore itself apart. Those that were fighting the good fight were equal parts crazy and suicidal. But this time, Blade had promised himself that he would be there in the end, and if Espre was going to go to hell in a bucket, he was going to be one of the people left to hold the handle.

As Kiara continued her work, Blade became aware of commotion around them. He heard weapons drawn by some of the soldiers, while others he saw snap to attention. Others dropped to their knees and began to pray. It was a truly strange response, and then Warron saw two pair of booted feet walking in the direction of the command tent, trailing a group of soldiers behind them. Warron looked up at the on-coming duo, only to feel his heart catch in his throat. His eyes caught those of one of the duo and he could not help the frown that curled his lips.

"Oh no," Warron said in a tone loud enough that only Kiara could hear him, "not him."

* * * * * * * * * * * *

Inside the command tent, everything was frozen. From the position that Tolon was in, even with Dane's increased speed and powers there was a very good chance that he would not be able to prevent the Knight of the Flashing Blade from severing his brother's head from his shoulders. Korrd by his own admission wouldn't have had enough power left to deflect such a blow, and even with his abilities as a swordsman, the chances were slim for survival. The Amethyst Knight was in perfect position for a killing blow, and from what Dane knew about the man, he was certainly to be considered an efficient killer at any range. There was a tickle in the back of Dane's mind and despite himself the look of quiet concern and concentration melted away from his face and he could only smile. In what must have looked like a gesture of supreme arrogance, the smile widened on Dane's face, and he eased himself back into the chair that Korrd had made available for him. Korrd's eyes widened for a moment but the trust in his brother's motives and actions would not allow for a more severe reaction. For the Amethyst Knight however, the action was greeted with the color rising in his cheeks, and his teeth visibly clenching behind tightly drawn lips. The frown had deepened on his face, and it threatened to stretch into a violent sneer. When the tent flap flipped open Tolon's eyes darted to the sudden flood of light but neither he nor Korrd moved a muscle. When Tolon's eyes found the woman's who first entered the tent, he kicked hard with his right foot, sending Korrd skidding across the dusty ground then crouched down low, his body shielding as much of Jerrica's fallen form as he could while still keeping his body and weapon ready for the assault he knew would be coming in a matter of moments. But as the seconds passed, it became more apparent that the assault would not be coming. In fact, the woman though she was looking the Amethyst Knight squarely in the eyes had made no move toward her weapon. Despite that fact, the hairs on the back of Tolon Morr's neck stood on end, his practiced warrior's danger sense alerting him to the growing danger. Mere heartbeats later, another form entered the tent, stepping into the space between the woman and the Amethyst Knight, and though Tolon had never seen the man before, he knew that the danger posed by this new arrival was greater than any he had ever experienced. What irritated Tolon was the fact that the man, though clearly in harm's way, had not even looked in Tolon's direction. Instead, the man's focus was purely on the one named Dane who sat smiling and now shaking his head in the chair on the far side of the tent.

"Just like you to be in the middle of a warzone," the stranger said to Dane. "But then again, at least this time you didn't cause the war."

There was a slight chuckle that escaped Dane's lips as Korrd had regained his composure and knelt near the map table.

"As I recall, starting wars was always your forte."

Finally the stranger looked in Tolon's direction. Instead of reacting to the threat that the man posed, he instead cocked his head to one side and looked first at Tolon and then at Jerrica.

"Don't you have someplace else you need to be?"

Tolon felt his features fall. Whatever grim expression had been painted on his face moments before was now replaced by a combination of puzzlement and annoyance. What did this man know about his mission, about his aims, or about his desires? But then he saw what he could not believe. Strapped across his back was perhaps the most famous of the Sacred Weapons. It was certainly the largest and to be wielded took more than just a master of the sword, but one possessed of such strength and balance that they would be considered a superior warrior in all respects. It had once been the weapon of Gregor Quicksilver, the most renowned member of the Knights of the Flashing Blade now branded a traitor, and now it hung from the back of this seemingly common man. A low growl escaped Tolon's lips and he charged forward with the blade of Strength held high and waiting to find flesh. The man held out one hand and the razor-sharp blade stopped just inches from his tender palm. However, it wasn't anything done by the man that caused Strength to not find its target. Instead it was Strength itself that resisted the strike. Just as it had when Tolon had tried to strike down the Maldovrin Triplets, Strength had intervened of its own volition and refused to strike its intended target. This time however, the weapon began to vibrate in Tolon's strong hands. As the vibration became stronger, it was accompanied by an incredible heat. In a matter of seconds, Tolon had no choice but to relinquish his hold on the weapon. It clattered to the ground loudly, and for a moment Tolon felt as though disappointment rolled from the weapon. The stranger looked down at the weapon for half a moment, as if he too were surprised at what had just occurred, and then when he looked back up at Tolon, he snapped the fingers on his outstretched hand. Heartbeats later, a large swirling portal appeared beneath both Tolon and Jerrica, leaving the pair no choice but to fall through. Just as quickly as the portal had appeared, it had closed, and the Amethyst Knight and his companion were gone, leaving the pair alone with the two brothers.

* * * * * * * * * * * *

While Tolon crashed to the hard snow-packed ground, Jerrica floated softly through the air like a feather on a light breeze, coming to rest as though she had been laid carefully by loving hands. It took only a moment for Tolon to scramble across the distance between them, and cradle Jerrica's head in his lap. He was surprised to find that her color was much better, and it seemed as though some of her strength was starting to return. Her eyes fluttered softly and then gently cracked open. Despite the chill in the air, she wasn't shivering, and her skin was still quite warm to the touch. When Jerrica's eyes found Tolon's, a smile cracked her pale lips and she blinked softly. He started to open his mouth to ask a question, but she gently raised a hand and placed two fingers at his lips. There was a gentle shake of her head before she spoke.

"This isn't the time for questions," she said in a voice that had more strength that it had in several days. "I know now what we must do. I have been touched by the divine, and I know what lay ahead of us."

It wasn't until that moment that Tolon felt a chill run through him.

* * * * * * * * * * * *

Aerith Seth reached down and recovered the Sacred Weapon Strength and held it for just a moment before looking at his companion.

"If we leave this war to the mortals, it will be like leading lambs to the slaughter."

There was a look in Hannah Ironheart's eyes for the briefest of moments that could have been interpreted as either disgust or insult, but then the look faded. Inside Hannah still felt that she was mortal, but the more that her mind worked on the powers at her disposal, the voices and memories in her mind, the more she began to reshape her ideal of mortality. Aerith wasn't talking about the condition of being able to be killed. Even gods could be killed. Aerith spoke purely of those who had no true power, those who were pawns in the game started by the Creator and his children; those whose importance could not be underestimated, but whose impact on the game itself was limited. The game had always been influenced only by those with power, with few exceptions, and the pawns that were destroyed in the process never knew exactly why they died. The few rare times that a mortal had stumbled into a greater role, it had only been at great personal suffering and the strength to rise above it.

"So you're Aerith's new protégé."

For a moment Hannah didn't know if she had heard the voice with her ears or if it had only been in her head. It was a voice that she had quickly become familiar with. Her eyes shifted to the man sitting in the chair, and her gaze was greeted with a sly smile. Still she didn't know how the words had come to her, but for the moment it mattered little. At the same instant,

Hannah's mind came up with two identities for the seated man. The first was much less flattering to her sense of order than the second, but the second in the greater scope of things was more infuriating. In her world before she had met Aerith Seth, Hannah knew the man before her as Dane Rhuiden. To all members of the Church of the Creator, Dane Rhuiden and his Order were a pebble in the boot of every upright individual who loved the Creator. He constant questioned, harassed, but stayed just at the edge of inflammatory speech. Hannah and Gregor both had occasion to speak with Dane with the express desire to silence him, however his evasions and careful words proved that he was more than just a fanatic. Each time the efforts to bring an end to his cult were rebuffed and the attempts only seemed to strengthen his resolve. But now, with memories and voices transferred with Aerith's mantle, Hannah knew the man for who he truly was. Logan Ranthall, the *Chosen One*, the fallen hero, the Lord Phoenix of the phasia, savior, herald, annoyance, and perhaps one of the few reasons that there was an Espre. But as Hannah stole a glance back at her patron, she knew instantly that his eyes were focused on the other man, and the look on his face was one that Hannah was only familiar with through memories. It was surprise.

"You shouldn't be here."

There was stress in Aerith's voice, but he made no move to either conjure or draw one of his weapons. The man across the room, again a man with two identities in Hannah's mind, stood slowly, his hand never moving toward his own weapon that sat on the table half a stride away.

"I'm hearing that a lot today," Korrd said slowly and with an uneasy tone. "Why am I the one out of place? Being dead isn't really that big of a deal on this world."

Hannah's mind identified the words and tone as a joke, but she couldn't fathom why it was funny.

"And you," Aerith said turning his attention to Logan, "you should be hundreds of miles from here. What possessed you to come this way?"

Logan leaned back in the chair.

"Had an unfortunate run in with some very insistent people. And you know me; I can't resist helping a damsel in distress."

Hannah could feel the shock from both Aerith and Korrd. Finally Logan smiled and laughed.

"You see how annoying that is, Aerith?"

Korrd eased a little at the comment and leaned against the map table, resting his hand on his helm for what seemed to be comfort, but Hannah felt certain there was something more to it. Aerith put his hand on Hannah's shoulder and pointed at Logan.

"As you no doubt have determined, this ungrateful annoyance is one of the lucky people to have worn my mantle, and as you can also tell he's none the better for it. But then again, he also had Halicon's influence buried inside of him, and that could be the cause of all his trouble-making ways."

Before Hannah could speak, Logan interjected.

"We've met," he said with a hint of comedy.

"Collided," Hannah corrected.

"Collided," Logan accepted. "But that was another life, for both of us."

There was a curt nod from Hannah. While her connection to the man before her was undeniable, she didn't have to like him because of it. It would take her a long time before she could see him as anything other than a nuisance.

"Stories will have to wait," Aerith said finally, his eyes still locked on Korrd. "I'm here for a very specific reason. I need to know where he is."

Hannah caught the slight emphasis on the word 'he', but despite the connection that the two shared, Hannah had no idea who Aerith was referring to. Korrd seemed to flinch a little at the unspoken implication, but after a moment straightened his shoulders and stood. Whatever joviality had been sucked completely out of the tent, and even Logan looked as though his mirth had been seriously dampened.

"I don't think you really want to know that, Aerith," Korrd said finally. "You know that could end badly for both of you."

Aerith set his feet firmly, and Hannah could feel a cold begin to wrap itself around the ancient man.

"Right now," Aerith said, steel filling his voice, "I'm asking. You know as well as I do, if I wanted to, I could take the information from you, and you're in no position to stop me. I could tear this whole camp apart and kill every last one of your soldiers, and it would take a fraction of the power I have at my disposal now. I could level your whole country and still not work up an appetite. Don't make the mistake of making an enemy out of me paper dragon, you won't like the outcome."

Hannah barely kept her jaw from dropping open, and she could see that Logan was not as adept at controlling the physical manifestations of his emotions. Aerith had a violent streak, that much was assured, but he was never to be confused with cruel or sadistic. He would never kill innocents in the manner he was describing, but even being in the man's head, and knowing the millennia of his history, she wondered if she was wrong. Did he truly have the capacity to carry through his threat? Aerith was possessed of great ability to compartmentalize and segregate his emotions from the task at hand, and perhaps the lifetimes of killing had taught him to see the goal as justifying the means, even when that means called for such horrors. Logan started to stand, but Korrd extended his hand toward his little brother, his eyes never leaving Aerith's.

"And what if I said that I didn't know where he was?"

"DON'T LIE TO ME!"

The voice that thundered through the tent shook not only the people within the small space but also seemed to shake the ground itself. Hannah heard shouts from outside as the ground shifted and moved with Aerith's anger. A small fissure opened from Aerith's foot across the ground to within a few inches of where Korrd stood. Whatever shock Hannah and

Logan felt from the outburst, none showed on Korrd's face. In fact, when the shaking stopped, Korrd only smiled.

"Careful old man," he said mockingly. "You haven't had a chance to adapt to your new powers yet. Sabrina may have been smart enough to save her own life, for now, but you have no idea what it's done to you. He said you'd be unstable. He said you'd be violent. But I know you're not stupid, no matter how reckless you may be. You're not the only one whose been planning and plotting for millennia, Aerith, and some people actually have scores to settle."

Aerith's face held pure rage, but Logan's held more disbelief than anything else.

"Korrd, what are you talking about? What's going on?"

Korrd's eyes never left Aerith.

"I'm sorry little brother. I had hoped it wouldn't come to this. But as the seer said, it was much too early for us to meet again, and I had hoped the only moment you would have known that I had returned to this world would be when you were staring up at me with my sword through your heart."

Korrd extended one hand, and a wave of energy erupted, filling the entire tent. Both Hannah and Logan were knocked to the ground, but Aerith stood like a beacon in the storm, seemingly unfazed by the assault. The waves of power continued to pulse from Korrd's hand, and while Hannah was eventually able to shield herself with a bubble of power, Logan appeared to be suffering. It took a great deal of effort to extend the shield to cover the heretic, but Hannah managed. The exertion however crippled any ability she had to counter attack, but if there was going to be a counter to Korrd's treachery, it was going to come from Aerith. Hannah blinked, and Aerith had crossed the room to where Korrd stood, a sword in his hand, the tip of the blade thrusting through where Korrd's throat should have been. It took Hannah's mind a moment to catch up to what her eyes had seen. Aerith speeding across the intervening space, and Korrd simply being somewhere else a split second before Aerith's sword struck. There was a flash of motion from beside Hannah, and Strength leapt from where it lay on the ground and struck at where Korrd stood, but again he shifted to a new position.

"Too slow old man," Korrd taunted.

Then just as suddenly as the fight had started, it was over. But when Hannah looked at Aerith, she was shocked to see Korrd's sword jutting from the middle of Aerith's back. However, Aerith looked as though he didn't feel it at all. Korrd was gone, but a moment later his voice rang out again.

"Emries has had lifetimes to learn all of your tricks and master techniques you've never seen to counter them. If the two of you were to meet right now, you would be no match for him, even with the strength that Sabrina has gained you. But simply killing you isn't worth the effort now, and certainly won't be enjoyable. You're going to suffer first, Aerith. Think of everyone you've ever touched, everyone you've ever loved, everyone who owes anything to you. And now think of how it's going to feel as every last one of them is taken from you in the most vile and sadistic manner possible. If you thought what Dorovar was going to do to this world was something to be feared, wait until Emries unleashes the hell he has planned for it."

The voice fell silent for a moment, and then spoke again.

"Cedric knew what was going to happen. He was weak. But even his suicide at Jeroch's hands could not prevent him from fulfilling Emries' plan. Tried though he might, he proved that he was nothing more than a weak failure whose destiny from his birth was to be led to completing the tasks his betters had for him. Together we will make you all pay. You won't know who you can trust, you won't know who secretly belongs to us, and is just a time-bomb waiting to explode."

When the voice disappeared for good, the anguished and angry roar that escaped Aerith's lips would have rivaled that of any dragon.

Chapter LXIX

Reflections of the Infinite

Year Four of the Just Emperor Kaitain "Dragonsbane" Lorien, Creator's Calendar Year 1871

"We have nothing to say to one another, pretender."

Draven tensed and balled both of his hands into fists as his eyes locked with Wolf's. Power rolled off of both men, not for any offensive purposes, but rather to show the other that they were ready and willing to strike if the conversation went a direction they did not like. With a sneer coming to his lips, Draven continued.

"You showed yourself to be a coward when you would not face me as Onea fell. You hid behind Evan and Gwydeon and were not brave enough to take the fate of our world in your own hands. Even Jeroch showed more courage than you did. You proved to be exactly what I knew you to be the moment I laid eyes on you. An imperfect copy, corrupted by thin Ranthall blood."

Wolf's only reaction was to blink once before refocusing his eyes on Draven.

"Are you finished?"

The matter of fact tone in Wolf's voice struck a chord in Draven's heart, and the sneer deepened into a frown. The younger looking man continued to sit on the rock that he had been seated on when he first made his presence known to Draven, and he had not seemed to be ready to relinquish that posture. Draven had continued to gather strength, and at a moment's notice would be ready to unleash a torrent of energy that would have reduced the cliff-side to a crater. There was no way that the so-called hero wouldn't have been able to feel the increasing strength of his opponent, and yet maddeningly, he continued to sit there as though he were talking to some old friend. When Draven made no effort to continue his jibes, Wolf exhaled slowly and lowered his eyes to the ground.

"You hate me, I hate you," Wolf said finally, his tone low and resigned. "So what? Do you think that really matters in the grand scheme of things? We could kill each other here, and it wouldn't matter a bit. And to be honest, I know you're stronger than I am, and I certainly know that you are quite a bit more practiced with your powers. Besides, you've found yourself a new tutor, and I'm sure that he's shown you all kinds of new tricks to put an end to his rebellious former followers."

Wolf didn't need to look up to know that Draven's eyes had gone wide.

"Don't act so surprised, Draven," Wolf continued. "Just because Emries thought he was pulling the wool over everyone's eyes by laying low so long and recruiting creatures like you to his cause secretly doesn't make it so. There are far more eyes on this world and what happens around it than you know."

Wolf looked up finally.

"But then again, you were never the most astute of the phasia."

Draven let the jibe wash through him. He should have been above such comments after all of this time floating between worlds in that hellish limbo that Emries rescued him from, but for some reason, the calm words of the man sitting before him gave the insult far more weight.

"But I didn't come here to trade insults with you, Draven," Wolf continued dropping his gaze back to the blacked sand at his feet. "And to be honest, if I didn't want to see you, I could have been far away from here with my family."

Draven scoffed, louder than he intended.

"So you came out here to protect your shining tower? To sacrifice yourself so the rest of the cowards who call themselves Dark Gods can run away? Truly the best of you was cut down far too early in this game. I would have liked to see the look on Gwydeon's face when I tore his citadel apart with my bare hands."

"You may well get that chance," Wolf mumbled to himself before putting his hands on his knees and pushing himself up to his feet.

It felt good to be back on his feet again, and it felt good to feel the wind in his hair, and even though his slumber had been one without consciousness, his body certainly knew that it was slumbering. Every one of his muscles was sore, and even though he had spent the last few days trying to repair the Dark Citadel, there was still too much stiffness. If Draven was not willing to listen to reason, then there would be nothing that would prevent the former member of the phasia from cutting him down with little effort. Wolf wouldn't be surprised if Draven's first attack was enough to end things. But if it came down to a fight, Wolf had lost anyway.

"So the magnanimous Emries found you floating in the depths of the space between worlds and out of the kindness of his heart he brought you to this world, took you under his wing, and taught you all of the tricks you needed to get your revenge. Then what? What is the end game, Draven? You're going to rule at his right hand when he's destroyed all of his enemies and he's welcomed back into the loving bosom of the Creator's love? Or maybe you'll be standing there beside him when he turns his blade on his maker and tries to wrest control of the Cosmos, waiting for your own opportunity to do the same."

Draven felt the blood run from his face and the frown deepen on his face.

"Well, whatever your designs, and whatever you think Emries is going to do, or has done, you're wrong."

Draven blinked hard, and then found his frown melting. A sly smile was on his face the next moment, and he felt the laugh before he heard it.

"And what do you know, Ranthall? You've been sleeping since your fall. Emries told me that your powers were stripped from you, and that you've been nothing but an invalid since you were cast down to this rock. How could you know anything about what Emries had planned, or the state of any war for that matter? I can feel your powers are diminished."

Wolf shook his head. The next moment he was gone, and Draven turned several times trying to find where his opponent had gone. Then, just as suddenly as he had gone, Wolf had returned to his previous position. However, his clothing had changed. No longer did he wear the simple pants and black shirt that he had been wearing only a moment before. Now he was dressed in full armor, the kind that Aryx Terian made famous, with a cloak stretching behind him of white with the symbol of his uncle, the Dragon, stitched into it. A sword hung from either hip, and the look in the man's eyes was much more confident and much clearer. Then Draven noticed something, Wolf's eye color had changed. No longer were they the confident yet sullen brown eyes of all of the men of the Ranthall family. Now they were a bright a clear blue, full of emotional refuse like compassion and humility that turned Draven's stomach.

"I think, Draven," Wolf said, the pitch of his voice slightly higher and filled with a more whimsical tone, "that there have been a great many pieces of information that you have not been privy to, and moreover that your new patron has continuously lied to you since you so-called rescue."

Another form materialized to Draven's left, just inside the edge of his vision. From the moment that Draven set his eyes on the new arrival, his blood went cold. What he was seeing should not have been possible, and yet at the same time, it was impossible to ignore. The form was lithe, bordering on unhealthily thin, and yet Draven knew that the form was powerfully if diminutively built. The man had midnight black hair, and his eyes glowed yellow with a power and a knowledge that defied description. It was as though the man had seen into the beyond and had been forever altered by what he had seen. He was dressed in all black and trailed a gray cloak behind him that scraped the ground as he walked. On his right hip he wore a sword, free of its sheath, the black metal of the blade drinking in all of the light that tried to reflect off its polished surface. His shoulders were pulled back hard, and his head was held higher than even a proud man would have held himself. Though his hair was long, the strong breeze did not move so much as a hair. In Draven's mind's eye, he could see the man with a haughty and cruel smile plastered onto his lips, a glimpse into the mind of a man who had once been feared for his deviousness and cunning. The tenacity of the man known as the Lord Raven was well known and well feared, even though Basille Mystic had been dead for millennia.

The new arrival stopped several paces short of where Wolf and Draven stood, and as Draven's now wide eyes went back to Wolf, he was shocked to find that the man's features had changed once again. The long brown hair had shortened and lightened, bright platinum blond even in the moonlight that filled the sky. It was as though the streaks of fire that were lighting the sky had caught in the man's hair, giving it an incredible radiance. Wolf's features had changed too. His cheeks had filled out slightly, making those high cheekbones less visible, and all traces of stubble on his upper lip, chin, cheeks, and jawline had disappeared. His skin too seemed more vibrant and luminous. In a word the man who had once been Wolf Ranthall appeared more angelic. The mystery deepened that next moment when Draven caught movement out of the corner of his right eye, and any pretense the former phase had tried to keep of not being impacted by what his eyes had seen shattered when Wolf Ranthall took two long strides to stand beside the blond man.

Basille was the first to let his voice find the air.

"I think there are some things you should know, Draven."

* * * * * * * * * * *

Deep in the Citadel of the Dark Gods, Lissa Ranthall and her oldest daughter Mirana were making preparations to level the Citadel and leave no traces that could be used by anyone who would come after. It would take only a few applications of power to bring everything down now, and it could be triggered at any time. Liara had been conspicuous by her absence ever since she had felt the portal forming outside the Citadel and Wolf had gone to investigate something that he clearly had been expecting. From a nearby chamber Lissa heard the sound of breaking glass, and before she could make a move to investigate, Liara came staggering through the doorway, blood streaming from the corners of her eyes and from both of her nostrils. Without a word Lissa was there at her youngest daughter's side, catching her as she collapsed.

"Lee!"

Mirana was also there at her sister's side quickly, holding her hand and dabbing at the blood with one of her sleeves.

"We have to leave here," Liara said in a voice that was filled with distance and weakness, "now."

Lissa looked up at Mirana.

"Tell Darrien and Alderin that they have to move, now. Send them to Celidar to meet Jerrard, and tell them that we'll meet them when we can."

Mirana hesitated, her eyes intent on her sister. Finally, Lissa put her hand on her oldest daughter's shoulder and pushed hard.

"Go!"

It took the young woman only a moment to gather herself and rush off to do what she was told, leaving her mother and her sister in the quiet of the chamber. After a long moment, Liara locked her eyes on Lissa, the blood still streaming down her face. Lissa's breath caught in her throat when she saw her daughter's eyes. All of the color had drained from her iris, and only a light green ring remained to separate her iris from the white of the rest of her eye. The stark and disturbing white eyes stared up at here like those of a corpse.

"He's free, mother." Liara said in a quiet and pain-filled voice, "Dorovar is free."

* * * * * * * * * * * *

Draven took a half-step backward before resetting himself and letting his fists relax. He spread his fingers and let the powers of the Blaze fill his hands. He drew deeply on the ancient energy source, and suddenly felt his powers limited. It was as though someone had curtailed his access to the depths of the Blaze, but what power was available was still going to be enough to crush the three men standing in front of him, especially with the augmented abilities that he had gained through his tutelage at the foot of Emries. Wolf was the first one to put his hand up in reaction to Draven drawing on his powers.

"Draven, this isn't an ambush. We need you, and we need you to listen."

Draven couldn't keep himself from laughing.

"You're still pathetic, Ranthall, and you're delusional if you think I'm going to stand here and listen to anything that you and that ghost have to say."

Basille's lips fell into a frown and Wolf opened his mouth to speak again, but it was the blond man's voice that caught the air.

"Then listen to me."

Draven's hold on the Blaze slipped. The man's voice was filled with a combination of comfort and familiarity that distracted Draven for a moment from his murderous intentions. It was as though calm radiated from the man's voice like a blanket that wanted to wrap itself around Draven and smother him. But Draven reached deeper and pushed past the interference and redoubled his grip on the powers at his disposal.

"Did you ever wonder why you were the only one that was cast into the void?" the blond man continued. "Did it make sense that all of the other phasia managed to be brought here to Espre? Why would Emries have had to rescue you? All of the creations and touched of the Children of the Creator as well as the children themselves are here on Espre. The only one that would have been outside this mandate would have been Basille. And he was on the Other Side because he had given his string of power to Wolf. And yet, even Basille felt pulled here, through his connection to Wolf. He was trapped in this web just as surely as you should have been."

Draven wanted to shake himself. His head was being clouded by these meaningless words. Even though there may have been truth at the core of the man's words, they were so wrapped in lies that Draven found it hard to stomach even the illusion of a possibility. And still the blond man persisted.

"Emries is the reason you were in the void, Draven. He saw early on in the formation of this world what those with power would be capable of, and with the interventions of his brother and sisters on this land, as well as the grasp at power made by some of your fellow phasia, he needed something that would help him turn the tide. All those that had once acted in his name had been pulled away from him, had turned their back on him, or had been killed early on in the conflicts of this world. Cedric Binosear was the one most dedicated to the destruction of his former benefactor. Even Logan Ranthall did not have the venom and vitriol within him to take the steps of hunting down all of those who once bore the touch of Emries upon their souls. Cedric easily found the first men that served Emries, those that were the precursors to the Erieal, as they made no attempts to hide themselves. Their powers were not as developed as those that would come later and were no match for the man who once called himself the Lion."

There was a sadness that entered the man's voice, one that permeated every word and impacted Draven in a way he did not expect. Draven had not been made to feel pity, remorse, or sorrow. It was simply not in the makeup of his being. But somehow, the words of this man were piercing through to the core of Draven's being, touching emotions that even the King of the Devils did not know he had.

"Though it pained him, Cedric set his mind to eliminating his former allies; the ones who wore the name Erieal. The ones who had not made the choice to ascend to the heavens as Aryx and Diana Terian did. The wizard Mailock and the brave hero Arathorn Geoffry. It was Cedric that cut them down early in the wars that would put Terrik Lorien on the throne of Cadaria. Arathorn was using the banner of the Lion in an effort to build an army that would put down both Grawn and Terrik. But Cedric would not allow an army shackled to his fate to sway the course of this world. So he slew his best friend in single combat. But it could not end there. His heart broken, Cedric allowed his hunt to continue, tracking down any of the so-called heroes and villains from your world. Any that he found met their ends at the tip of Cedric's blade."

Draven smiled.

"I didn't think the old man had it in him."

The blond man frowned, and suddenly the sorrow in his voice gave way to pain.

"Every death weighed on Cedric in ways you could not imagine. But he knew that sooner or later as touched as he was by the hand of Emries, that he too would have to be brought to justice for his role in the death of Onea, and for what he had done in the name of giving this world a fighting chance. Cedric knew that he would not be able to finish the task ahead of him, to destroy all those who shared his fate. He made a pact with Aryx and Diana Terian, as he could not bear to bring an end to their lives after all of the blood on his hands. They would not reveal the fates of the fallen Erieal to the rest of the Dark Gods, nor would they be hunted if they agreed to give their powers away and fade into the mists of memory. That left only Lissa Terian from the Erieal among the Dark Gods. Pike Rhuiden though once a member of the Erieal had long since renounced that title and had given up his powers to Halicon. That may have saved him from Cedric's machinations, but certainly not from the minds of others."

Draven's teeth shown with his own murderous thoughts.

"Cedric felt his death coming, and wanted to live no longer," the blond man continued, "and so he sought one that could finish his task. One who could make right the things that went wrong, and to cleanse the stench of those who one wore Emries' mantle, as well as those who were touched by Halicon. Cedric trained a successor, one that could wield his powers without owing either Halicon or Emries their allegiance."

Draven could feel his patience running out.

"So the old man groomed a pet," the demon scoffed, "and why should I care?"

"Because you've allowed yourself to become a pet yourself," Basille answered. "Emries knew what Cedric was doing and needed someone to do his dirty work while he hunted Aerith and those who followed him. Aerith and the others are the real threat to Emries and Talisia, and Emries will stop at nothing until Aerith lies dead at his feet. Nothing else matters. Not you, not the Dark Gods, not the dragons, not Dorovar, and certainly not the Cadarians. It's always been about killing Aerith, and to do that he needs you to keep the others distracted."

"You and the other *Coromors*," Wolf added.

Draven scratched his chin and smiled.

"Say I believe you," Draven said finally, the scheming part of his mind taking over, "and say that I accept that Emries was going to eventually betray me, if I didn't choose to betray him first. Say I believe that he is the reason that I didn't come here immediately as the other phasia did. So what? I'm alive and most of them are dead. I'm in a position to make my vision of this world and this universe come true, and they aren't. Emries did me a favor and I'm going to repay him by spilling his blood all over the ground and walking over his corpse to take the throne of the Creator."

Wolf sighed and shook his head.

"And you don't think that Emries knows you'll betray him? You're not that naïve."

Draven's smile flared wider.

"Of course I'm not, and neither are you. Emries is going to get himself killed long before I need to raise a finger. Whether it's Aerith or one of you, or one of the Dark Gods, or anyone else, it won't matter. He's careless. That's why he lost on Onea, and that's why he'll lose here."

The blond man's face fell. The disappointment hung palpable in the air.

"I thought we would be able to convince you to work with us peacefully. I had only one chance to ensure that someone would be there to make things right for me and for those who followed me. For those who proved to be the heroes that they were destined to be. But I see now that you are too wrapped up in your own hatred to see anything else."

Before Draven could react, the blond man's right hand shot forward, and a stream of flame erupted toward Draven. Instead of burning, the flames wrapped themselves around Draven's body like a thick fog. Draven was rendered immobile by the tumultuous flames.

"Death surrounded me," the blond man was saying, the words barely piercing the roar of the flames. "Thousands had died fighting for me, and fighting against me. I could see the wings of angels burning, their glowing spears piercing their hearts. Monstrous dragons broken in half, their jaws askew, wings riddled with holes. But as I looked up, all I could see were the cold and vindictive eyes of my sister staring down at me, her long slender fingers wrapped around my throat. Out of the corner of my eye, I could see Gwydeon Sandar struggling to get to me, wanting so desperately to save me from my fate. But when Talisia launched her attack on the Throne, I knew what the end had to be. My love, Raenera, was gone. My brother, the strongest of us, Halicon, was in seclusion, and only the angels and those gods loyal to the Creator stood between Talisia and her goal. Even the heralds were nowhere to be found. Though I was not a warrior, I could not stand by and let her evil touch the Cosmos. So I sacrificed myself to sate her hunger for power."

The fires raged brighter around Draven, and it clouded his vision. He could no longer see the blond man, only his voice penetrated the flames.

"So there I languished in the formlessness of the limbo. Forever to be forgotten in the annuls of the Cosmos. But I found that I was not alone. The other souls of the lost were there looking for comfort, and I gave them that comfort. I became the shepherd of the lost. But I began to hear whispers of this new world, souls coming from the great wars that were shaping this place. It was by chance that I crossed paths with a phantom that seemed to straddle between the land of souls and the land of the living. Through him, through Basille I felt the Dark Gods fall, and it was my chance. I reached through Basille, made him my conduit to touch the mind of the man whom I had known as Wolf Ranthall. But the crossing was difficult, and it changed all three of us. Wolf was incomplete, as was Basille, as was I. Together Basille and Wolf would not have been enough to house my power, to act as my vessel as others now act as the vessels for my brothers and sisters. But then you emerged, Draven, and you will be the last piece of the puzzle."

Draven began to feel cold creep into his fingers and his toes. His entire body was starting to go numb, but his mind was on fire.

"The three will no longer exist after this night," the blond man's voice echoed from the nothingness. "Only the vessel will remain."

* * * * * * * * * * * *

Wolf Ranthall's eyes slowly slid open, and he felt as though every part of his body was freezing and burning at the same time. It took several long moments for his eyes to refocus, and when they did, he saw the perfect features of a blond man staring down at him. So many thoughts swam through his mind, and so many voices. Equal with the voices was the power. Power unlike any he had ever experienced before. He tried to push his way to his feet, but his legs would not support his weight, and Wolf went crashing back to the cold hard ground. Finally, after a long moment, the blond man extended a hand and helped Wolf up until he was sitting on a boulder.

"It will take quite some time before you will be able to adjust to the new powers that you have at your disposal, my friend. And it will take even longer for you to integrate all that you have been given with all that you were. The Wolf Ranthall that you once were no longer exists. You now are Draven Batoe and Basille Mystic as much as you are Wolf Ranthall, and that will take some time for you to come to terms with. And while you cannot erase the horrors that they have done, you can use the knowledge of their lives to make this world better and prevent similar horrors from being visited upon these people."

The blond man fell silent for a moment before adding.

"You are a collection of reflections no more, my friend."

The blond man stood from where he sat and started to walk away.

"Where are you going?"

Wolf's voice sounded alien to him. Tones and pitches that his throat had never made, but as strange as they sounded to his ear, he knew them as though they had been there all his life.

"Halicon showed the way. We were once the future, and we were once the pattern by which all would be judged. But we are flawed. We are reflections of an ideology that cànnot work without the other ideologies to give them context. Talisia is nothing with Raenera, who is nothing without Halicon, who is nothing with Emries, who is nothing without me. Together we could have made something that would have lasted forever. Something that could have defined infinity. But now we are squabbling children, content to kill in the name of our own flaws. I will be a part to it no more, and like Halicon, I will pass from this reality and hope that one day those who come after us will discover the infinite that should have been ours to forge."

The blond man stopped and turned back to face Wolf.

"The being I once was, the being I was destined to be, now lives within you. Seek out those who are the vessels of my siblings and bring peace to this war. Perhaps then, the name Pyrrus can be remembered with honor, and not be forgotten in the stardust of a Cosmos torn apart by our own selfishness."

With that Pyrrus, the youngest child of the Creator turned and disappeared as the night sky filled with streaks of fire and light.

Predators

The plains surrounding the Academy of Arcane Arts in Jelan still resounded with the echoes of battle, the dying screams of men and monsters, and the reverberations of the name of the pale woman who floated opposite a child of the Creator. Talisia Masile's face showed the contempt that she had for the interloper that dared to resist her attempts to reduce the whole of the valley to rubble. Many had already met their end in the battle for Jelan, and despite all appearances, none of the four armies that had taken the field had a decided advantage. The Iron Legion under the command of the Moonstone Knight, Bernhardt Yeoman had been reduced to less than a hundred men, and though they kept fighting, their wills had been all but broken. The shattered body of the Moonstone Knight still lay on the field, the light long since extinguished from his eyes. The last standard bearer for the army stood over their fallen leader's body desperately trying to rally the men of Pellatori to his banner. The men of the Iron Legion would never flee, would never abandon the battlefield, but any chance they had of fighting as a unit was lost the moment their leader had fallen. The vivisected body of the great dragon Phantasma Graverobber lay as a mountain of death under whose shadow the Iron Legion rallied, but the death of the dragon had shown that the battle was not yet lost. In equal turmoil was the pieces of the detachment of the Jade

Army, and though their leader still lived, many of the remaining soldiers had begun to doubt whether or not the renowned Jade Knight of the Flashing Blade was still in command of her own faculties, let alone able to rally her troops for a counter-attack. Though Leonora Wastri was still very much alive, she lay face down in the blood soaked mud, her breathing ragged and erratic. But faith in their leader had not totally eroded. This seeming pause in the great battle for Jelan had given the Jade Army the opportunity they needed to rally, using the crest of the broken hill as their new staging ground, surrounding their fallen leader with a wall of bodies.

The army led by the twin members of the Dark Gods and their progeny had not fared much better in the battle than the mortals, and the two other great dragons had done much to thin their ranks. Trece Starlin lay unconscious in a pool of her own blood, a ring of Shadowwalkers gathered around her, defending her fallen form. Rael Starlin was still conscious and ready to fight, but he worried at the silent portion of his mind that always contained the thoughts of his sometime sister and sometime wife. Their relationship had been complicated since the day of their birth, and would be until the day of their death. From where Rael stood he could not tell how many of their children were still alive, but he knew for certain that he had seen the death of three of them. But mourning would have to wait. Talisia still hung above the battlefield, and she had the power to kill every one of those who still stood, and there might be no one left to do any mourning in the heartbeats that followed. Rael's eyes would not leave the ghostly woman, and he felt something inside that he could not shake. He knew the woman somehow. The familiarity was certainly not imagined. However, while it was clear that Talisia was quite aware of everything that had taken place below her watchful and disdainful eyes, it was not as clear if Jerah was aware of anything but Talisia.

Jerah floated as though nothing from the turbulent environment touched her. Lightning flashed all around, and bolts of white heat flashed by so close that they would have caused a mortal's hair to stand on end, but Jerah only noted their passing as though it was barely worthy of her notice. The whipping wind and rain were held at bay by the sheer force of her will, and not even her clothing could be disturbed. Her opponent however responded to the turbulent nature of the environment destabilizing around them. Talisia was like the eye of a hurricane, riding the winds and feeling the hot rains streaming down her skin. Her hair was already matted by the deluge, but her wild eyes showed that the woman thrived on the chaos. She raised one hand in the air and spread her fingers. Several bolts of lightning struck her hand simultaneously, the collected power coalescing in her palm. A sly smile came to her face for a brief moment before her lips twisted into a snarl. The huge concentrated bolt of lightning leapt from Talisia's hand the next moment, crossing the gap between the two floating women in the blink of an eye engulfing Jerah. Crackles and explosions could be heard for miles, the light blinding, and waves of heat scorching the ground in all directions. The shockwave from the blast leveled one of the towers of the Academy of Arcane Arts. When the smoke and light finally cleared, Talisia's smile faded. Jerah hung in the air, completely unaffected by the blast, not a single singe on her clothing.

"Pathetic."

The single word from Jerah brought a change to the storm. Freezing cold filled the air, frost forming on the ground and on the armor of the soldiers. The rain changed to ice, and with a simple gesture, the falling ice became needle-thin and razor sharp. Where once she reveled in the falling rain, Talisia cried out in pain as the shards of ice ripped through her body, sending plumes of blood spraying in all directions. On the ground too, the indiscriminant assault had impact. Soldiers fell to the ground, ducking under shields and whatever other cover they could find. One member of the Jade Army provided what cover he could to Leonora Wastri's fallen form, while several of the Shadowwalkers sacrificed their bodies to shield Trece. Finally, whatever otherworldly power was keeping Talisia in mid-air was overwhelmed by the pain of Jerah's assault, and the Child of the Creator fell to the blood-soaked ground.

* * * * * * * * * * * *

Aris Ebonsight stared in disbelief as the battle had turned from a clash between mortal armies to a clash between nearly immortal powers. The arrival of the forces of the Dark Gods, was dwarfed by the arrival of the dragons, and then the two incredibly powerful women who floated in mid-air. The soldiers on the battlefield could only see the devastation being wrought by the power being brought to bear, but Aris had a different perspective on the battle. She could see the flows of arcane and divine power being employed. Where the Dark Gods and their forces seemed to exist in harmony with the natural flows of power coming from the air and the land, the one calling herself Talisia seemed to create power out of thin air, a kind of power that was reserved for the Servants and Children of the Creator. Everything that Talisia did was pure creation, something that no mortal could ever replicate. But the woman called Jerah, she was different. Mortals who could see the flows of arcane power could touch and manipulate the subtle flows to generate effects. Young and inexperienced sorcerers wielded such power with the subtlety of a club, while the well-trained practitioners had the same level of fine control that a sword-master had over a blade. The ones called Rael and Trece seemed to work with the natural flows of power, almost requesting their compliance with the Dark Gods' will. It was as though they themselves were one with the arcane energy.

Then there was the one called Jerah. The natural flows of arcane power seemed to just bend around her, as though they were trying to avoid contact altogether. But when she did exercise her power, it was as though she bent everything around her to her will. She seized control and twisted all of the arcane flows in unnatural, even obscene ways. Her power was unbelievable and frightening. Aris watched in horror as the tower was destroyed by Talisia's attack. Luckily all of the external towers had been evacuated when the two mortal armies had appeared. Only the single internal tower still had anyone inside of it, and that was only the four remaining Masters. Aris' mother, Fiona, the ranking Master of the Council had retired to meditate, hoping to find some way out of this impossible situation that did not result in the death of all who called Jelan home. Only Ashinica Maupin held vigil with Aris in the tower. She had been shaken since her return to the Academy, a product no doubt of the failed negotiations that was the spark that lit the fuse of the conflict that raged outside.

But Ashinica could not have known the horror that would come after. There was no way that she could have foreseen the arrival of the army of the Dark Gods, the dragons, or anything else that occurred.

"What can we do, Aris?"

Ashinica's tone was harried. She was feeling the strain of the combat as though she had been personally involved in all of it.

"Nothing that doesn't violate our code."

There was a spark of irritation in Aris' voice. For all of their power, the Masters were restrained by their adherence to the code of conduct created by the first Masters of the Academy who ruled at the birth of the Cadarian Empire. Those who used the powers of the arcane to harm others would be corrupted by the power they wielded. They would become tyrants, and the devastation that they could do to the world was without measure. That was why the oaths were created. That was why all safeguards were put into place. No master or student of the Academy would ever be allowed to become a threat to the Emperor or the Empire.

"Damn the code."

Ashinica pounded her fists on the table.

"You sound more like Ayden every day," a voice said from the doorway.

Ashinica turned her attention to the form of Jastra Mythryn. The Master of Energy leaned against the door frame with a defiant yet pained look on her face. Aris knew that the young woman could feel the lives on the battlefield being snuffed out as the moments passed. She could feel the essence of every life both in the Academy and on its grounds, and in that way, the Master of Energy had the greatest burden of any of the other Masters.

"And maybe that isn't such a bad thing," Ashinica countered. "There is so much that we could do to help those people out there."

Aris' calm yet sullen voice answered.

"I don't think even our power would be of much use out there now. Between this Jerah and Talisia, they could swat us like flies, with or without the code."

Ashinica grimaced.

"Perhaps it's time to start discussing what happens when the battle is over. If either of those powerful creatures is victorious and decides to use the Academy as a base of operations, or worse."

The implication was clear. Jastra meant the final invocation of the oaths. The destruction of the Academy of Arcane Arts, and the death of every one of its members everywhere on the face of Espre. A final blow to keep the secrets of the Academy from falling into the wrong hands, and a final fulfillment of the promises made by the first Masters to the First Emperor of Cadaria. Aris looked over her shoulder at Jastra for a moment, barely restrained tears in her eyes. Then she looked back to the battle, and she could not help her mouth from falling open.

"The sky," she said shocked and disbelieving, "it's bleeding."

* * * * * * * * * * * *

Rael looked up and watched in a mixture of horror and shock as the deadly rain of ice tore through Talisia's body. Blood splattered everywhere, leaving streaks in the sky as though an artist had flicked a huge brush full of red paint at the sky and it had hung there. Talisia's head rocked back, the rain still assaulting her flailing form, more blood splattering in all directions. Finally a scream ripped from the woman's tortured body. The scream shook the ground in all directions, causing great cracks to form not only in the ground, but in the walls of the Academy buildings. The scream arched out in all directions, finally causing a reaction out of Jerah, as it pushed her back several feet in the air. The assault of ice ceased, but the rain itself did not. However, it did not fall to the ground as rain any longer. The drops of water became thick and viscous, taking on the character and feel of blood. The red droplets fell from the sky, coating everyone and everything. When the scream finally subsided, Talisia hung limp in the air like a broken doll and then fell to the ground. Her impact created a crater that slowly began to fill with the thick liquid. Jerah continued to float in mid-air, watching the scene with a cold and dispassionate look. Only she was unaffected by the bleeding sky, her white dress and pale features still clean.

For several long minutes Rael looked on, his eyes never leaving the crater created by Talisia's fall. He fully expected her to immediately pull herself back to her feet and launch her counterattack at Jerah. But each moment, each breath that escaped Rael's lips, the more doubt began to creep into him. Perhaps Jerah had done more damage than even a Child of the Creator could sustain. More and more of the blood fell from the sky, filling the crater into an obscene pool, the stench of death hanging heavy in the air. Finally, after what seemed like an eternity, large bubbles broke the surface of the pool, and Talisia began to rise from the gore. Her gown was ripped, her body caked with blood, some of which was her own, and her hair was matted to the sides of her face. But it was her eyes that disturbed Rael the most. He had never seen eyes burn with that much hatred, not even during the height of the wars on Onea. This hate and rage knew no boundaries, and Rael feared that Talisia could burn every living thing on Espre into nothingness, and her hatred wouldn't be sated. What was clear however, was that Jerah's attack had done significant damage to the Child of the Creator. She did not leap into the sky; she did not laugh or threaten. She simply floated to the shore of the lake of blood and looked up at her attacker. Jerah's impenetrable features cracked for the briefest of moments, one corner of her mouth creeping into what for her could have been referred to as a smile, and her brilliant green eyes flashed.

From out of the lake of blood, forms began to appear. They grew slowly, closest to the edges of the crater, almost congealing into being. The forms were unmistakable to Rael's eyes. Huge four-legged creatures with snarling teeth, broad feet, and tails wagging in anticipation of a kill. This pack of constructed wolves moved lightly from where they had formed, circling Talisia, their red eyes never leaving their prey. To her credit, the Child of the Creator seemed impressed by the display of power, but raised one hand toward one of the creatures. A spray of fire leapt from her extended fingers, engulfing one of the wolves. The smell of charred flesh filled the air, but only the sound of sizzling could be heard; there was no cry of pain from the beast. Rael wasn't sure that the thing could even feel pain, or anything at all but the lust to kill. From the roaring flames, the huge wolf erupted, catching Talisia completely by surprise. One huge paw crashed into the side of Talisia's face, turning her head violently. Rael thought for a moment that he heard Talisia's neck snap. The force of the blow sent the woman flying backward, another cry of pain ripped from her. The other wolves leapt in the next moment, clawing and snapping, ripping at flesh and gnawing on bone. Shrieks and cries of pain filled the air, impossibly loud. But whatever advantage the constructs had was short-lived, as a wave of brilliant light flashed from where Talisia lay and enveloped the pack of bloody carnivores. Many were thrown clear of their prey, and when they managed to fight their way back to their feet, the creatures simply began to dissolve. Talisia was slow to get back to her feet this time, long jagged scratches clearly visible on her arms and legs, and large bite marks remained where chunks of her flesh had been ripped out. Her face and neck were marred, almost beyond recognition, but the indignation and fire still burned in her eyes. A moment later though, the Child of the Creator began to laugh.

At first the laughter was distorted, a sickening sound filled with gurgling of blood from her ruined throat. But as the moments passed, the wounds on Talisia's body began to quickly repair themselves. The laughter rang louder as the woman's suddenly rejuvenated form stared up at Jerah.

"Parlor tricks may have worked on some of my weaker siblings, but I have had millennia to prepare for this war. I have killed angels, dragons, and gods by the hundreds. I am the most accomplished warrior in the Cosmos. I slew my own brother with my bare hands, and no abomination will stand before me and think she has enough power to end my existence."

Suddenly Talisia was gone from where she stood and was simply hovering in front of Jerah, so close that she could reach out and touch her. Talisia jabbed a finger into Jerah's chest with a wicked smile on her lips.

"Dissipate!"

Rael blinked hard twice and tried his best to wrap his mind around what happened next. There was the briefest flash of light from where Talisia's finger touched Jerah's chest, and then it seemed like an explosion began somewhere deep inside of Jerah and she simply flew apart. But this explosion did not send huge pieces of the woman flying in all directions, no; the destruction was more complete and complex. Pieces no large than pebbles were cast in all directions, a haze of blood and flesh. However, as Rael was coming to grips with that attack, his eyes seemed to play tricks on him. The pieces of Jerah simply froze in mid-air, and then were pulled back to the source of the explosion. Just as quickly as she was deconstructed, the reconstituted form of Jerah floated before Talisia. The Child of the Creator fell back as if she was struck.

"That's impossible! Nothing can withstand concentrated Divine power!"

Jerah's counterattack was equally vicious. She sped forward, one hand wrapping around Talisia's throat, the other hand pushing into her chest. The hand ripped through the sternum, skin, and muscle, until the hand found the swiftly beating heart that lay beneath. With a single deft motion, Jerah pulled the heart out of Talisia's chest. It beat several more beats, before Jerah closed her hand, a burst of fire enveloping the vital organ. In a matter of seconds, the powerful muscle was reduced to ash. Jerah held her opponent there for several more moments, staring into Talisia's eyes, watching all of the light fade. Finally she released the lifeless husk of the Child of the Creator, and let if fall once again to the ground below. Bones could be heard breaking upon impact, but this time there was no crater, and no thought in Rael's mind that the woman would ever rise again. This time, Jerah floated down to the ground, standing over her fallen opponent. After a moment, Jerah raised her boot and brought it crashing down onto the side of Talisia's face, and then ground her heel down onto the fallen woman's head, adding a final insult.

Jerah's eyes found Rael's for the briefest of moments, and then she moved to where Trece lay. Jerah didn't so much walk as she glided across the ground. Her legs moved as if she was walking, but her feet never seemed to come into contact with the ground. Jerah covered the distance quickly, and as she approached, the Shadowwalkers began to move as though they would block Jerah's advance. Jerah paused, looked back over her shoulder and met Rael's eyes again. Rael made motion with one hand and the Shadowwalkers ranks parted. Jerah knelt and placed one hand on Trece's back. In a matter of moments, Trece began to move again, her wounds completely healed. She did not stay to admire her handiwork, and turned back to Rael. When she was close enough, Rael could feel the waves of cold radiating from the woman, as though Jerah was the cold of the grave personified. But whatever she was now, he knew what she once was. Her tactics, her eyes, everything spoke only one name.

"Thank you, Caris."

If Jerah had any reaction to the name, it didn't show on her features. She instead cast her glance to where the Jade Knight, Leonora Wastri lay.

The woman still had not moved from where she had fallen, but even at a distance, Rael could tell that the woman was still alive. Jerah lifted one hand to point at the fallen form.

"Take."

Rael could not hide the confusion from his face. Was this Jerah speaking, the woman who had just killed a Child of the Creator, for whomever she served now, or was it Caris speaking, his old ally? Jerah kept her eyes locked on Rael's for a moment, and images began to flood in his mind. He saw the creature calling itself Dorovar. He saw the other servants of that abomination and the hell they were about to unleash. He saw dragons, demons, angels, and gods clashing in the skies above them. He saw more blood raining from the skies. Then a blazing symbol floated across his vision. A symbol that held only one meaning. It was Caris speaking to him. And he knew now what he needed to do, and where to take the woman Leonora. Jerah nodded slightly.

"Take."

Rael nodded and turned toward where Trece was just getting to her feet with the assistance of several of the Shadowwalkers. There was so much Rael wanted to say and wanted to ask, but he could only form one statement in his head.

"I'll tell Logan you're alright."

Jerah turned away, lifting her eyes to the central tower of the Academy of Arcane Arts. No matter how much she was allowed to deviate from her assignments to fulfill her own whims, she was still a servant of Dorovar, and she still had a mission she had to complete. If she did not, one of the other Heralds would, and their brutality would remove any usefulness that the Academy could have to their master. To Dorovar, the souls in the Academy had two uses. Either they could bend their arcane powers to help defeat Dorovar's enemies, or they could simply become new members for his Chorus of Souls that would sing him to the Heavens.

* * * * * * * * * * * *

Aris Ebonsight watched the battle end, the anxiety twisting the pit of her stomach and causing the bile to rise in the back of her throat. It felt as though the world was coming to an end, at least the world that she knew. Now the woman called Jerah stood in the middle of the blood soaked battlefield looking up at the central tower. Aris could practically feel the woman's eyes on her, even from that great distance. A moment later, Jastra stood beside Aris, looking down on the pale woman whose bright green eyes were staring at them. Jastra sighed deeply.

"I think we have no choice now," Jastra said, her voice grave and full of gravity, "I, the Master of Energy petition the Master's Council to enact the Final Oath. The Academy of Arcane Arts must be destroyed, and its secrets protected from the evil that threatens us."

Risk Versus Reward

Year Four of the Just Emperor Kaitain "Dragonsbane" Lorien, Creator's Calendar Year 1871

The hour was getting late when the knock came at the door. The servant opened the door but a crack to announce that dinner would be served within the next hour in the formal dining hall. When the door closed again, Quyhn stretched indelicately, complete with curling toes and a long groan. Though her belly was rumbling from lack of food she wasn't sure that starvation could have pried her out from under the covers. Her eyes fell to the form beside her, and found her own gaze met by the dark eyes of Rhionna Winter. Lying on her stomach, Rhionna had propped her head up, resting her chin in the palm of her right hand and leaning slightly on her elbow. Her long delicate fingertips rested just above her full upper lip, and all of her expression was held in her eyes. It looked as she too was disappointed they would have to rouse themselves. After a long blink that seemed to take the place of a nod of her head, Rhionna rolled away, onto her back for a moment before popping up to a seated position and turning to put her feet flat on the floor. Despite herself, Quyhn found herself pulling the covers up to her neck before she too turned to put her feet on the floor. She held the covers like a shield, her modesty suddenly overwhelming her. She felt the blush all over her body, and was thankful that Rhionna had her back turned and was not paying attention. Quyhn was just making her way to her wardrobe when she felt Rhionna's hands snake around her waist. Instead of soft skin pressing against her back, Quyhn felt the rough fabric of Rhionna's simple white shirt. The taller woman kissed Quyhn lightly on the back of her neck before squeezing her tightly, almost too tightly for Quyhn to breathe, if the woman's sheer presence wasn't already making it hard to find her breath.

"Wait for me, and I'll escort you to dinner. We must keep up appearances."

Quyhn felt the shy smile creep to her lips and her head nod slightly. The slight blush in her cheeks deepened and she could not help but watch the older woman as she slipped through the door and moved toward her own quarters further down the hallway. Left alone again, Quyhn could feel her ability to think and breathe return. She had only been drunk once in her young life, and that moment standing in front of the wardrobe felt much like being drunk and being hung over at the same time. It had been shortly after Dominique's marriage and the attack on Emperor Lorien that a vigil dinner was held in the sleeping Kaitain's honor. Long after the royal guests had been shown from the palace, Dominique, Chelsea, and Quyhn had sequestered themselves in Dominique's spacious room and had drained the better part of four jugs of wine. There were toasts to fortune and to misfortune. To loves lost and found, and to a sisterhood that had formed under the most bizarre of circumstances. Quyhn had never felt warmer in all of her life, both because of the wine, but also because of the safety and love she felt. Despite all of the tragedy she had endured in her young life, Quyhn had survived it all, and had found something she never thought she would have again, a family that loved her unconditionally. Though the next morning the feeling was more like that of riding in the back of a wagon over an uneven and rock-filled road, there was still a glow and glimmer of satisfaction. Here the afterglow of love held her, her mind spinning and drunk on sensation and contentment.

Letting the sheets finally fall to the floor, Quyhn reached into the wardrobe and thumbed through the different dresses hanging there. Some had been brought with her from her time at the Academy of Arcane Arts, while others had been created for her while at the Imperial Palace of Aldere. Several new ones hung there as well, gifts from Gabrielle Peregrim, designed to befit her new station in life as the Imperial Heir. It was that new station in her life that she could not reconcile in her heart. Even finding love in an unexpected location was more acceptable that the sudden realization that if anything happened to Emperor Kaitain that the responsibility for guiding the direction of the Cadarian people would fall to her. She had been in the Academy of Arcane Arts when her childhood friend Aris Ebonsight had been elevated to the position of Master within the Academy. Though she had been bred for it from the time that she was able to touch the flows of magic, the sudden realization of overwhelming responsibility was difficult for her to adapt to. Quyhn had seen something similar once she became closer to Dominique. Though she came from a low station in life and struggled every day to learn more and be better than anyone thought she could be, Dominique tackled all challenges and increased responsibility with a grace that belied anything that could be expected of one person.

Picking a light purple dress with cream colored accents from the collection that followed her from Aldere, Quyhn's thoughts went to Chelsea, and then by extension her daughter Rhionna. The two women were so strong but in completely different ways. Chelsea was a practiced warrior and general who had fought in and led many battles, and at the same time she tried to hold a Kingdom together, a truce, and a failed marriage. Then suddenly her husband's mistress is thrust into her life, but unbelievably as her better and her charge. How Chelsea had been able to not only adapt, but also to form a friendship with the woman spoke more to her character than anything she could have ever done on the battlefield. Though there was more to that relationship. There was a connection that existed between Dominique and Chelsea, one that very few would be able to see. But Quyhn knew it was there. There were stolen moments. Not on the level of intimacy that Quyhn had found in the arms of her protector, but it was more than respect, and more than friendship. It was as though the two women needed each other to survive what was coming; a need so deep and primal that there were no civilized words or thoughts to describe it. But it was not Quyhn's place to figure out such things; not when they were so far away and her new responsibilities were staring her in the face.

The evening's dinner was one of those new responsibilities. The feast in honor of the upcoming Days of Star Fire was a well-held tradition in all of the royal houses of the Cadarian Empire. Usually the invitees were restricted to members of the royal families, but while Quyhn's father had held the position of Court Sorcerer and advisor to the Emperor of Cadaria, Quyhn had had the opportunity to attend these feasts. Depending upon where the feast took place, there were several traditions that were observed, including readings from ancient books about the Day the Heaven's Fell, and about the great triumph of the first Cadarian Emperor over the leader of the Dark Gods and then of the Shadow War. But many of the houses spoke of their own heroism in those battles, casting their accomplishments as the turning points in the wars. However, in a place like Lordhill under the control of Connor Peregrim and the people who followed him, Quyhn was sure that there would be very little traditional in the feast other than the actual inclusion of food. Moreover, Connor Peregrim did not strike Quyhn as a man who would stand on ceremony regardless of who was sitting at his table. He was not one who was famed for his adherence to protocol, which is what earned him his exile in the first place.

It took only a few minutes for Quyhn to be dressed in her gown, and a quiet knock on the door announced Rhionna's return. Quyhn wasn't sure what she expected Rhionna to be wearing, but it certainly wasn't the stark white gown that she wore. There were simple gold accents on the sleeves and at the hem, as well as a simple tasseled gold belt and shoes. She looked amazing in the dress, and for the first time Quyhn saw modesty color Rhionna's eyes, and a slight color come to her cheeks.

"This wasn't my idea."

Her voice was not gruff, but Quyhn had enough exposure to the woman to know that she was not pleased with the way that she looked. She was not comfortable with the finery of court. She was born and bred to be a warrior, and had spent her life becoming one of the deadliest women to ever serve in a Cadarian army. She was every bit her mother's daughter, and Quyhn was sure that even her uncertain and shady parentage would not have prevented her from ascending to the ranks of the Knights of the Flashing Blade. Perhaps if Quyhn became the Empress of Cadaria, Rhionna would take a position similar to the one that Chelsea held now, not only a member of the Knights of the Flashing Blade, but also the personal protector and advisor of the Empress of Cadaria. Quyhn pulled her thoughts away from the idyllic future and back to the present with Rhionna's next words.

"I'm afraid if we stay here too much longer that Gabrielle will make it her personal mission to civilize me."

Quyhn could not stifle her laugh.

"I suppose you being civil might take away from your charm. But then again, I'm sure there are some expectations of the consort of the Imperial Heir."

Any color that was in Rhionna's features suddenly drained away and her eyes became cold. Rhionna took two quick steps forward and stood practically on top of Quyhn. At that distance, Rhionna's height advantage over Quyhn was much more pronounced, and the older woman towered over the younger woman who greatly exceeded her in social rank. Rhionna brought her hand up and took hold of Quyhn's chin. She didn't grip hard, and if Quyhn had wanted to, she could have pulled away, but Quyhn let Rhionna raise her chin and stare into her eyes.

"Listen to me," Rhionna said her voice low and conspiratorial. "Whatever we are here, and in private wherever we are is for us and us alone. Outside that door and in the view of the public we are what we are supposed to be. You are the Imperial Heir, and I am a soldier. You are my charge, my responsibility, and if the need arose, I would give my life to protect you, because that is what is expected of me. You are the Imperial Heir, and as such your life is for the people that you might one day rule. Time will require you to marry, to have children, and fulfill your responsibility to protect and extend the legacy of the family that you now belong to. You may not be a Lorien by birth, but you are a Lorien by name, and so the royal blood will be your burden to shoulder and to one day pass on."

Rhionna held the gaze for a long time, and though Quyhn wanted to let the tears flow from her eyes, she held her emotions in check. The words were hard and harsh, but the sentiment and the gravity were not. Rhionna believed, and more than that, she believed in Quyhn and the responsibility of her station. Saying what she said was less about convincing Quyhn, and more about expressing an understanding of what they were to one another, what they had to be, and what they could never be. Rhionna was a tactician, and she was laying out their relationship the way that she would lay out a plan of battle. The thought wiped away the troubled emotions and allowed Quyhn to bring a smile to her lips. The response caused Rhionna to release her chin, but before she could step back, Quyhn reached up and put a hand on either side of Rhionna's face and returned the intense stare.

"But no matter whom my station tells me I must share my bed with to preserve the Imperial Line, my nights will be ended in my own bed beside the person I choose, even if that person has to bring bow or dagger to bed in order to fulfill her role as my protector."

That caused a smile to come to Rhionna's lips. Quyhn let go of her protector's face and crossed past her toward the door. Just before she took hold of the handle, she turned back to face Rhionna with a mischievous smile coming to her lips.

"Though I suppose a little civility isn't such a bad thing, if it means you continue to wear clothes like that."

* * * * * * * * * * * *

Quyhn wasn't quite sure what she was expecting from the Feast of the Days of Star Fire, but it certainly wasn't the light and story-filled evening that it proved to be. In the fine royal houses of Cadaria, Rhionna would have been forced to stand through the whole painful ceremony, only allowed to get something to eat after her charge was safely tucked away in her private chambers. In Lordhill however, things were much different. While everyone was dressed well, there was nothing stuffy or elitist about any of the people around the table, and they all seemed to know that they were in the positions they were in not because of any breeding or heredity, but because they had worked and fought for everything they had. Rhionna sat to Quyhn's left at the moderately sized table, and while she felt out of place in the dress, it was not out of place with the examples set by Gabrielle and Quyhn. In a pinch, the table could have been set to accommodate eight, but there was no need for this intimate dinner. Connor Peregrim sat at one end of the table, near Rhionna, while Gabrielle Peregrim at the other end of the table at Quyhn's right. Across from Quyhn and Rhionna sat the seemingly inseparable pair of Arent Fox and Strum Anvilguard. In the time that Quyhn and Rhionna had been in Lordhill, they had gotten to know the two men quite well, and an interesting pair they were to say the least. They bickered constantly about everything, but always respectfully. Some of the time it seemed as one took the other side of an argument just so they could argue. But what was obvious was that both had very good minds. Strum was well-read and could quote passages from some of the great writers in Cadarian history. Arent was the master of history, both military and civilian. This was usually the breeding ground for most of their conflicts. Strum pulling on the more flowery and philosophical while Arent leaned toward precedent and fact. Rhionna had enjoyed her talks with Arent, learning more about the battles that pre-dated her involvement in the military, but also providing him with details from the battles she had seen with her own eyes. Strum and Arent were in the middle of another one of their debates when a page entered and handed Connor a message.

"How can you sit there and call the conflict at the Plains of Steam anything other than an act of war perpetrated by Thorigald?" Arent was saying, "And a desperate one at that. Anyone who would openly march his troops across that wasteland has only one intention, and that would be to launch an attack on Saldarine."

"History may reflect that point, my friend," Strum's deep voice registered. "But those who have reflected back on the policies at the time see the action for what it was. The war between Thorigald and Saldarine was never going to end. It was never going to be anything more than a series of holding actions and defensive retreats. Someone needed to be bold. Someone needed to elevate the level of the conflict and force the Emperor to take action to end the war once and for all. As long as things remained on the small scale, the Emperor would never get involved. It wasn't in his best interests."

"Strum has a point, Arent," Gabrielle interjected. "It was that conflict that led to the Emperor forcing the peace accord that culminated in the marriage alliance between the two kingdoms."

"A lot of good that did," Rhionna mumbled.

Rhionna's voice carried more than she intended, and while Gabrielle's face remained even, Arent laughed.

"You see, this is why regardless of how the writers and poets and well-wishers want to remember the political motives of that battle, the truth is found in the history. Thorigald and Saldarine are kingdoms that have hated each other long before the formation of the Cadarian Empire. The fact that they are tied together by the crucible called the Plains of Steam only means that they can't move en masse to wipe each other out without drawing the attention and ire of the creatures that live in that hell hole. Any peace between the two kingdoms is temporary at best, and ultimately futile. The soldiers know it. The generals know it. Even the royalty know it, but they play at peace to advance their political aspirations only, and care little for how many of their troops are sacrificed to create those gains."

"It's no wonder the Creator chose to insinuate you into my life," Strum countered. "You have no poetry in your soul."

"It's not a lack of poetry in my soul, my good and dear friend," Arent retorted, putting his hand atop Strum's, "it's your complete lack of perspective for anything other than flowery sentiment."

Those comments, as well as the touch of the two men's hands caused Quyhn to see the two men differently. Like relationships between women, relationships between men were not unheard of in Cadaria. It was even said that one of the Lorien emperors far preferred the bed of his favorite general to that of his wife. However, while most turned a blind eye to a tryst between women, there was an uncomfortable judgement placed upon the dalliances of men. Perhaps it was the expectation to carry the linage to the next generation, or perhaps it was the failing of the male ego and the inability of one to recognize the softness and vulnerability in one's self. Men were rough, brutish creatures that lived to be the strongest, or the bravest, or the most dominant. And the most tragic part of their existence was the fact that though they wished nothing more than to be judged on their strengths, they defined themselves by their weaknesses. Even her father had not been immune to the hypocrisy. While the Academy of Arcane Arts discouraged relationships between students, they were not totally forbidden. However, there was a little known rule dating back to the formation of the Academy that ordered the immediate expulsion of any male student found to be in a relationship with one another. As the Grand Master of the Academy, it had been within her father's power to excise that order, but his own prejudices and frailties could not be pushed that far.

The exchange between Arent and Strum sparked another peal of laughter and a lighter topic of conversation shared by everyone at the table, except for Connor. Out of the corner of her eye, Quyhn could see the tension in the man's face. Some of the color had drained from his cheeks, and he looked from the paper in his hands up to his wife once and then back to the paper. Finally, Gabrielle sensed something was amiss and turned her attention to Connor. It was not long after that the rest of the conversation around the table died, and all waited for Connor to break his silence and share the contents of the message he received. Finally Connor exhaled a long deep breath and leaned back in his chair.

"It seems that our dear Emperor Kaitain Lorien is far madder than we ever expected he would be."

It was as though all of the levity and good feelings were sucked out of the room at the mention of the Emperor's name. Quyhn could see Arent balling his fist and Strum's jaw clenched tightly. Gabrielle seemed visibly saddened, but did her best to keep more composure than the men at the table. Rhionna's military training kicked in, and the stone face of a soldier returned. After another moment, and another breath, Connor put the paper down on the table and looked first to his wife and then Quyhn. When he started speaking, it seemed to Quyhn as though he was speaking only to her, as if explaining something that everyone else already knew.

"Even though Lordhill technically falls within the borders of Aldere, we get treated no differently than some of the Great Kingdoms in several regards. Information coming out of the Royal Palace is usually very tightly controlled, which is why each of the royal families does their best to keep spies inside the palace to ensure that all of the news gets back to the right ears in a timely and uncensored fashion. Obviously with the loss of the Royal Palace itself, much of the formalized structure of spying, bribery, and graft that has existed for over a thousand years has been destroyed. Information is harder to come by now, and the cost of getting secrets is high. Unless of course you have a source."

"And that letter comes from your source close to the Emperor?" Rhionna asked.

Instead of Connor finishing his thought, Gabrielle commented.

"I can't imagine what sources we would have near the Emperor," she began, "especially now. With the Imperial Palace gone, I would imagine that Kaitain is keeping the people with access to him or those who have secret information to a very few, and most of them wouldn't like us."

Rhionna cocked an eyebrow, which Arent caught.

"We aren't exactly popular in Imperial circles."

Connor quickly shook his head.

"No, it isn't a source that owes us any allegiance; in fact we owe knowing any of this information to our guest here."

Quyhn was shocked for a moment, and then a knowing smile came to her lips. If anyone could have gotten word out of the inner circles of Kaitain's power, it would have been Dominique or Chelsea. Such information could be easily disguised as correspondence from mother to adopted daughter.

"It's quite obvious that this information comes from Lady Zarova," Connor said finally, "and what she outlines here is a nightmare scenario for anyone who doesn't share the same world view as Emperor Kaitain. Jacob Aldora was executed for crimes against the empire, and namely against the Emperor himself for failing to protect the Imperial Palace. Similarly Chelsea Zarova would have met the same fate if she hadn't ensured the life of the Empress."

Shock rippled through everyone sitting at the table, and Rhionna paled even more with news about her mother's brush with death. Though Quyhn was concerned, she was happy to know that both Chelsea and Dominique were safe enough to even send word with that madness going on.

"But there is much more. It seems that the Captain of the Imperial Guard, Korin Melcab has now become the de facto right hand of the

Emperor. Geoffry Aramour has fallen out of favor and seems to simply be skulking around. It appears as though the whole Shadow Guild is out of favor and a new layer of subordinates have risen to the Emperor's notice. Worse still, the Emperor has outlawed the practice of worship of the Creator, and anyone who fails to live up to the letter of this new law will find themselves stripped of all rank, station, and possessions and sent either to work here in the mines of Lordhill, or be pushed into slavery. Priests are being rounded up and executed."

Quyhn could not keep her mouth from dropping open.

"He's become a monster," Rhionna said quietly.

There were many blank looks around the table, as the enormity of what had begun to occur simply defied any rational explanation.

"Unfortunately, there is more," Connor said after a moment. "It seems that Kaitain is not content with letting his decrees unravel the Empire. It says here that he has started to mobilize his army in an effort to take direct control over all of the kingdoms. There are also standing orders to arrest any remaining members of the Knights of the Flashing Blade."

"Does Chelsea say what she and Dominique are planning to do about any of this?"

Gabrielle's question was pointed, and there was an implied meaning behind it. The leadership of Lordhill had been plotting a move against the Emperor, and now that the Emperor was taking a more active role in tearing down any who opposed him. The time for gathering strength was at an end, and the time for a move was at hand. If Chelsea or Dominique had designs to resist the Emperor and his madness, then the members of the Lordhill rebellion would be in the best position to help them.

"Dominique has been sentenced to exile in Rashaleb. She's been tasked with acting as the Emperor's agent in that Kingdom, exerting direct influence through her. Chelsea managed to convince Kaitain to allow her to accompany Dominique to Rashaleb instead or returning to Saldarine, which she has now been appointed the military governor of. They will be leaving from Aldere the morning after the Night of Star Fire, and are worried that Kaitain or Korin Melcab may attempt to kill them both and make it look like the action of a rebel faction or at the order of religious fanatics, or Marlae. She has asked if we could provide escort to Rashaleb and ensure their safety."

Quyhn put both of her hands on the table and stood.

"We must ensure the safety of the Empress."

Connor leaned back.

"We certainly can't allow Kaitain to use the death of the Empress to turn the populace against his opponents. And Chelsea Zarova is too valuable of an ally to lose. Not only that, I'm sure the Imperial Heir would not be too happy with us were we to ignore this request for assistance."

Quyhn folded her arms and nodded slowly.

"Very well," Connor said finally. "I'm sure I can find someone I can send."

The Religion of the Gods

Year Four of the Just Emperor Kaitain "Dragonsbane" Lorien, Creator's Calendar Year 1871

The first streams of dawn began to peak over the eastern horizon, and though the sky was alight with the trails from the moon rock being ripped from Espre's moon during its pass through the coronas of the twin suns, dawn was still striking in its beauty and majesty. Korin Melcab stood outside the door of the room that now served as the private suite for the Emperor of Cadaria, Kaitain Lorien. Korin knew that the young emperor had spent all of his night interrogating a prisoner, one of such importance that it could shift the balance of the war with the Dark Gods. When the door cracked open, the Emperor emerged, one half of his fearsome mask coated with dried blood. The red liquid had crept into the carefully carved filigree turning the fine silver coloration a deep crimson. Korin chanced a look past the Emperor into the room and saw the form of a naked unconscious woman bound to a chair in the center of the room. Her head was down, and her long hair obscured most of her upper body from view. Pools of dried blood could be seen on the floor at her feet, and there were streaks of it staining her legs. Quickly Korin gave a shallow bow to the Emperor and returned to a sharp attention waiting for orders.

"Report."

Kaitain's voice was smooth with just the hint of malice. If there were any noticeable effects from his long slumber under the effects of an assassin's poison the principle among them was his more vicious attitude toward everything. Ire was his default position, and any transgressions were met with the harshest reprisals. Korin fell into step a half pace behind the Emperor as they made their way in the direction of the small room that served as the quarters for the Empress Dominique Lorien. The door to that room already stood open and there were guards both on the inside and outside of the doorway.

"There were a number of disturbances during the night, my Emperor, several of which should be of considerable concern. The first relates to the Empress and her guardian."

The guards at the doorway both bowed quickly and moved to the side to allow the Emperor and the Captain of the Guard access to the room. In the far corner of the room under the only window was a wide pool of dried blood. Beside the blood lay an ornamental sword that bore the crest of the Lorien family etched into its blade just above the hilt. Two guards knelt in the opposite corner of the room, two of their fellow guardsman on either side, weapons at the ready. Kaitain took in the scene for a long moment before turning to face Korin.

"Explain."

Korin quietly cleared his throat before beginning.

"This is one of four connected incidents that seem to have been engineered by Chelsea Zarova and an unknown number of collaborators. The first actually took place in the cellar under the inn. As you recall, my Emperor, the Sacred Weapon Tenacity, which until her removal from the position of Garnet Knight of the Flashing Blade was held in trust by Lady Zarova, was being stored in the cellar until such time as the Just Emperor deemed it necessary to appoint a new protector to that post. It appears that there was a disturbance created by a group of religious zealots that were opposed to the recent decrees about the illegality of the worship of the Creator. They distracted the guards who were responsible for ensuring that there would be no entry into the cellar without permission. This distraction allowed someone, and for now we believe that person to be Lady Zarova, to slip into the cellar and steal the Sacred Weapon."

Kaitain put his hand up for a long moment to interrupt his Captain of the Guard's report. Annoyance was growing within him, but the explosion was being kept at bay. Korin's silence showed the level of respect that someone in his position had to show at all times, and also showed an understanding that Kaitain Lorien was not a man to be tested. Lorien's eyes still had not left the pool of blood under the window, and when he spoke, the rage in his voice was clear.

"Were both the guards and the rioters put to death?"

Kaitain couldn't have seen Korin's nod, but he nodded just the same.

"I saw to it personally last night, my Emperor. Fifteen rioters as well as the four guards in question met their ends. The heretics will be burned as is the law. I have taken the liberty of mounting the heads of the guardsmen on pikes and placing them at the corners of the inn as a motivational tool for the remaining men."

Kaitain gave a curt nod and with a flourish of his hand beckoned for Korin to continue his report.

"The second incident took place sometime before the riot, but we don't know exactly when. The exact nature of this incident is unknown as it was not considered to be related until my investigation in the early hours. A serving maid from the common room was murdered in the stables. The body was hidden well, but during the thorough search of the grounds that I ordered in the early morning hours, it was easily discovered. The murder was quick and would have been relatively painless, as if some level of care was extended toward the girl."

Korin fell silent for a moment, letting his words germinate meaning in the mind of the Emperor. His gaze still fixed on the pool of blood, he responded.

"And who was this girl? And why would she have such import as to be connected to Lady Zarova's treachery?"

"The girl was of no true consequence, other than serving as a distraction for me from time to time. But this was reason enough for her to be murdered and replaced with an assassin."

This last caused Kaitain to turn and face his Captain of the Guard.

"A face-dancer?"

Korin nodded curtly. Though not many knew of the secret techniques of the Shadow Guild, Kaitain was one who prided himself on knowing all weapons at his disposal. Though Geoffry Aramour, the resident Master of the Shadow Guild, was never fully transparent with the information he had concerning the techniques of the guild, enough pieces seeped through that a man of Kaitain's intelligence could glean a fuller meaning. Face-dancing was a cherished and guarded technique that allowed very specialized and skilled assassins to perfectly impersonate a single person. This allowed them to get very close to their targets before striking a fatal blow. But the act of copying a person required the death of the person being copied. It was a powerful tool, one that would be extremely dangerous in the wrong hands. And now it appeared that the technique had been turned against Kaitain's own inner circle.

"And you were the target?" Kaitain questioned.

Korin again nodded. But instead of allowing his master to come to his own conclusions, Korin continued his explanation.

"The assassin was well trained and used all of the techniques at her disposal to attempt to remove me from this life. However, I proved too difficult a quarry for her skills to vanquish. However, in addition to preventing me from interfering in the theft of the Sacred Weapon, the distraction of the assassin also allowed someone to steal my sword and place it here in the Empresses' room in an attempt to implicate me in either her disappearance or death. If the assassin had succeeded, it would have been easy enough for them to place my body in the Empresses' room, and allow Lady Zarova to take credit for protecting the Empress from me, undermining your power and casting the Empress as the sympathetic figure."

"A bold plan," Kaitain said with a mixture of emotion, more of respect than of anger. "But utterly fruitless. Even were they to deprive me of your services, it would be simple enough to cast you into the role of an ambitious and self-interested man who wanted to make the Empress his own and was thwarted by one of the most decorated members of the Knights of the Flashing Blade. There are many who would accept that explanation, and those who didn't will see vipers in all shadows."

When there was a flutter of doubt that crossed over Korin's features, Kaitain was quick to continue his train of thought.

"But regardless, these conspirators would have deprived me of one of my most loyal subordinates. Which I assume leads us to the incident that occurred here."

Korin's curt nod caused Kaitain to turn back to face the pool of blood on the floor. For several long moments the two men remained silent before Korin began his explanation anew.

"This is the incident we know the least about. All we know for certain is that the guards who were ordered to keep post at the Empress's door were sent by Lady Zarova to assist with putting down the riot outside of the inn. This allowed Lady Zarova to enter the Empress's room and for whatever occurred here to transpire without witness. When this room was investigated in the early morning hours, all of the Empress's clothing was still hanging in the wardrobe and folded neatly. There was no sign of a body, or any track or trail that could be followed, either leaving the room through the door or out the window. Two horses have been reported missing from the stables, however there are reports that they were seen running wild during the riot. There have been no reports of sightings for either Lady Zarova or the Empress."

Kaitain walked over to where the two guards knelt, and turned back toward Korin, his hand sweeping in the direction of the two prisoners.

"These were the men who left their posts at Lady Zarova's orders. When they returned to their posts and discovered that their charge was missing and possibly dead, they surrendered themselves to custody."

Deftly, Kaitain drew a dagger from one of the guard's belts who held the captive men and slit the throat of the guard closest to him. Blood spurted in all directions and the last dying gurgles escaped his lips before he fell face-first to the floor, the growing pool of blood flooding around his fallen form. Tension filled the room as Kaitain held the blade to the other man's throat.

"Dereliction of duty will not be tolerated. Any failing, any measure of disloyalty, any measure of incompetence will be met with swift and brutal reprisal. The incompetence of my protectors nearly cost me my life, and may well now have endangered the life of the Empress. There are traitors who have dug deep into the flesh of this Empire, and I will not rest until I have cut free every malignant parasite who feeds on the flesh of the righteous."

With his other hand, Kaitain took hold of the captive soldier's collar and pulled him to his feet. He pressed the hilt of the blood knife into the soldiers hand and stared him hard in the eyes. The soldier's eyes widened and his pupils contracted to pin points as he stared into the dead eyes of his Emperor.

"Follow every track, follow every trace, turn over every rock and scour the landscape from here to the end of the world. You will search until the Empress is found, and the traitor Chelsea Zarova is brought to justice. If the Empress is found dead, once Zarova is dealt with, you will end your own life in penance for your failure. If however she is found to be alive and is returned to Aldere, I will consider only stripping you of your rank and sending you to the mines to work for the rest of your life."

Kaitain paused here to let his words have the full measure of impact that he had intended. When he was sure that the young soldier understood the gravity of his situation, he leaned in closer and spoke in a violent tone.

"If you try to run, if you turn your back on your duty again, or if you cast your lot in with the traitors who would see me ripped from my birthright, I promise you with every drop of blood that flows through my veins that you will suffer pain unlike any man has ever suffered. I will make sure you beg to die with every breath, and that you live in pain and humiliation until I no longer draw breath."

Kaitain turned his back on the soldier.

"Get this disgrace out of my sight."

The two soldiers were quick to take the shaken prisoner by the arms and lead him from the room, leaving the Emperor and his Captain of the Guard alone. The silence was deafening. Finally it was Kaitain that spoken.

"What are you doing about this, Korin?"

The implication was clear. The responsibility for the disappearance of the Empress sat firmly on the head and shoulders of the Captain of the Imperial Guard.

"With a face-dancer involved," Korin began, "it's clear that the Shadow Guild is involved. To that end I've had Geoffry Aramour arrested under suspicion of treason. He's under guard in the cellar right now, protected by ten of my hand-picked Imperial Guardsmen."

Kaitain turned to face Korin again, and this time Korin could feel the heat of his master's gaze digging into him. The barely restrained fury was being pushed to its limit. And then as if something had occurred to the Emperor, he began to chuckle behind his vicious mask.

"Excellent," Kaitain said finally. "Geoffry has been operating on the very edge of what is acceptable for far too long, and his trustworthiness was beginning to be called into question. There is a chance that he also has information on the assassin that made the attempt on my life. However I doubt highly that we will be able to break any information out of him."

A cruel smile came to Korin's lips, but Kaitain dismissed his next words with a wave of his hand.

"Oh I have no doubt that your torture techniques are sound enough to get the information out of him, Korin. However, I highly doubt that the Shadow Guild would ever allow one of their Masters to be broken. They know certainly by now that we have him in custody, and they have never been an organization that has been slow in acting. They will either attempt to rescue him within the next day, or they will eliminate him if they feel he has outlived his usefulness. And I can assure you that no amount of your hand-picked guardsmen would be able to prevent either eventuality."

Korin again began to object, but the Emperor's raised hand prevented him from doing so. Kaitain had fallen silent and returned his gaze to the pool of blood under the window. There was something about the blood that seemed wrong, but he just couldn't place his finger on it.

"Find Yaron Telsin. I'm sure he hasn't strayed far, even after the fall of the palace. And where he is, so shall be his students. Yaron will have a better chance to defend Geoffry unless the Shadow Guild chooses to send their very best. Provided of course he's still alive while we are speaking. Until those provisions are in place, I'm holding you personally responsible for our captive's safety."

Korin bowed slightly and crossed the room to where his sword lay at the edge of the still wet pool of blood. As he knelt down he quickly looked out the window to see the ruins of the Imperial Palace of Aldere in the distance and the bright trails of fire in the sky. Upon retrieving his blade, he stood straight again, but this time when Korin looked out the window, he saw the form of a man standing in the middle of the open area, looking up at the window. Korin could feel the power rolling off the man, and he squeezed hard the hilt of his sword. The two men stared at each other through the distance, when suddenly the man standing outside the inn lifted his right hand. As Korin felt the whole of the inn shake, he turned and dove for Emperor Kaitain, pressing him to the floor and shielding him with his own mass. An invisible force ripped through the walls of the inn from the foundation to the roof, opening a foot-wide gash. Guards burst into the room the next moment, and as Korin stood, he pulled Kaitain to his feet and practically threw him to the guardsmen.

"Flee with the Emperor. Take him toward Zevarit. Go, now!"

The guardsmen held the Emperor firmly by each arm and started to pull him from the room. Shock held the Emperor's will at bay for only a few moments before Kaitain regained his senses and pulled himself from the guards.

"No. Aldere is mine! I will not flee like a mewling babe in the face of a threat. The Imperial Palace was lost, but I shall not lose Aldere. Not now, not ever."

The guards fell back and instantly had their weapons at the ready for whatever battle was to come. While the guards were filled with pride and spirit, Korin could only feel disappointment. With what faced them outside the inn, defending this position was impossible. To attempt any defense of a worthless plot of land was suicidal at best. But the Emperor was not of sound mind, not any more. The only thing that propelled the man was rage, hate, and vengeance. And none of those emotions allowed for the possibility of retreat, even in the face of a greater enemy, or in the face of utter destruction. There would be no retreat, which meant there remained but one alternative.

Korin took one short step toward the crack in the wall before sprinting into the gaping opening. He leapt into the opening and floated into the nothingness for a long moment before crashing down toward the ground. When he landed, both feet touched the ground and left deep imprints. Korin paused for only a moment before raising his blade and charging toward what could only have been a member of the Dark Gods. A full two paces from his prey, Korin hit what felt like a brick wall. However, instead of bouncing off and falling down, he held his ground and struggled against the force that was trying to propel him backward. From inside the bubble of force that protected the Dark God there came a sound like thunder, and a wave of power exploded outward; a shockwave that sent Korin sprawling backwards. He landed hard on his back, but the wave of power didn't relent. It was as though the Dark God was trying to squash him like a bug beneath the sheer force of his will. Were Korin an ordinary man, or were he even one of the members of the Knights of the Flashing Blade, such an assault would have crushed the life from his body in a matter of moments. But Korin was not an ordinary man, nor was he going to allow himself to be beaten like this. He would not allow himself to become an afterthought in the Dark God's rampage to murder the Emperor of Cadaria. Digging into his inner reserves of power, Korin forced his way back to his feet and stood firm against the onslaught. After a few moments, the oppressive waves abated, and the Dark God's vengeful sneer lightened slightly and the left corner of his mouth cocked in a show of mock respect.

"Not one of Kaitain's normal lackey's, are you?"

Korin's only answer was a frown that turned into a sneer.

"What are you," the Dark God continued, "one of those pathetic Flashing Blade imbeciles? I hope not, they die far too easily."

"My name is Korin Melcab, and I am the Captain of the Imperial Guard and personal protector of Emperor Kaitain Lorien. The Knights of the Flashing Blade have become populated with traitors and should be crushed under the boot of those who are truly dedicated to the future of Cadaria. Emperor Lorien's vision for the future of Cadaria…"

"Is a rotting corpse," the Dark God interrupted. "As he will be soon enough."

Korin let the jibe pass through him. He took a step toward the Dark God, squeezing tighter the hilt of his sword until his knuckles turned white. Before he could continue his rhetoric, the Dark God pointed one finger at the center of Korin's chest. The half-smile disappeared, and the face of a killer replaced it.

"My name is Pike Rhuiden, I am the leader of the Dark Gods, and you and the traitor Ivan Quicksilver have my wife. You will return her to me now, along with the head of the traitor and your pretender of an Emperor, or there will be no Cadaria for your Emperor to rule over. I will leave this Aldere of yours to watch the rest of your empire crumble around you, and just before the last embers of your burning landscape go out I will personally rip Kaitain's heart out."

After a long moment Korin dropped his sword to the ground and reached up to un-clasp the breastplate from his armor. A metal shell would not avail him in the battle that was to come. When the armor had been removed, Korin stretched his neck first to the left and to the right before balling his fists and taking another step toward the Dark God. The gesture caused a peel of laughter to burst from Pike's mouth. The absurdity had become too much for him to bear.

"I've only experienced stupidity like yours one other time in my life, Korin Melcab, Captain of the Imperial Guard. A man thought he could change the world just because he thought he knew a different way. He thought he was better than the rest of us. He thought he was smarter. But like you, there was only one fate for such a man. He's dead. And I'm still here. I'll always be here, and in the end, I'm going to be the one that shapes the world according to my whims. Not him. And anyone who stands in my way will burn."

The air around Pike began to sizzle with energy, and Korin could feel his hairs begin to stand on end. Power rolled off of the Dark Gods like waves and crashed into Korin like breakers against the shore. For just a moment, Pike's eyes fluttered shut. But then when they opened, all of the color had drained from them, and they were pure white.

"And now you will burn."

Pike extended his hand once again, only this time it was wreathed with writhing white peaks of flame. A stream of fire exploded from the spread fingers, traveling the distance between the two men in less time than it would have taken to blink. The massive gout of flame took the Captain of the Imperial Guard full in the chest. Pike expected the flame to burst through the man's chest and erupt through a massive hole in the man's torso. However Korin kept his feet and seemed to be withstanding the onslaught. Reaching deep, Pike increased the power flooding out of him, trying to overwhelm the stubborn mortal. Not only did Korin seem to withstand the assault, but the man took a step toward Pike, bringing both of his arms to his chest as though he were trying to block the Dark God's attack. Then suddenly there came an explosion from where Korin's crossed arms met the stream of flame. A wave of force erupted in all directions, sending both Korin and Pike sprawling to the ground. Trees were felled by the force of the explosion and the nearby stables collapsed. Pike's head felt as though someone had hit him with a thousand pound sledgehammer and when he got himself back to his feet he started looking for the surprising man who had proven to be far more of an impediment than Pike had expected. Smoke rolled across the plain, creating a fog that proved to obscure Korin from Pike's sight. However after a moment enough of the smoke had cleared that the Dark God was able to spot his quarry. Pike could not believe his eyes.

Instead of a man, Pike saw the form of a massive beast, its face covered in blackened scales, and burning red eyes glaring hatred. Horns protruded not from a helmet, but from the top of its head; it's snarling mouth full of razor sharp teeth. The being seemed to have grown to double his previous size, with legs as thick around as tree trunks. Large bat-like wings protruded from places just below the shoulder blades. Seeing the new creature facing him, Pike let twin blades of ice form in his hands. This time it was Korin who extended a razor-sharp talon in the direction of the Dark God.

"Now, I will make you burn."

CHAPTER 69

Chapter LXX

The Heart's Reason

Year Four of the Just Emperor Kaitain "Dragonsbane" Lorien, Creator's Calendar Year 1871

Though she was well known in the Kingdom of Celidar, Taya felt uneasy as she ascended the long flight of steps that lead to the gates of the palace. Celidar itself had come a long way since Jerrard and Erika Mistic were named regents of the kingdom, and while neither of them were considered to be of royal blood on this world, they were respected equally by all the lords and ladies of all the other Kingdoms of Cadaria. The fact that they gained their position through Imperial mandate and not through inheritance was rare, but demanded a level of respect. Though Celidar did not have access to the same kind of riches that many of the other kingdoms did, Celidar did have the greatest trading and fishing ports in all of Cadaria. Strangely enough, when the spate of pirate assaults began on the fleets of Cadaria, Celidar suffered the least amount of losses and attacks which allowed their economy to prosper. The only downside of course was as their profits soared, so too did the burden of taxes required to support Kaitain's wars. Almost every piece of gold that wasn't being used for upkeep and improvements to the kingdom was sent to Aldere in one form or another. Most of it was in the form of steel, the other chief resource that Celidar had in abundance. Between the mass smelting operations in the north close to the borders of Zevarit and Rashaleb, and the foundries on the southern coast, Celidar produced more workable steel than the rest of the Cadarian kingdoms combined. The steel brought some money into the economy of Celidar, but due to ancient laws and traditions, the largest portion was simply given to Aldere for Imperial use. Kaitain had tried to increase that amount as well, but fortunately for Jerrard and Erika, the Imperial decree that gave them control over Celidar also guaranteed that as long as they were alive, the production quotas were protected, and it was a decree that could not be violated, even by the decree of another Emperor of Cadaria.

As was her tradition when she came to Celidar, Taya's fleet would stay close to the coastline, and only a few ships, those that could be viewed as trading vessels would come into port. However, under the circumstances, such precautions could not be taken. It was time for Taya to bring her entire armada into port but all ships were striking Celidar colors. Though this irritated some members of her anti-Cadarian crew, they all knew enough not to question the motivations of their Captain. Even still, they would all remain at their highest level of vigilance while in port. Taya took none of her crew with her on her visit to the palace as it was not necessary. There were none in Celidar that could have caused her harm, and with Sabrina and Rhain at her side as well as two members of the Knights of the Flashing Blade, the chances of any interference were staggeringly low. Though Devlin and Gabriel were unarmed, they did have their reputations to keep all but the bravest or stupidest at bay, and while most who observed the small group would have regarded the two men as the most dangerous of the group, that assertion could not have been farther from the truth.

As the group ascended the long flight of granite stairs, Sabrina stopped just short of reaching the landing at the top of the stairs where the large iron-banded wooden doors barred entry to the royal palace. She put her hand out and instantly found Rhain's shoulder. The diminutive and pale woman supported herself for a long moment before being able to find her balance again. The powers that she had inherited were still destabilizing her system and making it difficult to adapt to the changes that flooded through her. Contact with others who had power, and those who had similar power helped for a short period of time, and seemed to give her the opportunity to catch her breath. And with what waited for them on the other side of the door, she would need all of the fragile stability she could manage.

There was overwhelming power that surrounded Sabrina, and no matter how she tried to control her breathing, it felt more and more as though she were going to lose consciousness. There was more power on the other side of those massive doors than she was prepared for, and the flares of power within her seemed to grow with every step. Sweat had already begun to form on her brow, and as Rhain gave her a comforting smile, Sabrina knew that she had to be deathly pale. How she was able to hold herself together at all was a credit to the years that she had to learn the intricacies of the abilities that Aerith had granted her. She knew that she had always impressed Aerith with the way that she had excelled, and over the centuries she had even been able to teach the old man a thing or two. Though she knew that Bryn would have frowned on the stolen time that Sabrina and Aerith spent together, every second was precious to both of them. However, the stolen moments were not for carnal pleasure, or for any purpose other than to make sure they were both ready for the fight ahead. Even without his full powers, Aerith was a master of tactics and strategy, though few would have noticed since his mouth gave a completely different impression of the man. But then, misconceptions had served to keep the man alive this long, and anyone who underestimated him now showed only their own ignorance. Aerith had limitless depths, both positive and negative. Those who dared to tap into them were met with wonders and horrors that defied description. Many nights Sabrina had awakened, drenched with sweat and heart racing from nightmares that were not her own. The horrors and pain that Aerith dealt with every moment of his life were staggering, and inwardly Sabrina wondered if the old man would find peace even in victory.

When the doors finally opened, after what seemed like an eternity to Sabrina, the procession entered the long receiving hall that led to the improvised throne room. Jerrard and Erika disdained the oppressive throne room that originally held the center of the royal palace, so they had it dismantled in favor of something far less formal. The thrones were replaced with more reserved high-backed chairs, to continue to promote the air of approachability that the couple wanted their subjects to feel. The receiving hall on the other hand had very little of the comforting air that the Mistics tried to foster. Perhaps it was less the fault of the chamber and more the fault of the discomfort that was growing in Sabrina's gut. There was something waiting for her on the other side of the doors ahead, and the uncertainty was not something that she was managing well. Part of her wanted to reach out for Aerith, to draw comfort from his presence in her mind. But things had changed so drastically for the both of them that she didn't know what that would do. Did she have the power now to pull him through time and space to where she was? Would reaching out to him in that manner send up a flare alerting all of their enemies to where they each were? Until she had better control of her powers, perhaps she would chance such a connection, but for now, she would just have to show more strength than she had been able to muster alone for a long time.

Sabrina had grown up in a world at war, a reality that should never have existed, and one where atrocities were the rule rather than the exception. Men died by the hundreds daily, and very few heroes dared rise up against the tide of villainy. And yet, when a hero did rise, he shown like the brightest beacon in the darkest night. Sabrina grew into her teen years in the shadow of one such hero, a man who she came to love as a father. Even now, all these millennia removed from those days, she would sacrifice anything for him, and while proximity to some of the heroes of her world had created a tarnish upon their legacy, Logan Ranthall still shown as brightly as the day he stormed into her life. A close second in Sabrina's estimation, and perhaps greater in reputation for heroism was Gwydeon Sandar, and when the doors to the throne room opened, it was his eyes that Sabrina first found looking back at her. She had known he would be here. She didn't know how she knew, but she knew. Before the doors were even fully open, she found herself sprinting across the distance between them and throwing her arms around him. She squeezed him tightly for a long time before finally regaining herself and pulling away. She barely realized she started to speak until the words had already escaped her lips.

"You're much easier to hug without wings," Sabrina heard herself saying, a comment met by laughter from the woman standing to Gwydeon's left.

Despite herself, Sabrina found herself throwing her arms around Midarin next, though for a much shorter amount of time. The two women had never been close, but had usually found themselves on the same side of most issues that faced the Dark Gods. Loss had created a need for distance within Midarin, which forced her to keep everyone at arm's length. Perhaps there was also trepidation within Sabrina to push for fear that Midarin would have seen the truth in Sabrina's eyes. Midarin put her hands on Sabrina's shoulders as the younger woman pulled away.

"I forgive you," Midarin said calmly. "I can't imagine how difficult it has been to hold on to the secrets you have inside you."

Sabrina could barely manage a smile in return.

"So this is the famous Gwydeon and Midarin...."

The voice came from the red-haired woman behind Sabrina. Rhain had taken several steps away from the rest of the group and was standing with her hands on her hips taking in both Gwydeon and Midarin.

"I don't see what all the fuss is about."

"Who the hell do you think you are?"

Midarin started to take a step toward the impertinent girl, only to find Gwydeon's hand resting on her shoulder, resisting her attempts to advance. Her puzzled glance melted with his smile and soft laugh.

"You must be Rhain," Gwydeon said, the smile still wide on his face. "Midarin, this is Aerith and Bryn's daughter."

After a long moment of the two women regarding one another, Midarin softly clicked her tongue and let a small frown curl her lips.

"Explains her manners," Midarin said just softly enough that only Gwydeon and Sabrina could hear.

"I see we have guests," Jerrard's voice came from behind Gwydeon and Midarin.

Jerrard and Erika approached quickly, and Taya crossed the distance and wrapped her arms around her mother in a tender embrace while favoring her step-father with a mild smile before stepping back.

"We're sorry to drop in on you like this," Taya said quickly, "but there is much we need to discuss and time it seems is growing shorter."

Jerrard saw the look in Taya's eyes, and then moved toward the rest of the group.

"My hospitality and the hospitality of my court is at your disposal. Let's move this conversation to the dining hall where we can talk."

Sabrina's features went cold.

"There isn't time," she said her tone suddenly deathly serious, "at least not for Gwydeon's portion of this conversation. You need to leave now. You need to be in Rashaleb. There is someone there waiting for you that you must see. And very soon, otherwise things will go horribly wrong. You know why. It's time."

It was this moment that Felicia Lorien emerged from an adjacent corridor, and she was just pulling the sword belt tight around her waist.

"What are we waiting for?" Felicia said pulling her hair back into a tail. "Let's go."

Midarin took a long hard look at the princess before speaking.

"Are you sure you want to do this?" Midarin asked with a note of genuine concern in her voice. "I'm sure that Jerrard would appreciate your assistance in defending Celidar."

"Celidar is well defended," Taya bristled, "both from the land and from the sea. There's nothing a spoiled Cadarian princess is going to be able to do to help, especially if she spends all of her time painting her nails and brushing her hair."

Felicia made a move toward Taya, but it was Sabrina that spun to face her ally.

"Taya, put away your hate. There will be plenty of time to make Kaitain pay for his crimes. Felicia is not your enemy. Not now. But she has to go with Gwydeon and Midarin. She is needed there. Perhaps more than either Gwydeon or Midarin."

Sabrina put her hand on Gwydeon's chest, and his eyes opened wide.

"You'll need this," Sabrina said softly. "For now, and for later."

In the blink of an eye, Gwydeon, Midarin, and Felicia were gone. Multiple portals opened in the throne room a fraction of a second after the trio had disappeared, and then just as quickly closed. Sabrina placed a hand on her chest and took a long deep breath.

"With a few seconds to spare…"

Rhain saw Sabrina's knees go weak and the woman begin to collapse. She and Taya got to Sabrina's side at nearly the same instant, supporting the girl. Sabrina was flushed and sweating profusely, and her eyes fluttered open as though it took great effort to fight back her eyelids. Finally her eyes came to rest on Rhain's face.

"Whatever happens, don't interfere. We can't lose you now."

Without an answer to her puzzling statement, Sabrina lolled her head to one side so that she could fix her eyes on the intent gaze of the Onyx Knight Devlin Rannoch. Tears streamed from the woman's eyes the next moment, and her weakened voice barely touched his ears.

"I'm sorry."

* * * * * * * * * * * *

Darrien and Alderin stood looking down at Tess's sleeping form, the unspoken conversation about the events outside the Heart of Stone binding them in silence. Already plans were in motion around them, that much was clear. Mirana had burst in only a few moments ago to inform them of the impending destruction of the Citadel of the Dark Gods, the only home that they had ever known. It was a day that Darrien's father always knew would come, one that he had planned for since well before her birth, and one that he had trained her for. Despite what Wolf, Lissa, or any of the others desired, Darrien's place was on the path that her father had set for her. Finally Darrien turned to Alderin and could not suppress the frown.

"Tess is your responsibility now," she said, a tear coming to her eye, "take her to Jerrard and make sure she's safe. Father made you our protector long ago, and you have to stay with her. Especially now."

Alderin's face held no expression, but his stormy eyes were full of raging emotions. Alderin was the mirror image of his father in temperament, passion, and power. He had learned every lesson at White Lightning's feet and perhaps was the strongest of the children of the Dark Gods. Unlike Darrien, both of Alderin's parents had powers, and that had made certain concepts of the use of power easier for him to grasp. Also, he was much older than Darrien, so he had the advantage of centuries more practice. Before Alderin could make his thoughts known, Darrien leaned in and gave him a long deep kiss. As she pulled away, a portal was already opening behind her. However, before she could make her way through the event horizon, the portal snapped shut. Darrien whirled to face the bed just in time to see Tess sitting up on the small bed, her eyes glowing with bright golden light. The blow hit her the next moment, sending her crashing through the stone wall behind her. Alderin received a similar blow the next moment, except this one was much stronger, sending him bursting through the exterior wall of the chamber to the muddy ground outside the citadel.

"The traitor's life is mine!"

Before Tess's words had finished lingering in the air, her form had disappeared from the chamber.

* * * * * * * * * * * *

Two portals opened on the far side of the Royal Palace of Celidar, one slightly before the other. Bryn dropped to the ground and waited for the weakened form of Jeroch Yetre to follow. Jeroch was gravely wounded, and the chances were even that he would survive the trip through the portal. Traveling through portals created by someone else was disorienting at best, nauseating at worst. After laying Jeroch on the grass-covered ground, she began to look around for some landmark that would ground her. Finding none, she looked back down at Jeroch, whose eyes were open and squinting to try to focus on the structure of the palace.

"Celidar."

His voice was weak and strained, but better than it had been prior to their abrupt retreat from Iltorp. When his head shifted back and his eyes found Bryn's, there was the faintest hint of a smile on his lips.

"Jerrard."

When Bryn heard the name, she too smiled. Ellis had not only protected them, she had made sure that Bryn would find the help she needed for Jeroch. Jerrard's wife was a fine healer even before the Fall, but now that she had the powers of a Dark God, she was perhaps the only person on the face of Espre who Bryn knew would help Jeroch without question, despite the rocky past they all shared. She made a move to lift Jeroch from the ground, but he put a hand on her shoulder and let his eyes fall to the direction of the palace again.

"Wait. Something isn't right."

It was then that Bryn felt it too. There were massive powers coming from the direction of the palace. Several of them were familiar but all wrong, as though they were not supposed to be there at all. Then Bryn homed in on one that was too familiar. Too close to herself. Her eyes widened with realization. Her eyes went back to Jeroch, but his restricting hand had already begun to push her away. Jeroch may not have known exactly what she was feeling, but the strong ripple of concern that floated between the two could not be mistaken.

"Go."

Bryn put a reassuring hand on the middle of Jeroch's chest, and then quickly stood and reached for her powers. The portal formed seconds later and Bryn was gone. Jeroch lay there for several long moments before attempting to get to a seated position. It took longer to be able to get his feet under him again, and though the poison was rushing through his system at incredible speed and attempting to eat him from the inside out, he trusted in the abilities of the Blaze to keep him alive at least until a permanent solution could be had.

"Stubborn to the last, Shadow."

Jeroch didn't have to turn around to know the voice.

"Was wondering when you were going to slither out of your hiding place, Saurn."

The violet-eyed Saurn simply appeared in the space in front of Jeroch. It was obvious to the oldest member of the phasia that his younger sibling had been perfecting his tricks.

"Hiding in plain sight has been far more rewarding than I thought. I've been able to watch you and the others scurrying around trying to eliminate one another. But as you say, it's time to come out of hiding. Unless I miss my guess, the endgame is just beginning, and I wouldn't want to miss that."

A blade had appeared in Saurn's hand. Jeroch could have used some of his powers to conjure a weapon, but it would have stolen from the valuable life-sustaining functions that the Blaze was currently performing. And, if this confrontation devolved into a fight, it would be severely one-sided.

"You don't need that, Saurn, and you know it," Jeroch said, color coming slightly back into his cheeks. "I've made sure that you have stayed out of sight all this time. Do you honestly believe that someone as intelligent as me wouldn't have known that you were at the heart of the Shadow Guild? Do you honestly think for one second that you could have stayed out of Cedric's notice, or Logan's, or any of the Dark Gods' for that matter if it wasn't for me? You're good, Saurn, but you've never been that good."

Saurn opened his hand and let the blade's hilt fall from it. A moment before the blade would hit the ground, it dissolved into thousands of grains of sand.

"It seems we have much to talk about then. I have the antidote for the poison that is ravaging you, and once administered, you should be feeling back to your old self in no time."

Jeroch took half a step forward and then stopped.

"How did you know I'd be here?"

Saurn's smile widened slightly.

"That is a much more interesting salve to ply on old wounds."

* * * * * * * * * * *

As Taya lay on the floor, it felt as though hell's mouth had opened beneath the throne room and was yawning widely into the world of the living. It took only a few moments for everything to go wrong, and now, as wind and fire whipped around the whole of the throne room, even the powerful members of the Dark Gods were taking shelter to weather the storm. It had only been a few moments before that Gwydeon, Midarin, and Felicia had disappeared from the throne room. Then everything went wrong. The portal opened on the far side of the room, and from it stepped the form of a lithe young woman wearing only a thin white night shirt. Her hair was wild as though she only just had awoken from a long sleep, and her face held no expression. But what was clear was the terrible golden light that streamed from her eyes. There was no chance for anyone to make any moves, and the young woman raised both of her hands toward the small group in the center of the throne room. Twin bursts of fire, light, lightning, and what could only be described as super-heated energy exploded in all directions from her outstretched hands. Everyone was sent flying in various directions, only Sabrina and Rhain able to hold themselves in position. Sabrina must have known what was coming and had created a shield around herself and Rhain to defend from the impetuous assault. Jerrard and Erika recovered next, also able to erect defenses; they had to also shield Gabriel, who if it weren't for their intervention would most likely have been ripped to shreds by the tides of energy. Taya was the last of the Dark Gods to find defense to the assault, and when she did, she plastered herself to the floor, minimizing the amount of energy that impacted her directly and maximized any options she had to counter attack. The only one who seemed to be spared any direct assault was the Onyx Knight Devlin Rannoch. He seemed to be trapped in the eye of the storm, and had not moved one inch from where he stood the moment the portal opened and the deluge began. Wordlessly, the young woman walked across the distance that separated her from the Onyx Knight, her bare feet resting on slabs of stone that only heartbeats before were molten. The seconds passed with agonizing slowness, but finally the young girl stood before the towering and imposing figure of the Knight of the Flashing Blade, but there was no question as to which of the two were gripped by utter and complete fear. The piercing golden eyes looked up into the clear eyes of the half-dragon, and they stayed there for a long moment before the young woman reached up and put her hand on Devlin's chest. She held it there for a long time before she pushed forward, her hand disappearing into the larger man's chest. There was no wound, no visible means of entry, the young woman's forearm simply stopped half-way and seemed to connect seamlessly to Devlin's chest. Devlin immediately went pale. It was then that the girl finally spoke.

"Do you feel my hand around your heart, Devlin? Do you feel me squeezing your heart?"

Blood spurted from Devlin's open mouth, dripping from the corners. His eyes were beginning to glaze over, but the young woman didn't relent.

"This is what it felt like when you betrayed me. It felt as though you were reaching into my chest and squeezing the life out of me. You stole what was mine, you stole what was dearest to me, and you made me suffer so many indignities that they scarred my heart. Now it's your heart that is in my hands Devlin. And I shall crush you, as you crushed me."

On Lines and Strings

Year Four of the Just Emperor Kaitain "Dragonsbane" Lorien, Creator's Calendar Year 1871

Midarin's fingers were numb, but not because of the cold. She barely felt the cold wind that whipped around her, her blood was boiling too hot for that. However, out of the corner of her eye, she was sure that Gwydeon was shivering. Whatever he was now, somewhere between mortal and god, the elements would be a factor in the battle that was facing them. From her experience, Midarin knew that Nightwing would not allow the fragile princess Felicia Lorien to be affected by the temperatures, but she was still extremely unpracticed with her powers. She would be a liability in the battle to come. Setting her jaw, Midarin reached inside herself and drew upon the powers granted to her as an ascended being. She never was comfortable with direct applications of power, but with the fight that was looming, there would be no choice. The arrow appeared out of thin air, a construct of light and fire. It took only the beat of an eye for the bowstring to be drawn back and her aim to lock on the heart of the man who once could have been called her son. Now, the creature wearing the name and the face of Nathan Sandar was nothing more than one of Emries' puppets. Killing the creature would finally put her son's spirit to rest, and she would be doing a service to the Cosmos by ending him here and now. However, before she could release the arrow, Gwydeon reached out and put his hand on her arm. His touch always had the effect of ebbing whatever emotion she was feeling, filling her with a kind of calm and serenity that she could never find when he was away from her. The target was locked in her mind, and she easily could have looked at Gwydeon and held a conversation and still taken the shot. However, she only turned her face slightly in his direction, enough to regard him but still keep Nathan at the center of her focus.

"We're not alone."

Gwydeon's words were accompanied with a sidelong glance toward a form that was just finding its way back to its feet. Gwydeon looked slightly up and nodded. From her elevated position, Felicia glided gently in the direction of the rising form. Nightwing's metallic voice filled the void the next moment.

"It's one of the Flashing Blade. Orren Eldrath I think."

"Yes," Nathan's cold and mocking voice answered. "Emries and Draven were enjoying toying with the mortal. Apparently he is the new vessel for White Lightning's powers. Not that it did him much good against Emries. Though I'm sure none of you stand much of a chance now. Especially after Emries took so much joy in gutting Aerith's pathetic boy. I wish I could have seen that first hand. I owe the old man almost as much as Emries does. Perhaps I'll get my chance to introduce myself to Aerith's daughter before all is said and done. It should be much more fun making her scream."

Midarin's fingers twitched, and she wanted more than anything to let the arrow fly, but Gwydeon's hand would not relent. With his new sword in hand, Gwydeon took a step forward and patted Midarin's arm slightly before withdrawing his hand and sinking back into his practiced defensive stance. Despite herself, Midarin took a step back and let the arrow disappear from her hand. However, the sword that replaced it was an indication that she would not be caught off guard should Nathan employ unconventional tactics.

"So, do you remember anything about noble combat, Nathan?" Gwydeon asked coolly.

"What good is noble combat to someone such as me who has no equal? Would a fly receive noble combat from a spider? Why should I lower myself to your level? You are nothing. Emperor Lorien robbed you of your divinity, and you are nothing more than a bug that I will squash with my boot. My so-called mother on the other hand, she could prove to be at least a brief challenge. But father, if you want me to end your life before you have to watch your wife suffer, I suppose I can show you some magnanimity."

Midarin almost didn't see the strike before it was too late. Two separate beams of power emerged from Nathan's hands. The first struck at Midarin's feet, and would have enveloped her if she had not thrown herself back. Gwydeon on the other hand raised his blade and parried the assault. But what he did shouldn't have worked. Mortal weapons should not have been able to remain whole against divine fire, but something within Gwydeon told him that the tactic would be successful. Midarin looked at the point where the stream of energy was contacting the blade. She had expected to see the metal of the blade beginning to become superheated to the point of melting, but to her surprise, the blade wasn't even beginning to glow from the heat. What was present however was the faintest purple glow coating the length of the blade. When the assault ceased, Midarin wondered which of the two combatants was more surprised with the outcome, Nathan or Gwydeon. Regardless of his surprise, Nathan was not one to let his opponent breathe. A rain of fire and light erupted from the boy's fingers. Instead of attempting to block all of the attacks, Gwydeon began to run toward his opponent, sword blocking unseen assaults before they were on top of him. At the last second, Gwydeon planted his left foot hard in the ground and leapt. He glided through the air, his sword held before him blocking the deluge, until at the last possible moment, the sword flashed and a plume of red erupted. However, when Gwydeon landed, he fell to the ground clutching his side. It was Nathan who had struck the blow, bringing an eruption of red from Gwydeon's side. Midarin could not help but grimace. A similar wound had ended the life of the Gwydeon she had known once upon a time. The Gwydeon from the Light Reality, where Logan and the others had triumphed and set their world on the right path. This Gwydeon had lived through the assault on Shau-ling's palace, had seen the world fall to darkness after. Had watched his own love die at the hands of their son, only for them to find one another again. Just as they had on this world, and Midarin would not stand by again as the man she loved was taken from her.

With a thought, the sword in her hand split into a dozen arrows. In the blink of an eye, they were on her bowstring and a heartbeat later they were in the air. The ten arrows became twenty, which became a hundred, which became five hundred. The rain of death struck where Nathan floated, but instead of striking him, they passed through harmlessly. Instead they rained down on where Gwydeon knelt, striking him before he knew they were upon him. Midarin looked on in horror as dozens of the arrows of light pierced his body, and he lay motionless on the ground, some of the smoldering arrows still lodged in his back. Midarin gritted her teeth hard when the only sound to emerge was Nathan's laughter.

"Did you honestly think that I would fall for such an obvious attack, mother? A bow? Really? How could you think that I wouldn't know every tactic you would employ before you would even think of it yourself? It was foolish for either of you to engage me in combat. I know all of your tactics, I know all of your moves. You lost before you even began to fight. You should have run while you still had the chance. Now, I will enjoy ripping you apart."

The next outburst of power came not from the smug boy, but from the two in the distance who had yet to stake their claim in the battle. The first assault was a wide beam of white flame that fanned out across the air where Nathan floated. The pure Blaze flame, strong enough to erase a mortal being from existence caught the boy by surprise, but not enough that the assault would strike a target. Nathan simply was somewhere else the next moment, the flames passing harmlessly below him. The next assault however struck true. Several bolts of lightning lanced out from Orren Eldrath's extended hand, one of which flashed across Nathan's face leaving a nasty burn. But the Knight of the Flashing Blade was not content with a single strike, and another hail of bolts sped toward their target. This time however Nathan would not be caught unawares. Each bolt was either parried away or sent back in the direction from which they came. Orren and Felicia scrambled, each going their separate ways, but neither letting their assaults relent. More gouts of fire as well as blades of dark steel erupted from Nightwing, while a combination of lightning and balls of fire were sent toward Nathan from Orren. Midarin shook herself out of her pain and grief and added her own contribution to the assault, as more and more arrows of light and fire sped toward their target. Nathan crossed both of his arms in front of his chest, extending power around him like a bubble of pure energy. When the strikes from the trio struck the bubble they exploded in nearly blinding flashes of light. More and more the trio poured on the assault, until the bubble exploded sending a shockwave of force outward so intense that it caused great cracks to form in the ground all around and triggered an avalanche from nearby mountain peaks. Midarin was thrown to the ground by the force of the explosion, and Nightwing was knocked out of the air. Orren had gone to a knee when he felt the explosion coming, but his tattered clothing and the blood streaming from his nose and ears showed that he was worse for wear from the conflict. Nathan hung a little limp in the air, one of his arms badly mangled. Still the boy laughed.

"You're going to have to do much better than that if you are going to defeat me."

In a matter of seconds, Nathan's arm was healed and the burn on his cheek had disappeared completely. Midarin was just getting back to her feet when Orren, from one knee let out another strike. The single bolt of intense lightning arched across the sky. Nathan extended his hand as though to catch the strike, but a moment before impact with his palm, the bolt split into a mesh of interconnected bolts forming a ball around the cocky youth. Over scant heartbeats, the cage shrunk around Nathan until the sparking bolts struck his flesh. The smell of burning hair and skin hung thick in the air, and Nathan cried out in pain for the first time. However, the cage could not close tighter than simply contacting the skin, as the boy's control and power were too great for someone without fine control over his abilities. Orren's attack had the element of surprise, but now it had been reduced to a battle of will and control, a battle that a novice like Orren could not hope to win. The cage of lightning shattered that next moment, sending the errant bolts flying through the air in all directions. When Midarin looked back up at Nathan, all of the wounds from the encounter had already healed, and the haughty smile on his lips had been replaced by a cruel sneer. He pointed a single finger in Orren's direction and a beam of pure white light crossed the distance impossibly fast and claimed the young knight square in the chest. The man cried out in pain and was thrown backward, the breastplate of his armor a ruined mess that still smoked. The melted steel scalded the skin below almost totally incapacitating Orren.

"I suppose if this went on long enough," Nathan said frowning, "the three of you might get lucky enough to score a significant blow. That would not do. But, just as my dear mother and father did not come to this battle alone, neither did I. Let me introduce you to my little helpers."

Just below where Nathan floated, two swirling blue portals winked into existence. In unison, a man stepped from the portal on the left while a woman stepped from the portal on the right. Each was dressed simply, like commoners, with simple pants and shirt. However, Midarin immediately knew the identities of the man and woman, and could not help the horror that rose up within her. The man was the spitting image of his father, with the exception of the broader shoulders and the closely cropped black hair. The woman was slight of build, with long dark hair. But where Midarin had expected to see the sharp blue eyes of their mother, she saw only white.

"As my erstwhile mother has no doubt recognized my little troupe of puppets, I will gladly introduce them to the interlopers in this family squabble. Please meet Storm and Taya Mystic. They were supposed to be the servants of my weaker reflection on our world long ago, but they will content themselves by serving me here. Mother and I can have some quiet time now that the sides have been evened considerably."

It was then that Midarin noticed the glowing golden gauntlets on the hands of the new arrivals. Emries had pulled out all the stops when he assembled his army for this war. With former members of the *Erieal* resurrected and obviously enslaved to Nathan's will, and with the power of the *Debuisa* at their disposal, these puppets would be the match for any of the Dark Gods, and would easily over-match anything the Cadarians would bring to bear. Slaughter did not even begin to describe what lay ahead for the uninitiated who challenged Emries' will. The automatons advanced on Felicia and Orren, Storm's gauntlet beginning to turn blue while Taya's became a ghostly translucent. Nathan looked down at Midarin again.

"Now mother, shall we continue our conversation?"

* * * * * * * * * * * *

Felicia needed all the speed she could muster as the winds of the tornado conjured by the girl Nathan had called Taya buffeted her. Felicia had briefly met the other Taya, the one who was one of the Dark Gods, and while the two had some similarities, there were many differences. Thanks to the memories and knowledge from Diana and Nightwing, Felicia knew that this Taya was from the Light Reality, born to Jerrard and Erika Mystic, the loving couple that were the rulers of the Kingdom of Celidar in Cadaria. However, the Taya that they claimed as their child on this world was really the daughter of Erika and a thief named Gideon Viruci, and she came from the Dark Mirror version of Onea. The whole thing made Felicia's mind spin, but she did not have time to worry about lineage or obscure history while the very air around her was trying to destroy her. There was no expression on the girl's face as she pointed the ghostly gauntlet in Felicia's direction, instructing the tornado to do its work. Felicia called on every bit of speed that Nightwing could muster, and she was barely able to keep up with the torrent. Small stones and pieces of ice from the ground and surrounding area were being caught up in the spinning funnel and were battering the hardened shell that surrounded Felicia. Nightwing's armor could take a lot of punishment, but Taya was pushing that to the limit. Lightning arched from side to side inside the funnel, testing Felicia's reflexes and concentration. She was totally on the defensive, unable to even think about a counter-attack. Then an idea came to her mind. Tucking her wings back, Felicia threw herself into a dive, hurtling toward the ground at unbelievable speed. At the last moment, she pulled herself up hard, her belly and toes scraping the hard ground sending shocks of pain all through her body. But there was no time to hurt. The increased speed shot her from the base of the funnel as though she were shot from a cannon, but too fast for even Nightwing's other-worldly abilities. Felicia tumbled out of control, colliding with Taya and sending them both sprawling. Felicia heard bones cracking and from the pain that radiated through her, she could not tell whether the bones were hers or Taya's. When the two finally skidded to a stop, they were a tangled mass of limbs and blood. The Nightwing armor retraced beneath Felicia's skin, as her concentration could no longer keep the shell intact. Red clouded the edges of her vision, and from her own ragged breathing she knew that several of her ribs had been broken. Beneath her, Taya was barely breathing as well, the now golden gauntlet lodged between their two bodies and hanging precariously from her broken arm. Bone protruded from skin and had impaled itself in Felicia's side. From where she lay atop Taya, Felicia could barely turn her head enough to get a look at the other woman's face. Taya's eyes were closed, and blood streamed from the corners of her mouth and her nose. Her breathing was erratic, but she was breathing. Though she fought to retain consciousness, Felicia knew it would only be a matter of moments before she too could no longer keep her eyes open. Fighting through the pain was not an option, and she wasn't able to concentrate enough on her abilities to start the healing process. As blackness started to claim her vision, Felicia silently prayed that Taya would not wake up and finish Felicia off before she had a chance to fight back.

* * * * * * * * * * * *

Gwydeon's whole body felt as though it were throbbing. He could feel the arrows still stuck in his spine, and they were preventing him from moving in any meaningful way. There was a numbness that was beginning to flood through his feet and legs that was worrisome. Despite how much he wanted to pull himself together and get back into the fight, he couldn't. But something was nagging at him, he was missing something. He tried his best to calm his mind, shutting out the screams and the sounds of fire and laughter. Images floated through the blackness of his mind, and one face kept coming to him over and over again. Sabrina's voice nagged at his mind. The touch of her hand on his chest and the warmth that filled him. The words, 'you'll need this, for now and for later.' There, deeper in the blackness of his mind, he saw something. It was a flicker, a faint green glow. He recognized the descriptions that Aryx and others had given over the years of the Blaze, and how it looked, but there was something different about this flickering flame. The peaks were not a brilliant green as it had always been described to him. There was a faint tint of blackness at the peaks of the flame. And then just as suddenly as the faint glow was there, the fire burned brighter, leaping and roiling like a living being.

"Touch me."

The voice was a mixture of tones, pitches, and gender sources. They were all mixed together so completely that Gwydeon could not pick out any of the specific pieces of the voice.

"Open yourself, reclaim what was lost."

Gwydeon extended his hand in his mind's-eye. But hesitated at the last moment. He had done so much all this time without power. During his seclusion he had spent many days thinking about the last days on Onea. How much had changed because he did have power. How much had gone horribly wrong because of others who could not be trusted to use the power that they had. He thought of his son, and the corruption that had spread through him because of Emries' influence. But Sabrina's words tugged at him. There would be no way to fight those that needed to be fought unless he could match them with power. Gwydeon could only hope that his own will and strength would be great enough to resist the temptation that so many had succumbed to. Suppressing the last doubts in his heart and in his mind, Gwydeon allowed the phantom hand to reach into the dancing green flames, and felt the fire burn what was left of him away.

* * * * * * * * * * * *

Orren was getting tired. The one Nathan had called Storm had begun his assault from nearly the moment he had stepped onto the battlefield. Waves of ice, driving rain, and crashing walls of water battered the weakening shield of lightning that Orren had managed to erect. But as the strength began to flood out of his body, more and more of the seemingly constant and endless assault was slipping through. Several open cuts on Orren's face and arms poured blood, caused by razor sharp daggers of ice that had slipped between the bolts of lightning that were the body of the large shield. Orren had been unprepared for the force of the wave of water that impacted his shield, and his control over his new powers had slipped for the briefest of moments which allowed the daggers to slip through. Despite his powers, Orren was still very mortal, and as more blood escaped from his body, the more the cold and the exhaustion began to overtake him. Storm was a machine, sending wave after wave of attack, leaving no time for Orren to breathe, and if something didn't change soon, the shield would fail and Orren would be ripped to shreds. It was time for a change in tactics.

Calling on his last reserves of strength, Orren channeled all of his power and intensified the shield. Storm's expressionless and cold face registered nothing, but it seemed as though the man increased the power of his assault to match the power of his opponent's defenses. That was what Orren was counting on. He changed the angle of the shield, forcing Storm's entire torrent into the rock face that loomed over them. By the time Storm realized what was happening, it was too late. Huge chunks of rock and ice were streaming down the mountainside followed by a blanket of thick snow. Boulders struck the ground all around the combatants, one striking a glancing blow to Storm's back and head. The man was sent crashing to the ground, quickly lost from Orren's sight, buried under the avalanche. Finally, the assault from both Storm and the avalanche grew too great, and the shield of lightning shattered. Before he could even cry out, Orren found himself buried, and the cold and pain overwhelmed him in a matter of seconds.

* * * * * * * * * * * *

Midarin could feel Nathan's glare. The evil and knowing smile twisted his lips into a sneer, and the glow that surrounding him was anything but angelic. The bow had fallen from Midarin's hand, and though she was not as comfortable with a blade, the weapon created from pure energy seemed at home in her hands. Gwydeon's training was flooding through her mind, and there were dozens of things that could happen next. However, one thing was clear, Nathan had the advantage at range, and if Midarin was going to stand a chance in this battle, she would have to close the distance and stay in the boy's face. As if reading her thoughts, Nathan let a laugh hit the air.

"Do you really think you stand a chance against me in single combat, Mother? Try as much as you like, and delay the inevitable as long as you can, but the result will be the same. You will not leave this field with your life. I will snuff you out just like I snuffed out my father, and just like I will snuff out any of you so-called heroes that dare to stand in my way. Emries has given me all the power I need to settle all the old scores, and when all is said and done, when this world is a cinder, Emries will lead those of us who are loyal to the throne of the Creator, and we will watch as the Light of the Cosmos is extinguished and a new ruler shapes the future of all life."

Midarin drew herself up. Indignation filled her.

"Emries failed once. He'll fail again. Shau-ling failed. Talisia failed. I've watched gods, dragons, angels, and Children of the Creator fall and beg for mercy at the hands of these people you scoff at. You may kill me Nathan, you may kill others that resist you, but as long as you serve Emries, your humiliating defeat is assured."

Nathan snarled and sent beams of energy crashing down upon Midarin. The blade in her hand came up and instantly changed shape into that of a shield. The huge dome of darkness created by Midarin's will deflected most of the assault, but the force nearly caused her knees to buckle. However, Nathan's anger was making his strikes wild. Beams of energy struck all around Midarin, creating fissures and craters. One struck close enough to nearly cause Midarin to lose her balance. The snarl became maniacal laughter, a feverish madness overtaking Nathan as he rained death from above. Midarin caught motion out of the corner of her eye. Where Gwydeon lay motionless, she was sure that she saw something. Yes, she had seen movement. Gwydeon was making his way to his feet, and from where Nathan floated, he couldn't have seen it. Just then a stronger blast hit Midarin's shield and threw her off her feet and into one of the craters behind her. The shield broke when she struck the ground, and she lay defenseless. Nathan raised his hands above his head, a ball of brightness forming above his upturned palms. At the last moment, a massive gout of flame struck the boy in the back, causing the ball of light to fly past its intended target, striking in the heart of the dead city, destroying dozens of buildings. When Nathan spun around, Midarin was sure there was a look of pure shock on his face. Gwydeon Sandar stood firmly on his feet, his whole body wreathed in green flame, and a pair of black feathered wings extending from his back.

Responsibilities of Power

Year Four of the Just Emperor Kaitain "Dragonsbane" Lorien, Creator's Calendar Year 1871

Lissa Ranthall sat on the floor cradling the head of her daughter in her lap. Blood still trickled from the corner of her eyes, and there was a smear on her cheek from the blood that had gushed from the side of her mouth. Of the twins, Liara was always more delicate, a trait that her sister continually pointed out was an oddity in the history of the families. But the jokes and laughter could not hide the obvious. The abilities that Liara touched innately weakened her physical form, and she had a connection to something greater than any of them realized. This latest display, her physical reaction to the freedom of the evil creature that wore the name Dorovar was another reinforcement of that fact. Lissa was dabbing the blood from her eyes when Mirana emerged from the dark corridor supporting Alderin on her shoulder. Lissa's brother looked much worse for wear, his clothing singed and his face and arms already beginning to blister from burns. But there was more than just his physical injuries, in some ways Alderin seemed diminished. It was as though something had been robbed from him, ripped away from him in the same way his arm had been.

"Darrien's gone," Mirana said after a moment, "Tess too."

Pulling himself away from Mirana, Alderin stood straight, patting his niece on the shoulder lightly before moving to kneel beside Lissa. He spoke softly, more due to his injury than any worry for who would hear.

"Darrien was going to join Pike, but something happened. The portal closed and Tess just disappeared. But there was a wake, this incredible wake of power. Darrien was swept up in it and just disappeared. It passed through me like steam, scalding me from the inside out. Whatever other damage it caused, it has suppressed most of my abilities. I can't even create a simple portal."

"She's getting stronger."

Wolf emerged from the shadows slowly, his footfalls not making a sound. Lissa looked up and smiled, relieved to see that her husband was safe, but the smile melted from her lips in a moment. There was something different about his eyes and the way he held himself. Liara too seemed to sense something as she curled up tighter to her mother, a small shiver beginning to roll through her body. Wolf approached slowly and bent to smooth his daughter's hair back away from her face. His touch caused her to recoil for a moment but finally whatever had triggered her fear ad seemed to ease. When Wolf looked up and met Lissa's eyes, she had to blink twice. His eye color had changed, and the same sweet vulnerability that she had fallen in love with had returned. It was clear that something had happened, and Wolf had been changed by the experience, but the old Wolf was still in there somewhere. Liara sensed it too, perhaps more than any of them, but the fact that her shaking had abated said everything.

Wolf turned his attention next to Alderin, putting his hand on the man's chest and closing his eyes. It took only a moment for a warm glow to envelop Alderin and the scabs and wounds on his face and arms begin to fade. From her vantage point, Mirana could see the flows of power being used, and they were unlike she had ever seen. Instead of directly influencing the wounds and pulling them closed, mimicking the natural healing process, just at a much faster rate, this application of power seemed to just remove the wounds. It was as though they were being erased, or more accurately that they were made to have never existed in the first place. However, when the flows of power attempted to touch and heal the stump of Alderin's arm, they simply passed over as though there was nothing to heal. All of the energy then gathered in the center of Alderin's chest.

"Well, let's see how much damage she did."

Wolf's voice had a haunting quality, filled with such wisdom but at the same time with palpable sorrow. Whatever changes had happened Wolf it was as though he was still trying to cope with them all. Mirana watched as the power penetrated into Alderin. His whole chest glowed with golden light that pulsed along with his heartbeat. After a few moments the color of the light changed to a bright white, and then disappeared. Wolf was sweating when he finally sank back from Alderin, nearly falling backwards. Mirana crouched by Alderin who also seemed shaken by the experience. By this time Liara also had started to sit up, her own eyes wide watching the powers that her father was bringing to bear, and it was Liara that spoke first, her voice filled with wonder.

"Dark Gods can't do that."

Wolf smiled and shook his head.

"No, they can't."

Liara sat forward and took Wolf's hand into hers. She turned it over and ran one fingernail over his palm, a trail of golden glittering power following the track of her nail as though she were drawing in living sand.

"That's the Creator's power."

Lissa's worried face went to shock, and then horror, and then confusion in a matter of seconds. The constantly morphing emotional canvas finally settled on something close to neutral acceptance before she was able to speak again. The question she managed to push out encapsulated all of the questions that she wanted to ask but didn't have the words to express.

"What happened?"

Wolf's smile seemed to fade at the question, and when grim determination replaced it, there was yet another change in the character of his eyes. The center of the eye was bright blue, clear and filled with power with a corona that consisted of concentric yellow circles. The confused eyes were matched by the confused aura that everyone but Alderin could see, Liara and Mirana because of their abilities, and Lissa because of her intimate knowledge of her husband's love.

"I wish there was time for an explanation, and I wish more that I had an explanation that actually made sense. So much has happened, and yet it is only a beginning. Not the beginning, because Halicon has already seen to that. And in his own way, so has Aerith. Now Pike is trying to bring everything crashing down, and he may well succeed even if it isn't the way he intended."

Wolf paused then, as if unsure how much he should say, but there was more to it than that. He seemed unsure of the words themselves, as though he weren't exactly speaking them, but that he was reciting them as though channeling them from another time and place, conscious only of what he was saying after it had crossed his lips. Looking over at Alderin, Wolf continued.

"I wish there was more that I could do than simply heal your wounds, brother," Wolf said finally, the word sounding alien to his ear, "but it seems that Tess's abilities are accelerating faster than anyone thought. And now that she is making rash decisions like the ones her father would make, things have gotten complicated."

Mirana's eyes widened.

"Is Tess dangerous?"

Wolf nodded.

"More than even she knows. If Pike had the kind of power that Tess had at her disposal, he would shake not only this world but every world that the Creator has ever touched. But even he couldn't envision remaking the Cosmos in his image. That arrogance is purely in the minds of the Children of the Creator and their twisted progeny."

Liara spoke next.

"And Dorovar. Dorovar would use that power to destroy everything."

Again Wolf nodded. Alderin's gaze didn't relent. Now that the pain of his wounds had been removed, all Alderin could feel was the hole in the middle of his being. There was an emptiness that he had never felt before, and besides the fear that he had for Darrien's safety, it was as though everything else inside of him had been muted.

"What did she do to me?"

Lissa knew the look on Wolf's face. He had something very unpleasant to say, and he was trying to work out the best way to say it. Finally his eyes narrowed which meant there was no good way to say what he was trying to say, and the only option he had left was to just let it out.

"Understand Alderin, that she could have just as easily killed you. Back on Onea, Emries and Halicon demonstrated that they could suppress the powers of those that they had endowed with abilities. At least to a degree. We've all known for a while that if the Creator willed it, He could remove access to power. It seems that Tess has stumbled on a way to turn her reality-shaping powers into something practical, but I doubt it was done as anything more than a reflex. Her rage activated her abilities and as such caused her to lash out unconsciously. I'm sorry Alderin, short of your immortality, you're very mortal now."

Part of Lissa felt sorry for her younger brother. For his entire life, Alderin had been a child of the Dark Gods. His life had been shaped by the powers that he had at his disposal and the things that he could do that no mortal could. In that way, Alderin had more in common with Mirana and Liara than he did with Wolf and Lissa. On Onea, Wolf and Lissa had spent the majority of their lives without extraordinary abilities, and as such they were not as ingrained into the fabric of their identity. Perhaps that was why Alderin was always closer to their father, and Lissa was always closer to their mother. Aryx Terian had been born as a child of Halicon, and his entire existence had been lived in the reality of power. Diana was a noblewoman who lived life as a mortal until extraordinary circumstances found her. Now Alderin would have to make his way in a world that was shaken by those who could move mountains with their bare hands, and he would have to find now weapons to topple titans. When Lissa brought her eyes back to Wolf's face, she saw the regret for what had been said, but she also saw a glimmer of hope in his eyes.

"But?"

Lissa knew enough to know that there was something that hadn't been said, and Wolf was still debating whether or not he should say anything at all. Finally he closed his eyes for a moment, gave a small nod, and then opened them again.

"Sabrina could help you."

Lissa balked a little at the name. Though the Sabrina that had been saved from the world of Onea was not the same Sabrina that Lissa had grown up with as a sister, there was still some discomfort and healthy distance between the two women. Part of that was because of the painful memories of the loss of the woman who was her sister in every way but blood, and the other part was the knowledge that this Sabrina had been a servant of the Creator and was also linked to Serrina Mistic, which did not ingratiate her to many of those who had fallen from the heavens. After a brief pause, Wolf continued.

"And I think that is where you should go. You'll find her in Celidar with Taya and Jerrard. They're going to need all the help they can get after what is about to happen there. Or perhaps what has already happened."

Wolf's voice trailed off, and his eyes focused on something far in the distance. Without much effort, Alderin found his way back to his feet, and after a brief check of the sword belt that hung from his hip, he ran his fingers through his blond hair and firmly set his jaw.

"Would someone open a portal for me?"

Lissa got to her feet quickly and wrapped her arms around her brother. When she pulled back, she looked him squarely in the eyes.

"You don't have to do this. Your powers aren't you. We can find another way, we can fight another way."

Alderin leaned in and kissed Lissa on her forehead and forced a smile.

"You don't understand, Lissa. There isn't another way. Darrien needs me. No matter where she is, no matter where Tess sent her, she's going to do everything she can to get to her father. She thinks that she can protect Pike, or at the very least try to save him from himself. That kind of thinking puts her right in the line of fire of some of the most powerful people, especially considering how good Pike is at making enemies. I need to be there at her side. I have to be there to protect her from those threats, protect her from Pike, and if necessary protect her from herself. I can't do that like this. I need to be able to stand toe to toe with anyone who threatens her."

Despite her disappointment, Lissa understood. She nodded her head once, and then started to channel the flows of power necessary to open a portal.

"Then I'm not going to let you go alone."

Alderin put his hand on Lissa's shoulder.

"Wolf is right," Alderin said shaking his head. "Too much is happening, and we can't afford to be traveling together. What if Tess had had her outburst here in the middle of all of us? What if we were all taken out of this conflict and trapped by our powerlessness? We have to be smarter. Whatever is waiting for me in Celidar, I can take care of myself until I can find out if Sabrina can help me or not."

A tear came rolling from the corner of Lissa's eye, but she could not help the smile that came to her lips. She gave her brother another long hug and then a kiss on the cheek before turning her head to look at a space beside him. A portal winked open that next moment.

"You're too much like our father sometimes," Lissa said as Alderin took a step toward the portal.

"Which is why I need Darrien to keep me grounded and remind me that I can't do everything," he replied as he stepped through.

The portal closed behind him, leaving Lissa staring at the empty space, another few tears streaming down her cheeks. After a sniff and a moment to regain her composure, Lissa turned back to her husband who was helping Liara back to her feet.

"Tell me I didn't just send my brother on a suicide mission."

"I don't think Alderin is in any direct danger," Wolf said finally. "Though what happens after Alderin meets with Sabrina is anyone's best guess. There is too much in motion to see clearly. And even the things I know will happen are starting to become cloudier. This world is teetering on the brink of destruction the same way that Onea did near the end. Dorovar makes all of the work that has gone into this world and in to the plans of great and terrible men that much more perilous. Dorovar cares for only one thing, his vengeance. He doesn't care how he accomplishes it, he doesn't care who he has to kill to get it, he just knows that he wants it, and he has spent too many lifetimes preparing himself for it. We've never faced an enemy like this. There is no agenda, there is nothing to be manipulated, and there is no better nature to appeal to. He will not manipulate. He will not bargain. He will only destroy. So for now we have to focus on saving and protecting what we can. Unfortunately there are too few of us, and too many to protect. Now is a time we have to make hard choices. Probably some that are harder than we have ever had to make in our lives."

Mirana moved to stand beside her sister, half supporting her and half comforting her. Lissa extended her hand to her side, and a moment later, a thin rapier of fire simply came into being.

"So, what does this mean for us? What should we be doing now? You said you wanted us to go to Celidar, but obviously that's changed since I just sent Alderin there alone. What plan have you got churning away in that brain of yours?"

Wolf grimaced for a moment before speaking. His mind was full of so much information and from so many different sources it was hard to keep it all straight. From what Draven knew about Emries' plans, his aims would be to punish Aerith Seth and remnants of the heroes that led to his defeat during the fall of Onea. But that was far too many targets for the four of them to protect, and more than that, Emries was far beyond them now. Draven knew what Emries was capable of. Knew all about his new tricks, and more importantly, knew how viscous the Child of the Creator had become. It was the thoughts of Basille and Pyrrus that were far more reasonable. Those with power had to protect those without it. As much of a threat as Dorovar and Emries posed, the madness of Emperor Kaitain Lorien could not be overlooked. To that end, those who drew his ire, those who could help to pull the quickly shattering world back together outside of his destructive grasp, had to be protected at all cost.

"Liara and Mirana need to go to Aldere. Pike is going to rip that place apart, and someone needs to be there to find and protect the innocents so they don't get caught in the crossfire. Liara is sensitive enough to keep track of everything that's happening, and with Mirana's ability to hide, she will be able to keep them safe. They are perfectly suited for this."

Wolf turned his gaze to the two young women.

"No taking chances," he said gruffly. "And under no circumstances are you to have any contact with Pike or Kaitain Lorien. They are too dangerous and unpredictable. Focus on protecting the mortals. The image of the Dark Gods is as invaders and destroyers. If we are going to really win this war, we are going to have to convince the people that we are their salvation and the misguided people trying to rule them are their true enemies."

"We understand," Liara said.

"And if something goes wrong?" Mirana asked.

The older of the twins was always the more pragmatic. She always wanted to know about all the contingencies, and asked questions that most considered to have answers that were already understood. However, she almost always proved to be wise in her caution and thoroughness.

"The only safe place we have left would have to be Aerith's island. I don't know that there are many outside the Dark Gods that know of its existence and fewer still that would actually go there. As long as you stay away from the actual house I don't think there is any risk, and can serve as both a place to hide and a place to plan. If Pike discovers you, or if you have no other option but to fight and then retreat, that is where you should go. Don't try to find us. We'll come to you."

The twins nodded in unison. Mirana turned and kissed her mother on the cheek while Liara hugged her father. After another moment, a portal appeared behind the twins and then each waved as they stepped through leaving their mother and father standing, looking at one another.

"Should I infer from your statements that we won't be travelling together?"

Lissa's tone was abrupt and harsh. She was just barely containing the anger that she was feeling, more at the situation than Wolf himself. She didn't want to admit he was right, and she certainly didn't want to admit that there was a lot of logic to his plan. All she wanted was to slap him, and to kiss him, and for them to just hide somewhere together with their daughters. The warrior that Lissa had once been had been subsumed by her new role as a mother, and while she would fight more fiercely than ever to protect her family, she also would not fight with reckless abandon if it meant that she would not see them again. There were just some sacrifices that she was no longer willing to make. Perhaps Wolf was counting on this new protective instinct when he suggested the change in tactics, or perhaps it was just the most prudent course of action. Either way, its logic trapped Lissa into following the strategy of her husband, for now.

"I have to see my father," Wolf said, his voice failing on the word, "and you need to see the mortals who inherited your parents' powers."

Lissa felt her heart skip a beat. Before they left the Citadel, Diana and Aryx had taken their daughter aside and explained what was about to happen. Though she listened with tears streaming down her face, her heart broke with every word. She would never see her parents again, and in a way they were sacrificing themselves to protect the world from what they could be made to do. As chosen of Emries in their roles as *Erieal* of the prophecies there was a chance that Emries could exert some control over them and force them to do something drastic. Though Lissa too was touched in this same way, they cautioned her on not acting until there was no choice left open to her. But to that end, they explained the process of passing on their abilities and passing beyond the veil. The thoughts were like a splinter in her mind's eye, tugging at her consciousness with every moment, wondering when and if that moment would ever come. Lissa had known the moment that her parents ceased to be. She felt her father's pride and acceptance, and she felt her mother's sorrow and ultimate relief. Wherever they were, they were there together, and they were free. For millennia they had been at the core of conflict, without ever knowing true peace or true joy. There were pockets of emotion for them, pockets where they found solace. Now they would find it in each other's arms for eternity.

"And when I find them?"

Wolf's face held little expression.

"Teach them how to live up to the gift they've been given. Start freeing the kingdoms of Cadaria from the yoke of tyranny they now suffer under. Don't take control. Let the mortals make the choices they need to make. Eventually, free from the machinations of the church and the aristocracy, they will make the right choice."

Lissa frowned.

"What makes you think they will?'

"If they don't," Wolf said finally, "then we've already lost, and we're just going through the motions."

Lissa nodded.

"And your father?"

Wolf's frown deepened further. The fact that there was no surprise in Lissa's voice concerned him a little, but then again, she was always much more observant than she chose to let people know.

"Even though he wasn't the man who raised me, and came from a world in which I wasn't even born, we are still blood. We are still family, and I can't let him continue to wander without direction. I am however concerned that his connection to Aerith Seth won't enable him to hear what I have to say, and if that indeed proves to be the case, then my road becomes much harder. But there has to be a way to defeat Dorovar, and I think between my father and I, we can find it."

Lissa considered that for a moment.

"Is that why you didn't want any of us to go with Alderin? Because of Sabrina?"

Wolf couldn't help but laugh.

"You always could see right through me. Sabrina has changed the game, both in terms of Aerith Seth, but in terms of the Children of the Creator. She's become the inheritor of Halicon's power, and that makes her dangerous for me to be around."

"Because of the power you've inherited."

Lissa's tone was matter of fact.

"Should I bother to ask how you knew?"

Lissa shook her head.

"With Basille using you as a conduit, it wasn't difficult to see once I saw your eyes. I can only assume that our earlier visitor was Draven?"

Wolf nodded.

"The three of us are together now. Thanks to Pyrrus."

Lissa nodded at the name.

"So all of the Children are accounted for. I guess you're right, the end is rapidly approaching and I'm not sure we're ready."

Wolf lifted his wife's free hand to his mouth and kissed the back of it lightly.

"It's up to us to make sure we get ready, and quickly."

Chapter LXXI

The Genesis of War

Year Four of the Just Emperor Kaitain "Dragonsbane" Lorien,
Creator's Calendar Year 1871

In the far reaches of the Frozen Wastes, closest to the northern pole of Espre, the Day of Star Fire, the first day of the moon's pass through the corona of the twin suns, was far less spectacular than it was in the wide equatorial zone within which most of Cadaria sat. The land was perpetually coated with ice, and most days of the year, snow fell in a constant curtain of white. This was a different kind of wilderness, a wilderness untouched by the race of human, and untouched by most creatures that crawled or walked on Espre. It was also perhaps the most inhospitable of environments on the whole of the world. Standing alone in the middle of the wastes stood Mariti Brightblade, her glowing talons dug deep into the thickly packed snow and ice. For many long hours she had just stared up at the burning sky. How many times had she seen the pieces of rock fall from the heavens, burning as they fell to the planet? Now though, as she looked to the heavens, she no longer saw massive chunks of moon rock. All she saw were bodies. The bodies of the angels that she killed, the bodies of the angels killed by the forces of Talisia Masile, the forces of the dragons that served Gwydeon Sandar; so much killing and so much death, and for what? Before the war broke out, the heavens were a mass of confusion and uncertainty. Raenera had gone into seclusion following the destruction of her world. She had been so wounded by the betrayal at the hands of her brother and sister and the abomination that was created. The dragons had been complicit in the destruction of Dorovar's world, but had not been responsible. That burden had fallen squarely on the shoulders of Emries and Talisia. The eldest of the dragons had sensed the treachery, but Raenera would never have taken steps to prevent what would ultimately come to pass. She could not; it was not in her nature to interfere directly. That was why Talisia and Emries were able to inject the poisonous doubt into the minds of Raenera's followers. But there were more effects than just the destruction of one world and the creation of a scourge like Dorovar. There were deeper implications, ones that would make the war in the heavens possible to begin with.

When the dragons were informed of the possibility of a new home on Dorovar's world, the Council was divided, and the debate raged for many long months. However, instead of waiting for a decision, instead of waiting for a directive for action, Stormbane and Shadowweaver conspired with Emries and Talisia to concoct a plan. And while the debate raged on within the Council, the deal between Shadowweaver and Dorovar was finalized and signed with blood. The deal would be announced in the Council by Stormbane, forever marking him as the Traitor, though anyone could see through the lies and see Shadowweaver standing at the center of the travesty. And though many of the members of the Council despaired at the possibilities and loathed the manner in which the deal was done, none would openly speak against the deal. However, this would never be disguised as acceptance, and Lord Tarot along with those who supported him would begin to look into the manner in which the deal had come to pass.

Mariti had never been one to concern herself with the politics of the gods, or the politics of the Children of the Creator. To the elder dragons, the ones who had been born into the formlessness of the Universe, the Children of the Creator were spoiled cousins who were enabled by the Creator to do whatever they wanted whenever they wanted. But the dragons were the intelligent designers of the cosmos. They named most of the things that walked and crawled on every world under the Creator's control. And so, when the Children of the Creator began using those creatures and those worlds as their ideological warzone, the dragons could not stay silent and would eventually have to choose sides. The true betrayal came when those creatures were turned against the Dragons. After several traitorous acts motivated by the Children of the Creator, tolerance of and patience with the tenuous relationship deteriorated and bred incredible amounts of distrust. It was the destruction of Dorovar's world, and the betrayals at the hands of Emries and Talisia that proved to be the final nail in the coffin. Sides had to be chosen, and the division of the dragons began following the escape from Dorovar's world. Shadowweaver and Stormbane would never be directly held accountable for their actions, but the devastation that would follow would serve as penance not only for the architects of Dorovar's fall from grace, but also for the whole of the race of dragons.

The skirmish that happened in the heavens after the death of Dorovar's world was nothing compared to what would happen after the destruction of Onea, and the ascension of the heroes that would become the Dark Gods. It was Halicon that had kept the skirmish from escalating. Small groups of dragons had aligned against Talisia and Emries after the truth about the betrayal came to light. Angels came to Talisia and Emries' defense, as did other dragons. There were only a few deaths before Halicon with the Heralds put an end to the hostilities. An accord was reached, and Emries left the heavens to shepherd the humans on Onea. His real purposes came to light soon after his arrival on Onea, when he presented the laws of the Creator as his own, and the humans of Onea saw no separation between Emries and the Creator. This led to Halicon becoming Shau-ling, and the generations' long ideological war between the brothers began anew. The dragons never had a presence on Onea, largely because Lord Tarot knew what would have happened. Inclusion in that war would have spilt the dragon race down the middle, and as Onea was torn apart, so too would be the dragons. Perhaps also it would have made it impossible for the humans to be driven to the point of awareness of their place in the universe. There probably would have been no Gwydeon Sandar or any of his confederates, and when Emries and Talisia made their play for power, perhaps there would have been nothing to prevent the Children of the Creator from toppling their maker. The dragons just watched the conflict from afar, gaining respect for the race that had been only their tormentors and prey historically.

After the cataclysm on Onea, Emries and Halicon disappeared. Emries was assumed dead by most, but those who knew the inner workings of power in the heavens understood that he was simply recuperating in the formless void, waiting for his opportunity. Halicon had been drained by the conflict and he too was in the void not only recovering his strength, but also reflecting on what he had learned from his experiences on Onea. Raenera still hadn't been seen in the heavens since her loss, and many wondered if she would ever be seen again. Some, especially those who understood the nature of power, were concerned that she never recovered and that perhaps she would fade from existence altogether. Of the remaining Children of the Creator, Talisia was the one who was spoiling for a fight, and saw her opportunity to create an advantage that she didn't have in the previous skirmish. She took her time, rallying a large amount of dragons to her side, waiting for the right moment to strike. Then, inexplicably, all of the Heralds were dispatched at nearly the same time on important missions for the Creator. Never in history had the Creator been so unprotected. Talisia had to be salivating over the opportunity. The attack was swift and brutal, a frontal assault on the ethereal palace of the Creator. Warrior angels and all other forces that could be brought to bear lent their arms to the defense of the Creator, even the newly ascended humans from the shattered world of Onea. They had never seen dragons, let alone fought against them, but still the heroes threw themselves into the fight with reckless abandon, the kind that only the foolish or the brave can wield. Talisia's forces had been fought to a standstill, but that was when Talisia launched her true master plan. Stranded in the middle of the fight, leading a group of dragons that included Mariti Brightblade, Pyrrus cut down enemies in a manner overshadowed only by the might of Gwydeon Sandar and Pike Rhuiden. But when Talisia rounded on him, he stood no chance of combating her superior martial skills. Gwydeon Sandar was too late to save Pyrrus, and it was the intervention of the Will and the Wrath that would prevent Gwydeon and Pike from having their revenge on Talisia. However, Mariti and the other dragons would not be denied so easily. Many were in striking distance, and the arrival of the Heralds had broken the will of most of Talisia's forces. Nothing stood between Mariti's talons and the throat of the Child of the Creator, and she would be struck down just as easily as her brother had been. But at the last moment the Spirit was simply there, interposed between Mariti's talons and Talisia's throat. Even possessed of all of the power that the Spirit had at its disposal, the creature was still made of weak flesh that was no match for the deadly sharpness of Mariti's claws. One shining claw ripped through the Spirit, tearing the creature in half and sending glistening blood splattering in all directions. Mariti became the first dragon to kill a Herald, the first one to draw the Creator's blood. From that day forward, her claws glowed as an eternal reminder of what she had done. For her actions, and the actions of all dragons during that war, the entire race was banned from the heavens under penalty of death. Never again would they be able to feel the voice of the Creator upon them, and never again would they know his divine presence. Like all the other creatures that called the universe their home, they were outside the Creator's love, and would only know His thoughts through the decrees of the Heralds.

There was a flare of light from the moon above as more of the crust of debris, ice, and rock was stripped away by powerful celestial forces from the impregnable and indestructible core. From behind Mariti there was the sound of crunching snow. The footfalls were small; human-sized. Mariti made no move and waited as the footfalls took the creature to the massive dragon's right. When the creature stopped, it stood beside Mariti, barely far enough away to be able to dodge a quick outward strike from the dragon's claws. There was no fear coming from the creature, no awe, no power, and no presence at all. It was as though the creature was a hole in the fabric of the universe. This could only mean that it was one of the Creator's Heralds. When Mariti shifted her gaze to take in the form of the creature whose actions could only be cause audacious, a wave of revulsion passed through her.

Each of the Heralds had attributes that made them special, and so marked them for the rest of the universe. The Voice constantly had an aura around it that inspired trust and cooperation. This enabled the words of the Creator to be heard regardless of the tenuousness of the situation that the Voice had to step into. Unlike the rest of the Heralds, the Voice rarely displayed its wings, and usually only as a last resort. The Voice liked to remain closer to those beings that it would ultimately be communicating with. The Will was a towering figure that could not be confused with any of the other beings that directly served the Creator. Known more for its impressive shimmering armor and helm, the Will was imposing in every aspect. Most fearsome of all of the Heralds was the Wrath. Known mostly for its adherence to the most violent and brutal applications of the Creator's desires, the Wrath would appear wreathed in fire and divine light, its four angelic wings sending waves of destruction in all directions. It was a being of pure rage, and could not be reasoned with or evaded once loosed upon its designated target. The last was the Spirit, a creature that could only be described as the corporal vessel of the Creator's power. Each of the Heralds had access to a level of divine power, but only the Spirit could actually contain a measure of the Creator's power and allow it to become manifest in the world of the mortals. What actual powers the Spirit could call forth were largely unknown, and no one had been foolish enough to test the Spirit's limits in any real way. The being that now stood to Mariti's right could only have been the Spirit.

The being stood silent, large white wings folded to its back, not a feather being rippled by the freezing breeze. A black cloak was wrapped around the form, and it too seemed totally immune to the elements. Snow would not even cling to the fabric, and shadows fell perfectly within the cloak's hood obscuring all of the being's features. The way the cloak fell on the creature also prevented Mariti from determining the gender of the Spirit's host. Power surrounded the Spirit, flowing in and out of it like breath. After several long moments of the strange pair watching the sky falling above them the Spirit began to speak. When the voice came to Mariti, it was a mixture of tones, languages, accents, and pitches. There was no way to determine race, gender, or anything else about the host.

"Mariti Brightblade, the killer of angels, you are now the foremost of your race, and as such you are to hear the words of the Creator."

That single sentence was so pregnant with meaning that Mariti felt as though she had been struck. When Lord Tarot had ordered all of the dragons to abandon the Great Tree, and he chose to stay behind, the implication was clear. The Great Tree would burn, and the oldest of the dragons, perhaps the first dragon ever to walk the universe, was gone. But more pressing, and perhaps more frightening than the loss of their leader was the manner of his death. Even at his advanced age, Tarot was still the strongest of the dragon race. Shadowweaver and his brood liked to think themselves capable of overpowering Tarot whenever they wished, but the truth stayed their hand at every turn. If the enemy created by their own hand was indeed free from the Vault, and if he had learned the secrets stored there, then no dragon, no hundred dragons, would be able to stand before him. Dorovar would hunt them to extinction.

Mariti lowered her head and said, "The dragons have tried to silence those words, and it has cost us our leader. Some fancied themselves above the command of the Creator or his heralds. Lord Tarot believed that all deserved their opportunity to speak, which led to the rule of the mob and our costly failures. Dire times require extreme responses, and now is not the time to ensure that all voices are heard. Speak, and those loyal to me will follow."

The Spirit remained silent, the snow and wind calming over the tense seconds. Finally, there was only silence. No wind blew, no snow fell, and when the Spirit finally let its voice find the still air again, it seemed to Mariti as though the whole of the world reverberated with its words.

"Now, here at the edge of oblivion, the dragons deem it worthy to heed the words of the Creator. Now, left with no other choice, left with no other option, pushed to the brink of extinction, they seek a way to atone for their myriad of sins, not the least of which is immutable pride. While pride may goeth before the fall, so too may the blood of the prideful wash away the sins of those who suffer under the yoke of tyranny. It will fall to you, Mariti Brightblade, slayer of angels, murderer of light, to choose which path your race will follow, and whether or not there will be a tomorrow for the dragons."

The words were an assault. Every emotion, every sentiment that floated in her immense heart was battered by the jibes of the Herald, and the impact was felt even more strongly when the mind could find no fault in the words. The truth was more damaging than any falsehood. The dragons were a prideful race, and had made every decision as though they were infallible. They had been proven wrong again, and now perhaps for the last time. Mariti didn't have long to let the words soak in before the Spirit began speaking once again.

"In the days and weeks to come, the race of dragons shall know suffering unlike any they have ever known. Any chance that you had to escape this fate died when Evan Sinn ceased to walk among the living. The abomination is loose, and he will not stop until the last of the dragons has been crushed at his hands. Even now his heralds have taken to hunting down and slaying the weaker of your breed, and they are as efficient killers as any this world or any world has ever known. Dorovar has spent many millennia plotting and planning for this day, shaping his followers for two deadly purposes; the extinction of the dragons, and his ascension to the heights of the cosmos. He plans to topple the Creator and to reshape all of existence in his image, but perhaps in this he has made the error that will allow his defeat."

Mariti felt her tail twitch slightly. Perhaps all was not as bleak and hopeless as she thought following the loss of their leader. If there was in fact as way that Dorovar could be defeated... But of course the Creator would have to protect itself from the wrath of the abomination. Tarot had spoken to Mariti at length over the millennia about the drives of the Creator. Perhaps the words of the oldest of them had not been as blasphemous as Mariti had once felt. Perhaps the Creator had baser and fallible drives after all.

"Do not mistake my words for hope," the Spirit chided. "The fate of your race has been determined. Should any dragon survive this conflict, it will be by sheer happenstance and fortune at the hands of those you feel are beneath your notice. There are plans in motion now that have uncertain outcomes for all, including the Creator. Perhaps there was an error allowing this wager to proceed, but that time is passed, and all must be held accountable for their role in this conflict."

Mariti finally shifted her weight and turned to fully face the Spirit, but the angelic creature did not return the gesture. The cloaked figure continue to look out into the nothingness, its sight piercing the veil between worlds seeing both into the realms above and beyond Espre, but also into the very hearts of all those that dwelled upon the world that had become a battlefield.

"Ideology was the genesis of this conflict. However, the motives and the desires of those that began this war have grown far beyond their control. Ideas and ideals have melded and given rise to new sides within the ranks of the children of the Creator, and those ranks swell with every passing day. The so-called Dark Gods and their followers, the mortals of this world, the dragons themselves, as well as the damnable Aerith Seth and his progeny have splintered the power of this world to such an extent that there may be no salvation for anyone, and the last one left standing may only inherit a cosmos of ash. But Mariti Brightblade, slayer of angels, leader of the doomed and the damned, do you have enough power and pride left within you to have an impact in this conflict, or will you sit here, watching the falling of the heavens, only to be taken in the end by that which you created?"

Mariti considered for a long moment, the silence that wrapped the two figures as immutable as the fate that the Spirit had decreed for her race. When finally Mariti spoke, it was not full of the pride or the pomp of her position at the head of the oldest and most powerful of the races, but rather as one who knew the full weight that her words carried.

"I can only speak for myself now," Mariti began, "and if I can convince any of those who still consider me their leader to follow me, then they too will abide by these words. Dorovar is my only enemy. I renounce the war against the Dark Gods. I renounce the war against the Cadarians. Aerith Seth and his followers need not fear me. They need not worry about my motives or my greater goals. There is no hatred to be manipulated. There is no rage to blind me. There is only truth. Truth that I must risk and endure all to see my enemy slain. More than that, I cannot do."

The Spirit considered for a long moment. Suddenly the form of the creature was gone, and only the echo of its voice was left as the sound of the wind and falling snow returned.

"Then turn your sights to Jelan. There you will find a weapon that will give you the ability to do what you say you will do."

* * * * * * * * * * * *

Gregor Quicksilver stood looking down onto the fields of snow below, and saw the massive dragon spread its wings and launch into the air. There was something akin to annoyance that roiled in his stomach, but he wasn't sure whether it was disgust at the sight of a dragon, or disgust at the fact that the dragon had been placed on the path that she had been placed on. Now that the power of the Voice inhabited his body and his eyes had been opened to the greater truths of the cosmos, Gregor felt himself changed. The veil of ignorance had been lifted, and he saw the futility that he had dedicated his life to before that moment. He had been a servant of the Creator in name only, and most of the tenants that he held himself to were only shadows created by the bright light of truth. The truth was so much simpler. Service was not its own reward, it was the only truth. Each being served the Creator whether it wanted to or not, and the more it struggled against that servitude, the more it brought suffering upon itself. Service was the only way to avoid pain and loss; the only way to avoid regret. Now that Gregor knew the truth, the futility of his former life was like a wound upon his soul that would never heal. Moments later, he felt the presence of the Spirit. The being appeared not through a portal or through any visible disturbance; one moment the Spirit was just there. Though the Voice inhabited his mind, Gregor had no idea who or what the Spirit was, its identity was completely hidden from him. Whether that was done by the Creator or by the Spirit itself was the real question.

"Was it wise to send the dragon to Jelan? You know what's going on there."

Gregor's question was half his own, and half the Voice's. Being a dual being was still a strain on Gregor's mind. Though he had control of the abilities of the Voice, sometimes he spoke with the Voice, and sometimes the Voice spoke through him. He knew what the Voice wanted him to know, while other times he felt as though he was completely in the dark. Perhaps the Voice didn't fully trust him yet.

"This war accelerates whether we wish it to or not," the Spirit replied. "Dorovar is a threat that must be dealt with, and the only piece on the board now that would not topple it is the dragons. Whatever happens, the heretic must not be allowed to face the abomination."

Hatred boiled in Gregor's heart. The heretic was the Creator's name for Aerith Seth, the man who had humiliated Gregor the last time they met.

"The heretic is mine."

"No," the Spirit answered. "The Wrath will deal with the heretic. You have more pressing matters. The dragons will distract the abomination for a time, long enough for our forces to be marshaled. But you must ensure that the path is open for our forces when the time comes. The loss of the Will will be felt for some time, especially now that the Dark Gods have learned that the limits they once thought their powers had can be broken. Aryx and Diana cast themselves into the void rather than be used for our purposes, and the influence of Pyrrus and Halicon complicates everything. The Brother of Angels is no longer mute, and if he discovers that which Dorovar overlooked...."

The Voice nodded Gregor's head.

"Then he would be our equal, and upset everything the Creator has put in motion."

The Spirit scoffed.

"You have never understood the Brother of Angels. His motives are not selfish. He would never keep such power for himself. But if he were to give it to the Phoenix, or to the heretic, then there is no chance to prevent the collision."

The Voice turned to regard the Spirit.

"Then why am I not going to kill the Brother of Angels?"

The Spirit bowed its head.

"I am afraid that task is left for me."

The Voice nodded.

"And the Will?"

The Spirit looked out onto the horizon.

"The Will has already chosen its new vessel. Or maybe the vessel was the one to do the choosing. However, who will be in control still remains to be seen. Either way, the heretic will be distracted, and with any luck it will be enough of a distraction to allow the Wrath to do its terrible work."

What Once was Lost

Year Four of the Just Emperor Kaitain "Dragonsbane" Lorien, Creator's Calendar Year 1871

Tolon Morr took a long deep breath and exhaled slowly, watching as his breath crystallized in the crisp cold air. As he looked up into the sky, he saw the streaks of fire as they bounded through the atmosphere. Inwardly he wondered how long it had been since anyone from Cadaria had stood where he was standing. How long had it been since the Frozen Wastes in the far northern reaches of Espre had known anything other than peaceful and natural tranquility? But left in this barren wasteland, no matter how beautiful it may have been, Tolon had nothing to do but think on all that had happened. Tolon was a gladiator and a soldier, two professions not highly regarded for their capacity for reason and logical thought. Men like Tolon were trained to be living weapons, their only need for reasoning was the ability to determine who the enemy was and how best to approach destroying them. But in all that Tolon had seen in his short time as a member of the Knights of the Flashing Blade, that distinction between enemy and ally was becoming blurrier by the day. Despite everything he had been taught, Tolon could not help but see the tenants of his former life as a lie. The Emperor of Cadaria was not infallible, and was not the moral compass of the world. Kaitain Lorien was a brute and cared for nothing but his own agendas. Perhaps in some ways he was worse than the so-called Dark Gods that had been regarded as enemies since they fell from the heavens almost two millennia ago. And now there were dragons and monstrous beasts that served someone called Dorovar. All of them seemed intent on destroying anything and everything in their path.

But there was more to the war than just the fighting, and the dying, and the unknown motivations of those with more power than Tolon could grasp in ten lifetimes. There was a secret war, buried so far under the surface that it had gone unnoticed for almost two millennia. There were hints, innuendo, and half-truths, but one thing had become painfully clear to Tolon; the Sacred Weapons were at the heart of this secret war, and learning about the Secret Weapons had to take priority. Of course Tolon could have been on the front lines, as he had in the Plains of Steam. He could be fighting against dragons, and men, and Dark Gods. But the battle at the Plains of Steam showed him just how pointless his intervention in this war would be. He would fight, and he would die. In time one of the beings with real power would strike him down and he would become just another victim of a war he didn't understand. But what had also become clear in his time as a Knight of the Flashing Blade, was that the Sacred Weapons were more than just creations with wills of their own. They had a destiny, a terrible and ominous destiny.

When he heard rustling behind him, Tolon turned and returned to the makeshift camp that he had constructed. After arriving in the frozen wastes by way of a portal created by the strange man who was accompanying the supposed traitor Hannah Ironheart, Tolon had found a pack containing rations, clothes, bedrolls, and a small tent. It seemed that whoever the man was who sent them there was more than just an arrogant bastard, he also knew where he was sending them and what they would need to survive there until they found what they were looking for; whatever that was. Jerrica Maldrovin was just pulling on one of the heavy coats that was in the survival pack when Tolon pulled back the flap of the tent. He regarded her for a long moment, and was encouraged by her color. She had been so pale for so long, it was good to see her with color back in her cheeks. She still moved as though she were weak, every exertion exaggerated.

"How are you feeling?" Tolon said kneeling beside her. "Your color looks better this morning."

Jerrica smiled weakly and nodded.

"The longer I am away from that place, the better I feel. I'm sorry you have had to tend to me so intensely over the last few days."

Tolon reached out and smoothed her hair away from her face. It was an intimate gesture, and as the two had been together these gestures were becoming more frequent.

"Are you ready to talk about it?"

She took his large and callous-laden hand into hers and held it tightly. There was so much caught up in her suddenly jumbled mind, and there was no good way to make sense of it all. For all her life she had lived with her two sisters, Jordyne and Jania. Together they were not just seers, but they were reflections of one another. They could see into each other's minds and hearts, and together the three of them were able to make sense of what one could not alone. For nearly three centuries they had lived like that, the three together, teaching and learning from each other, never alone with their thoughts. Now that she was separated from them, now that she was alone in her head, it was nearly impossible to keep the flood of unfamiliar information straight. She was out in the world by herself, seeing sights with her own eyes that she had only seen in vision to that point. She had been within reach of dragons, Dark Gods, and mortal heroes. But whatever excitement that had engendered within her, the side effects had been much worse than she could have anticipated. Once long ago the Dark Seer Jehna Feris had warned the Maldovrin Triplets of the dangers that lay ahead of them. Jehna Feris had been the first of the Seers to have direct contact with the Dark Gods, and it had changed her. Her visions had suddenly become more powerful, and more precise. It was as though an area of reality that had been closed to her was suddenly thrust open. But with her new and powerful visions came a strange disease, one that robbed her of her physical strength and vitality. She said once that she felt as though she constantly walked around with a great weight on her shoulders. In her short time close to the Dark Gods, Jerrica got the briefest glimpse of the overwhelming weight that the Dark Seer has described.

"I'm not sure how to describe this to you, Tolon," Jerrica said, her voice suddenly weaker and more pensive. "I'm not sure how to even describe it to myself."

She looked down at their joined hands and then exhaled slowly.

"How much do you know about the Seers?"

Tolon grimaced a little.

"I was raised on a diet of superstition, tall-tales, and outright lies," he said slowly. "When I was growing up around the arenas, and then as a gladiator, the only thing that passed for news were the ramblings and gossip we heard from the traders and guards. Good stories were currency to us. So I've heard Seers described as witches, or just another kind of Dark God. I've even heard them called the angels, and voices for the Creator."

Jerrica reacted little to the description, except for the last one. Tolon thought he saw her wince slightly.

"Seers are rare in Cadaria, True Seers rarer still," she said after a moment. "Only a handful of children are born into each generation with the ability to glimpse the future. As the generations pass, there are more that are born, but because of the dilution of the bloodlines, their abilities are weaker, and sometimes completely out of their control. Most don't even realize they are glimpsing the future. It comes to them as dreams, or even as a feeling they can't describe of knowing something is going to happen, but not exactly what. These people could barely be considered Seers at all. Those closer to the bloodline have some control over what they can see, but most of their visions will come unbidden in dreams. It's only the True Seers, the ones directly descended from the bloodline of the First Empress, Liette Lorien, who can actively control their visions. But more than that, the visions become like another sense, no different from smell or hearing."

Jerrica paused there, considering her words. Tolon's world had not allowed for much delicate communication with anyone, and he was more comfortable with the blunt, straightforward etiquette of battle than he was the circular etiquette of polite conversation. For that he had often been considered an unsophisticated brute. In some measures that was a kind assessment.

"You winced when I said that Seers were the voices of the Creator."

Jerrica kept her eyes down, then closed them for a long moment before looking up to meet Tolon's gaze. There was a deep and profound sadness in her eyes.

"Perhaps in some ways, the True Seers are glimpsing the mind of the Creator with their visions. The greatest of us, the Dark Seer however has said that the Creator has only granted us the ability to see what He wants us to see. That is why the Dark Seer left Cadaria. She glimpsed the rest of the reality that had been hidden from her because of her exposure to the Dark Gods. The longer she stayed with them, the more clearly she could see. But mortals were not supposed to see the truth of the world and the Cosmos around them. There is just too much for the fragile human body and mind to make sense of. Exposure to that truth changes and weakens you. Stretches you out and weighs you down with the sheer enormity of it all. Whatever Jehna saw, whatever she was exposed to, she needed to see more, it was important that she see it all. I do know that whatever it was, it was horrible, and it scared her more deeply than anything any mortal had ever seen."

Jerrica fell silent again, and Tolon was not sure whether he should press her for more information or not. There was more she had to tell, that much was obvious, but he decided to try a different line of questioning.

"Is that why you were so weak when we were in the Plains of Steam? Because there were Dark Gods there and it started to change your visions?"

Jerrica nodded meekly.

"I felt them," she said softly and slowly, "long before we were at the Plains of Steam, I felt them. It was like a swarm of spiders crawling around in my brain. My visions were always calm, but the closer we came to that place, the more violent they became. I saw the dragons; I saw the beast calling itself War. I saw the people wielding power that no mortal should ever wield. But the more I saw, the tighter my chest became, and the harder it was to breathe. I feel now as though I am at a crossroads. I am no longer what I was, and yet I have not fully crossed over to becoming what Jehna became. I am floating somewhere in between, as though I am being given the option to pull back, to not take the plunge."

Tolon considered for a moment more before speaking, but before he could, Jerrica pulled her hand away and smiled.

"I feel as though we are close to our destination, Tolon, and that there are a great deal of important questions that we are going to find answers to, and still more that we did not even know existed. We should begin to travel while we have light, before the cold makes it impossible to make progress."

Tolon nodded and started to assist Jerrica in breaking down their meager campsite. Perhaps they would find answers, but Tolon's thoughts drifted toward the inevitability of questions that had no answer.

＊ ＊ ＊ ＊ ＊ ＊ ＊ ＊ ＊ ＊ ＊

The day of travel had been uneventful, but very difficult. While much of the snow was packed so densely that travel over it at reasonable speed was possible, there were also stretches that Tolon would find himself in snow drifts that came up to his knees and sometimes higher. For those stretches, he hoisted Jerrica onto his back and trudged through as best he could. There were times when the wind blew so hard it felt as though it were cutting through them, the cold penetrating them to their bones. During the late morning and afternoon hours, the sun was able to mitigate some of the biting cold, but Tolon knew that as night approached, it would be impossible to travel, and perhaps difficult even with the camping gear and clothing that they had available to them to stay warm through the night. It would not be enough to kill them, but it would certainly not make their night comfortable. However if they were not able to find their destination within a couple of days, the elements would certainly be their undoing.

It was approaching nightfall when Jerrica finally tugged on Tolon's sleeve and pointed in the direction of the horizon. At first, Tolon thought that she was pointing at the streaks of fire shooting across the sky. This far north, the Rain of Star Fire was much more brilliant, making the stars seem dull by comparison. But quickly Tolon realized that it wasn't the brilliant streaks that Jerrica was calling his attention too, it was a small pillar of gray smoke that emerged from somewhere. It couldn't have been more than a few miles away. Even it if wasn't their ultimate destination, smoke meant fire, and fire meant warmth. The opportunity to find some respite from the brutal and oppressive cold was too much to pass up. Their faces were covered with cloth to protect their mouths and noses, so Tolon simply nodded his understanding of Jerrica's gesture, and turned their path toward the smoke in the distance.

It took several hours to cover the distance to the source of the smoke. As the time passed, Tolon was able to begin to make out the outline of a structure in the distance. At first there was little in the way of definitive features that could be seen, but the closer they got, the more Tolon was able to make out. The pillar of smoke they had seen was not one pillar, but was several pillars that billowed from at least four separate chimneys. If Tolon had not known any better, he would have thought the place to be an inn of some kind. No windows could be made out from the view they had of the structure. It was nightfall by the time Tolon and Jerrica were standing before the broad wooden doors that led to the interior of the structure.

Tolon reached up and knocked as hard as he could manage three times at the large doors. After several long moments, Tolon could hear movement behind the door, and he stepped back, pulling Jerrica with him. The large wooden door separated in the middle after a moment, light streaming out of the opening into the advancing darkness. A young woman with long, straight, shiny black hair stood in the opening, a gentle smile coming to her lips when she saw Tolon and Jerrica. She had lily-white skin that was even more stark compared to the plum colored dress that she wore.

"Please, travelers," she said after a long moment looking over both Tolon and Jerrica, "you must have come so far to be here. Please come inside and warm yourselves near the fire."

Jerrica did not hesitate to accept the invitation, moving past the young woman in the plum dress and into the large open area that served as the receiving hall for the structure. Tolon moved past a little slower, his warrior's senses not allowing him to give in even to the cold that was ravaging his body. The young woman took two steps back away from the doorway, allowing Tolon to pass into the room proper before closing the door behind them. Tolon was struck immediately by how warm the room was, even in its spaciousness. There were many tapestries hanging from the walls showing vistas that Tolon had never laid eyes on before and could not place. As he pulled the cloth away from his mouth and nose, Tolon was struck by the sweet smell of flowers and fruit. Jerrica had already made her way to a large fireplace that stood in the center of the large room. It was made of light gray, nearly white stones that seemed to radiate as much heat as the flames themselves. Jerrica perched on the edge of the fireplace, on a low wide bench that would have been perfect for Tolon to lay flat across and bask in the warmth of the fire. But he was not ready to let his guard down just yet.

There were several doors leading out of the room, and the woman in the plum dress was making her way towards one of them.

"I'm sure you're hungry," she said in pleasant if stilted tones, "I'll have some food prepared for you, and once you are properly warmed up, dinner will be ready for you in the dining hall. After we will see you are well bestowed with rooms and baths if you wish. Wherever you are bound, you should not be travelling again until the morning. It is far too cold for civilized being to be out on a night like this."

She smiled a weak smile, bowed slightly and then turned to go through a door. Tolon was left looking around the room once more, making his way toward the roaring fire. Even at a distance it felt good to be warm once again, though his bones and muscles still ached. It would probably take several hours before the core of him would feel warm again, but perhaps a bath would speed the process.

There were two winding staircases that stood at the back of the room, and after several moments Tolon could hear footsteps descending the staircase to their left. Tolon placed his hand on Jerrica's shoulder and then suddenly realized that he was unarmed. Even if there were a threat posed to them in this place, Tolon had nothing but his bare hands and formidable strength to meet it with. The situation did not fill him with optimism. However, Jerrica reached up and put her hand on his and look back at him with a reassuring smile. It was obvious that she did not perceive the same sense of danger that he did. She was the Seer, and he was only a soldier who was trained to see danger everywhere. Perhaps he needed to put more faith in her prophecy and less in his own paranoia.

The footsteps soon resolved into a pair of high quality leather riding boots and then green pants fringed with white and gold. A white shirt came into view next, followed by shoulder-length brown hair. At the bottom of the stairs, the man turned to face his guests, and both Jerrica and Tolon finally were able to see his face. He had bright blue eyes and a short but well-groomed beard. At first glance, Tolon thought that he was in his early thirties, and that he had the look of a man who had seen many battles in his short life. However, there was no air of menace from him, and the gentle smile on his face reached his eyes and was meant to set his guests at ease.

"Welcome my friends, to Glacier's Rift. I'm sure you can imagine that we don't get many visitors here, so of course I am curious as to what would bring you this far north."

Tolon started to open his mouth in answer, but Jerrica responded first.

"The world has become a violent place, full of wars that seem to stretch without end. Dragons and Dark Gods clash daily with the armies of Cadaria, and there is no place on either Cadaria or Mythryn that is safe. We heard rumors of an island away from the madness, a place where we could be safe. Tolon did not want to come with me, but we felt it was the only way we could be safe."

The man regarded first Jerrica for a moment, and then Tolon.

"Tolon? Tolon Morr? The famous gladiator?"

Tolon gritted his teeth for a moment. If Jerrica was going to craft a lie, she should have done so without using their real names. Finally Tolon nodded, trying to looking as pensive as he could. Perhaps the man did not know of his elevation and did not know that he was a member of the Knights of the Flashing Blade. There was no clear idea of exactly how much news made its way to the Frozen Wastes.

"I saw you fight once," the man said, "many years ago in Rashaleb. You were very impressive, and I was happy to hear that you earned your freedom. No man should be left to fight those battles. Man was not meant to be fighting every day for his life, knowing that one mistake will end his existence. There are too many things that we do not know about that threaten to kill us as it is. No need to tempt fate."

He took several steps forward, but stopped five paces short of where Tolon and Jerrica were. His eyes had gone to Jerrica, and there was a moment that Tolon was sure he saw the man's jaw clench. But however long that the smile faltered, it would have been for no more than the blink of an eye.

"But I do forget my manners, don't I? I'm sure that it comes as no surprise to you that we do not get many opportunities to practice our hospitality or our manners. If you would have come a few years from now you may have found nothing but savages. My name is Jared, and I am happy to welcome you and offer you any respite that you desire."

Tolon could feel Jerrica's smile, but there was something about the man that Tolon instantly distrusted. One would have to be blind to not realize that the man was covering a growing discomfort with a smile.

"Perhaps you would be willing to answer a few questions then," Tolon said after a moment, "since you know about me, and I know so little about you."

Tolon didn't wait for Jared to respond before launching his first salvo.

"You said that you saw me in Rashaleb, is that where you're from?"

Jared paled for a quick moment but then seemed to regain his footing.

"No, not Rashaleb. You might say that the Frozen Wastes have always been my home. I have been here for a long time, and I can barely remember anything before I came here. Though, I would be remiss if I didn't say that I did not come here of my own free will, like most of us here on the grounds. You could call Glacier's Rift a home for lost children."

A sympathetic groan came from Jerrica.

"So this is an orphanage, and you're an orphan?"

Jared's smile widened.

"After a fashion. I like to consider myself more a refugee from a life that no longer had room for me. I would imagine that the rest of those here would feel the same way. But if you have more questions, I'm sure that I'm not the person to really answer them. Follow me, and I'll take you to someone who will answer any question you have, including the real reasons you came here."

Jared turned back toward the staircases and took several steps before Tolon was able to speak.

"We told you why we were here."

Jared turned back, a sly smile on his lips.

"Knights of the Flashing Blade and True Seers don't come to Glacier's Rift looking for refuge from wars that they have large roles in. You are here for information, and you are here to find something to help defend your people against the growing darkness in your world."

Tolon tried hard to keep his jaw from dropping open.

"We may be removed from your world," Jared said turning away again, "but that doesn't mean we don't pay attention."

Jerrica looked back at Tolon, and he could see some concern in her eyes, but he smiled down at her and helped her to her feet. For some reason he seemed reassured that Jared knew who they were and why they were there. Before he was cautious, but now the potential for real answers filled him with a hope he had not known for some time.

Instead of ascending one of the staircases, Jared moved between them and opened the door that stood in the far wall. The door led to a long corridor that had doors at consistent intervals down its length. Jared continued down the length of the corridor, stopping before the door at the end of the hall. He knocked twice and then opened the door without waiting for a reply. Standing in the hallway, Jared motioned for Tolon and

Jerrica to pass by him into the room before entering behind them and closing the door. It didn't take Tolon's eyes long to find the other man in the room. He stood near the fireplace with his back to the new arrivals. After a long moment, the man turned to face Jerrica and Tolon. The man's hair was short and seemingly unkempt, but it seemed an organized chaos. His eyes were cold gray, and his cheeks and chin showed just the start of a beard, but his features made it almost impossible to guess his age. His clothing was a patchwork of common farmer's garments and royal finery. Though he was not armed, Tolon could not shake the feeling that this was perhaps one of the most dangerous individuals that he had ever laid his eyes upon.

"Our visitors, Sir Tolon Moor, the Amethyst Knight of the Flashing Blade from the Kingdom of Steel Celidar, and the True Seer Jerrica Maldovrin."

The unnamed man cocked his head to one side, and flashed a quick smile.

"No need ta be so damned formal, Jared. Not much done 'ere is anyt'ing like ye'd find back in da kingdoms. But den again; maybe dat's not such a bad t'ing."

The man's accent was so thick it was hard to understand him. However Tolon did understand the motion from his hands that invited them to sit. Instead of sitting, the man instead chose to lean against the side of the fireplace.

"Ye 'ave questions, so let's talk. Ye can call me Gideon."

Rewards of Service

Hedorah, the Flying Kingdom had become renown over the centuries for a great many things, not the least of which were its history of legitimizing graft, blackmail, bribery, and assassination as a means to achieve greatness within the Kingdom's borders. It was the worst kept secret in the whole of Cadaria that the right amount of money could buy anyone without shame or scruples as much influence and power as they wanted. However, it was also no secret that those who achieved power in such ways often had trouble holding onto it. The same guard that could be bribed to poison the food of a member of one of the royal families could just as easily be bribed to turn his sword upon that original employer. This rampant corruption had created a battle for power that prompted the creation of a royal council instead of a single voice to shape the policy for the kingdom. Over several hundred years, the royal families of Hedorah became infested with wealthy merchants, brigands, and con men who had bought their ways into the halls of power. Various schisms formed within and between families creating splinter families that had the same name but different agendas. All told, there were ten royal families of Hedorah, all of whose principle allegiances were to themselves. Even in the best of times, there was a fragile peace that held between the families, the gentleman's agreement preventing assassinations of the heads of the families holding, but just barely. There were always rogue operations that claimed the life of some unsuspecting would-be noble. However, the unwritten law in Hedorah was that if one was unable to protect oneself at all times, then the fault lay not with the aggressor, but with the victim.

Recent events had done nothing but exacerbate the barely restrained conflicts in Hedorah. Following the execution of the Topaz Knight, Jaccob Aldora, the representative of the Kingdom of Hedorah in the Knights of the Flashing Blade, and the new decrees by the Just Emperor Kaitain Lorien, an emergency session of the royal council had been called. Several of the families were directly affected by the decrees, largely because of their ties to the Church of the Creator. The Church had always had a significant presence in Hedorah, and it was said that the only Kingdom that the Church had more sway over was Albitonin. Another complication facing the royal council was the fact that their history had deprived them of direct representation in the Imperial Court. Jaccob Aldora had been the only member of any of the royal families that could find himself in the presence of the Emperor. Now that door was shut to the rulers of Hedorah, and that fueled more debate amongst the bickering royals. Already several hours into their running arguments, the volume of the shouts had reached a crescendo. Finally a singular voice cut through the din. It was the voice of Terrance Aldora, Jaccob's older brother, and often recognized as the voice of reason within the royal council.

"We're getting nowhere," Terrance's strong voice rang out. "The question before the council is not whether or not the Emperor's decrees are in the right or not. Kaitain Lorien is recognized as the Emperor of Cadaria, and therefore his wishes are his to make manifest and those loyal to him can do nothing but obey. The question before this council is whether or not we shall remain loyal to the Emperor of Cadaria, of if we shall lend our voices to those of dissent that have rung out in Thorigald and Albitonin."

A rotund merchant named Pelis stood. He had been elevated to the royal council after the mysterious death of his brother. Pelis' family had bought their way into nobility, and most were certain that it had been Pelis behind the death of his brother, though none were interested in proving the suspicions to be either true or false.

"And we will be crushed just as surely as those rebellions have been. Haven't you heard the news coming out of Albitonin? The Stone has been broken. Hannah Ironheart is dead. Marlae Lorien has been brought to the Emperor's justice. It's said that the entire Army of Fire is crossing the Plains of Steam to wipe out any voices of decent in Thorigald. The Wolf of Saldarine is leading the army personally and she's going to rip the heart out of her husband, the traitor Seraph Kore if it means bringing that rebellion to an end. All will be made to bend their knee to the whims of Kaitain Lorien. He's turned the tide in the battle against the dragons. I've even heard stories of sailors seeing explosions on the Dark Continent. They say that ill winds are blowing from Mythryn. The scent of death, and that the Dark Citadel has fallen."

A hard peel of laughter bellowed from another of the royals, this one a man called Herren. He was a gaunt sickly looking man, but his powerful voice belied his fragile visage.

"Ghost stories and propaganda. If the Dark Gods have been defeated, where are the bodies? Where are the heralds championing the great god killers? If Hannah Ironheart is dead, why does Albitonin still fight? Chelsea Zarova has been disgraced and stripped of her title as Knight of the Flashing Blade, and yet she is leading the most important offensive in the history of Cadaria? You're more of a fool than your brother was, Pelis, and I didn't think that was possible. My aunt's dogs have more sense than you, and they eat their own droppings."

This brought a new salvo of accusations and arguments from the assembled royals. Whatever manners and grace the assemblage purported to have had obviously been left outside of the council chambers. Again Terrance's voice called out for silence, but it was not his words that filled the emptiness next, it was the softer but powerful voice of the Reverend Mother of the Church of the Creator in Albitonin, Amallia.

"Kaitain Lorien believes that he has been betrayed by the Church of the Creator. He believes that the rebellion against his reign instituted by Lady Hannah Ironheart was a coup designed to place a more moral leader on the throne, one that would be a puppet to the Church, but this is far from the truth. Had the Church wanted to wrest control from Kaitain Lorien, then it would have been Lady Ironheart herself, or Sir Quicksilver to replace the boy upon the throne. But in her wisdom, Lady Ironheart proclaimed Marlae Lorien as the rightful heir to the throne, and Hedorah should recognize that proclamation as ordained by the Creator."

Pelis scoffed.

"Ordination by the Creator means nothing if we are stripped of our possessions and forced into servitude. Your fate is clear Amallia. You have no choice but to fight for the cause of the Church. If you fail you will die, and if you do nothing you will die. You cannot even renounce your faith because the mandate of the Emperor is clear. All members of the clergy are to be put to death. So your words can be seen as nothing more than self-serving drivel."

"Spoken by a man who knows how to say nothing other than what is self-serving," Herren retorted.

"This is getting us nowhere," Terrence called out again. "Whether we agree with the Reverend Mother or not is immaterial now. What we must decide is if Kaitain Lorien has overstepped his authority as Emperor of Cadaria, and whether the decisions that he is making now are out of madness. If the Emperor is leading us on a road to destruction, we cannot simply be led blindly to slaughter. I call for a vote. What shall be the fate of Hedorah? Shall we follow the will of the Emperor, or shall we join those who have vowed to remove him from power?"

It was then that the doors to the council chamber exploded open, the huge wooden doors thrown off their hinges and slamming to the floor with a sound like thunder.

* * * * * * * * * * * *

News of the death of Jaccob Aldora, the Topaz Knight of the Flashing Blade had been met with many responses in Hedorah. A great many were of disbelief, while others were of shame and disgust. Most who knew Jaccob had always considered him a kind if misguided man whose demons would consume him if the drink did not end his life first. Though he slept more often in the bed of a prostitute then in his own, he did keep a modest estate near the royal quarter. The lower element of Hedorah had wasted no time in looting everything of value from the estate within the first few hours after Jaccob's death had become common knowledge. Windows were broken; doors were flung open and hung precariously from their hinges. What could not be taken for a quick sale was vandalized, and what remained of the home was nothing more than a hovel. However, no one was careless enough to make the place a squatting ground, except the wild animals and rodents that were commonly found running through the streets. It was encroaching on the first evening hours when a portal opened in the center of what had been the common room of the estate. The swirling blue portal hung in mid-air for almost a minute before the first form emerged. Ayden Seth immediately turned back toward the portal and waited as the form of Marlae Lorien stepped through. He supported her gently as she found her balance again. But just as quickly as she seemed to be stable, she fell to her knees and vomited. Ayden knelt beside her and pulled her hair back away from her face and supported her gently as she continued to heave and cough. After a few long minutes, the young woman seemed to regain her bearings and sat back gingerly on her heels. Ayden wiped the sweat away from her brow gently and smiled a supporting smile.

"Portal travel can be rough the first couple of times, but you get used to it pretty quickly. It seems to be harder on people who don't have powers."

Marlae felt the bile burning the back of her throat, and when she tried to answer, she could only cough. Thinking better of anything she could say at that moment, she forced a weak smile and began to look around the room. The place looked like it had been gutted and abandoned, and no one of her station in life would be caught dead anywhere near a place like this. When he saw the distress on her face, Ayden too began to look around their surroundings. His countenance changed to a deep frown, one that spoke of both sadness and anger.

"This was Jaccob's home," Ayden said finally, the anger creeping into his words. "I guess the looters in Hedorah wanted to keep up their reputation as ruthless and efficient. If I wasn't escorting you, Empress, I would hunt down every last one of them."

The word Empress rang in Marlae's head, and she shook off the sickness that was still twisting her stomach and her head. So many things had gone wrong over the past day, and Marlae was determined that whatever fate was waiting for her, she would meet it on her feet and not on her knees. She would live up to the title that she had fought for, and she would make all of those people who doubted and turned their back on her pay for their lack of vision. It seemed that with Ayden at her side, she had a chance to make all of her wishes come true, and the dream that she had of Jaccob would soon prove to be more prophecy than imagination.

"This was the place you thought would be safe for us, Ayden?" Marlae said as she slowly got back to her feet. "I thought you would take us to a fortress, or somewhere that we could raise an army to take the throne away from my father."

Ayden's frown changed to a more neutral look, but there was still fire in his eyes.

"Jaccob set us on this path, so Jaccob's kingdom is where we have to start, Empress. It is isolated, protected, and a strategic point to strike at Zevarit, Rashaleb, or Iltorp. Getting a foothold on the continent of Cadaria will be the next goal, but if we are successful in turning this den of thieves into your own personal island stronghold, Heodrah's navy will be of great benefit in the war to come. Your father doesn't understand anything other than force. So that is how we must teach him the depth of his mistakes."

Marlae saw the wisdom in his words, but did not like the feeling that he was taking control of the situation, and telling her what was best. But this new warmth inside of her, this part of her that had awakened instantly trusting the man who was bleeding to death on her floor, knew that he was not trying to usurp power. His intentions were exactly what he said they were, and whatever thoughts he had for himself were being set aside to ensure that her goals were realized. Ayden was obviously a dangerous man. But he had been chosen as her protector. Sent to her through flame and by the hand of the Creator. If there were any man whose council she would respect, she would have to learn to let it be Ayden's.

Ayden looked more purposefully around the room, and spotted something in the far room that caught his interest. He softly squeezed Marlae's shoulder and then went to the room, retrieved something from under several overturned chairs, and returned. Marlae saw quickly that it was a bottle that was still stoppered.

"It looks like the thieves didn't get everything. Here, drink some of this; it should help with the portal sickness."

Marlae looked at the non-descript bottle in Ayden's hand for a long moment before finally taking it from him. This was so different from the life that she had lived. Never had she been given a bottle to drink from like a common drunkard. All liquids were properly presented to her in a goblet or other vessel that was properly adorned to befit her station. Even when she was exiled in Albitonin, she was treated to the fineries of her station. Just as she pulled the stopper from the bottle and got a first nose-full of the pungent aroma, a strange feeling tugged at the back of her mind. Something flared within her, something akin to the strange ability that had allowed her to heal Ayden's wounds, though part of her still did not believe that was anything other than an incredibly vivid dream. It was as though there was someone in the room with them. But as Marlae tried to shake off the ridiculous feeling, she caught a look at Ayden's eyes. It seemed that her ridiculous feeling was not so ridiculous after all. Ayden seemed to sense a presence with them as well.

Suddenly a form was simply there in the room with them, standing opposite them near two broken windows. The form was in the shape of a person, but it seemed to be nothing more than an outline of pure white light. But instead of being in the shape of a man, it was more in the shape of a boy, standing just tall enough to come to Ayden's waist. The form of light stood for a long moment, and it was impossible to determine which direction the form was facing, or if it was even aware of their presence. Finally the form seemed to take one step toward the pair. A voice sounded the next moment, young and barely mature, but instead of coming from the form it seemed to come from everywhere at once.

"Marlae Lorien, first born daughter of the so-called Emperor of Cadaria, the blasphemer known as Kaitain Lorien, step forward."

Marlae hesitated for a moment, reaching out to take Ayden's hand. She squeezed it hard, as though drawing strength from him, before releasing her grasp and taking two steps toward the form of brilliant white light.

"Marlae Lorien, your father, Kaitain Lorien has renounced the Creator. He has decreed the worship of the Creator to be against mortal law, and that those who worship the Creator shall have their possessions and rank stripped of them and reduced to poverty, servitude, and slavery. Moreover, the vile man has decreed that any who have dedicated their life in service to the Creator through His Church shall be put to death. Your father sees himself as the giver of life and death, that he should be the only voice calling out from the wilderness, shepherding the lost. He sees himself as the moral authority, justified in his vice and violence. Killing in his own name, without sin or fault. Killing those who have served to protect the weak, give comfort to the helpless, and to lead the Creator's flock into the arms of salvation. But there will be no salvation to those who follow this demon's call. There will be only damnation, pain, and endless torment. Do you, Marlae Lorien, follow the path of your father? Do you hate the Creator, and see yourself as His equal? Do you cast stones at those who have sacrificed for His greater glory? Does blaspheme permeate your being so that it rolls from your tongue with every word?"

Marlae felt her heart in her mouth. She tried to breathe, but it caught, her chest aching with the exertion to force the breath from her lungs. Finally her voice pushed through the fear and the shock.

"No."

Her voice sounded meek and hollow. It rung in her ears the way it had when she was a little girl, awed by the presence of her powerful grandfather and the impossibly virtuous and upright men and women who wore the mantle of Knight of the Flashing Blade. She swallowed hard, remembering the hard lessons she had learned at the hand of her father; the brutal lessons that failure and timidity brought.

"No."

This time there was conviction in her voice. She pulled herself upright, standing straight, her shoulders pulled back, trying to look as regal as her title depicted. The light around the being dimmed for a brief moment and then intensified, almost as though the being had taken a breath; either of relief or frustration. When it spoke again, the tone was less intense, but no less commanding.

"The Lorien line is corrupt. It has been touched by the mind of evil and has descended into madness so severe that it cannot be redeemed. A Lorien will not lead this world into its next age, and so now, Marlae Lorien, you must choose if you will renounce your father, renounce your family, renounce your name. Will you renounce your father and the crimes he has committed?"

Marlae hurt all over. Her mind racing and her soul feeling the weight of the questions being put to her. But her course had been chosen, she could not turn back now.

"Yes."

The being of light continued.

"Will you renounce the family that sired you, and all of the horror they have wrought on this planet?"

"Yes."

The glow intensified around the being.

"Will you renounce your name?"

Marlae swallowed hard.

"Yes."

The being reached out with one ghostly hand and touched Marlae lightly on the forearm. In that instant, she felt a warmth coursing through her body unlike any she had ever felt before. She felt as though her skin was glowing, covered with a phantom fire that only she could see and feel. Then just as quickly as it started, the warmth and heavenly lightness was gone and Marlae felt as though she had been renewed and reborn. The being stepped back and spoke again.

"The child that you were exists no longer. That creature died on the floor of a room in the holy city of Albitonin. You have been reborn, a new creature; a child of the Creator. You have earned a sacred name, a name revered for wisdom, strength in the face of adversity, and unwavering loyalty. These are traits that are crucial in the days to come. Your soul swims now with one who has passed from this life, may you find together what you were not able to find apart. You are henceforth Marlae Tamerlane, the Enlightened, Scion of the Creator and Divine Empress of Espre."

Marlae felt something well up within her that she had never known. She had always been brimming with confidence in her adult life, but she had never felt conviction, only entitlement. Now she felt as though she was finally on the road she had been destined for since birth. The sovereign of not just a continent but of a world as ordained by the Creator. The being of light now turned its attention to Ayden.

"You, child of abomination, you must also renounce the demons of your origin. The Creator teaches that the son shall not bear the burden of the sins of the father, and though you have been raised to despise all that the Creator has wrought, now you stand with the possibility of redemption. Your life has been spared the torment of an eternity of pain by the power of the Creator through his newest child, and that debt will be paid with service or with blood. So you are given a choice, Ayden Seth."

That moment a helm and suit of armor appeared beside Ayden, floating in a haze of smoke and light. A flaming sword hung there too, brimming with divine fire.

"The Divine Empress requires a protector, and a general of her armies. As a Child of the Creator, she shall command the very armies of the Heavens; angels, dragons, and gods alike. Accept what is being offered of you, Ayden Seth. Renounce your family, renounce your abomination of a father and demonic whore of a mother and become the new vessel for the Will of the Creator, and dedicate your existence to protecting the Divine Empress."

Ayden felt his blood boil. For so long he had resented his father. Resented that he would never be more than he was, resented that he would always be fighting his father's battles. Here was a way to escape, here was a way to become more than he would ever be on his own, to escape the trap that his father had placed him in from the moment he was born. Most importantly it would keep him at Marlae's side and allow him to help her craft a new world. A world free of strife and hatred, and more importantly a world free of the Dark Gods and the blight that followed in their wake.

"So, Ayden Seth, do you renounce your father and mother? Do you renounce your name?"

Ayden pulled himself up to full height, and nodded.

"I do."

The being of light pulsed slightly.

"Then grasp the sword and accept the mantle that has been offered to you. Leave the life of Ayden Seth behind. Become a Chosen of the Creator, and dedicate your new life to His service and to the service of the Divine Empress."

Ayden didn't hesitate to reach out and take hold of the flaming sword, and immediately felt the rush of power through him. The heavy suit of armor over the next few seconds began to change color, shifting from the neutral tones of steel to a deep almost blood red. The transformation complete, it disappeared from where it floated and reappeared wrapped around Ayden's body. He felt no weight from the armor itself, but felt the weight of the huge wings that had sprouted from his back in a matter of seconds. The broad helm settled onto his head, and he could see as though he was not wearing a helm at all. With a thought the helm and armor disappeared, and he was left with only the flaming sword and his wings.

"In your life, Ayden, you lacked the commitment and focus to make your gifts anything other than your own amusement. Your soul has been bonded with a soul who was taught the value of endurance and unwavering fortitude. The life of excess and fallacy that you once lived have ended along with your name. Henceforth, you shall be known as Ayden Crill, Soul of Fortitude, Will of the Creator, and Guardian of the Divine."

With that the being of light faded from view. A long moment passed between Marlae and Ayden, their eyes locked, a flood of emotion and relief passing between them. Then, in the only gesture that would matter, Ayden fell to one knee and bowed his head. Marlae looked on for another moment, a wave of pride filling her. Finally she crossed the distance between the two and put her hand on Ayden's shoulder. He looked up at her and then rose. With a snap of his fingers, the blood red armor and helm reappeared, and with a simple gesture of his hand, two warrior angels appeared on either side of him.

"Shall I announce your presence to this Kingdom's ruling council, Empress?"

Where once, a cruel smile would have curled Marlae's lips, now an impassible look of calm held her features.

"By all means."

* * * * * * * * * * * *

The royal council of Hedorah was in disarray, each member's personal guard drawing weapons and rushing toward the door that had been opened with incredible destructive force while some of the royals themselves cowered under tables or behind overturned chairs. But before the first of the guards could make it into the entryway, two angels swept into the room, each armed with long spears tipped with bright fire. Most of the guards stopped in their tracks, while others fell to their knees, weapons clattering to the ground. The chaos caused by their entry suddenly calmed, disbelief taking over. The cowering and hiding royals all rose to their feet. Into the room came a regal woman in a gown of pure white. Any of the royals who had ever set eyes on the girl had to look twice to realize it was the same woman they had known. Empress Marlae Tamerlane stopped just inside the large meeting room, looked first to one side of the room and then to the other, her eyes briefly stopping on the older woman at the back of the room. The Reverend Mother instantly fell to her knees and dropped her head in supplication. Marlae felt Ayden behind her, and she let her voice hit the suddenly calm air.

"I believe this meeting is to discuss the future of the Kingdom of Hedorah," she said calmly and coolly. "I have a few thoughts on the matter."

Chapter LXXII

Allies and Enemies

Year Four of the Just Emperor Kaitain "Dragonsbane" Lorien, Creator's Calendar Year 1871

"Bastard!"

Aerith Seth brought his hand down hard on the map table, and from where Logan sat, he could hear the wood cracking. Unlike Hannah, Logan had had long enough wearing Aerith's mantle that he had felt the temper that Aerith possessed, and though he had never known the man personally during his time as the *Chosen One* he had been able to glean enough. In fact, this was the first time that the two men were in the same place at the same time. But even still they were more like estranged brothers, both knowing that the other existed from afar and that one day their paths would cross. The shock in Aerith was echoed in some levels in Logan, but the betrayal that Korrd had just perpetrated somehow made sense. He should have seen it coming. It was that thought that continued to echo in Logan's mind. From the moment that Korrd started explaining his time on Espre, he should have seen something. Korrd was a hero. For lack of a better word, and regardless of his motivations, the character of the man could not be denied. He was not a soldier, he was not an artist, and he was not a family man. He was a hero who would not stop until the cause that he was fighting for was victorious. There was no way that a man like that would spend generations serving the whims of men who could not fathom the wonders and horrors he had seen. He would have been on the front lines, fighting against the forces of Dorovar or the Dark Gods or anyone else that he could find to fight. But the influence of Emries had turned him into something else. Much like Nathan Sandar had become on the Dark Mirror reality, Korrd had become the shadow of the man who stormed Shau-ling's palace, and was now a puppet under the control of the mad god Emries.

"He played us," Aerith said turning back to Hannah. "I thought for sure that he was going to be on our side, but I underestimated how much power Emries would have over him. At least we know now that anyone who had ties to Emries on Onea can't be trusted."

Hannah started to open her mouth with a question, but Logan cut her off.

"If the *Erieal* are compromised to, that puts us in a worse position than even I thought we could be in. With Korrd working for Emries, and it being a safe assumption that Nathan is back too, the numbers aren't stacking up well. At least Cedric is out of the game."

Aerith cast a forlorn glance at Logan, but then his eyes shifted back to the entryway of the tent a second before the flap opened to admit three newcomers. Logan came to his feet gingerly and crossed the distance to the newcomers, clapping a hand on Warron's shoulder first before resting both of his hands on Jillian Corven's shoulders. He looked into her eyes for a long moment before turning back to Aerith.

"Aerith, this is Kiara Aren, Jillian Corven, and of course you remember Warron."

Aerith saw Jillian and Kiara's eyes open a little wider at Warron's introduction, but whatever shock was there was quickly internalized. Warron slowly crossed the distance to the much taller man, his injury slowing his mobility. They seemed to size one another up for a long moment before Warron extended a hand to his long-time enemy. Aerith took Warron's hand quickly and held it for only an instant before he saw Kiara fall to one knee in front of Hannah.

"Your grace," Kiara said quickly, "I had no idea you were here."

Hannah looked first at Logan and then down at the kneeling young woman. Her face was familiar but she could not immediately place it. But before Hannah could make any move or say anything to the kneeling girl, the red headed woman that Logan had introduced as Jillian pulled Kiara to her feet and placed herself between Hannah and Kiara staring defiantly in Hannah's eyes.

"You don't owe this bitch any deference, Kiara. Remember, it was her who threw you out of the Church of the Creator. She's the reason you're here and not safe in the Heart of Stone."

Hannah felt as though she had been struck. The silence and tension held after for a long moment before Logan, Hannah, Jillian and Kiara began talking over one another. Their words were not clear to Aerith's ears, but as the seconds of cacophony dragged on, his annoyance and anger increased. Both Hannah and Logan felt the explosion before it happened, but we equally caught in its wake.

"Shut up!"

The force of Aerith's anger manifested itself not only in his booming voice, but also in a wave of power that silenced the entire tent. The argument between the four was cut off and every attempt any of them made to make a sound was thwarted by Aerith's will. Inside, both Hannah and Logan could feel not only Aerith's anger, but also his confusion. He shouldn't have been able to do what he just did, and it seemed as though the powers that he had inherited through Sabrina's actions had for the first time since his powers manifested when he was a child created doubt. He no longer knew what his limits were, and no longer knew just how far he could push his abilities, and by extension, himself. He hadn't so much lost his composure, as he had been able to enforce his subconscious will that he could make all of them unable to speak. Now that that had been accomplished, Aerith met the eyes of each of the people in the tent one by one before opening his mouth to speak. He saw the threads of power now that held them in silence, and he would not release it until he had made his point clear.

"We can't afford this now. We've just been stabbed in the back by one of our own, and we don't know how many of the people that we've counted on as allies are now on the other side. Emries is smart; a smarter opponent than he was the first time around, and he has the advantage of having seen us at our best. Well, it's obvious we're far from our best now, and we're not unified in the way that we once were. We have to figure out who we can trust, and who we can't. Back on Onea the sides were much clearer. Here everything is muddy. Dorovar, the dragons, the dark gods, the Cadarians, Emries, Talisia, the Heralds, and on and on and on. We can't take chances, and we can't bicker amongst ourselves if we're going to survive. So, if you have personal business you need to work it out and quickly, otherwise you'll find yourself on the wrong side of my blade, and in a hurry."

Aerith let his words sink in, and then final released the strings of power that guaranteed silence. No one spoke for a long time, and everyone took a long time glancing from one person to another. Finally it was Logan that cleared his throat and walked toward Aerith.

"You can put Pike on the wrong side of the register. He doesn't care about anyone but himself and his own agenda. As for his kids, I can't say for sure. We'd need someone from inside the Citadel to let us know for sure. Between Darrien and Tess I would have been more worried about Darrien. From what I know, she is the one who is most like her father, and most likely to follow him into hell. But after what I've seen recently, I think Tess may be the greater threat."

Warron spoke up next.

"With Cedric gone, and most of the phasia and *Erieal* gone with him, there aren't a lot of strings for Emries to pull on. We know Saurn, Taron, Draven, Jeroch, Ellis, Rael, Trece, and Bryn are still out there from the phasia, and from the *Erieal*, you have Diana, Aryx, Pike, Taya, and Lissa."

Hannah swallowed the irritation that she still felt over not only Jillian's words, but also Aerith's intervention and moved to join the conversation.

"Taron is off the board," she said gripping tightly to the still very silent Sacred Weapon, "we saw his body when Aerith and I destroyed the Will."

Jillian's voice adding to the group was unexpected.

"That's still a lot of names that are unaccounted for. How can you be sure how many of them are going to be on our side? And what about Dorovar, and what about the Knights of the Flashing Blade, and the Emperor?"

Aerith scratched his chin absently.

"Or my kids for that matter."

Hannah's quizzical look found Logan's eyes first. As much as Logan wanted to reassure her, he knew exactly what Aerith was thinking, and not because of their connection. Ayden and Rhain were wild cards, even more so than Aerith himself. They had power, but like Aerith they were beings rooted in neutrality. They could be swayed to one side or the other, but they didn't have to follow the same set of rules that Aerith always held himself to. They could be used as tools by the Creator, or Emries, or Talisia, or anyone else if they wanted. Aerith's greatest fears were that he would end up on a different side of this ideological battle from his children or from his wife. On Onea, Aerith had the luxury of staying out of the war and letting things unfold. Here on Espre though, it seemed that Aerith was going to make things unfold the way he wanted them to, and if it meant putting his wife and children in the ground, then that's what he would do. Aerith didn't seem to dwell on his words very long before nodding silently to himself.

"We need to cut down this number. As much as I hate the idea of splitting up, and making ourselves ripe targets for Emries and those people who are loyal to him, we need answers."

The tent flap flew back again, and a new form entered. He walked with a staff that resonated with so much power that even simple mortals could have felt it. His eyes were full of pain and the strength derived from that pain, and what normally could have been called a comforting gaze was full of thunder. He regarded everyone in the tent for a long moment before settling his eyes on Logan. He took in the young man for a very long few seconds, measuring and judging him before walking over to Aerith and shaking his hand.

"I was wondering when you were going to get here," Aerith said with a bit of annoyance.

"I figured that little display of power you've been sending out was intended for me."

Warron's face was the one that showed the most shock. It had been a long time since he had set eyes on Arin Ranthall, and it had never been under good circumstances. When Warron had known him, he had just been a soldier in the Lion's Mane, fighting to free Lakestone from the phasia in the first generation of the prophecies. It wasn't until much later that it was discovered that Arin had been the first *Chosen One*, the first person to inherit Aerith Seth's mantle. He was Logan and Korrd's father, but he hadn't lived long enough to see the men that his children would become. If there was a man who was an innocent in this whole war, it was Arin. He wasn't involved in the politics, but now he had been brought back to the world of the living for the final ideological clashes.

"It's been a long time, Aerith," Arin said finally.

"Wasn't by choice," Aerith returned. "The Creator and his children are responsible for all of this. We just need to make sure that it all ends here for good."

Arin nodded and looked over to Logan.

"I hear you've done pretty well for yourself. Your mother would have been proud of you."

Logan seemed a little crestfallen at the comment, but Hannah was surprised to see how quickly he recovered. There was so much that she still didn't understand about all of these connections, and how dead men from one world were being pulled back into this war. But soon enough she would have to understand. This however was one of those times that she needed to listen instead of asking questions. Before Logan could respond to his father's words, Arin continued.

"One of Kaitain's assassins hit Iltorp. Ellis is dead, and Jeroch is seriously wounded. But Bryn has him. Not sure where they're going."

Hannah saw the quick grimace that flooded across Aerith's face.

"If Bryn is with Jeroch, she knows about the game and the wager. Which means she's not going to be happy. It also means that another member of the Knights of the Flashing Blade is off the board."

Jillian asked the question before Hanna could.

"What does that mean?"

Logan was the one who answered.

"Vallic Ultiv, the Serpentine Knight was one of us. He was a Dark God."

Hannah couldn't suppress the curse that escaped her lips, one that brought a smile to Logan's face, and a look of shock to Kiara's.

"I wasn't sure that the High Priestess knew words like that," Logan teased.

"I blame Aerith," Arin countered.

"Bryn's influence," Aerith added absently as he looked back at the map table.

Jillian, her shyness waning, moved over to where Aerith stood and looked at the map table and then up to his eyes. She followed the line of his gaze to Iltorp. It took a moment for Aerith to realize that Jillian was looking at him, but once he did, his eyes slid over to her face and he regarded her for a long moment before speaking. His voice was low, but anyone in the tent would still have been able to hear him.

"So, Jeroch is wounded, my wife has him, and they were last in Iltorp. Where would she go? Where could she get help?"

"Why not to the Dark Citadel?" Kiara asked.

"Too dangerous, my little healer," Warron answered. "If Pike is in the Citadel, then Jeroch won't live long enough to be healed. Besides, none of the Dark Gods there are talented enough healers, and Bryn would never put herself in that kind of jeopardy."

Jillian was biting her bottom lip.

"Go ahead," Aerith said low enough for only her to hear.

As if his voice snapped her out of whatever line of thought she was trying to follow, Jillian blurted out her last thought.

"What other Dark Gods are hiding among the Cadarian elite?"

Aerith smiled.

"She's smarter than most of the mortals I've come across lately. Good thing you aren't one of the Knights of the Flashing Blade. We might be in trouble."

Hannah frowned. Aerith didn't have to see the gesture, he felt it. But it was Logan that interjected.

"Ever since Gwydeon fell to the first Emperor, and even during the Unification Wars, it made sense for some of us to live among the Cadarians to keep an eye on things. If I had to guess, I would say that Bryn would go to Erika."

Aerith nodded.

"Lord and Lady Mistic of Celidar," Aerith said in answer to Jillian's silent question. "She's the best healer of all of us, and Jerrard has always been a little more tolerant of his extended family than the rest of the Dark Gods. Seems like the most logical place."

Hannah felt an itch in the back of her mind. Aerith was avoiding something, something he didn't want to think about, and didn't want to face.

"Aerith," Hannah said finally, "what about Ayden and Marlae?"

Aerith shook his head.

"I can't deal with Ayden right now. He's going to have to take care of himself. We have to figure out what is going on with Tess and we need more intelligence in regard to all of the pieces on the board. Too many variables, too many questions, and too little time."

There was silence for a long moment. It was Warron who spoke up.

"How are we going to do this?"

Aerith seemed to think for a long moment before finally answering.

"Hannah and I will head to Mythryn. We need to continue to follow the trail that Tess is leaving behind. There is something important about her."

Logan shook his head.

"That isn't good use of our resources," he said gruffly. "Hannah is powerful enough now to take care of herself, and if you keep the two of you together, you're limiting the amount of ground we can cover."

Aerith's jaw clinched.

"She's had her abilities for less than a day, Logan," Aerith said with a hint of irritation in his voice. "What if she runs into Korrd, or Nathan, or Emries for that matter? How is she going to handle herself in a fight against Pike or one of the Dark Gods who isn't on our side?"

Color flooded into Logan's cheeks and he took a step away from Aerith. Hannah didn't need to share the man's thoughts to know that Logan was irritated and on some level insulted by the assertion that Hannah couldn't take care of herself.

"No offence old man," Logan said, the frustration creeping into his voice, "but I didn't need you holding my hand when the world was crumbling around me. Sabrina seemed to do alright for herself without you too. Neither of us had seen the kind of combat that Hannah has seen, and she's one of the Knights of the Flashing Blade. I wouldn't think that you would need to nursemaid her after everything she's been through. Besides, didn't you say that you took on the Will together? Doesn't that qualify as a pretty good test of her abilities?"

Logan knew where the argument would lead, and he was not fighting for Hannah's sake. He needed Aerith to see how unreasonable his actions were.

"I won't lose another one of you for no reason. Sabrina can take care of herself now, and so can you Logan. And even through Arin has never had to really use the powers that he has available to him, he has the advantage of not being a known quantity in this war. In some ways he is in the best position of us all. He can operate in the shadows, which is why I want him to go to Aldere and find out what Kaitain is up to. He may not be as large a player in all of this as Emries or Talisia or Dorovar, but if he has somehow been compromised by one of the major players, we need to know that, and we need to know what he intends to do. Besides, you know as well as I do that there can't be any wild cards unaccounted for. What we don't know in this war is going to be what ends up killing us. I won't sacrifice anyone else the way that I sacrificed Evan."

That was what Logan was waiting for.

"You didn't sacrifice Evan," Logan said harshly. "Evan made his choices, and he had some made for him. He had faith in you, and he had faith in the Creator. Unfortunately the two couldn't coexist. You did everything you could to make sure that he had the tools to survive and to thrive in this war. It was the Creator that killed Evan. It was the Creator that let him fall. Not you. You can't cripple yourself and you can't cripple us by holding on to the arrogant assertion that you could have saved him. That ship has sailed. Get your head back into this game and let's finish it. You've got to let Hannah fly, and you can't worry about her falling or being sacrificed."

Hannah felt the bile rising in the back of her throat.

"Logan's right," she said finally. "We're all expendable in this, Aerith, and you know it. You've known it from the first moment you set foot on this world. It has to end. I signed on to fight, not to hide behind you. Tell me what you want me to do."

Aerith's eyes blinked quickly, and then he let them close for several long moments. Jillian felt as though the man was going through a lot of pain, and he was steeling himself for another round of the argument. However, when his eyes opened, the pain had been washed away from his features, and the hardened look of a warrior replaced it.

"Arin's going to go to Aldere. Warron, I want you to go with him. It's not that I don't trust Arin, or don't think he's capable, but there's a lot to deal with in the Imperial City and a lot of different plot lines to keep mindful of. Between the Shadow Guild, the Court Sorceress, the Emperor, and the various rebel factions that are going to make a move at some point, we need all the eyes and ears we can get there. Logan, go see Jerrard. If Bryn does end up going there with Jeroch, you can coordinate with them. Just be careful of Serrina. If she ends up checking in on her parents, then I'm not sure exactly what could happen. She's in Pike's pocket and has been for a very long time. Try to lay low as much as you can. Sabrina is on her way there if she isn't there already, so make sure that she knows what we're up to. If you can take any of our opposition off the board, do it, and don't hesitate."

Aerith turned to Hannah.

"I'm going to go to Mythryn and see what I can track down there. And Hannah, you'll go to Jelan. Ayden was there for a long period of time, and if he doesn't feel safe going anywhere else, he may go back there. I have a feeling that he's made alliances there that he may trust more than he trusts me. On top of that, I know that everyone is courting the Academy of Arcane Arts for alliances. Kaitain wants them, Marlae wants them, the Dark Gods want them to stay neutral. Too much uncertainty and power there. Find out what their leanings are. If they are on the wrong side or have been corrupted somehow, do what you can to turn them to our cause, or if you have to, take them out of the game."

Hannah's eyes widened.

"I'm not a killer, Aerith."

Warron scoffed.

"You are now, little girl."

Hannah felt the snarl come to her lips before the sound escaped. Though her ire was up, Warron stepped into Hannah, just close enough to be intimidating but far enough away that the shorter man didn't have to crane his neck to look up at the priestess.

"In this war, you're either a killer or a victim. There are no in-betweens. Emries is a killer. He sacrifices hundreds of thousands at a whim, to prove a point. Talisia is a killer. She'd burn this whole world to a cinder for nothing more than a chance to settle her vendettas. Aerith is a killer, Logan is a killer, Arin is a killer, I'm a killer, even the girls over there are killers. The only constant in the days and weeks and months to come will be blood and death. And you'll either be the one bringing death, or you'll be among the dead."

Hannah's heart raged, and her knuckles were white gripping Spirit.

"That's your way," she insisted, "not mine. That was what got us all into this situation, created this world, created this conflict. Do you really believe that killing all those who won't agree to your way of thinking is any different than what Emries is doing? Or Talisia? Or the Creator? There has to be a better way. There has to be some other path to ending this experiment than killing all of your opponents."

Warron clicked his tongue in response.

"And while you're talking, Korrd will gut you."

Aerith was about to step in, but it was Kiara who stepped in.

"Your grace, as much as it pains me to say," the diminutive woman began in a slightly wavering voice, "I must agree with these people. I abhor killing as much as you do, but even the Church teaches that in defense of one's own life, the taking of life is sanctioned. If these killers that Aerith is talking about are truly willing to kill all those on this world, surely we must be willing to defend the innocent with every power at our disposal. You have always been a champion of the helpless, your grace, and you have always acted in the best interest of the innocent. The only difference I would see here would be the scale. Whether these people are right or not is immaterial. If this Emries or this Talisia kill indiscriminately for their cause, would not the best course to protect the innocent be to prevent them from doing this harm? And if these people are right, and they are set on their course, how can you expect to find diplomatic solutions?"

Hannah thought for a moment, and finally relented. She didn't have to like the concept of killing, but to prevent the death of innocents; it would be the only way.

"And if you'll have me, your grace," Kiara continued, "I'd like to accompany you on your trip to Jelan."

Hannah smiled.

"It would be my privilege."

"And I'll be going with Logan," Jillian announced.

The tone was that of finality, not suggestion. Logan smiled and laughed slightly which drew a shake of the head from Aerith.

"Alright," Aerith said finally. "Here's the plan…"

Of Gods and Monsters

Year Four of the Just Emperor Kaitain "Dragonsbane" Lorien, Creator's Calendar Year 1871

It had been a long time since Pike Rhuiden felt anything other than superior to any who stood against him. From the time of his ascension after the death of his home, Pike had felt himself better than those who stood around him. He had faced down children of the Creator; he had killed enemies by the hundreds, and had even bested a perverted version of himself. He had lived in a suspended hell while his world had torn itself apart, and in the end he had crawled his way through mystery and lies to reach the final battle. As phasia and heroes had fallen around him, there was only one target in Pike's sights, only one battle that really mattered. It was as though his entire existence had led him to that point. The loss of the woman that he loved, the treachery at the hands of his friends, watching everything he knew and cared about perverted by the Creator and his son Emries into a living blasphemy; striking down his own older reflection, the one that should have been from the darker reality, not from the one in which the heroes had triumphed. He had looked into his own soul and saw the self-loathing and the haunting need there, and had the strength not to succumb to that weakness. With the revived love of his life beside him, he was ready to face down Emries, to end his perversion, and to bring salvation to his broken world. But his position as the hero of the story had been usurped. Evan Sinn, a man of little consequence except for the powers taken from another, fancied himself as the only one who could end Emries. But he had waited until both Eldar and Gwillim had their lives stolen. His delay, his arrogance had cost Pike again, and proved that he cared only about his own glory and not about those that he claimed to be working to protect. So Pike stood aside, mute, as the final battle raged, his knuckles white as he watched the two usurpers and cowards circle each other. And then it was over. The heroes of Onea had triumphed, but for what? Everything they had known, everything they had loved, had been destroyed. Emries had brought their world to an end because of his arrogance, and Evan Sinn had not lifted a finger in the entire war and had watched from the shadows until the last moment. How many could have been saved if he would have used all of those powers at his disposal to do something more than run errands for Aerith Seth?

When it was all over, and Emries had been defeated, there stood Evan Sinn, glorious in his triumph, and after the heroes of Onea were elevated to their new positions in the heavens, what was Evan Sinn's reward for the pile of dead created by his arrogance? Pike, Sabrina, Wolf, Lissa, Jerrard, Gwydeon, and Midarin were treated like invaders in the Creator's heaven. There were other gods there, servants of the Creator and the Creator's children who had been mortals on other worlds, and they felt that the Oneans should have been left to burn. The angels did their best to ignore the new arrivals, and only Pyrrus, the youngest child of the Creator showed any level of interest or care for the heroes. Even Gwydeon's position as the vaunted Brother of Angels did not prevent him from being looked down upon. But Evan Sinn was different. He had parlayed his 'heroism' into a position at the right hand of the Creator. His 'victory' had elevated him to the level of the man that he had defeated. Evan Sinn became the Voice of the Creator, tasked with spreading the word of his love and his law to the far corners of the Cosmos. He looked down upon those that were his betters as though they owed him something, and as the years stretched into decades and then into centuries, the survivors from Onea created their own little niche in the Creator's domain and had gained a level of acceptance from the denizens. However, Evan Sinn still looked upon them with disdain, his heart corrupted by the power of the Creator, his mind addled by the lies being fed to him every moment.

For years tension was mounting in the heavens, gods who owed their allegiance to different children of the Creator began to take their eternal posturing to new and violent levels. The angels, who existed as only servants and warriors were swept up into these imagined and ideological conflicts and were forced to fight by those they served. There were times that Evan Sinn arrived to quell the fighting, but it seemed as though he felt he was above such interventions. And in the end, his interference in the powder keg whose fuse was slowly burning would prove to only delay the inevitable explosion. Talisia Masile's army was full of viciousness and hatred for everything other than their goddess, and those that owed their allegiance to Emries found themselves carried away by the frenzied tides. Their strike against Pyrrus and his allies was swift, brutal, and had the feeling of a long-term plan coming to fruition. The combined force of angels, gods, and dragons seemed as though it would rip its way through the heavens and burn everything in their path. Pyrrus to his credit turned out to be more of a hero than Pike had given him credit for. Pyrrus had always seemed like one who valued peace at any cost, one who would rather allow himself to be destroyed for the principle of peace than to take up arms to defend that which he loved. But there stood Pyrrus in the middle of the dead and dying, his rippling blade of divine fire striking down all that came toward him with malicious intent.

Though the heroes of Onea owed him no allegiance, Gwydeon could not stand by and allow Pyrrus to be destroyed by Talisia and Emries' combined might. By this time, Gwydeon's abhorrence for the politics of the heavens had created in him a streak of valor and genuine righteousness that were to be both admired and feared. Pike however had felt his disdain for everything divine growing with every passing moment and as the battle was joined and he drew the blood of any who stood against him, the hatred burned in him hotter than the brightest star. As much as he hated the enemies that stood against him, his true hatred was targeted at those who were not there to take an active role in the combat. Where were the servants of the Creator as the life of one of His children was being threatened? Where was the supposed 'hero' Evan Sinn as Talisia stalked her brother with murderous intent? Why was it Gwydeon Sandar who tried to stop the killing blow and not the Voice, the Will, the Wrath, or the Spirit? Whatever questions or doubts dwelled in Pike's heart before that point exploded into full bloom. His hatred and disgust manifested and became like blood pumping through his veins. Ever the architect and planner, Gwydeon hatched his plans with Sabrina, but Pike had only one plan, find and kill any that served the Creator. To take vengeance against the Creator and His servants for every death they had ever caused, for every mortal who was left behind or sacrificed for His greater glory.

Upon his arrival on the world called Espre, Pike Rhuiden saw a different kind of fanaticism manifesting. The people of Cadaria, a fledgling nation, were just beginning to cling to the teachings of the Creator, the beginning of the dangerous and deadly path lying before them. Veiled threats and fear became a full scale war between the mortals and the threat that they called the Dark Gods. As much as Pike wanted to crush the resistance and ascend the throne of Cadaria himself, his judgment and will were wrangled by Gwydeon yet again who preached patience and caution. But that caution has cost Gwydeon his life. That patience only resulted in generations of death caused by those who followed the whims of fear and misguided hatred. But Pike had made a promise to keep the peace until there was no alternative. The arrival of the assassins with weapons that would kill a Dark God was the last straw. But there was more to it than that. Evan Sinn had fallen. Evan Sinn, the man who had betrayed them all, the man who had been at the center of all of the loss had been destroyed by his former mentor. Some of Pike's vengeful rage had been thwarted. But many of the long nights in the Citadel of the Dark Gods had been spent in the company of his closest friend and confidant. Her council was invaluable, and in time Pike's daughter joined the silent conspiracy. Evan Sinn's neutrality and lack of intervention in the devastation on Onea had been forced not by his own cowardice, but some misguided orders given him by his benefactor. In truth, it was not completely Evan Sinn's fault for the blood on his hands. While he could have disobeyed his orders, while he could have showed the courage of his convictions and defied the one who made him into what he was, the true fault lay at the feet of Aerith Seth. His role in everything had never been clear to Pike, other than being the one whose blood moved the millennia-old cold conflict between Halicon and Emries into a full blown bloody war. With Evan Sinn dealt with, Pike turned his attention to tracking the movements of Aerith Seth, trying to learn where the man would be so that vengeance could be paid in full.

Treachery though would distract Pike from his ultimate goals. Ivan Quicksilver, a former Knight of the Flashing Blade sent on the laughable mission to kill a member of the Dark Gods, had been shown the error of his allegiances and been shown the depth of the deception perpetrated against him. He had been welcomed into the fold as an ally of the Dark Gods and given shelter in the Citadel of the Dark Gods and a home on Mythryn. But the man had had ulterior motives all along, and his ultimate betrayal had nearly destroyed the place he had called home and had delivered Pike's own wife into the hands of the mortal enemy of the Dark Gods. Kaitain's motives with regard to Sadrina were not clear, but one thing was painfully clear to Pike, both Kaitain and Ivan would be made to pay for their hubris. Pike had expected some resistance by those that called themselves the servants of the Emperor of Cadaria upon his appearance, but he had not expected the hulking beast that stood between him and the object of his ire. Korin Melcab, the Captain of the Imperial guard, or so he called himself, was not a man at all. He was a demon hiding under the skin of a man and now stood nearly twice his former height, broad wings stretched behind him. To Pike's eyes he resembled something like a Shadowwalker from his home on Onea, but much larger in every aspect.

"Now, I will make you burn."

Korin charged the next moment, his wings beating once, injecting his charge with a combination of speed and power. Pike was caught between actions, one half of his mind wanting to sidestep the charge, while the other wanted to take the charge head-on. The indecision cost the Dark God, and a hard set of talons raked across the right side of Pike's face, leaving long bloody and painful trails down his cheek and across his neck. Had Pike not reacted to the pain by throwing himself backward, the strike would have ripped his throat out instead of leaving only light gashes. The defensive motion lasted for only a heartbeat before Pike threw himself forward again, this time slashing with his twin blades of ice. The first went high while the second went low, aiming at the much larger creature's upper thigh. Korin feinted to one side, avoiding the low strike and reached out with his right hand and caught the frozen blade. A trickle of blood flowed from the wound, but no pain showed on the creature's face. Pike pulled back hard on the blade, and while the move caused more blood to flow from the wound, Korin's grip would not relent. The other blade flashed again, which

Korin caught in his other scaled hand. That moment a cruel smile flashed across the creature's face, and he closed his hands tight around the twin blades, his long black claws digging into the smoking blades. The sound of shattering ice could be heard for miles around as the will of the huge hands won against the manifested power of the Dark God. The blades broke in half and then disappeared completely. Pike was caught off-guard again by the power of his opponent, and never saw the counter-attack coming. Korin punched hard with his right hand, the balled fist connecting flush with Pike's breastbone. The force of the impact threw the Dark God backward a hundred feet, and his impact created a small crater in the ground. It wasn't until he made it back to his feet that he realized that blood was trickling from the corner of his mouth. Absently Pike wiped the blood away with the back of his hand. Obviously this Korin Melcab was no ordinary opponent and was not one to be taken lightly, but Pike could not help but crook one corner of his mouth into a smile. Reaching to his belt, his right hand fingered the cold steel of Fury and finally wrapped around its solid haft. Korin remained in the same position he had been when he struck Pike, making no moves to advance on his wounded opponent. With Fury in his hands, Pike slowly advanced on his stationary opponent.

"Let's see you catch this," Pike said as he suddenly accelerated toward Korin.

The larger man fell back, unprepared for the speed of his opponent. Korin was also unprepared for the range and ferocity of Pike's assault. One of the blades of Fury struck true, leaving a long jagged gash across Korin's chest. However, Korin was made of stern enough stuff to bring one of his massive fists to bear, connecting with Pike's wounded jaw and sending him flying again. This time when Pike landed on the ground, he felt the blood spewing from his wounded face. The vision in his right eye was gone, and he was sure that his cheek and jaw were broken. A trickle of power mended the bones quickly enough, but more concentration would be required to knit his eye. The strength of his opponent was incredible and unlike anything Pike had ever faced. Even Taron didn't hit as hard as Korin, and now that Pike had the power of an ascended being, he didn't feel like he could be tossed around as easily as Korin made it seem. When Pike was back to his feet again, he set his base wide and motioned for Korin to come at him. It was time for a change in tactics, and he would have to outthink his opponent rather than overpowering him. Korin stood straight, glaring down at the Dark God, and brought his hand to the wound in his chest. The wound oozed thick black ichor and it coated the creature's fingers.

"You'll pay for that."

A hard bat of the wings later, Korin was on top of Pike, large fists pounding down like hammer blows. The first came crashing down with such speed and power that it almost ended the fight, but Pike's reflexes proved to be faster than his own mind. Fury's haft met the crashing blow, the immortal weapon absorbing most of the force, with the rest shaking Pike's body, nearly causing his knees to buckle. As the second blow came down, Pike shifted his weight and used Korin's own arm as a fulcrum. Fury went from blocking a blow into a blow of its own, the gleaming blade striking Korin on his wrist with such force that it severed muscle and shattered bone. The great hulking beast roared in pain as its hand dropped to the ground. Black blood sprayed from the open wound like a fountain, and as it hit Pike's exposed skin it felt like burning tar. But Pike endured the discomfort and continued in his improvised attack, spinning into the great hulking beast, jabbing the blunt end of Fury's haft into Korin's stomach. Korin stumbled back half a step, allowing Pike to plant with his left foot and spin his body with all of his might. The broad axe-head cut through the air at incredible speed, until it lodged itself fully into the already gaping wound in Korin's chest. The blow stuck with the sound of an explosion and propelled the massive Captain of the Guard backward and off his feet. This time it was the larger man landing in a crater of his own making. Pike stood, his empty hands shaking from the force of the blow he had just struck, a small pool of his own blood forming at his feet. Blood streamed from the side of Pike's face as well as both corners of his mouth, and every breath felt as though it had to be dragged through his lungs. But it was the larger Korin Melcab and not Pike Rhuiden who was lying on his back in the mud with an axe protruding from his chest and missing a limb.

Pike let his hands fall to his hips, his white knuckles starting to return to a normal skin tone. But his reverie was short lived as impossibly the hulking figure began to move. It took only a few moments, but Korin found his way to a seated position, Fury still obscenely emerging from his broad chest. Korin grasped the haft with his remaining hand, ripping it from the wound and tossing it to the ground as though it were nothing more than a troublesome splinter. However Fury took more than its pound of flesh on its expulsion, bringing massive gouts of blood spraying in all directions. Korin however seemed to pay the oozing liquid no mind as his crimson eyes burned with hatred locked upon his enemy. The two men circled now, Pike moving toward his discarded weapon, and Korin crossing toward his severed limb. At nearly the same time, the two bent, their eyes never leaving one another. When Korin straightened, the look of hatred eased for a moment into a cruel and knowing smile. Holding the severed hand to its stump, the oozing black blood congealed and pulled the useless flesh back into its former position. In a matter of seconds the hand was moving again, balling into a fist. Pike did his best to not let his shock and disgust show on his face. The cruel smile on Korin's face widened.

"Pike Rhuiden, the hero of Onea. You're everything I'd heard you'd be; I just didn't think that I would be the one to get the chance to end you."

There was something in the tenor of the man's voice that filled Pike with a feeling of dread. It was clear that there was more to Korin Melcab than had even been revealed to this point and it made Pike wonder how much the hulking beast was holding back. Of course Pike had reserves he had yet to call upon, but there was doubt as to whether direct application of his divine power would have any more impact on the creature than his blade had. Besides that, Pike was never as practiced with his unearthly powers as he was with his more martial ones. While it was true there were many among the Dark Gods who could have helped him hone that side of his abilities, he never felt it necessary. What could stand against his power as an ascended being? What threat would he face that Fury could not cut through? Perhaps that confidence would be his undoing.

"Did you think you Dark Gods were the only divine creatures suffering on this stupid rock? Do you think that your children are the only ones who were lying in wait, blending into this mewling bed of refuse until the time of the Great War presented itself? I could have squashed that fool Kaitain like the bug that he is, but that fool will end himself long before he becomes a threat to any scheme that matters."

Pike felt the cold sweat on his brow and suddenly realized his heart was beating faster than it should have been. Korin must have sensed the change in Pike's demeanor and took a step forward, his fists clenched.

"Halicon's children are fools and weaklings, and those that carry Emries power are nothing but parodies of something greater than they could ever understand. Raenera's chosen are slaves and puppets, and Pyrrus had no children to live up to the disappointment that he proved to be. But my mother, the true inheritor of the Creator's position in the heavens, Talisia Masile, she bred her children to be as vicious, as conniving, and as brutal as she herself is. Her partners were the strongest of their race, and her progeny, my brothers and sisters, are stronger than any who have ever walked on any world. We have been groomed to take the place of our mother's fool siblings. And we are more than capable of disposing of what passes for heroes on this ball of dust."

Korin was on Pike the next moment. He moved so fast that he simply blinked from where he stood to in front of Pike. The first blow took Pike straight in the gut, knocking all of the wind out of him. The second blow was a strong downward strike that landed flat on the top of Pike's left shoulder, dislocating it. The force of the blow propelled Pike to the ground face first. Not letting his opponent breathe, Korin brought his right foot crashing down on the back of Pike's head, driving it deeper into the mud. Pike could feel his skull crack and blood stream from his eyes and nose. Another hard stomp caught Pike between the shoulder blades, causing his spine to crack like dry straw. A third stomp came down on the already separated shoulder, sending waves of pain rocketing through Pike's body. Just before the boot came down again, Pike rolled in the mud, suppressing the agony and his own defiant muscles, and brought Fury swinging with as much might as he could. The gleaming blade struck the back of Korin's weight-bearing knee. Tendons and ligaments snapped and Korin cried out in pain before falling backward. Pike continued the strike, rolling through and across the intervening distance, bringing Fury up again as though it were attached to the spoke of a wheel. Fury crashed down on Korin's exposed chest, biting into his breast bone and splitting it in half. Korin's roar of pain manifested as a wave of force that lifted Pike from where he lay on the ground and threw him through the air where he landed in a heap with Fury clattering down at his side, its blade coated in black blood. Not knowing whether or not Korin would recover from the blow, Pike pushed all of his energy into healing as many of his extensive wounds as he could. It took scant seconds for the Dark God to find his way back to his feet, regardless of how shaky his footing was. Even as Pike's shoulder was pulling back into its socket, Korin was beginning to move. When the massive beast found its way back to its feet, he pulled his wings around his body to protect the wounds on his chest. Though he was able to put some weight on his wounded leg, it was obvious that the wound was compromising his balance. Pike could see that the man's fortitude was formidable, but it was also obvious that while he was nigh invulnerable, he was also not able to heal as quickly as Pike could. If the battle went on long enough, and Pike could avoid the staggering strength that Korin could bring to bear, it was possible that Pike could outlast the much larger man.

The two men stared at each other, each measuring the other and taking stock of the repercussions of the battle thus far. His hands soaked in blood, the haft of Fury felt slick in his hands, but his grip was still solid. The sky above them had begun darken as the conflict wore on, and now the dark foreboding clouds had blotted out the suns. Streaks of fire still darted across the sky, but with the backdrop of the clouds, they took on a more ominous aura. Then, just between them, a figure was simply there. A simple black robe with gray trim barely buffeted by the breeze; long hair refusing to heed the wind's call. His head was turned away from Pike, looking directly at Korin, and then just as suddenly as the new arrival had appeared, Korin was gone. One moment he was there, the next moment, he simply wasn't. The form turned finally to face Pike, ancient eyes glaring from deeply inset sockets. Pike couldn't understand what was happening, but something inside of him identified this new arrival as a larger threat than even Korin posed. Steeling himself, Pike brought Fury to bear, charging the distance between the two men in the blink of an eye. At the last moment, Pike brought the ancient axe up and brought it crashing down onto the seemingly unarmed man. At the last moment, the man brought his hand up and blocked Fury's strike with a single outstretched finger. The hand and finger did not waver, did not move, and Pike found himself feeling as though he had struck the hardest unforgiving stone. That next moment an unseen force struck Pike full in the chest, sending him backwards to the ground again, Fury slipping from his grasp. The robed man towered over Pike now, looking down at him with a mixture of disappointment and pity.

"I've been waiting for this moment, Pike Rhuiden of Onea," the robed man said in a cold and even voice. "I am Dorovar."

Eternity in a Heart Beat

Year Four of the Just Emperor Kaitain "Dragonsbane" Lorien,
Creator's Calendar Year 1871

The air around Rhain groaned. Whatever the young girl was doing, it was torturing the elements in ways she had never seen before. She had known the power of the Servants of the Creator, she had felt the elements go cold and silent around her when they were near, but she had never felt the tortured burning that permeated everything the young woman touched. Even within the shield of energy that Sabrina had erected they could feel the power rippling from the girl. It was then that Rhain looked at the wall closest to where the girl held Devlin. Stone and wood rippled like water, but did not show any sign of damage. They were simply being warped by her unconscious exertion. Rhain began to fill herself with the power that was hers since her birth, but felt Sabrina's grip on her shoulder tighten. When Rhain locked eyes with the woman who by her appearance was no more than a girl, she could see the immense pain written there, and the unspoken warning. Becoming involved in the events to come would be too dangerous, and probably ultimately fruitless. They would have to remain silent witnesses to the painfully slow murder that was taking place. Rhain chanced a look around the room and found that no one else was attempting to make any kind of moves, though Taya seemed to be the only one in position to do so even if she wanted to. It was then when the girl's voice rang out again.

"I could keep you like this forever," her vicious voice calm and clear over the tumult, "just on the edge of death, tortured and in more pain than a body should ever know. Every beat of your heart would bring a century of torment, and that wouldn't begin to equal what you have done to me. Your betrayal and callousness are so complete that they will scar me for the rest of eternity. So I shall make you suffer an eternity's worth of pain in these last few seconds that you draw breath. Make no mistake Devlin Rannoch; your life will end as soon as my hand finishes closing around your heart. Every drop of life will be crushed out of you. I take no joy in this, for your damage has already been done. But that does not prevent you from paying for your unconscionable sins."

Another tortured moan escaped from Devlin's lips and his wings spasmed and dipped a little lower around him.

"Devlin!"

Gabriel's cry could barely be heard above the drone of death that circled around them, but Rhain could feel the anguish in his voice. It was at that moment that Rhain felt pressure in the back of her mind. Something was happening close to the palace, something familiar. Rhain's mind clicked and she knew the presence that was so close she could reach out and touch it. A small smile turned up the corners of her mouth and she found Sabrina's eyes again. The pain had been replaced by shock, and then an intense sadness. Finally a sparkle hit her eyes, as though something was about to change. It was then that Rhain felt the change in the woman who was equal parts stranger and family. She was drawing on impossibly deep reserves of energy, filling herself with divine power.

"Get ready," Sabrina's weak words came to Rhain's ear. "We're either all about to die, or we may have a chance to escape. No matter what, open a portal and get out. You may only have seconds."

Rhain wanted to protest. She had been ordered out of a battle before, and she was not about to turn tail and run again. She drew deeper on the powers inside of her and filled herself to almost overflowing.

"No running," she said finally. "Not this time."

Sabrina sighed.

"Don't move until I do."

It was then that Rhain felt the familiar flows of power in the room. Someone was opening a portal into the throne room. The exertion was not lost on the young girl, and Rhain watched as she lifted the large form of Devlin Rannoch off the ground and tossed him through the air like a doll. He crashed hard into one of the stone walls, and crumpled to the ground, blood flowing from his mouth, nose, and ears, one of his legs bent in an unnatural direction. The next moment not one but two portals opened at opposite ends of the throne room, one to the girl's left and one to her right. Out of one of the portals emerged a man in monk's robes and a woman who had the look of noble woman because of the light blue dress she wore. Out of the other stepped a woman in a scandalous dress that only she could wear. Rhain felt the hope in her swell at the sight of her mother. Bryn wasted no time in letting a pillar of fire erupt from her hands and speed toward the girl. A shield of light intercepted the blast a foot from the girl, but she was given no time to counter attack. The monk let fly with an attack of his own after roughly pushing the noblewoman behind him. Twin beams of light and darkness lanced out of his extended hands, striking the shield and forcing it back slightly. Seeing her opening, Taya forced her way to a knee and let fly a hail of stones. The flood of stone battered the shield along with the fire, light, and darkness, and seemed to be forcing back the shield of the girl. From the far side of the throne room, another beam of darkness and another of light added to the assault. Jerrard and Erika had joined the attack, and their efforts pushed the shield even farther back, almost to the girl's outstretched hands. Sabrina's signal finally came and Rhain added her stream of fire to the assault. Sabrina seemed to take no direct action, as though she was waiting on something. That something came in the form of an increased push from the monk and Bryn, which forced the shield all the way back to the girl's hands, and then caused it to shatter. Sabrina struck then, a massive column of pure Blaze fire erupting from the ground beneath the girl's feet, engulfing her completely. Bryn, the monk, and Jerrard shifted their assault that moment, adding their own streams of Blaze energy to the one from Sabrina. For long moments nothing happened, the roar of the Blaze filling the room. What happened next was as unexpected as it was impossible.

A bubble of golden energy pushed from the perimeter of the column of Blaze, disrupting the tornado of energy. The glow from the golden bubble seemed to leak into the column itself, changing its color slowly from green to gold, stopping its rotation. Suddenly the column simply melted, splashing around the unscathed girl like puddle of melted snow. But while everyone had been concentrating their attention on the girl and the powers that tried desperately to contain her, no one had seen Gabriel Shadowfall move from his position by Jerrard and Erika. It had taken only a moment for him to reach Taya's side, where he pulled a sword from the sheath on her hip and turned it deftly in his hands. As soon as the column of Blaze had disappeared, Gabriel was already at a full sprint, and the next moment he buried the length of the blade through the chest of the young girl. Time froze. The girl, her mouth wide with surprise; Gabriel, his face etched with determination. The next moment, the girl's eyes flashed, the bright golden light flaring brightly, and her hand reaching out to take Gabriel by the throat.

"I was going to spare you," the girl said. "I was going to spare you all. I only came for the traitor. He had to pay for defiling my Camille. Now you all share his sin. You will all pay for his crime, and you will wish you were never born."

A razor–thin wave of golden energy shot from the girl in all directions the next moment, cutting like a scythe through the air. Everyone in the room was able to erect a defense, but some were less successful than others. The strength of the assault was incredible and it was all that Jerrard and Erika could do to keep it from cutting them in half. Taya also seemed to be struggling with her defenses. Bryn and the monk on the other hand were holding the assault at bay with one hand while planning their counter-attack. Sabrina had enveloped Rhain again in a bubble of Blaze fire, and it seemed to be keeping them safe, but as Rhain stole a glance at her protector, she could see the blood beginning to leak from the woman's nose. The exertion was slowly eating her from the inside out, the newly inherited powers from Halicon too much for her frail body. But there was no doubt the woman would keep fighting. Rhain saw her mother and the monk lock glances, an unspoken plan of attack floating between the two. As if Sabrina had been privy to the silent conversation, she smiled and began to draw deeply on the Blaze.

"Get Gabriel free."

Before Rhain had a chance to answer, the phantom plan materialized. Bryn and Sabrina launched a devastating assault of Blaze fire, directed at the young girl's chest. Her attention turned to defense, blocking the twin blows with her free hand, but she did not relent in her grip on the Knight of the Flashing Blade's throat. It was then that the monk let fly his attack, but when Rhain saw was he did, she could not help but feel a little disappointed and confused. Instead of lashing out with the Blaze of some other application of godly power, the monk reached into a pocket, pulled out a rock and threw it at the girl. Half-way to its target, Rhain's eyes widened.

"You've got to be kidding."

Rhain couldn't help herself as she began moving toward Gabriel. The girl obviously didn't understand the danger that the rock posed, and so when it collided with the arm that held Gabriel by the throat, she made no attempt to block or dodge it. When the stone connected, it opened instantly into a swirling blue portal that severed the girl's arm at the wrist. Gabriel fell backwards, and the girl screamed in pain, her defenses lowering for the briefest of moments, which allowed Bryn and Sabrina's assault to strike her full in the chest, sending her crashing hard into the stone wall behind her. At the same time that Rhain was pulling Gabriel away from the fight, the woman in the blue dress was streaking in, her sword held high. The girl staggered a step or two away from the wall and didn't know she was being attacked until the blow was upon her; the sharp steel flashing down and connecting with the back of her neck. The strike was clean and efficient, passing through skin, muscle, and bone, severing the young girl's head from her body just above the shoulder. When the head and body hit the ground, they dissolved into thousands of grains of golden sand, nothing left of the girl but dust. The victory was short-lived, as the girl reappeared where she had been a moment earlier. She reached out with one hand and slammed it hard into the noblewoman's chest, sending her flying backwards into the monk. Another blast of energy followed, striking Bryn full in the face, sending her to the ground. A cage of lightning appeared around Rhain and Gabriel pinning them to the ground where they lay. Taya, Erika, and Jerrard were still neutralized by the previous attack which left only Sabrina standing against the girl. Golden eyes bored into Halicon's vessel.

"I thought of anyone here, you would understand Sabrina. You know what I have to do. You know that the traitor has to be punished."

Sabrina drew herself up to her full height.

"You can't do this Tess," she said with all of the strength that she could manage. "Your mother wouldn't want this. Your father wouldn't want this. You're not a killer."

A disturbing and malicious laugh tore from the woman's chest the next moment. The cackling filled the room and made everyone's blood run cold. A ghostly aura appeared around Tess the next moment, appearing like a monster standing behind her.

"You don't know anything about me Sabrina, nor do you know what my parents would want. My father would want me to hunt down and kill each and every person who has ever wronged me. There is nothing that motivates my father stronger than vengeance. It is like the blood that runs through his veins. He eats, breaths, and lives revenge. That is why my mother chose him. She has wanted revenge against those who have wronged her for longer than you have drawn breath. And she will have her revenge, through me. Talisia will pay for what she did to Pyrrus. The dragons will pay for what they did to Dorovar. And the Creator will pay for letting world after world fall to pettiness and ignorance. I will topple them all."

The golden light flared in Tess's eyes once again, and as she reached out her hand, black tendrils emerged, whipping toward Sabrina. An instant before they struck there was a flash of moment, and a form interdicted the strike. A hard bat of dragon-like wings pushed Sabrina backwards, and the tendrils of darkness wrapped themselves around Devlin Rannoch's throat, arms, and legs. Tess's eyes went wide, but the attack had already struck and she could not call it back. The tendrils constructed, breaking bones and crushing Devlin's throat. At the last moment of the Knight of the Flashing Blade's life, he knew he had sacrificed himself for a greater good, and he closed his eyes and thought one last thought of Camille as the tendrils ripped him to pieces. Devlin's broken body fell in pieces to the ground, causing Tess to scream in frustration. It was obviously not the way she had wanted her prey to meet his fate, and the shock of Devlin's interference gave the others in the room one more chance to strike.

The monk and Bryn were seconds behind one another with their attacks, the monk starting the assault with pure Blaze energy, a staggering amount. The exertion caused the man to sweat and blood to pour from his nose. Bryn too, her newly scarred face clenched in determination pushed all that she had into a similar attack. Jerrard joined the attack, though the amount of Blaze he could draw upon was limited. Erika, instead of turning her powers to assaulting Tess directly instead reached out with her powers to heal and bolster the others in the room. The strike from Sabrina came at Tess from every direction, battering her and buffeting her. No matter what defense she tried to erect, it seem that Sabrina struck where she wasn't ready. Tess sank to her knees, the golden light fading from her eyes, Devlin's death seeming to take some of the fight out of the girl. But as the weight of the assault pressed in, the golden light seemed to reignite, pushing back all of the combined powers and forming an impregnable golden shell. Then, just as suddenly as Tess had appeared in the room, she was gone. The combat over, Sabrina collapsed to the ground. The monk was to her side a split second before Rhain. The man held her head in his lap and stroked her hair lightly, dabbing some of the blood from her face.

"I didn't expect a family reunion," the man said smiling.

Sabrina smiled weakly.

"You're starting to sound like Aerith," Sabrina's voice rasped.

The man chuckled.

"There's no need to be insulting. After all I did just save your life."

Rhain was too concerned for Sabrina's safety to let her incredulousness show on her face. When Bryn knelt beside her daughter, she looked not at Sabrina, but at the monk.

"How is she?"

The monk sighed and shook his head.

"Weak. Halicon's power is taking a lot out of her. Aerith knew that something bad was going to happen and that Sabrina would need support, and figured she might come here. He also thought you might bring Jeroch here."

Bryn's face was a mixture of anger and confusion.

"I'm not going to ask how that bastard knew I was with Jeroch."

The monk shook his head.

"My father."

The anger leaked from Bryn's face.

"I felt him, Logan," Sabrina said softly. "I hope I get to meet him."

Rhain felt her blood go cold. Logan Ranthall, the man that her father had told her so many stories about. The unlikely hero. The thorn in the side of everyone who had power. The second greatest champion from Onea, and one of the people who held Aerith's mantle. But he was supposed to be long dead. Logan leaned down and kissed Sabrina lightly on the forehead. In another life, another place, another world, Logan would have been Sabrina's step-father. He would have raised her as his own and shown her all of the love and care that he had left in his heart. But Draven came between that, so had the rest of the war.

"You will, Sabrina, I promise."

Suddenly serious, Logan looked up at Erika who had just knelt beside them.

"I'll do what I can for her."

Logan nodded and pushed his way back to his feet. His body hurt. The girl packed a punch that was for sure. His next thoughts were for Jillian who was just pulling herself back to her feet. She made her way back to his side, taking in each of the others in the room.

"Would someone care to tell me what the hell that was?"

Bryn was beyond annoyed.

"That was Tess Annis, Pike's youngest," Jerrard offered. "Though I dare say that she is quite a bit more powerful than I think anyone had the right to expect."

"She was using divine power," Logan added. "The kind reserved for the Creator and Children of the Creator. But I never saw Emries or Halicon do anything like that."

Bryn clicked her tongue.

"I need to get Jeroch. He's injured and I don't know that he'll last much longer."

"He's gone," Sabrina's weakened voice offered. "Saurn came for him, and they left together."

The curses that flowed from Bryn's mouth the next moment were the kind that Logan instantly recognized as the ones reserved for when Aerith had truly upset her.

"Will that bastard never die?" Bryn offered finally.

"Saurn is the least of our problems," Logan growled, his own grudges against Saurn coming to his mind. "Emries is on the move, and he has help. Korrd flipped to the other side, and is working for him. Nathan is back on the board too, and we're pretty sure that any of the remaining *Erieal* may be compromised. Aerith gathered those of us that have held his mantle and we're trying to divide our enemies and get the numbers down without jeopardizing the mortals. Dorovar's last herald is on the move, and he's a bit of a challenge. Sorry Jerrard, but Aerith thought you might be ready to lend some support to us."

Jerrard folded his arms.

"You know my thoughts on this Logan," he said grimly. "I'll provide a safe haven when needed, and I'll do my best to keep innocents from getting caught in the middle, but I won't fight."

Taya rose to her feet and glared in Jerrard's direction.

"I never thought you were a coward!"

Gabriel put his hand on Taya's shoulder.

"A man who values life and the protection of those who cannot protect themselves is not a coward. Those kind of convictions are what I have always strived to follow. When I met Aerith on the road to Albitonin, I knew he was a man of conviction, which is why I couldn't let him be executed. If you'll have me, Lord Jerrard, I'd like to offer my services to help you make this place into your safe haven."

Jerrard smiled.

"I would be glad for the help. I'm sure Prince Feyd would be glad for it as well. I have a feeling that as Kaitain Lorien destabilizes the whole of Cadaria that more and more refugees will be looking for safe places to hide."

Taya scowled.

"I'll give orders for my fleet to help protect Celidar's coastline. And any of my sailors will be seconded to your military. They're pirates, but they're all good men."

Jerrard smiled.

"Thank you, Taya. I had thought you might be ready to continue your crusade."

Taya sniffed.

"Vengeance is ugly. Besides, Sabrina needs me, and I'm not going to leave her side. And maybe it's time I got to know my aunt a little better."

Rhain's face went pale.

"You're going to make me hate you if you keep that up, Taya."

Bryn crossed the distance to Logan and got in his face.

"Start talking," she said with deadly venom on her tongue, "and don't leave anything out."

* * * * * * * * * * *

Deep in a forest on the edge of Albitonin, a small pond sat barely disturbed by the soft wind that blew through the high branches of the trees. Very few creatures frequented the pond, but those that did perked their ears up at something they did not hear, but rather sensed. When the portal opened, all of the creatures scattered. The girl in the tattered white shirt stumbled from the portal, and fell to her knees at the edge of the pond. The only sound that escaped her was an inconsolable sob. For several long minutes she knelt there, crying, her chest heaving and hurting. Finally, the wave of emotion broke, and she was left in the silent wake of pain and depression. That was when the confusion set in. Looking around, she had no idea where she was or how she had gotten there. Wiping the last few tears from her eyes, Tess found her way to her feet and then sat slowly on a hollow log close to the edge of the pond and dipped her toes into the cool crisp water. For a long time she sat looking at the pond, the reflection of the streaks of fire from the heavens. Finally she looked up and watched the dancing lights play in the heavens.

"Cosmic thoughts, my dear?"

Tess turned her head, the strange voice somehow comforting and not alarming. She took in his features without speaking. He had beautiful and comforting eyes like her mother Sadrina, and his hair was thick and long like her father's. There was a soft smile that curled his lips, and he had a very common and unassuming look. He looked like he could be a priest, or at the very least a father who had seen many years of raising children. Without another word the man approached and sat gently on the edge of the log near Tess. He looked at her for a long time before reaching out with one hand and wiping the last few tears from her eyes. The gentle touch of his hand sent another wave of emotion through Tess, and she began to sob. The man took the girl in his arms and held her gently as she cried.

"There there, my dear," Emries said sweetly. "Everything will be alright.

Chapter LXXIII

Words to a Lonely Mountain

Year Four of the Just Emperor Kaitain "Dragonsbane" Lorien, Creator's Calendar Year 1871

Lightning crackled overhead as Aerith Seth stepped out of the simple swirling blue portal onto the broken hilltop that overlooked the Citadel of the Dark Gods. Using portals always filled Aerith with discomfort, which is what led him to crafting his stones in the first place, but one of the limitations of the stones was that he had to have been to the place he was going at least once. This marked the first time in all of his centuries on Espre that he had ever set foot on the Dark Continent of Mythryn. Of course there had been many times when he had been tempted to look in on the people who had fallen from the heavens. But there would be too many questions, too many conflicts, and to stand in the Citadel of the Dark Gods and lie straight faced to the people who would eventually pay for his arrogance was more than he could bear. Lying to Bryn and his children was different.

Bryn was a monster, a beautiful monster no doubt, but a monster nonetheless. She wasn't human, and she was born with the express purpose to turn the weaknesses of humans against them and to stand laughing as she wanted them burn from their own failures. Her calling was to murder and sow chaos, to bring misery to everyone who set eyes on her, and she was very good at her birthright. Domestic life always felt temporary, and though she tried her best to play the part, Aerith knew that she would never be happy until she felt the blood of her enemies on her skin once more. She had played the diplomat, the detective, and the general in her past, and mother and wife to her were no different than those roles. They were necessary in the grand scheme of things, but they were not really her. She was a warrior. A killer. A monster. Of course she would be angry that he had lied to her for so long, but that anger would not be focused at Aerith for long. She would use it to stoke the long dormant fires inside of her and make her enemies pay for the lies that Aerith told both out of necessity and out of fear. If Bryn had known, if she understood the true breadth of what was going to happen, she would have wanted to strike early, before all of the pieces were in place, and she would have tried to stop Aerith from doing what had to be done. But now the Lady Fox was back where she belonged, in the thick of the fight, and there was nothing that she could do that would stop Aerith from continuing down the path that lay before him.

Just as Bryn was a monster, so too were Rhain and Ayden, each with their own role to play in the conflict to come. Ayden was his father's son; irreverent, ill-tempered, and always trying too hard to make everyone believe that he didn't care about what was going on around him. But Ayden and Aerith held the same secret. Not only did they feel everything that was going on around them, they felt it harder than most men. One of the advantages of being human was that one had a limited perspective as to the ramifications of actions. There were times when a person could see what was going to happen once they turned left or right, both to themselves and to the people who were in their life on a daily basis. But no human could honestly be expected to understand the full consequences of their actions as it related to people they have never met or places they had never seen. That kind of ignorance was necessary for sanity. Those who were blessed or cursed with the ability to pierce that veil, to truly know what the ramifications of their actions would be, tried their hardest to take no action at all. Aerith had stumbled on that truth far too late in his life, long after he had done more damage than could be undone in a hundred or a thousand lifetimes. He had lost count of the number of people he had killed, the number of lives he had destroyed, the number of families that would never be whole again. In the darkness he could see the faces of every man, woman, and child that he had ever been the final fate of. And while those phantoms tugged at his heart, they were nothing compared to those he had damned by his very existence. Arin, Logan, Cedric, Anabel, Gideon, Sabrina, Grawn, Bryn, Ellis, Hannah, Evan, Meredith, and the list went on and on and on. New names were added to the list all the time, and it was all Aerith could do to keep his mind and his efforts trained on the present and not the past. Ayden too had his father's gift for sight, but as a young man who had never tasted the hell of war, had never seen the true need for neutrality, he was destined to make the same costly mistakes that Aerith had made, and Ayden was more than capable of raining down more death upon the mortal world than Aerith had known was possible when he was that young and naïve.

Rhain was another matter, because she was so much like Bryn, too much at times. The monster in her was clear from the moment she began to look longingly at Aerith's swords, and marveled at the fire that her mother could summon to her fingertips. Rhain's casual grace extended to everything, including the natures of life and death. No different than her mother, Rhain was born and bred to be a killer, a silent and unintended legacy that could not have been avoided no matter what the parents wished. Bryn molded Rhain in her own image, more because she knew nothing else than any desire to corrupt her daughter. Neither Aerith nor Bryn had had parents, so they didn't know the first thing about raising children, never mind powerful and immortal ones. They did the best they could not to pass down the worst parts of themselves to their children, but at the end of the day, the children of two monsters had little chance to be anything but, no matter how good the intentions might be. And there was never a question in either Bryn or Aerith's mind that the war would be coming for them. It was only a matter of when. That was part of the reason that Bryn and Aerith sent their children into the world. They needed to be ready for what was ahead, and the only true way for a warrior to prepare himself for war is to know those whom he will fight and fight for. That was the subtle difference that had grown in Aerith and Bryn over the years they were fighting on Onea. In the beginning they had both been trying so hard to tear down everything around them, to see an end to their enemies and to revel in their suffering. So many events had conspired to change all that. But it had been Logan, and Elwyne, and Gwydeon, and Midarin, and all of the others who had the courage to ask questions. Who didn't hate. They were willing to sacrifice everything if it meant saving those that could be saved. Aerith always had marveled at the strength of those who inherited his mantle. In some ways they had done so much more with his powers than Aerith ever had, and unlike Aerith, they were better for the experience.

Aerith felt the tear fall down his face and knew that he was dwelling too much on the past. Nothing he had done could be changed now, and he had tried his best to put plans in motion that would save as many people as he could. If he and those who trusted and followed him were lucky enough and strong enough, they could change this world forever, and perhaps create a brighter tomorrow for all of the innocents caught up in a hell they had no concept of. There would be many hard days ahead, many losses, but the path was clear, and doubt would mean the difference between success and failure.

Looking down from the hilltop onto the Citadel of the Dark Gods, Aerith saw the destruction that was most certainly recent. Reaching out he searched the ruins for signs of life, and found none. He feared the worst until he felt the flows of power deep in the heart of the Citadel. Someone down there had survived, and more importantly they had not missed his arrival. He hadn't intended to approach stealthily, not that that would have been much of an option considering those who called the place home. It took only a moment to recognize that someone within the Citadel was coming to greet him.

* * * * * * * * * * * *

The Citadel of the Dark Gods was a shell of its former self, broken and leaking in the elements. Wolf stood in the grand foyer looking up at the architecture that had stood for almost two millennia and marveled. He wished he had seen the place in better times, and wished he had more of a connection to the place than a broken feeling of home. In truth, Wolf had not known a home since the day he set out on his fateful journey from the little farmhouse on the outskirts of Aradon. It had been the home that his father had grown up in, the place where he had first set eyes on the woman that would become Wolf's mother. It was a place where decisions that shaped the world were made, and the humble perfection had never been lost on Wolf. It was a monument to the thought that anyone could make the world turn if they had the will. But that place was long gone, destroyed with the rest of their world in the fires of pride and arrogance. Wolf wanted nothing more than to make sure that this world was spared that fate, and that no other world would ever be placed in the crucible of the Creator's judgment.

His pack thrown over his shoulder with a few days of provisions and a few days' worth of clothing and supplies, Wolf looked back toward the room where he had slept for almost two thousand years, and felt an emptiness grow within him. There were still no answers as to why he had been struck by the fall. No reason why his life had been interrupted. Even the blending with Draven, Basille, and Pyrrus had yielded no answers. Somewhere there would be a solution to the mystery, and perhaps that was what Logan would be able to help Wolf find. There were still too many questions that needed to be answered about this war, and how it could be won, if it could be won at all. That was still the possibility that tugged at Wolf's heart. Perhaps all this posturing and planning would be for nothing. Maybe Halicon, Emries, and the others would just wake up after the final battle for the fate of Espre and find themselves back in the graces of the Heavens where they could begin their pointless ideological battle anew under the watchful eye of the Creator. It was still possible that all of the fighting and the dying would turn out to be for nothing.

Wolf caught motion out of the corner of his eye and smiled when he saw that Lissa had emerged from their shared bedroom. She was dressed in a set of armor that was very familiar, a way that made Wolf a little uncomfortable. It was Basille's memories more than his own that knew the origin of the armor, as it had been Basille who had seen it the most when it was worn with deadly purpose. The tightly packed rings gave the appearance of a solid breastplate but had the advantage of the mobility of much lighter armor.

"Doesn't look quite the same without the cape," Wolf said regarding his wife for a moment, and then smiling. "But it fits you better than I thought it would."

Lissa put both her hands on her hips and pursed her lips into a small frown.

"Mother and father made some alterations to it before they left. Father didn't want his armor leaving the family. I'm not crazy about wielding their swords, but I suppose that mother was right. She always said that just because we can make weapons out of thin air doesn't mean you shouldn't always have steel at your side just in case."

The armor fit Lissa well now, almost as though it had been tailored specifically for her. The crest of the lion that was formed by the rings of the breastplate had not been replaced, and Wolf found it oddly fitting that the banner of the once great Cedric Binosear was still being represented in one way or another on Espre.

"Are we ready to go?"

Lissa pulled her pack over her shoulder and started to reach for the flows of power to open a portal. However, at the last moment, Wolf put his hand out and touched her softly on the arm. He wasn't looking in her direction, rather off to the south toward something beyond the walls of the Citadel. Whatever Wolf had felt, Lissa had been concentrating on creating the portal and was not openly feeling for anything else. For a long moment Wolf stood there, saying nothing. Finally, he took a long deep breath, and exhaled slowly.

"I was hoping we would get away before anyone else showed up. Guess our luck is running thin already."

Lissa put her hand on the hilt of one of the swords that hung at her hips.

"No," Wolf said finally, "I'll take care of this myself. You need to get to Rashaleb and deal with our new allies. You have to get to them before anyone else poisons their minds against us."

Lissa didn't move, her eyes moving from where Wolf looked to Wolf's face.

"I want to stay and fight with you," she said mournfully.

Wolf turned and looked into his wife's eyes. He could see the love and devotion that had kept her by his side through his long slumber.

"Hopefully this won't come to a fight, but if it does, I don't think you would do much but get us both killed. It's not that I doubt your fighting prowess my dear, but our new arrival could probably take both of us with both of his hands tied behind his back, and he knows it. If I go out there alone, I have a better chance of talking us out of this. If we both go out there, he'll think we've come to fight, especially with you looking like that. Either way, I'll run long before I cross swords with him, no matter what power Pyrrus has given me."

He leaned in and gave her a long deep kiss before letting the flows of power fill him, and a portal open. Wolf waited for a very long few moments before making his way toward the portal. He wanted their visitor to know he was coming long before he arrived. When the portal winked out of view, Lissa stood in the emptiness and reached for the flows of power deep inside of her. The portal opened the next moment that would take her away from her home, probably for the last time.

* * * * * * * * * * * *

Aerith waited impatiently, turning one of his portal stones over and over in his hand. Whoever was coming through the portal was taking their sweet time, probably to keep Aerith from killing him the moment he stepped through. Most of the Dark Gods were cagy, having lived very long lives, and after having been exposed to extreme power for a long period of time they were intelligent enough to understand exactly who was standing outside of the Citadel. Thankfully it would not be one of the more fragile and bullheaded of the Dark Gods coming to greet Aerith. It would have been a shame to have to kill anyone needlessly. Aerith breathed a silent sigh of relief when he saw who emerged from the portal. There we few among the ranks of the Dark Gods that Aerith would rather have dealt with than Wolf Ranthall.

While Aerith had some exposure to the young man, it was not enough to form a true opinion of the boy. However, what Aerith did not know from personal experience, he was able to glean purely from the actions and the reputation of his parents. Logan Ranthall was perhaps one of the bravest survivors of Onea, surpassed only by his boyhood friend and ally Gwydeon Sandar. Wolf's mother, Elwyne Tamerlane was remembered for her strength, her tenacity, her calm devotion and love. Together Logan and Elwyne stood against things that no mortal should have had to stand against. And even though Logan was the bearer of Aerith's mantle, he was never a true warrior, nor was he comfortable with the power that he inherited. Where Pike, Korrd, and many from the generation that followed coveted the powers that they had been granted, Logan never felt comfortable with power. He likened himself more to Gwydeon's normality in the face of insanity. Men such as Logan and Gwydeon were the reasons that humanity had a chance against Shau-ling and the phasia, and they would be the reason that the mortals of Espre would be able to stand against all of the terrors that were aligning against them. Perhaps a chance was enough to shine the barest light against the darkness.

"I never expected to see you here," Wolf said as he sat down on a stone outcropping near where Aerith stood. "But then again, I'm getting used to the unexpected happening around here. An old friend of yours stopped by not too long ago. He was less than pleased with the outcome, but there was very little that pleased Draven during his life."

Aerith's eyes opened wide for a moment, but the expression of shock quickly faded.

"How many of you are rattling around in there now?"

Wolf smiled.

"Actually, only one more than should have been. Basille, Draven and I were all the same sides of different coins to begin with. It's only fitting that we ended up together. Then I guess you could say that Pyrrus is the glue that is holding us all together. But I knew you wouldn't be surprised. After all, you've gotten a dose of divine power recently."

Aerith frowned.

"You're well informed."

Wolf looked down at the ground.

"Did you really think that one of the Children of the Creator could renounce their power without the other children knowing it? I assure you, they all know, as well as the Servants. Sabrina and I both have very large targets on our backs. However, the Servants won't act directly against us.

Emries and Talisia will have to do that. Not that there is much time for them to worry about us."

Aerith nodded.

"I can feel the toll that Halicon's power is taking on Sabrina. I can't imagine how she's holding herself together."

"Is that why you're here, Aerith," Wolf asked looking up again. "Were you hoping that there was something here in the Citadel that could save her?"

Aerith could feel his blood run cold.

"I didn't know what I would find here," Aerith said finally. "But I wouldn't be able to live with myself if I didn't find out. The Dark Gods have been here for too long without having amassed some kind of knowledge about the Children of the Creator and their abilities."

Wolf shook his head.

"There is no information here that would help you Aerith. The mortal form was not made to be able to house the kind of power that Sabrina has been given. When she was wounded by the Voice, her divinity was taken from her. It's only your mantle that is keeping her alive as it is, but because most of that power has been given away to another, it's barely enough to keep her body from trying to tear itself apart. It's not enough however to keep the power from slowly eating her from the inside out. And even you don't have enough power or tenacity to restore her divinity."

Aerith shook his head slowly.

"Which is why you don't look worse for wear for inheriting Pyrrus' power."

Wolf's glance fell back to the ground again.

"I only wish it was that simple."

Wolf kicked a rock away with his foot and sighed deeply.

"Even though I have divine power now, I am not a divine being. I was born, the child of mortals, and no matter what may have happened to me when Onea fell, nothing can change the fact that I was born a mortal. My ascended status only prevents Pyrrus' powers from burning me from the inside out. However, the more I use those abilities, or any abilities for that matter, the more the poison spreads through my body. If something else doesn't kill me first, this power will."

Aerith could feel himself gritting his teeth.

"How long?"

Wolf couldn't help but clear his throat.

"If I'm careful, a couple of years. No more than that. Obviously if I end up embroiled in any of the situations you constantly find yourself in, that number goes down."

Aerith's heart felt like it was in his throat. Wolf felt the unasked question.

"Sabrina is a smart girl. She'll keep herself together as long as she can. She'll avoid conflict, and she'll make sure that she invests her power in people she can trust. That was Halicon's greatest advantage over his siblings. He could extend his life force into his children. If Sabrina is careful, she can share the burden with allies, and create a new Brotherhood of Phasia. That should extend her life for a little while. At least until you find a resolution to your plan."

"What do you…"

Aerith's voice trailed off. He met Wolf's gaze and saw the soft yellow glow in the man's eyes.

"It isn't very difficult to see if you know what to look for, Aerith. Though I have to say it isn't one of your most intelligent plans. Do you really think that you have enough in you to take on Dorovar? You know what he is; you know what he's capable of."

Aerith nodded.

"No one else is strong enough."

Wolf shot up to his feet.

"And what happens to your allies when Dorovar rips you to shreds? Have you thought about that? What happens when you die for good this time? What happens to the powers that are holding Sabrina together? What happens to Logan, to Arin, to your new protégé? Have you even thought about them?"

Aerith felt the growl escape his lips. He was in Wolf's face the next moment.

"I haven't thought of anything but them, Wolf. I had to kill one of my own, one of the people that I trusted, that I gave my powers to. That was never part of the plan, and I never would have sacrificed Evan if I would have had any other option. I will not sacrifice another. I would sooner give up my life fighting Dorovar than let them take my place in the fire. No matter what, it's going to come down to Dorovar and me, and in the end, he's either going to kill me, or I'm going to kill him. That's the only way this ends. None of the rest of it matters."

It was then that Wolf and Aerith both became aware that they were not alone. A presence had joined them on the broken hilltop, a presence that reeked of divine power. One of the Servants of the Creator was there with them. Aerith let the twin swords form in his hand, and turned to face the new arrival. Floating several feet above the ground was a young man, his face covered by a steel mask that glowed with divine power. His muscular chest was clearly in view, with four angelic wings jutting from his back, beating in a slow rhythm. A sword wreathed in holy fire was clutched in one hand, while a shield that seemed to be constructed purely of light was held in the other.

"You need not worry about Dorovar," the Wrath said coldly in a heavily modulating voice. "You shall not live long enough to see that creature fall, for your abomination ends here."

Frailty Thy Name Was

Year Four of the Just Emperor Kaitain "Dragonsbane" Lorien, Creator's Calendar Year 1871

Dominique awoke with a start as the litter that she rode upon hit a divot in the road. Her sleep had not been restful as it was, filled with dreams of death and blood, always haunted by the frightful mask of the man who was her husband in name only, the Emperor of Cadaria Kaitain Lorien. Dominique and her trusted protector had fled the makeshift Imperial Palace which found itself temporarily housed in an inn on the outskirts of Aldere late in the evening. Chelsea had insisted that Dominique try to sleep, but no matter how hard she tried, she could not rest. It seemed that every time her mind tried to give itself over to sleep, something would jar her body back to wakefulness. This latest upset was the last she would allow. She reached out with one hand and parted the heavy curtains that blocked the windows. The suns were already starting to climb high in the sky, and the streaks of light from the falling stars and meteors were slightly faded in the brilliant light. She stretched the best she could in the odd confines of the litter, pulling her dress back up around her body. Gently she rapped at the front of the litter, trying to gain the attention of the driver. The sliding door opened to reveal the right shoulder of Chelsea's armor.

"We've made good time," Chelsea said, her voice gravely with fatigue. "But we're still within the borders of Aldere, and not safe yet. I don't want to pass too close to Lordhill, so that has made the going a little harder than it could have been."

"Is it safe enough to stop? Can we eat, and stretch a bit? Or do you think there are guards chasing us."

Chelsea stayed silent for several long moments until finally Dominique saw her pull up on the reins and bring the litter to a halt. The strong woman slumped a bit in the seat before dismounting the seat without another word. She was at the door to the litter the next moment, opening it slowly. Dominique was struck by the appearance of her protector. Chelsea's eyes were normally bright, her hair and features immaculate. This morning though the woman looked haggard, as though the journey had taken far more out of her than Dominique would have expected. Despite herself, Chelsea tried to force a smile when she locked eyes with her friend, combing one hand through her hair.

"I think we may be safe enough to stop for an hour. Even if Kaitain sent troops after us, we've got quite a lead over them. Our escort should be waiting for us at the border, and then we'll have little to worry about. The Imperial Guard may be able to move with impunity under Kaitain's new laws, but they won't dare engage us. And once you've taken control of Rashaleb, the Army of Ice is sturdy enough even with their losses to defend you, and the nobles of Rashaleb have never been friends of Kaitain's rule."

Dominique forced a smile of her own.

"Once they find Natalia's body, Kaitain will declare us enemies to the Empire. He'll take your control of Saldarine, and he'll issue orders of termination for the both of us. Do you think Rashaleb will stand beside me then?"

Chelsea chuckled slightly.

"Kaitain may be a lot of things, but he's not stupid. The Imperial Legion isn't enough to take Saldarine by force, which is what he would have to do to eliminate all of the members of the Army of Fire that are loyal to me. And even though he gave me direct control of the Kingdom over the nobles, they will hate Kaitain more than they will hold it against me. He thinks he's tightening an iron grip around Cadaria, but in truth all he has done is embolden his enemies. Arrogance has blinded him to how tenuous his position really is. Short of Aldere, how many kingdoms does he actually have a good hold on? Saldarine will stay loyal to me. Thorigald is under Seraph's control. Albitonin and Zevarit belong to the rebellion, along with Galateria, Oradrim, and Menoris. Bellnoc may call itself loyal now, but it's been a stronghold for the Shadow Guild for centuries, and I don't imagine the Grand Master will take kindly to one of his Masters killed and another held prisoner. Iltorp and Celidar will probably remain loyal to Kaitain for now, and Hedorah is anyone's best guess. But Vallic Ultiv is anything but predictable, so Iltorp could switch sides at a moment's notice. Lord and Lady Mistic in Celidar were appointed by Kaitain's father to their positions in Celidar, but they have no loyalty to Kaitain. Their loyalty has always been to their subjects, and I don't expect them to stand for the persecution that Kaitain is trying to invoke. Cadaria has become a fractured land for the first time in two thousand years."

Dominique smiled and put her hand on one of the holds at the side of the door and began to pull herself toward the door of the litter, but Chelsea put one hand on Dominique's hand and another on the Sacred Weapon on her hip. She spun on her heels the next moment, putting her back to the entryway, blocking Dominique's exit, and drawing the twin blades from their sheaths. Though she may have been at the point of exhaustion, the Wolf of Saldarine's senses and reflexes were still second to none. It took her only a few heartbeats to find the source of the threat that had raised the hair on the back of her neck. On the hilltop just to the east stood a woman dressed all in black, the dress coming up across her throat, stopping at her jawline. Blond hair was neatly arranged in ringlets on the top of her head with a group of straight strands falling to either side of her face. Even at that distance, Chelsea could see the woman's bright blue eyes staring down at them. There was no doubt the woman was a threat, and Chelsea prepared herself for what could become a combat situation at any moment. The woman's voice broke the silence of the morning a moment later.

"Chelsea Zarova, I have no quarrel with you. Surrender Dominique Lorien to me, and you shall be allowed to leave here alive."

Chelsea snarled.

"If you want Dominique," she said with venom on her tongue, "then you certainly do have a quarrel with me. And if Kaitain thinks for a second that I'd value my life over that of Dominique, he's more deluded than I thought he was."

The woman in black laughed.

"I'm not here on behalf of that fool. My name is Serrina and I am here of my own volition on a mission for my lord Pike Rhuiden. Your Emperor's treachery nearly destroyed the Citadel of the Dark Gods, and has placed the wife of my master at risk in Kaitain's custody. Pike believed that one good turn deserved another, and sent me here to procure the delicate little flower that calls herself an Empress. You should surrender her to me, or I will take her by force."

Chelsea tightened her grip on Tenacity and bent slightly at the knees.

"You'll get Dominique over my dead body."

An evil smile curled Serrina's lips.

"I was hoping you would say that. And believe me, I am more than happy to oblige."

With that Serrina raised her hand and snapped her fingers. Multiple swirling blue portals appeared all around the litter, spewing forth dozens of red-skinned Jeresei. Two attacked immediately, coming in from Chelsea's left and right. One slashed hard at Chelsea's head with razor-sharp black claws. Chelsea easily ducked the blow, and retaliated with a strike of her own, Tenacity's blade tearing through the Jeresei's throat sending blood spraying in all directions. Chelsea flowed into the next strike, burying the other blade into the second Jeresei's heart. The other creatures seemed to hesitate for a moment, which gave Chelsea the opportunity to launch an attack of her own. Chelsea dove into the ranks of the Jeresei, blades flashing in every direction, finding throats, legs, and chests. Many fell to the assault, but several of the Jeresei took the opportunity to charge the litter. Sensing that she had over extended, Chelsea doubled-back, leaping from the ground to the top of the litter and then diving blade-first onto two

Jeresei who had gotten too close to the litter. That had given one of the Jeresei the opportunity to follow Chelsea's defensive move, leaping onto the litter and then diving down upon Chelsea. A moment before the claws would have found flesh, an arrow sped from out of nowhere and slammed into the side of the Jeresei's head. The creature wasn't even able to scream and fell like a stone to the increasingly bloody ground. Chelsea was too busy extricating herself from the dead bodies to immediately look up to find the source of the arrow. But when she made it back to her feet, she saw that the ranks of the enemy had pulled back slightly at the appearance of a blond woman with a bow and a slight woman in white pants and a purple shirt. Chelsea smiled at the sight of Rhionna Winter and Quyhn Ravenheart Lorien rushing toward the litter. Rhionna quickly moved to the top of the litter, bow in hand, an arrow quickly flowing from her quiver to the bow string. Quyhn was at Chelsea's side the following moment.

"You weren't at the border by sun-up," Quyhn answered Chelsea's unspoken question. "There is a squad of soldiers from Lordhill waiting there, but Rhionna and I wanted to scout ahead to find out if something had happened. If we're not back soon, they'll come after us."

Chelsea looked over the ranks of the red-skinned beasts. They had stopped to reassess the situation, but that would not last for long. Three against hundreds were not good odds, even with all of Chelsea's abilities brought to bear. Then there was the problem of the Dark God. The woman calling herself Serrina would tear through them as though they were paper in a matter of seconds, and there was nothing that the vaunted Garnet Knight of the Flashing Blade would be able to do to prevent it. Out of the corner of her eye, she saw a twitch in the hands of one of the Jeresei. They had worked their courage back up and were preparing to charge.

"Quyhn, I hope you can hold your side. Rhionna, you'll have to take care of everything that gets close."

Without waiting for an answer, Chelsea raised her blades, closed her eyes for a brief moment, and then bounded forward, starting a preemptive charge into the ranks of the Jeresei. It took only a moment for the shining blades of her Sacred Weapon to find flesh, blood spewing in all directions as she slashed throat after throat. Despite their superior reflexes and reach, the Jeresei weren't able to get a clean shot at the Wolf of Saldarine, as she darted through their ranks. But she could not occupy the whole of the Jeresei front. On the opposite side of the litter, the charge was just beginning in the front ranks of the Jeresei, and Quyhn steeled herself against what would be her first moments of combat. She had seen death around her most of her life, but she had never taken an active role in the taking of another life. Born and raised into the Academy or Arcane Arts, it had been drilled into her day after day that her abilities should never be used to harm another except in the direst of circumstances. And under the strict rules of the Academy, putting oneself in harm's way did not circumvent the first rule. Self-defense was not an absolute, and in most circles of the Academy of Arcane Arts, it was better to die than to take a life. But while the Academy abhorred violence for the sake of violence, they did teach many methods to create defenses.

Quyhn reached into the font of power available to her, pulling from the various elemental forces around her, and set her feet into the dense ground. She could feel the power welling up inside of her, sliding up her legs like vines, running over her like water. Her hands tingled with the exertion, and the sound of her heartbeat pounded in her ears. She felt an exhilaration and fear rocket through her, like standing on the edge of a cliff. The tingling in her fingers changed to burning, and in her mind's eye she could see the flames dancing between her fingertips. Her lips parted, silent incantations springing from her lips, and when she opened her eyes, a brilliant ring of flame sprouted up around the litter blocking any attacker from passing through. Several of the Jeresei fell back at the sight of the flames, while others charged, using their courage and rage as a shield. Upon contact with the raging fire however, they were turned back if not reduced to a cinder. Some tried to use their superior agility to vault over the flames, but the flames rose high to intercept the helpless attackers, dragging them down into fiery perdition. Seeing that the advancing attackers had been turned back, Rhionna turned her attention to picking off the creatures that were trying to flank Chelsea. After several more moments of intense combat the ranks of Jeresei had been thinned to the point that they retreated back from Chelsea and the wall of fire. Seeing that the threat had passed for the moment, Quyhn let the wall of fire around them disappear, and Chelsea slowly retreated back toward the litter. When Rhionna looked down at Chelsea, all she saw was a woman in brilliant armor that was coated in blood. Her hair was matter back with gore;

almost none of her exposed skin was spared the crimson color. Wiping sweat from her brow, smearing the blood, Chelsea let her gaze fall back to Serrina, whose lips had curled to an evil smile.

"Very good for a mortal," the Dark God said coldly. "Almost as good as those who you now call Dark Gods. But if you think for one moment that I am going to be so impressed by your heroism that I will let you live, you are quite mistaken. You see, I was never mortal. My whole life has been lived with the powers of the Heavens at my disposal, and I was taught early on how to use my gifts to inflict the most pain and suffering. I was bred to make mortals like you suffer. My lord Pike knew that one day war would come to this land, and that he was destined to rule over this world. But to do that, many of the so called champions would have to die. But Pike himself was once a hero, and he saw how the people rallied behind heroes, and how their deaths only pushed their followers farther. So death is not enough. Pike will suffer no martyrs made by his hand or the hand of his agents. So he taught me how to destroy, how to eviscerate, how to humiliate, and how to bring suffering unlike any a mortal could know. He took the lessons of his greatest enemy and made those tactics his own. Names that denoted such evil that mortals shivered when they were mentioned. Names that pathetic children like you would never know the true weight of. Draven Batoe, Taron Steen, Saurn Macco; those names stuck fear in whole nations. Now, I will teach you that the arrogance of would-be heroes has but one result. Pain."

Serrina extended one finger and pointed at Chelsea. The beam of pure black energy was on her before she could blink, and had she not been gifted with enhanced agility and reflexes from Tenacity, Chelsea would have had no defense for the blow. There was no time to dive out of the way, and no where she could have gone to evade the strike. If she would have dodged, the beam of energy would have passed into the litter and possibly hit Dominique. Though the woman said that she was to take Dominique alive, it was too much of a chance for Chelsea to take. At the last moment, Chelsea brought the twin blades of Tenacity up to intercept the strike. The force was stronger than anything Chelsea had ever felt. It vibrated up her arms, and threatened to shake her to pieces, but she set her feet and held on the best she could. The weapons began to glow with heat, and the warmth was beginning to transfer to the palms of her hands. Out of the corner of her eye, Chelsea could see Rhionna draw another arrow from her quiver and send it in the direction of the Dark God. The arrow struck true, piercing her chest where a mortal's heart would be. However, the Dark God paid the strike no mind and continued the assault.

"Do you really believe that a simple arrow could deter me from taking your life, Knight of the Flashing Blade?" Serrina mocked. "And do you truly think that even your Sacred Weapon will protect you from death at my hands? I will show you the true depth of your mistake."

Serrina redoubled the strength of her attack, pouring all of the divine power that she could manage into the single beam of energy. The force of the strike pushed Chelsea backwards slightly, but the force was still being blocked by the now glowing Sacred Weapon. Finally Chelsea felt as though she would not have the strength to hold on any longer. The next moment there was a hideous sound of screaming that filled the countryside followed by the sound of a thousand breaking mirrors. The blades of Tenacity broke in half in Chelsea's hand, one of the blades flying backwards and piercing through the plate of her armor, burying itself deep in her right shoulder. A force seemed to erupt from the Sacred Weapon that cancelled Serrina's beam of black energy. Chelsea fell to the ground, blood pouring from the vicious wound. Quyhn was at her side the next moment, trying desperately to arrest the bleeding with fabric she ripped from her dress. Serrina's face betrayed the pain that she was feeling in her now smoking hand and with her other hand she signaled again. The gesture was followed by the appearance of more portals; however these were suspended in mid-air. From the portals emerged huge winged beasts that Quyhn immediately recognized as Shadowwalkers.

"Destroy them!"

Quyhn looked on in horror as the creature began to circle above them, like large birds of prey ready to swoop in for the kill. However, the Shadowwalkers had no intention of diving on their target. Each of the five beasts opened their jaws and sent bright gouts of white flame crashing down upon them. At seemingly the last moment, there was a swirl of motion beside Quyhn, and a new form appeared, a woman with flowing red hair in a burgundy dress. She extended a hand above her, and the beams of fire struck a bubble of force. Undeterred, the Shadowwalkers continued to rain death down from the skies, but the shield projected by the woman continued to resist. Quyhn saw a slight smile come back to Serrina's lips despite the obvious pain she was in.

"I never thought I would see you defending the mortals, Liara. You were always too delicate for this kind of thing. And I see your nose is bleeding already. How long can you keep that up?"

Quyhn looked, and it was true, the woman Serrina had called Liara was visibly struggling against the attack upon them, and blood was trickling from her nose.

"I wonder what would happen if I do this."

Serrina's last statement was accompanied by another strike, this one a beam of pure white light that struck the invisible bubble. Sparks flew in all directions, and Quyhn heard Liara grunt slightly. More blood streamed from her nose, but the shield was holding. The next moment, another form appeared, this one right in front of Serrina. It was obviously the form of a woman in a white shirt and black pants, the long cuffed sleeves hugging her arms. The punch she delivered to Serrina's jaw interrupted the assault on Liara's shield and sent Serrina sprawling to the ground. The Dark God scurried back to her feet.

"I should have known the little snowflake wouldn't be far away from the delicate flower. Your mother must be so worried about you Mirana."

Mirana ducked the punch that Serrina threw, and delivered another to Serrina's jaw, sending the woman back to the ground.

"You always did talk too much Serrina," Mirana said coldly. "So unless you want to finally have the fight you've been threatening to have all these years, I'd take your pets with you and go. Dominique Lorien and her guardians are under my protection."

Serrina was back to her feet and scowling.

"You cannot stand against the Voice of the Council, Mirana, no matter who your mother and father may be. Lord Pike has spoken and the Lorien woman's life belongs to Pike. Either stand aside, or I will be forced to..."

Mirana's hands were filled with fire the next moment.

"Or you'll be forced to what? Run and tell Pike on us? Go ahead. See how many of the Dark Gods are standing with you when you try to make good on your threats."

A portal formed behind Serrina the next moment, as she stepped through she spat one more venom filled threat.

"This isn't over Mirana. Next time, I'll make you pay for your interference."

Moments after Serrina had departed the field, the Shadowwalkers broke off their attack and flew away, and the Jeresei scattered as well, fleeing in different directions. Quyhn could see Liara's shoulders slump as she released the shield, but she wasted no time wiping the blood from her nose and moving to where Chelsea lay. The loss of blood and shock had rendered the Garnet Knight unconscious. Rhionna had come down from her perch on top of the litter, and Dominique had emerged from inside, rushing to Chelsea's side and holding her blood-soaked hand. Liara knelt beside Chelsea and extended her hand toward the wound in Chelsea's shoulder. Dominique intercepted the hand with her own.

"What are you going to do? Who are you?"

Liara's lips rose into a genuine caring smile.

"My name is Liara. I'm here to help. I can heal her wound, if you'll let me."

Quyhn gave Dominique a reassuring look.

"She saved us, Dominique. Let her do what she can."

Frowning, Dominique relented, and Liara's smile faded as she laid her hand over the wound. Sweat began to bead on the woman's forehead. As Mirana approached and knelt beside Liara, Rhionna looked at the new arrival.

"Would you have won?"

Mirana's eyes found Rhionna's.

"I was bluffing. Serrina has a lot more experience in fighting than I do, and she probably would have killed me. But Serrina never fights unless she knows she can win. She doesn't like leaving things to chance. Next time though, she'll make sure she has the advantage. We surprised her this time."

That next moment, the shard of Tenacity pulled itself from the wound in Chelsea's shoulder and floated to the ground. Blood gushed in all directions for a brief few moments before stopping completely. The skin beneath the armor pulled itself together and in a matter of seconds it was as though Chelsea had never been wounded at all. Liara sat back, wiping the sweat from her brow. Dominique looked over the two women for a long moment and then down at Chelsea.

"Thank you," Dominique said meekly. "I can never repay you for the assistance you have given us."

"Serrina was out of line," Mirana said coldly. "Even if she was acting on orders from Pike, she should have known better. We aren't to involve ourselves with the Cadarians, no matter what. Even if your people have not kept their word, the Dark Gods would always abide by the bargain that Gwydeon made."

Quyhn found Mirana's eyes.

"So you are Dark Gods?"

Mirana nodded.

"I am Mirana, and that is my sister Liara. And I think it would be in everyone's best interest if we got moving."

Rhionna's face paled slightly.

"We?"

Liara smiled as she got to her feet.

"You're under our protection," she said lightly. "And we can't very well protect you if we don't travel with you."

Strange Bedfellows

*Year Four of the Just Emperor Kaitain "Dragonsbane" Lorien,
Creator's Calendar Year 1871*

Aris Ebonsight stood transfixed, looking out the window, her eyes never leaving the dead eyes of the woman calling herself Jerah. Over the next several moments several dozen swirling blue portals opened ushering the exodus of the army of the twin dark gods Rael and Trece Starlin. With them went the general of the Jade Legion, Leonora Wastri, and any hope that the forces of Cadaria would be able to save the Academy of Arcane Arts from its destruction, either at the hands of the forces of darkness or of their own code. Already Fiona Ebonsight had made her way to the chamber of the Masters and she and Jastra were deep in their debate about the invocation of the final covenant. The two older women thundered at each other, with Ashinica Maupin watching reservedly from the other side of the chamber.

"There is no choice now," Jastra said coldly, "there is nothing standing between Jerah and the Academy, and there is nothing that we will be able to do to defend ourselves from her. We must invoke the final covenant and remove the possible threat to Cadaria and the Emperor. This is what the first Masters intended when the code was put into place. Our powers can never be left to use as a weapon. They can never be left in the hands of those that would corrupt our purpose. How can you stand in opposition to this?"

Fiona's jaw was firmly set.

"Thousands of lives depend on the choices we make here in these moments. How many will be destroyed if we invoke the final covenant? How many deaths will be on our hands, including our own? Would you kill Ayden and Orren? Would you kill Quyhn and all of the children who cower in their rooms below us? Can we risk being wrong?"

"Can we risk not being wrong?" Jastra returned. "If that woman comes here and destroys us before we can invoke the final covenant, how many will die because of our inaction? Would you rather the whole of the world burns because we were afraid to do what we were entrusted to do?"

Ashinica finally slammed her hands on the table and broke the debate.

"There is no time for this. A vote has been called. No amount of vitriol will change the circumstances. The Master of Stone votes no."

Jastra grimaced, but did not let the disappointment register further on her face.

"The Master of Energy votes yes."

"The Master of Fire and acting Grand Master votes no."

Fiona's voice was crushing to the resolution, and Aris felt the pressure on her chest lighten slightly. The motion was defeated and she would not need to cast her vote.

"The motion is defeated," Fiona said with relief heavy in her voice, "and so we must turn our attention to protecting those here in the Academy."

Jastra's fist pounding the top of the table ended the conversation.

"The motion is not defeated. The Master's Council is not complete, and as indicated by the code, in situations where the Masters are tied in a vote considering the invocation of the final covenant, the Master of Energy holds all tie breaking votes. Aris must cast her vote, and if she votes for invocation, then the motion will carry."

Victory flashed across Fiona's eyes.

"Aris would never vote for the death of innocents."

Aris turned and clasped her hands at her chest.

"Which is why I must vote for the invocation of the final sanction. Too many will die if we do not do our duty, and if Alistair Ravenheart were here, he would agree. The Academy of Arcane Arts is too powerful to be allowed to fall into the hands of an enemy with the power that this woman Jerah represents. We would be fortunate if her goal were only to destroy us. If she does intend to kill us all, then we would be doing our students a favor by allowing them to meet their end peacefully and painlessly. If her intent is to bend us to her will, then we must save those who have trusted us with their fates. The covenant must be invoked, or we betray all of those who came before us, and all of those who placed their faith and their futures in our hands. May the Creator forgive us if we fail to do our duty."

Jastra did not allow an arrogant smile to come to her face despite her desire to display her victory in Fiona's face. They would all soon be dead, and there was no victory to be found in the ashes, no matter who ultimately would be proven right or wrong. Before she could turn to begin the incantations that would bring an end to everyone who had ever sworn their name and blood to the code of the Academy of Arcane Arts, Jastra was aware of another presence in the room. A swirling blue portal had appeared in the doorway, and for that moment Jastra thought the worst. When she saw the face of the woman who appeared, the feeling of dread did not immediately dissipate. The former Celestine Knight of the Flashing Blade, the High Priestess of the Church of the Creator, and the leader of the rebellion against the Emperor of Cadaria, Hannah Ironheart stepped quickly out of the portal followed by a woman that Jastra did not recognize, but from the way that she was dressed, she was obviously a disciple of the Church of the Creator. Once the portal closed, all eyes were turned to the former Knight of the Flashing Blade. Hannah walked to the window without a word and saw the carnage below. When she finally turned to face the assembled Masters, her face was painted with grim determination.

"I'm afraid, Masters, that your plans may be premature. The Academy of Arcane Arts is not lost, and I am here to make sure that it stays that way. But it is clear that Jelan is no longer safe. I have it on good authority that the estate of the Serpentine Knight in Iltorp is safe and would serve your needs well until such time it is safe to return to Jelan. Kiara will go with you to see to the evacuation of your students while I will do my best to hold your invaders at bay. Quickly now, before our time disappears."

No one moved for a long moment, finally Fiona broke the silence.

"Hannah, you are a traitor to the throne, and who knows where your loyalties lie now. If you are moving through the use of portals like that, you must have been corrupted by the Dark Gods or one of their kind. We cannot allow the students of the Academy of Arcane Arts to fall into the hands of the Dark Gods, no matter what happens. We have our own plan of action to protect our students from corruption."

Hannah growled.

"I don't think killing everyone is an effective means of saving your students, especially considering that one of the forces that would use the Academy for their goals has a creature serving them that calls itself Death. I don't think it would be against bringing the angry dead of your students back to this world to get their revenge for your shortsightedness and arrogance. I am offering you a way to keep your independence and your safety. All you have to do is follow Kiara, and hurry."

Jastra didn't move.

"And what is the cost for this assistance?"

Hannah felt her blood boil. Maybe Aerith was rubbing off on her far too much.

"Why is everyone constantly asking questions when there is no time for it? Just go. There will be time enough for negotiations later."

Jastra folded her arms.

"No, there will be no negotiations...."

Jastra's words were cut off by a hard punch from Hannah. The Master of Energy crumpled to the ground in a heap. For a moment Hannah wondered if she channeled a little too much of the flows of stone into her hand, but when she saw that the stubborn woman was still breathing, her fears had been alleviated. Aris was at Jastra's side the next moment, helping Jastra to her feet, but the woman was unconscious from the blow. Ashinica added her assistance, and the two Masters were able to get their unconscious fellow to her feet.

"We'll help get the students out," Ashinica said firmly. "And we will look forward to explanations after we are all safe. Lead the way, Kiara."

Kiara nodded, and waited as the four Masters flooded past her, through the door and down the stairs that led to the lower reaches of the Academy of Arcane Arts where the students were hiding in the safety of the basement. Before Kiara left to follow the Masters, Hannah unslung the small bag from around her waist and tossed it to Kiara.

"Remember what Aerith showed us. Just keep your thoughts focused on the portal and let the stone do its work. And only use the gray one, or there is no telling where you might end up. Even I don't know where all the stones go unless I'm looking at them."

"Light gray only," Kiara said bowing slightly. "I remember. We'll wait for you in Iltorp."

Kiara started to leave the room, but Hannah's voice made her stop.

"If I'm not there within two days, assume that Iltorp is no longer safe. Korrd is in charge of the Army of Fire, and the Army of Water is compromised by Seraph's leadership. Make for Albitonin. It is not the most ideal of destinations, but at least in the remains of the Stone the members of the Academy will be safe for a little while."

Kiara nodded again and this time bowed more fully.

"I understand your grace."

Once Kiara was gone, Hannah gripped tightly the hauntingly numb hilt of Spirit. The war mace had not felt the same since she had inherited

Aerith's powers, and at times seemed to put off waves of revulsion at her touch. But no matter how the Sacred Weapon may have felt about her at the moment, it still obeyed her commands in battle, and she would need its steady service in the minutes ahead. Letting her new powers fill her, a new portal opened in front of her and she stepped through. The blink of an eye later, Hannah stepped out of the portal and found herself only a few paces away from the pale white woman. Logan's memories flooded into Hannah's mind, and he immediately was aware of the woman's identity. She called herself Jerah, and she was a threat the order upon which Hannah had never faced on her own. When she fought the Will and the Voice, Aerith was by her side, but now she was about to enter combat with perhaps one of the most powerful creatures on Espre on her own. Brandishing the Sacred Weapon in her right hand, she summoned a bright golden sword to her other hand.

"The Academy of Arcane Arts is under my protection, Jerah, and I cannot let you or those you serve turn it to blasphemous work. Leave now. There is no need for this to escalate to conflict."

"Mistaken."

The single word flooded through Hannah like a wave of doubt. Her knees shook with a fear and hesitation that she could not explain, and no matter how she tried to calm her body, it would not respond to her orders. Finally, she reached deep and held onto the powers that the mantle of the *Chosen One* granted her. The next moment it felt as though she was made of stone, and no amount of fear or doubt could dissuade her from her work. Seeing that her opponent was not going to yield, Jerah closed her eyes for a brief moment, and when they opened, swirling red portals appeared behind her. Five people stepped through the portals, three that Hannah immediately recognized. They were the servants of Jerah that had attacked Logan in Hedorah. They were powerful to say the least, and would be a good test for Hannah's powers if it came to a fight. One of them was almost more than Logan could handle, but perhaps that had been because he was out of practice, or more likely because he was choosing to hold back what he was truly capable of. One of the things that Hannah had learned almost immediately about her predecessor was that he had never been comfortable with the powers at his disposal, and he would much rather have fought with his natural talents than lean on the powers that had been gifted to him. He never was able to see himself as anything other than a mortal that had some special abilities, and he was never going to let those abilities define him, even after the turns in his life turned him into something that could not be ignored or even fully defined as human. But to Logan, humanity was less about the state of being human, and more about what one chose to do with the abilities they had. To his credit, Logan was a better human than many of the nobles that Hannah had collided with over the years.

"Look at the poor little priestess," Lexa Silenti said coldly, "all alone and thinking that she can stand against the powerful Jerah all on her own. She should be spared her delusions."

Orchid Strages looked around and pulled on the Macero Furiae's sleeve.

"Look at all the blood Macero. We missed the fighting. You said we would be able to kill a lot of soldiers. We missed it."

Another woman walked up to Orchid and patted her gently on the head.

"Don't worry Orchid, there is plenty more killing. Once we are done with the deluded Knight of the Flashing Blade, you can carve your way through the whole of the Academy. I promise you can kill as many as you want."

The girl they called Orchid got a look of almost ecstasy on her face, tears forming in the corners of her eyes.

"Oh thank you Kyrie. You are so good to me."

"Then you should let me carve this one up," the other man said to the woman who Orchid had called Kyrie. "Especially after Macero had so much trouble with one little monk."

"You wouldn't have fared much better, Lucian. You were lucky to walk away from your little confrontation with a Dark God. So I don't think you are one to be bragging about your physical prowess."

"Enough."

The ground shook from Jerah's frustration. Each of the creatures that had appeared took a step back and bowed deeply to Jerah. It was obvious that there was more between them then fear. Without another motion, Jerah turned her attention back to the crater where Talisia's body lay, the move much too quick and violent to be casual. Jerah disappeared from where she stood and reappeared in the new place, and while the look on her face did not change, it was obvious that she did not find in the crater what she expected. The next moment, Jerah was gone. The disappearance of their patron seemed to shake the new arrivals for a moment, but a moment later, the one who had been called Lucian drew a sword from his belt and advanced on Hannah.

"I think perhaps you should lay your weapons down and let me end your life before something altogether horrible happens to you."

Hannah waited, not wanting to strike the first blow. She let her weight fall back onto her back foot and let the sword relax in her left hand. She had been right-handed through her whole life, but now that Aerith's powers and knowledge had transferred into her, she felt stronger in her left hand. Sensing hesitation in his prey, Lucian flashed in, his gleaming rapier crossing the distance between them in a heartbeat. However, Hannah had been ready for the obvious strike. She knew the opening gambit was coming, probably before Lucian himself knew what he was going to do. The rapier was a weapon designed for quick, nimble slashing movements, however the tip was sharp and light enough to allow for hard stabbing thrusts. For a master with the weapon, attacks could come from any angle with such ferocity that it would be challenging for all but the fastest opponents regardless of their skill with a blade. However, unlike most of Lucian's opponents, Hannah was much faster than any mortal, and faster than some Dark Gods. Falling back to just outside the fully extended range of the tip of the rapier, Hannah planted her back foot once more, and before Lucian could recover from his attack, she sped forward. She spun into Lucian's body, her left arm arcing up, letting the blade of her golden sword find Lucian's extended arm at the shoulder, severing it from his body. The spin also brought Spirit into her opponent at incredibly speed, and the heavy war mace struck true, the head of the weapon colliding with the head of her opponent with such velocity and force that the whole side of Lucian's skull was caved in. Blood splattered in all directions and the body of the abomination fell to the ground in a heap. For a long moment there were no reactions from the other four creatures as Hannah towered over the body of their compatriot. Blood pooled at her feet, and still Hannah stood, weapons in hand, her emotionless eyes locked on her other four opponents.

"The four of you together are no match for me," Hannah said with a cold confidence that sounded more like Aerith's voice than her own. "I don't want to destroy you, but I will if you give me no other choice. The Academy of Arcane Arts is under my protection now, and I will not allow you to defile it. Run while you have a chance. Please."

The please was hers and certainly would not have been in Aerith's vocabulary while facing down a group of armed individuals who were intent on killing him. But just as Aerith could not be anyone but himself, Hannah could not help but to be herself. She was raised and taught to be merciful in all cases except for the most dire. Even the wicked amongst the living deserved mercy. However after looking at the eyes of her opponents, Hannah knew that they would not be taking her offer of mercy. Silently they plotted how best to deal with the Knight of the Flashing Blade. It was Lexa that attacked first, with Kyrie right behind. The two women struck at nearly the same time, daggers flashing out of nothingness toward Hannah's face and stomach. The strikes were easy enough for Hannah to avoid, but her more bulky weapons did not allow for easy parrying and countering of the strikes. Spirit clattered to the ground and the golden sword disappeared from being that next moment, and Hannah coated her hands with pure light energy. It was a trick that she picked up from Logan's memories, and seemed to be something that could be effective in the moment. When Lexa flashed in again, Hannah caught one of the daggers with her right hand and then struck with her open left hand to the woman's face. Searing energy flared at the contact and Lexa screamed as her face was brutally burned by Hannah's attack. As she fell back, blisters began to raise on the burned skin. Undeterred, Kyrie struck, one blade barely grazing Hannah's right shoulder as she darted past. Stealing another technique, Hannah wrapped herself in a flaming sheathe and waited. This time when Kyrie flashed in, the blade struck the shield of flame and melted on contact before it could cause any damage to Hannah. The superheated metal splashed back onto Kyrie leaving burning craters in her chest. She shrieked in pain, and was unable to defend herself as Hannah charged in, a hard palm strike with her right hand catching the woman square in the chest. The blow caused Kyrie to explode in flames, the skin and muscle burned from her bones in a matter of seconds, the charred skeleton dropping to the ground. Not giving her other opponent a second to recover, Hannah pointed with her left hand toward Lexa, and the shield of flame extended like a whip, wrapping around the woman's throat searing her flesh. When Hannah pulled her arm back, Lexa's head was ripped from her body the next moment. When Lexa fell, Hannah released the shield of fire and turned her attention back to Macero and Orchid.

"There is no need for this to continue," Hannah said finally, letting the field of light disappear from her hand and summoning Spirit back to her right hand. "You have seen that you are no match for my abilities, and destroying yourselves will accomplish nothing. Flee while you have the chance, please."

A massive gust of wind passed across the countryside, and Hannah felt a presence of such power that it felt as though it were going to crush her. She saw the gleaming claws before she saw the body of the dragon, and it was the knowledge of the girl Sabrina that filled the gaps in Hannah's mind. The dragon was known as Mariti Brightblade, she had fought on the side of Pyrrus during the rebellion in the heavens and had killed many angels who had followed Talisia Masile. The massive dragon landed lightly on the ground a hundred feet behind where Orchid and Macero stood. After a long roar Mariti locked her eyes on Hannah.

"They are too stupid to flee, mortal. And no amount of pleading will change that. Kill them now, and be done with it. This world would be better off when all of their kind have been purged."

Hannah felt revulsion fill her.

"Then what, dragon? Would you purge all of the mortals and make this place for your kind alone? Then what? Would you purge those of your kind that did not share your beliefs, or perhaps your advanced age? Or maybe you would kill all those who were not on your side during the rebellion in the heavens."

Mariti roared again. This time Hannah felt the dragon trying to intimidate her. The roar was designed to make her doubt her abilities and flush her with fear. However, Hannah was not about to let herself be defeated so quickly.

"Your mouth and your arrogance betray you human," Mariti growled. "You serve the abomination. It's because of you and your kind that our lord Tarot has been destroyed. It's because of your Aerith that there was a war in the heavens, and it's because of you and your kind that we will all burn. Your arrogance is the blight that is choking this world. If it weren't for the threat that Dorovar and his ilk pose, I would rip you to shreds here and now. End the creatures and let us talk. They serve one of Dorovar's puppets and must meet the fire. Kill them now, or I shall."

"I think not."

On the hill where the battle for the Academy of Arcane Arts seemed to be the most severe a woman with wide bat-like wings stood with a legion of skeletal troops at her back. She brandished a massive spear that was tipped with fire. Beside her stood another woman, much smaller and more fragile in stature, but who resonated with power that Hannah could feel hundreds of yards away. Both of the women were instantly known to Hannah, and as she squeezed the haft of Spirit in her hand, she could feel the weapon screaming. The woman with the wings was the daughter of Talisia Masile, a creature called Seraphina, while the other woman was one of the servants of Dorovar, the creature known as Famine. Hannah could feel Famine's evil smile, and a flash of light later, Macero and Orchid stood at the side of Seraphina. Mariti roared again and crouched low to the ground. Hannah felt the dragon's voice crawl through her head the next moment.

"The fallen angel is yours," Mariti said as she launched herself in a charge toward the hillside. "Dorovar's pet is mine."

Where Divinity Meets Grace

Year One of the Divine Empress and Child of the Creator
Marlae Tamerlane, Creator's Calendar Year 1871

Hedorah, the Flying Kingdom, renown as the city of vice and corruption; but that was yesterday. Today, new power and new law swept through the streets, all under the command of the Divine Empress, Child of the Creator, and rightful ruler of Espre, Marlae Tamerlane. At the command of the Divine Empress, all of the royal families had been stripped of their positions and expelled from their estates, with the singular exception of Terrance Aldora, who had been named Regent of Hedorah. However, it soon became clear that the Regent's duties would be largely ceremonial, and isolated to only the direct issues that affected the people of Hedorah. The military of Hedorah, the former Flying Guard, had been all but dismantled in a matter of hours, replaced by the few paladins from the Church of the Creator. The more significant portion of Hedorah's new military consisted of warrior angels. Seeing the winged creatures walking through the streets of Hedorah had brought a mixture of shock and disbelief. There was also a mass exodus of the criminal element from the city. They were allowed to leave, if for no other reason than for them to spread the word that their kind was not welcome, and that the radiance of the Divine Empress would soon shine upon all of Cadaria. The Reverend Mother Amallia and her fellow priests roamed the streets, speaking of an end to the Time of Madness, a newly coined term for the rule of the False Emperor, Kaitain Lorien.

The changes happened swiftly in Hedorah, sparked by an address by the Divine Empress, a flight of angels around her, and the Will of Creator standing at her shoulder. It was a mandate from the Creator that things were changing, not only in Hedorah, but across the whole of Cadaria, and then the whole of Espre. The people who had been oppressed for so long by the history of graft and corruption could not help but cheer, while those who had lived off the fat of that dark enterprise could feel the pressure of the divine upon their souls. There would be no soft underbelly to exploit in the forces of the Divine Empress. Following the proclamations from the Divine Empress, she retired to the newly designated Royal Palace of Hedorah, the former palatial estate of Pelis and his merchant family, the largest estate kept by any of the former royals. It was made clear by Reverend Mother Amallia that the Divine Empress's visibility would be low in the days to come as she prepared for the battles ahead. It was decreed that the Reverend Mother and the Regent would speak for the Divine Empress in all courtly matters. Rumors circulated that the Divine Empress met in the seclusion of her palace with gods who had descended from the heavens that would take the fight not only to the False Emperor, but also to the Dark Gods, who it was said were already beginning their offensive on the shores of Cadaria. So much was changing, and wild rumor and speculation were the currency of the day.

Deep within the protective outer shell of the estate, past the series of guard check-points, and two dozen angels armed with divine weapons were the private chambers of the Divine Empress, a series of four rooms that would become the nerve center of the new empire. The most central room of the four was the Empress's bedchambers, off-limits to all but the Empress and her small retinue of trusted advisors and attendants. The smallest room served as a place of meditation, with a self-contained garden. The largest of the rooms was a meeting and private dining room with a long table and seats enough for two dozen, and the last room was a makeshift war room, with maps instead of tapestries lining the walls. This last room was where the Divine Empress found herself, listening to Ayden debating with a man who had called himself the god Azure.

"The logical choice would be to marshal our forces and wipe out Mythryn in a single strike," Azure was saying. "A direct assault would take the Fallen Ones by surprise and would give the Divine Empress a clear victory against arguably the largest threat to her rule. Not only would it prove that she is indeed the Child of the Creator, but it would also show that she can succeed where Emperor Lorien and his predecessors have failed time and time again."

The Reverend Mother shook her head. Though Amallia would never have openly disagreed with any voice that was showed itself to be from the Heavens, she could not let her awe override her good judgment in service to the Divine Empress.

"The Dark Gods and the False Emperor can continue to throw themselves at one another, the Divine Empress does not need to make such grand gestures. Carelessness is not an ally of a long and fruitful rule. The time for battle will come soon enough, we should not rush into one."

"Spoken like a human," Azure said, disgust clear in his voice.

Reverend Mother Amallia was not deterred.

"Humans are those who will serve the Divine Empress, and should not be overlooked, even if the majority of the Divine Empress's troops have wings and the powers of the Heavens at their disposal. The hearts and minds of humans are what need to be won, and no amount of Dark God blood will do that."

Azure scoffed.

"A decisive victory against the Dark Gods will win the respect of our enemies."

Terrence Aldora finally added his voice.

"But our enemies are not whose respect we need to win. The unwilling subjects of the False Emperor are not our enemies. That much has been proven by all those willing to die in uprisings. And how many more would flock to the Divine Empress's banner to protect their faith, or their loved ones who are devout followers of the Creator."

"The Creator teaches that you need not shine light in the eyes of those who are searching for it," Amallia intoned, "You need only shine that light upon the ground and they will follow any way they can, even if they must crawl."

Azure's cheeks colored with crimson.

"You dare quote the Creator's teachings to a god!"

Ayden was between the two the next moment, his searing gaze burning into Azure's eyes, while his sword flashed to the man's throat.

"We are not served by this," he said wearily. "As long as we bicker, the enemies of the Divine Empress gain more ground."

Marlae raised a hand briefly, and Ayden instantly let the flaming blade disappear from his hand. He took a step away from Azure, but did not let his spiteful gaze leave the god's face.

"Should I ask what side of the Dark Gods' rebellion you fought on? Or did you cower and hide like the rest of Emries' followers."

If Azure intended to reply to the challenge, the words died in his throat when the Divine Empress stood. Without a word, she turned and moved toward her private bedchambers. Amallia fell to her knees as soon as Marlae stood, and each of the angels in the room bowed low to show their respect. Only Azure and Ayden remained upright. As soon as the door closed behind her, Marlae could hear the bickering begin again. Whatever restraint they showed in front of her disappeared as soon as she had left the room. Passing one of the bowed handmaidens who attended her, Marlae stopped and put her fingers under the young girl's chin and lifted her head to get a better look at her face. To her credit, the girl kept her eyes down and would not meet the gaze of the Child of the Creator. To a common man, the girl would have been beautiful, but to Marlae she was just pretty. She was not in the same league as Rhain or Dominique, but she was certainly the most attractive of the group.

"How old are you, girl?"

The girl tried to speak, but her voice died in her throat on the first attempt. She took a ragged breath and then finally pushed out her response.

"Nearly twenty, Your Divine Grace."

She was only slightly younger than Marlae herself, but held herself like a girl instead of a young woman. She was intimidated to be sure, but that would not matter in time.

"You are all dismissed. Except for you," Marlae said looking back at the clearly shaking girl. "Return in one hour with a bathing vessel and hot water. You will attend me for my bath."

All of the handmaidens bowed in unison and moved carefully to leave the room, leaving Marlae alone with her thoughts. Standing there in the silence, Marlae could feel the ill-fitting dress rubbing against her hips and sides. Clenching her jaw, she moved to the large full length mirror which stood in the center of the room and looked at the image of herself. No, the dress would not do at all. It did not cling to her in any way that would be considered flattering. It bunched at the waist and had to be smoothed constantly. It would need to be taken in at the bust line and the neck line would have to be lowered considerably. There must be a plunge to show off her best assets, and a slit up the side so that more of her leg would show, perhaps up to her thigh. As she turned, her disgust with the dress grew. The dress made her look like a housewife. An elegant housewife of some minor lord, but a housewife nonetheless. It was not the dress of the most desirable woman in the whole of the world. At that moment she missed her wardrobe. She missed the decadent and provocative garments that she would wear to tease Gabriel. How she loved to watch his cheeks color as he tried to figure out where he could look without seeming disrespectful. She loved seeing the hunger in the eyes of men and women as she passed. It filled her with such a sense of power. Lost in her reverie, Marlae did not notice the image that she was so dissatisfied with disappear only to be replaced by another.

Marlae felt the disapproving eyes on her before she saw them. Shaken from her selfish thoughts, the Divine Empress looked back into the mirror and saw the woman standing there. She was dressed in a commoner's gown, but it was a beautiful shade of blue with golden accents. The blue was the same shade as the woman's stormy eyes. Her hair was also simply done, smooth and silky brown, cascading over one shoulder. Her features were soft, her skin radiant, but the strength in her eyes and her posture could not be ignored.

"I think, Marlae," the woman said softly, but with a power that hit Marlae like a punch, "that you and I should have a talk. Especially if you are going to be using my name."

* * * * * * * * * * * *

In the war room, the debate continued. Though as Terrance Aldora looked on, he began to feel as though it was less a debate, and more an old argument replaying for the hundredth time. The Will and the god Azure thundered at each other, though it seemed that most of the words lapsed into a language that Terrence could not understand. Amallia had said earlier in the day that it was the language of the Heavens, for lack of a better term, Angelic. There was one final exchange, and Azure simply disappeared. That was something else Terrence would have to learn to accept. The gods and angels could simply will themselves to be where they wanted whenever they wanted. Who knew that walking would make Terrence feel so much more mortal than it ever had before?

"He always was headstrong," Ayden said to no one in particular.

Reverend Mother Amallia kept her head down, but addressed Ayden.

"Does the Will of the Creator require anything further of this servant?"

Ayden looked down at Amallia and sighed.

"No, Reverend Mother, please attend to your many duties. I know you are more valuable to the Divine Empress out among the people than you are here holding your tongue through another needless argument."

Amallia bowed low, and after a moment stood and left the room, flanked by her angelic escort. Silence held the room for a long moment before Ayden looked over at Terrence. To his credit, the man did not avert his gaze from the Servant of the Creator, but the doubt and fear was clearly evident in the man's eyes.

"Is there any way we can prevent a strike against Mythryn?"

Ayden's question was a profound one, but one motivated more by frustration than anything else.

"Perhaps if I knew more about why Azure was so bent on striking at the Dark Gods, I could find better arguments against it."

Ayden regarded Terrence for a moment and then smiled.

"You and your brother are a lot alike. I knew that I would like you the moment I laid eyes on you."

Terrence wasn't sure how to take the comment. He and Jaccob had never been close. Terrence barely remembered Jaccob from his childhood days, as his older brother had been swept up by members of the Academy of Arcane Arts and taken to Jelan just before Terrence's fifth birthday. It wasn't until Jaccob's expulsion from the Academy that the two saw one another again. However, before they could really become acquainted again, Jaccob became a Knight of the Flashing Blade, and his time was divided between his drinking, whoring, and missions for the Emperor. Like most people, Terrence was ashamed of the man who called himself the Topaz Knight, but as the man's brother, Terrence tried to look through the attempts at self-destruction to see the man beneath. But all he ever saw was barely restrained pain.

"I wish I had known him as well as you did."

Ayden let the comment pass. He didn't want to reopen old wounds for his new ally. Instead he changed his focus to the question at hand. Taking the role of the Will of the Creator had opened new doors of understanding, and Ayden had gained access to history that he had only been able to guess at from the stories told by his former parents.

"Azure was once a servant of Emries, who is one of the Children of the Creator. Azure was elevated to godhood after the fall of his world, along with three of his brothers. Once, long ago, the men and women you know as the Dark Gods were mortals just like you, struggling to protect their homes and the people that they loved from an incursion they believed to be evil. Emries devised a series of tests for these heroes, in an effort to keep them on the right path. Azure was placed in charge of these tests. Let's just say that the heroes and Azure did not see eye to eye."

"So it's a grudge," Terrence commented.

Ayden nodded.

"One that worsened when the heroes were elevated to godhood themselves. It just got worse from there. There was a revolt in the Heavens, and the Dark Gods were cast down. But more happened there than any know, except those that actually fought. And as I'm sure you surmised, Azure and his brothers were not among the combatants."

Terrence slumped into a chair.

"So he sees this as an opportunity to get his pound of flesh that he wasn't able to get during the revolt."

Ayden sighed.

"Something like that. It's complicated."

Despite himself, Terrence chuckled.

"Complicated seems to be the word of the day."

For a long moment, silence returned to the room. Ayden and Terrence were both looking at the large map of Cadaria on the wall, and Ayden could feel something gnawing at his insides, like he had forgotten something. Suddenly it came to him.

"I think I have a way to give Azure his war without compromising the Divine Empress."

* * * * * * * * * * *

"I'm not in the habit of having conversations with reflections."

Marlae took a step away from the mirror and did her best to retain her regal tone and bearings. She had seen many fantastic things over the last year, and many more over the past few days, but this was different. Something inside her knew the woman in the glass. Though nothing would prevent Marlae from taking offence at the look in the strange woman's eyes. It was a mixture of contempt, disgust, and embarrassment. Finally Marlae turned away from the mirror and walked toward her bed. She practically threw herself down on the edge of the bed, sitting and looking at the back of the mirror, a defiant and triumphant look on her face. But as she watched, a foot, followed by the rest of the woman's leg emerged from the mirror. In a matter of seconds, the whole form of the woman had emerged from the mirror, and she rounded on the Divine Empress with her hands on her hips. Though Marlae was seeing the full form of the woman, she had a wispy, almost smoke-like quality to her. As though she were not really there, but an echo of something that she once was. The woman looked to be middle-aged, but no older than forty, but there was still a great deal of youth in her features. Her eyes were full of strength and wisdom, wisdom much greater than her physical age.

"Don't think that you're going to get away from me, Marlae," the woman said coldly. "I have plenty of experience dealing with spoiled, immature, entitled brats. And not a single one ever got the best of me, princess or farm-boy alike. I don't think a so-called empress will be much different."

Marlae felt her blood boil.

"How dare you…"

The phantom woman turned her head and raised her hand, and Marlae's contempt died in her throat. After a moment, the woman turned her gaze back to Marlae, the contempt clear on her face.

"Your days as a spoiled, pampered, privileged bitch are over. There is no room for that, and I won't have you disgracing my name. The Creator pulled me back from my rest and tied me to you, thinking that I would help you become the Empress that he wanted for this world. That you will bring some kind of new leadership, like the true calm voice from the wilderness to lead the faithful out of madness."

Marlae felt her pride well up.

"And what do you do? You stand here fretting about a dress. You're plotting how you can look less like an Empress and more like a whore. You want to be unattainable but desired by all. You don't want to be a leader, you want to be a temptation."

Marlae felt as though she had been slapped across the face, but the assault did not end there.

"And do you think your little dalliances with handmaidens and servants is how a true leader conducts herself? When will you learn that your life cannot be all about you? That is why your father is in the position he is in today. He doesn't understand that to lead means to think of others before yourself. Heroes are selfless, and this world needs you to be a hero. Heroes meet challenges on their feet, not on their backs."

Rage boiled up inside of Marlae and she stood, wagging her finger in the ghostly woman's face.

"And who are you to lecture me! What do you know of responsibility? What do you know of being a hero?"

This time the slap that found Marlae's cheek was real. For a long moment, Marlae's mind did not register that she had been struck, only that there was a pain in her cheek. It was when the woman reached out and shoved her back down to a seated position on the bed did she fully realize what had happened.

"I know more about heroes than you could learn in ten lifetimes, little girl," the woman said sternly and with conviction, but without any venom. "I fought alongside heroes, I was married to a hero, and I gave birth to a hero. I've watched heroes die for no other reason than to protect the ones that they loved. I've seen my friends ripped apart because they were strong enough to stand up for what they believed in. My husband died in my arms, knowing that he had done everything he could to prepare his friends and those who would come after for the road ahead. You could never understand that sacrifice. You could never think of others before yourself, and you will never find anything in this gift that has been given to you other than a way to pamper yourself. You're pathetic."

The ghostly woman let her words sink in for a long moment before she started speaking again. This time her tone was softer, more motherly.

"You have an opportunity now, Marlae. You can be more than you ever thought you could be. The Creator has reached down and touched you. This is your moment. My moment came once, and I was strong enough to grasp it. I could have stayed in my comfortable little life, been a farmer's wife, had many children and died comfortable in my ignorance. But I didn't. I fought. I fought against those I had no chance to defeat. And yet I fought. I stood before the embodiment of every nightmare that any person ever had, and was defiant. Even in the face of one of the Children of the Creator I stood my ground and would not relent. Can you find that strength Marlae? Do you have it within you to be something more than a puppet for your father? Or a puppet for the Church? Or even a puppet for the Creator?"

Marlae's eyes widened.

"That's right, Marlae," the woman continued. "Taking a stand means that for the first time in your life you have to make your own decisions. You can't blame others any longer. Be a force for good, or a force of evil, but do it on your terms, with your voice, and with real conviction."

After a long moment, Marlae stood. She still felt like a little girl looking into the eyes of the ghostly woman, but there was strength within her that she had never known before. There was warmth and a radiance that seemed to fill her. She set her feet, and squared her shoulders, and perhaps for the first time in her life felt as though she were standing alone, in the eye of a storm of her own making. The storm was small still, reaching only the walls of the room, but she knew deep inside that she now had the power to make that storm grow. Finally a smile came to the ghostly woman's lips.

"No matter what happens from now on, Marlae, you have to stand on your own two feet. Be smart, keep your eyes open, and know in your heart when people are telling you the truth or if they are only serving their own interests. Seek out real heroes, ones that will support you and follow you, not those who will serve you for the wrong reasons. Hold on to that strength inside of you. Don't be afraid to be afraid. Don't be afraid to not know. And don't hide behind your womanhood. There are people just on the other side of that door, and those that claim to serve you now that would put their hands around your throat and watch as you died. Just because they bow to you doesn't ensure they truly serve you. Perhaps I had it easier than you will, because I was never the leader. I was the glue that held us together. But maybe that is what this world needs now. Not a leader, but someone to hold it together while the heroes and villains try to pull it apart."

The woman turned back toward the mirror and took several steps.

"Wait," Marlae said, her voice weak, "there is still so much you can teach me."

The woman stopped and turned back, a pained smile on her face.

"This is not my world, Marlae, and this is not my war. I fought, I suffered, and I died for the people I loved. I earned my rest. I have friends and loved ones waiting for me. The Creator can't take that away from me, no matter how hard He may try. But if you are going to carry on my name, I had to make sure you were on the right path. I think you will be fine now."

The woman turned again. This time Marlae scrambled to her feet and tried her best to catch up to the woman before she made it to the door, but she stumbled and fell to the ground. When she looked up, tears were streaming from her eyes. The ghostly woman turned back one last time, her hand on the handle to the door that led not to the meditation garden as it would for Marlae, but to a place much more tranquil.

"There's no need for tears my dear. When I'm gone, you'll know what you need to do. Be more than you have been. And more than anything, be true to yourself."

The woman turned away again, this time, dissolving into nothing. The next moment, Marlae's mind was flooded with memories, thoughts, and emotions. Tears streamed down her face, but she could not suppress the smile the tugged at the corners of her mouth.

"Thank you Elwyne, for everything. I'll miss you, but I'll make you proud."

*＊＊＊＊＊＊＊＊＊＊＊

An hour passed, and the handmaiden returned, sheepishly opening the door. She would ensure that the Divine Empress still wanted her bath before ushering in the servants who would carry the vessel and the buckets of water. When the handmaiden's eyes finally found the Empress, she was standing in front of her open wardrobe, dozens of dresses lying on the floor at her feet. Sensing the girl's presence, Marlae turned towards her. The girl instantly dropped to her knees.

"Call for the seamstress," Marlae said, "and have her sent to me as soon as possible. Then I want to speak with Terrence Aldora."

The girl started to rise and leave the room, but Marlae's voice rang out again.

"Before you go, what's your name?"

The girl hesitated for a moment.

"Isabella, your Divine Grace."

Marlae smiled.

"Isabella," she said, rolling the name across her tongue. "Well then, Isabella, hurry back once you have delivered those messages. I have a job for you."

Chapter LXXIV

Sleight of Hand

*Year Four of the Just Emperor Kaitain "Dragonsbane" Lorien,
Creator's Calendar Year 1871*

The headquarters of the Shadow Guild was a mythical location that had sparked imaginations and nightmares for the whole of the existence of the Cadarian Empire. Such was true of all of the best secrets. There were those who claimed to know something, and circulated their falsehoods and speculations to the eager masses, perpetuating grand fictions of mountains of gold and libraries of secrets that could shake the foundation of the whole Empire. Closely guarded details of affairs, illegitimate children, assassinations, and lies so heinous that every royal family would be cast in the light of their own humiliations for generations to come. There were stories of a grand palace somewhere, guarded so well that if anyone came within line of sight of its black walls, that an assassin would emerge out of the shadows and make sure that person never saw the light of day again. No one returned to confirm the stories, and yet somehow the stories made their way to the ear of many eager listeners with details so precise that they had to be true. However, the truth was much less grand, and much more fitting of the nature of the Shadow Guild, and the well-appointed stories were nothing more than fabrications circulated by agents of the Shadow Guild to keep the mystique in the minds of the masses. The Grand Master taught that a good story was usually far more quickly believed than the unvarnished truth. Before the Palace of Aldere was constructed, there was once an abbey that stood on the edge of the borders of what was now Aldere. It was in the center of a small township that sprung up around the site. Rumor had it that the abbey was built over a location where a relic from heaven fell. The abbey was erected on the site, and soon people flocked to the abbey and built homes to be close to the divine presence. Like the mystique of the Shadow Guild itself, the legend of the abbey was only a facet of the truth.

What history remembered in the annuls of Cadaria was the Day the Heavens Fell. Cadaria was united under the rule of the First Emperor having just emerged from a prolonged and bloody civil war. The countryside was still littered with battlefield graves, but the wounds were starting to heal. Then the sky was on fire. The Days of Star Fire had trained the people of Espre to accept the streaks of fire in the sky, but it had not prepared them massive balls of fire that struck the ground on the Day the Heaven's Fell. When the balls of fire struck the ground, they sent flaming debris flying in all direction, reducing an ancient forest to smoking rubble in a matter of hours. The cataclysmic storm that followed darkened the sky for weeks, and the lightning caused more fires and damage to houses and farms. It was the first salvo of destruction that would harken the start of the First Shadow War. The War would end with the death of the leader of the Dark Gods, and the anointing of the First Emperor Lorien with his title of Godslayer. But long before the Day the Heavens fell, other refugees from the Heavens and beyond found their way to Espre. Most of the impacts were not seen by human eyes, and those humans that did witness a fall usually did not survive the experience. The few humans that did survive were permanently changed by the experience, some became creatures from legend, others were reduced to shells of their formers selves, obsessed with spreading the tales of the horrors they had seen.

One of these impacts happened just at the edge of Aldere, and the lone witness of the impact spent the next three years constructing the abbey that would stand at the site of the impact for hundreds of years. Many thought the man was crazy, and the feeling grew when he continually denied every offer of assistance. But he continued to work, day and night, until his fingers bled, no matter the weather and no matter the illness that wracked his body until the abbey was completed. The day he drove the final nail, the man dropped dead on the spot. The reason for his single-minded dedication, for his hysterical focus would never be known by another person, but the followers of the Creator who came to take up residence, the progenitors of what would become the Church of the Creator that would build the Heart of Stone in Albitonin, held the nameless man as a saint of the highest order. Before his true deeds were lost to the legend that sprang up around his actions, the man was a simple farmer who witnessed the impossible, after he was the Nameless Saint of Divine Faith.

But it was what was under the abbey that was of true interest. That was what the nameless farmer was building the abbey to protect. No one would dare desecrate holy land looking for natural resources, and the land all around the abbey would be protected as long as the structure stood and there were people to protect it. Beneath the foundation of the abbey several feet beneath the surface was a thick vein of thick stone. The impact from the heavens cracked the vein like a stone cracks glass. Shock waves from the impact travelled through the whole of the acres long stone slab, creating a web of twisting tunnels. The cause of the impact, Saurn Macco, spent months following his arrival on Espre turning the site into a secret base of operations that would serve him for nearly two thousand years. Excavating each of the chambers by hand took a long time, as he did not dare use his abilities for fear that one of the other Fallen would discover him. After the resolution of the war that began the reign of the Lorien family, Saurn Macco began laying the ground work for what would become the Shadow Guild. It took him years to recruit those he would teach the secrets they would need to serve the interests of the Emperor, the interests that could never see the light of day. Coming out of a civil war of such a degree, the Emperor would have enemies, enemies that would not have the clout or the strength to mount a military takeover of Cadaria. But a man with no army could still overthrow a king. Assassins were a constant danger, and the Emperor of Cadaria needed adequate protection. But even the Masters of the Shadow Guild did not know every chamber within the Shadow Guild's base of operations. The knowledge was reserved for the man who built it.

Deep in the deepest segment of the headquarters of the Shadow Guild was a secret chamber that Saurn retired to when he needed to think. Over the last two years, he had spent more and more time there, reviewing the way that the whole of the world was spinning madly out of control. From the day that he arrived on Espre, Saurn saw the way the wind would eventually blow; he just didn't know how long that would take. From his time on Onea, Saurn knew the value of long-term planning. Once Gwydeon and his minions had assured that the Lorien line would rule the Cadarian Empire, Saurn made sure to ingratiate himself and make the argument that he was indispensable. But the truth of the world that the Loriens would rule could never be revealed to them, even when agents from the heavens tried their best to interfere. Saurn knew about Dorovar, knew about the Children of the Creator, and knew that as long as Aerith Seth roamed Espre, that peace would never last for long. But Aerith kept his head down and tried his best to be a family man. The world continued to turn until Kaitain Lorien sat upon the throne. Dorovar's first herald walked, and death followed in his footsteps. War began with the dragons, and then the Dark Gods, and then there was the assassination attempt on the Emperor. It was sloppy work, but needed to be done. The poison had been of Saurn's own design, but the only reason he allowed it to be used was to keep Talisia's minions in the dark as to his true motives. In his disguise as Torda Safrick, Saurn had infiltrated the highest echelon of the Hand of Chaos, the secret inner circle of Talisia's followers. Whatever Talisia's schemes were, they were not entirely of her devising. Saurn had sensed a familiar hand at work, and his suspicious were confirmed when Emries was sighted just before the fall of the Imperial Palace of Aldere. The madness that followed could only be attributed to a mortal's lust for power, and it was clear that Kaitain had grown beyond the control of his divine betters. However, time had left behind the mortal, no matter his madness. Fate had turned again to the hands of those who had tasted immortality, which is what had drawn Saurn finally out of his comfortable hiding place.

In the secret meditation chamber, a portal opened and two men emerged. Jeroch Yetre was visibly struggling with every step, his blood soaked hand clinging to the gaping wound in his side. Saurn Macco followed quickly after, his violet eyes flashing for a moment which caused the portal behind them to wink shut. Jeroch slumped in a chair without being prompted, and Saurn moved wordlessly to a cabinet in the corner of the room. He retrieved a small vial from the cabinet and used a fraction of the power available to float it across the room to his older sibling. It took Jeroch a moment to become aware of the small glass vial floating before him, but once he was aware, he took it out of the air and in a single motion removed the stopper with his thumb and brought the vial to his lips. At that last moment he hesitated.

"If I wanted you dead Shadow, there are far better ways than to bring you here and poison you. I've had too many opportunities over the centuries to watch you draw your last breath."

Jeroch kept his eyes focused on Saurn for a long moment, the vial poised at his lips. Finally he closed his eyes and tipped the vial up, letting the small amount of liquid flow across his lips and down his throat. The thin, almost insubstantial liquid felt like fire running down his throat, and the burning spread through every part of his body in a matter of seconds. But just as quickly as the burning began, it was over, and the pain from the poison wracking his body was gone. Free of its influence, Jeroch poured all of his concentration into healing the wounds in his body and by the time Saurn eased himself into a chair behind the desk opposite where Jeroch sat, the most severe of the wounds had been mended. When the color had returned to his older sibling's face, Saurn leaned forward resting his elbows on the desk and resting his chin on steepled fingered.

"It's an interesting little poison I developed some time ago. But it is very difficult to make and only produces very small quantities. You see the principle ingredient is fluid from a living person's spine. And in such quantities I'm afraid that the donor would not live through the donation. Only my masters and a handful of special disciples know the formula for the poison, and fewer still know enough to perfect the brewing process. Of those few, I know only one who uses the kind of weapon that wounded you and would have the audacity to attack a member of the Knights of the Flashing Blade without orders from the Grand Master of the Shadow Guild. Would you care to know who it is and why?"

Jeroch leaned back in his chair. After a moment, he motioned with his right hand for Saurn to continue with his explanation.

"Her name is Alise Modrall. A vicious little creature that was created on orders from Emperor Kaitain Lorien. Even before he became the Emperor of Cadaria, Kaitain was a crafty soul, and far more suited to the position he would eventually inherit. He is much more like us than any of these mortals have been to this point."

Jeroch scoffed.

"He's human, he has limits. We're phasia, we have no limits."

Saurn's eyes narrowed.

"Don't be so quick to dismiss Kaitain. His eyes were opened early that a weak will would doom his reign before it began and trusting the establishment of his forefathers bred amazing arrogance. But more importantly, it bred carelessness. Kaitain grew up with a staunch distrust for anything that resembled structure. He distrusted the Shadow Guild because he felt they were too powerful and held too much leverage over the throne and hated the Knights of the Flashing Blade because they had a history of defying authority when it suited them. It burned in him that the people would rather have Gregor Quicksilver on the throne than the rightful Lorien heir."

"Perhaps we would be better off," Jeroch mused.

Saurn glowered.

"I'm not so sure given recent events."

Saurn's words trailed off, and he seemed to look past Jeroch into nothingness. The two sat there for a long moment in silence before Saurn's eyes snapped back to Jeroch.

"But I'm getting ahead of myself, now aren't I? Alise Modrall, she was a bargain struck with the darkness to keep my Guild safe. Kaitain wanted an assassin that was answerable only to him, that would kill on command and would never question orders. Alise was created with the help of some corrupted members of the Academy of Arcane Arts and some manipulation from me. She is a powerful and efficient killer, and can see and channel arcane flows as well as the masters of the Academy. She was taught to use her abilities to increase her speed, her strength, and her senses. She is the best tracker I have ever seen, and perhaps as efficient a killer as any of the phasia ever were. She is single-minded in her devotion to a kill, and once she gets the scent of her prey she will not relent until one of them is dead. Oh, and she is quite adept at not dying, even from blows that would kill one of us."

Jeroch shifted uncomfortably in his seat.

"I never imagined I would see you afraid of someone again, Saurn. But then again, I haven't seen anything like this Kaitain since we ruled our world with an iron fist. Perhaps if Kaitain had been one of our number we would have been more successful in eradicating Emries and his progeny before our world was destroyed."

Saurn's eyes widened.

"It almost sounds as though you admire him."

Saurn saw one of Jeroch's fists clench tightly.

"Just because I appreciate the man's abilities does not mean that I admire him. He is a monster of the highest order no different than Draven was. No different than Rane was. The difference is that Kaitain's madness will bring an end to everything we have been working for, and will hand the world over to either Dorovar or Emries, or worse, Aerith. Gwydeon and his kind taught us on Onea that the mortals were the true power that needed to be wielded and protected. With the dragons, and Dorovar, and Emries, and Talisia, and all of the others vying for control of this world, the people are suffering. Whole cities have been leveled, thousands of lives lost. And every day this war rages, more lives are destroyed and more opportunities to bring this to a resolution slip past us. I worked very hard in tracking down all of our brothers and sisters, and turning them to the proper side of this war or ending their lives. I slew Arathorn Geoffry before he became a threat to a Lorien ruling family. I ended Cedric Binosear, no matter how much of an asset he could have been these days. I let you sow your seeds of graft, menace and fear, knowing that when the time came you would not make the same mistakes that put you on your knees with Aerith's blade piercing you. As much as you may hate the man, and fear what he represents, you know as well as I do that we cannot end this without him."

Saurn smiled coldly.

"That remains to be seen. It seems that our father had something to say about just what fate Aerith Seth would have in this war."

Jeroch's eyes narrowed.

"Meaning?"

Saurn straightened in his chair.

"Meaning that there are still many acts in this play before we can see who is the hero, who is the villain and who will be left standing when the music stops. But that my dear brother is not why we are here. We are here because I needed to treat your wounds, and because I need your help in the part of this play I have been fated for, at least until it is forced to come to an end."

With that he stood and extended a hand, summoning another swirling blue portal. Jeroch stayed in a seated position for a long moment, watching Saurn move around the desk toward the portal before rising to his feet. Saurn motioned for Jeroch to enter the portal first, and after a moment of hesitation and a chiding stare by his younger brother, Jeroch stepped through. Saurn followed instantly. When the two emerged from the other side of the portal, they were in another part of the Shadow Guild headquarters. A woman waited for them, one that Jeroch instantly recognized as the Sunstone Knight of the Flashing Blade, Natalia Pressen. Natalia held her ground for a long moment, her eyes not leaving the man that she knew as Vallic Ultiv.

"Natalia," Saurn said slowly, "I know that you know our guest. But you do not know him as well as you think you do. The man you know as Vallic Ultiv is in reality my brother Jeroch. My spiteful older brother if you must know. Who is not possessed of the same kind and caring demeanor as I am."

To her credit, Natalia kept her face from showing any distress.

"He is here to help us with our other guest."

At this Natalia frowned.

"Grand Master, that is not necessary. We can break the woman any time we choose. She is hanging on by a thread as it is, and we need only apply the needed pressure. She is a simple woman, one that does not understand the forces she is meddling with."

Saurn smiled.

"Of course you can break the woman," he chided. "But that is not why we need Shadow here. It's what is locked in her mind that we must have. And that, I'm afraid is beyond your skill, and mine as well."

Natalia seemed disturbed by the realization.

"Shadow here was given the ability long ago to worm his way into the minds of anyone he chose, to ferret out the truth, and where necessary to overpower the will and make people do what they would ordinarily avoid. On our world, Shadow built a great black tower. He would have mortals herded in by the hundreds day after day. They would be subjected to tortures unlike any you could ever imagine, until they became twisted and subservient to his whims. This army of thralls would then be thrown at his enemies in relentless waves, caring not for their own lives, knowing only the need to serve. In his old age, Shadow has become more pedantic."

Jeroch grimaced.

"And you have become more long-winded. If that were possible."

Saurn ignored the comment.

"Our guest has secrets locked up in her mind that no amount of torture will wring loose. But the body needs to be weakened before the gates to the mind will be left unguarded enough to be approached properly."

Natalia nodded her head.

"I cede to your wisdom, Grand Master."

Saurn approached a door on the far side of the chamber and slid it open just far enough for Jeroch to see to the other side. He saw the woman sitting, her dress ripped, blood soaking it, her long brown hair matted with sweat and blood, tracks of her tears etched into her face. Jeroch recognized her immediately, and nodded his understanding to Saurn.

"A bold plan," Jeroch said finally. "But I understand your caution. If Irene Drage does still have a connection to Talisia Masile, it could put you at risk. And even if she does not, then the knowledge that Irene still possesses will be protected in a way that would kill anyone trying to get at it, including Irene herself. It is too great a danger to ignore, and a danger that few would know could be subverted. But you know that I cannot do this alone. Invading the mind of a mortal is one thing, but unlocking the secrets of a child of the Creator is a different matter. It will take a Dark God."

Saurn frowned.

"What you ask is difficult."

Jeroch cocked his head.

"But not impossible. You have favors that can be called in I assume?"

Saurn's frown deepened.

"None that would accommodate your request. However, I believe that Natalia here can make sure you have what you need. After all, now that she is dead, she can move without the Emperor's eyes finding her."

Both Natalia and Jeroch stared in response.

"I knew that Kaitain would soon put a price on the head of all of the Knights of the Flashing Blade, and I also needed to ensure that the Empress was out of Aldere before things became untenable for all of us. So I used Natalia's face to give everyone a proper push, and also ensure that all believed her dead. Now she will be able to move throughout the land with impunity. Natalia, you can collect on the debt owed to you in Rashaleb. Say no more than you have to, and no matter what happens, do not mention my name. You may after much effort mention the name Jeroch, but nothing more. Communicate with me via normal means once the assistance is procured and I will let you know where to meet us. Liandra will shadow you to make sure trouble does not find you."

Natalia's face curled in disgust.

"I don't need Liandra's help. I can make it to Rashaleb on my own."

Saurn smiled.

"It's not you I'm concerned about my dear Natalia. When you arrive in Rashaleb, there may be more opposition than you can handle between you and your quarry. Liandra is trained to fight, you are trained to lead."

Natalia ground her teeth, but nodded and bowed to her master. As she turned to leave, Saurn cleared his throat.

"Take the dagger with you. You will need a peace offering before your words will be heard. Show them how to break it, and how to defend against its power."

Natalia bowed again slowly and turned to leave. Once she had left the room, Saurn motioned Jeroch over to the door. He slid it open again, his eyes falling on the beaten and broken woman.

"Why must it be a Dark God, Shadow?"

Jeroch joined him at the door.

"If she does have Talisia's thoughts and memories inside her, I cannot use the Blaze to access them. Only divine power can influence divine power, and I'll need to use as pure a source as possible if I want to get out of her mind alive with the information you want."

Saurn nodded.

"Are you going to tell me what you are looking for?"

Jeroch looked over to Saurn and waited.

"Talisia's true plans, whatever they are. And just how she intends to defeat Emries and Dorovar."

Jeroch waited for a long moment, waiting to see if there would be more that followed. When no words were forthcoming, Jeroch smiled.

"That's good. And here I thought you were looking for the identity of the Dragon's Tear."

Restraint of the Ephemeral

Year Three of the Just Emperor Kaitain "Dragonsbane" Lorien,
Creator's Calendar Year 1870

Darrien's head hurt, that was the first sensation that struck her when consciousness flooded back into her mind. It hurt to move, it hurt to think, and it hurt to simply exist. Something irritated the back of her neck, and after several long moments she identified the sensation was sharp blades of grass brushing against her skin. She tried to force her eyes open, but they would not cooperate. Her whole body seemed to be rebelling against her will. Finally, the stubborn lids began to part, and her eyes were shocked by the bright light that shone down upon her. The lids snapped shut again, but finally seemed to be under some level of her control. Slowly Darrien forced her eyes open again, the sunlight causing them to water slightly, which blurred her vision, but only for a few moments. Her sight finally clear, she pulled her aching body to a seated position and looked around gingerly. She was in a broad glade surrounded by a thick forest. To her left stood a large tree that looked to have been recently burned. Smoke still rolled from the trunk and branches, and there seemed to be a massive split in the center of the trunk that ran from the base all the way to the highest visible part of the tree. As Darrien forced her way back to her feet, she became aware that there were bodies lying around her. The features of the three bodies were unrecognizable as they had been literally ripped to shreds by whatever had ended their lives.

Her legs felt weak as she began to walk toward the burned-out tree, but with every stride she could feel her strength returning. However, no matter how strong her physical form felt, there was another weakness that Darrien could not ignore. She felt diminished. Whatever her sister Tess had done to her had robbed her of all of her abilities that she had been granted as the child of a Dark God. Being mortal was a new sensation to Darrien, as she had never known life without her abilities. Even as a baby she had strength and intelligence that far out-paced that of any mortal that had ever lived. Sometimes it seemed as though her physical development was far slower than her mental and power development. By her twentieth birthday she had simply stopped physically aging, and as the centuries passed, she never looked one day older. At times it was irritating, especially when she was faced with the more mature beauties that were held by the likes of Midarin and Diana. Even the man that she loved, Alderin, looked as though he were ten years older than she was. Darrien's sister Tess seemed to have a worse situation, as she barely looked to be in her teens. The problem with Tess was that she never seemed to escape the awkward emotional phase that accompanied the journey to maturity that her physical appearance denoted. Most of the time Darrien felt bad for her half-sister, but she did not pity the younger girl. Though their parentage was out of their control, how they reacted to what they were was not. Darrien had strived every day to live up to the responsibility that was her birthright, and had been a model student, learning at the feet of some of the finest heroes that had ever walked.

With her father Darrien had learned the application of power, how to harness rage, how to strike fear into the enemy, and how to punish those who did not understand the significance of standing against a member of the Dark Gods. Those lessons were tempered by the words of Aryx and Diana, who preached responsibility in the face of everything. Power always had a cost, and though one may not have seen that cost, or even felt the repercussions of their actions, there would always be a cost that would eventually need to be paid. It could be delayed, but never avoided. But it was the time she spent with Sabrina that were the most enlightening. Sabrina constantly struggled with the life that she had as a mortal, the life that she had as a god, the life that she had as the Spirit, and the life that she had as a former *Chosen One*. Though none of the Dark Gods liked to talk about their time in the Heavens, or their time on their former world of Onea, Sabrina was the most forthcoming with information.

Sabrina openly spoke about Aerith Seth, and the manner in which she wore his mantle. She had been the last of the *Chosen Ones*, and as such she had the deepest connection to the man who had been her salvation and a surrogate parent for much of her life. Sabrina described hearing his voice in the back of her mind, and being able to share his memories, his lessons, his loves, and his struggles. Though Sabrina was far from forthcoming about the latter two, she did share many stories about the man, and his time on Onea, as a member of the Army of the Fox, or the Hand of the Light. Darrien did all she could to soak up the stories of tactics and battles that happened centuries before her birth. But the fact she found the most curious was the fact that Sabrina said that when she was serving as the Spirit that it had been Aerith's voice, and not the Creator's that comforted her through the many difficult times that her service brought her. Though after Sabrina had said that, she got a look on her face as though she had said something she shouldn't have and quickly changed the subject. There was a mystery there to be solved, but Darrien had never thought enough of it to pursue it any farther, and it was never spoken of again. For her part, Darrien had never mentioned it to anyone either. Whatever secret Sabrina was holding, it was not Darrien's place to bring light to it.

As Darrien stumbled through the wide crack in the side of the massive tree, she saw something that shocked her to the core. In the middle of the huge space that lay before her was the eviscerated body of a massive and ancient dragon. Its body lay in a slumped pile, surrounded by a pool of its own dry and congealed blood. Its massive head had been ripped in half, bisected at the jaw, the lower and upper halves of it gigantic mouth laying at right angles from one another. It's great eyes were still wide open, the brilliant blue glazed over with a coating of white, like a translucent egg-shell. Cautiously Darrien approached what was now nothing more than a great husk, her heart fluttering with trepidation. As she approached, the feeling of dread filled her, and her stomach turned. Just at the edge of the pool of blood she stopped, her heart racing, the feeling of pity for the great dead beast filling her. She didn't understand why she felt the way she did, but looking at the corpse she could not help but feel as though the creature laying before her was a noble beast that deserved better than his ultimate fate.

"Tarot's will not be the last senseless loss in this war," a soft female voice came from behind Darrien, "he was a noble and wise creature, too good to be cut down in the name of mindless vengeance."

Darrien turned, but not so fast as to overwhelm her already taxed physical form. Her reflexes were diminished and it was causing her balance to falter with almost every step. If she would have turned any faster, she probably would have fallen. When her eyes came around, she found a woman's form standing several paces away from her. The woman had a lithe but athletic build, her skin toned and tan, her straight brown hair hanging loose to the middle of her back. She was dressed in a simple white dress that had no frills or adornments, and a common cloak draped over her shoulders. She was slightly shorted than Darrien, but her presence was much larger. Her almond-shaped eyes held much strength, but at the same time such sorrow.

"But Tarot's loss will not be the last in this war, and the continued travesties will gain nothing but blood and pain."

"Who are you?"

The woman was looking past Darrien, her sorrow-filled eyes resting on Tarot's corpse and the burned remains of the Council chambers that had accommodated the leadership of the dragon race. Finally her eyes fell onto the child of the Dark God.

"For the last nearly two millennia I have been called Temperance, a trait that did not serve me well during my life as a mortal. But before that, many centuries before, many lifetimes ago, I had another name. It was a name that was revered and loved by many who called me their patron. Those that did not follow the name still respected it. In life, I was called Faelara."

Darrien's expression didn't change.

"That doesn't tell me who you are."

Faelara's lips curled into a subtle smile.

"You may not have your father's manner, but you have his pragmatism. Just as a name has power, if you don't understand the source of the name you cannot comprehend that power. And if I did not want you to understand what came before, I would not have appeared to you as I have now. Nor would I have ensured that you were brought here. Though I do not have the power that I once did, and perhaps it is better that I do not, the power that I do have has proven to be both useful and confining. Trusting others has been a struggle, and hopefully will prove more fruitful with you."

Faelara turned away from the carnage and stepped through the charred opening back into the grassy glade and the bright sunlight. When the sunlight hit the woman, to Darrien's eyes it seemed that she sparkled like the stars for a brief moment and become almost insubstantial. However when the woman turned back to face Darrien, her form solidified again.

"Like your father," Faelara began, "I was once mortal. I was born to the head of the dominant religious order on my world, Loinn, and fated to become the High Priestess from the moment of my birth. Our patron was Raenera, and our entire world was dedicated to serving her will."

Darrien found herself sinking down to sit on a small dirt mound. But apparently the blank look on her face betrayed her lack of understanding.

"You don't know who Raenera is, do you?"

There was a hint of disappointment in Faelara's voice.

"My father and the other Dark Gods didn't speak about their time in the Heavens. And they don't like to talk about Onea."

Faelara nodded.

"It makes things more difficult, but there are worse things I suppose. Sometimes correcting information is more tedious and difficult than relaying it for the first time. I'm sure you know the names Emries and Halicon."

Darrien nodded.

"The Creator had five children, Emries, Halicon, Pyrrus, Talisia, and Raenera. From time to time, each has been entrusted with worlds to shower their attention upon and to make in their image. My world was one of Raenera's worlds, and as such it was a pillar of order, law, and simplicity. Those who follow the teachings of Raenera value order over everything, and while Raenera does not forbid experimentation with art, she does prefer utilitarian expressions. As such all of the cities built in her honor consist of gleaming pillars of white, dotted with pristine buildings, straight roads, and perfectly kept gardens. The Disciples of Law roam the streets to ensure that those who dedicate themselves to Raenera's teachings do not stray. There is such beauty in the simplicity that it changes your perception of life and color."

Darrien could not suppress a shudder.

"It sounds so cold."

Faelara nodded slightly.

"Cold, perhaps, but no less beautiful. Just as the Disciples of Law were entrusted in enforcing the doctrine of our patron, there was an order that dedicated itself to the worship and furthering of the beliefs and understanding of Raenera's law and love. The high priests and priestesses of the temples dedicated in Her honor were given access to the tomes of Raenera's wisdom. When I became of age, I was allowed access into the great reliquary and given access to the tomes of wisdom. For days I stayed deep in the bowels of the church, pouring over the pages, trying to make sense of the words. But though it was written in the language of our people, it was as though I was seeing the words for the first time and didn't understand their meaning or their relation to one another. It was all gibberish. I began to doubt everything I had ever been taught. I began to think that everything I had ever believed was based on nothing but mindless and senseless ravings. But in time I began to see it for what it was. It took days, sleepless days, subsisting only on bread and water that I began to see the truth. The writings were gibberish, and the process was nothing more than a test of faith. I was not going to fail the test before me, so I surrendered myself and prayed for guidance from Raenera. I gave my will away, my doubt, my fear. Suddenly I was filled with such light and such power that I felt as though I was going to burst. It was as though her hands were caressing my face, and her love was filling me to overflowing. When I opened my eyes once again, the words on the pages had changed, and I could read them. For days I continued, my supply of food and water gone, but I continued. Raenera's power and wisdom filled me, and I no longer was fettered by the limitations of mortality. I had become her servant and become an extension of her love."

The sadness in Faelara's eyes was replaced for a moment with a look of such pride, but then the pride shattered and longing filled her eyes.

"I remember the day that doubt filled me again, and I have never felt whole again. But I have not arrived there yet. For years, my order held our world in perpetual peace and tranquility. All had everything they needed. There was no crime, no poverty, no hunger, no sedition, no rebellion, no war, no unnatural death. Raenera's love and wisdom and law created a paradise. But such a construct was not destined to last. Though my order was devout in their love, emptiness began to wake in some of my brothers and sisters. They longed for a more personal connection to our patron. They desired to walk with her and learn more of her wisdom. One of our brothers, a man named Dorovar, was approached with an offer, one that proved to be a poison that would plague our world. But he was devout, and believed that he was doing what Raenera wished of him. Others in the order were jealous of him, jealous of his visions given to him by the Goddess. He was ostracized. His near expulsion from our order was a great blow to me, as Dorovar and I were to be married as ordained by the High Priestess. "

A sudden understanding filled Darrien's eyes.

"That was the bargain that brought the dragons to your world."

Faelara nodded.

"The memory of that day is seared into my memory as though it happened only yesterday. I stood on the steps of my temple, its brilliant white stone gleaming in the sunlight. Then, above our heads, the sun was blotted out by huge winged shapes. They swooped and soared, filling the sky. Passing over us like an army preparing to wipe out everything in its path. A new fear could be felt in the streets of the city from that moment on. A feeling of impending doom that had not been there since the last rebellion, which was nothing more than a distant memory. As the days passed into weeks, and the huge beasts remained just on the edge of notice, the agitation in the people grew. It made no sense to those who tried to keep the peace. The dragons did not pose a direct threat and did not seem to be interested in our cities or in our people. And yet, the agitation of the people grew. Before long, people began to arm themselves and organize into hunting parties. There was a feeling that the dragons posed and imminent threat, and just because they had not openly struck against the people did not mean that they would not in time. Better to strike first than be caught by surprise. Even the Disciples of Law seemed bent on attacking the dragons, and no amount of preaching for patience and tolerance would do. Dorovar, though he had been expelled from the order moved among the people, trying to convince them to lay down their arms. He said that to attack such creatures would only bring destruction down upon the people. Those who were jealous of Dorovar suddenly changed from speaking of tolerance to speaking of the dragons as affronts to Raenera's law. That their very presence was a violation of the covenants held between the people and the Goddess. The fervor grew and spread. Whole cities began to turn into military complexes whose only goal was to eradicate the dragons and drive them from Loinn."

Faelara took a deep breath and closed her eyes for a moment. When she opened them again, Darrien could see that the woman was desperately trying to hold back tears.

"The war was over before it began, and if only we had been wise enough to see what was coming. We managed to kill one of them in the first days, but the retribution was terrible. For that one act, that one death, the dragons burned five of our cities to the ground, killed thousands of people, and inflicted such damage upon our farming and trade infrastructure that it would take months to recover. But what should have been a clear sign of our impending defeat only served to embolden our people. The attacks not only continued, but escalated. More cities burned, more people died, and the preaching for tolerance and patience quickly turned into the pounding of war drums. But people continued to die and suffer and they turned to my order for help. The only place we could turn was Raenera. But she had forsaken us for our arrogance and our violation of her laws. That was when Emries and Talisia appeared, offering us the power we needed to smite our enemies."

Darrien frowned.

"And you didn't ask what it would cost."

Faelara's expression was stone.

"The cost did not matter at that point. People were dying, cities were burning. Our world was being reduced to a cinder, and we were being offered the opportunity to take the fight to our enemies and save our world. In time we learned the depth of the deception that had been visited upon us. No matter how many we killed, no matter how much havoc we rained down upon our enemies, our planet was dying. In the end, the dragons made their deal with Dorovar, a deal that we necessitated with our arrogance. The few of us that were still standing when the war was over could do nothing but watch impotently as the fires consumed the world that we had worked so hard to save. But our misguidedness had cost us everything. But we thought the only things we were going to lose were our lives and our world. But the millions of lives of our followers necessitated that we suffer, and so our lives were not enough of a payment, our eternal damnation to the service of those who tempted us with power was the only possible fate that awaited us."

Darrien nodded.

"From what I know of Emries, no deal with him is without a terrible price, and he can't be trusted no matter what. His agendas are always more than anyone can see. Treachery to him is like breathing."

Faelara shook her head.

"It was not Emries who proved to be the one who made us suffer. It was Talisia. She had designs far past making her sister suffer. It was as if she had orchestrated everything all along. From bringing the dragons to my world, making the pact with Dorovar, starting the war, giving us our power, our fall from grace, Dorovar's immortality and madness. When we died,

Talisia rescued our souls from the void, held them chained to her will for years until just the right moment. Then, once Dorovar had been captured by agents of the Creator and was imprisoned in the Vault of Terrors, Talisia launched her rebellion. Her goal was to kill her brother Pyrrus, but her secondary goal was to cause enough damage that her expulsion from the Heavens was assured. Before she was cast down however, she entrusted our souls to one of her agents. When the gods from Onea began their rebellion, Talisia's agent was among them, and when they were cast down, our souls were brought along with them."

Darrien's eyes opened wide.

"One of the Dark Gods is Talisia's disciple? Who?"

Faelara shook her head.

"I don't know. Though I have spent much time trying to discover that truth. What I do know though is that after the Fall, we were left in the crater left by the Dark Gods' fall. Left there to be discovered by the master smith Arturious Demascious. The poor man was there only to find stone for his experiments. What he found was so much more than that. The stone that he sampled was the vessel in which our souls were stored, and free from our confinement we swarmed the poor man, invading his mind, and filling him with the horrors that we had seen, and the horrors that we knew Dorovar had committed during his time floating through the nothingness. By design, Arturious confined himself to his workshop, toiling sleeplessly on the weapons that would become the Sacred Weapons of the Knights of the Flashing Blade, the vessels for the souls of the fallen order. Now our souls would be imprisoned for all time in tombs of steel. Our souls, the only keys that could free our compatriot from his prison."

A dark light shimmered in Darrien's eyes.

"So how are you free?"

"The weapons that were our tombs were enchanted with abilities that mocked our failings. But at the heart of each weapon lay our damaged and tainted souls. Under the right conditions, each of the weapons could be broken and we would be released, breaking one of the seals on Dorovar's prison. But it didn't take all of us being freed to free Dorovar from the

Vault. But portions of Dorovar's power were sealed away as well, hidden away from his mind. He is diminished, but as more of our order are freed from their tombs, then more of his abilities will return. In time, he will be a weapon that will be unstoppable. Talisia's weapon. And she will use him to destroy everything that stands against her, including the Creator."

Darrien pushed herself back to her feet.

"If Dorovar is strong enough to destroy the Creator, then he could kill Talisia with a thought. How is that a weapon that she can use?"

"Make no mistake," Faelara answered, "Talisia is a being of treachery so vast that it defies description. She has had this planned for millennia, and she would not allow a weapon of her devising to be without weakness that she could exploit. She knows exactly how to destroy Dorovar, and she will use that secret when the need arises and not before."

Darrien felt her heart fall.

"So why bring me here? Why tell me this if everything is hopeless?"

Faelara put one hand on Darrien's shoulder.

"Nothing is hopeless for the daughter of a warrior. Nothing is hopeless for one who believes. I doubted my beliefs once and watched my world fall. I followed the beliefs of others, and was betrayed. Only your own beliefs matter, and I can show you a path that will lead you to the salvation of your people. There are more secrets in the Vault of Terrors than Dorovar could discover for he was blinded by his need for revenge. Perhaps there you will find a weapon of your own."

Rivals

Year Four of the Just Emperor Kaitain "Dragonsbane" Lorien, Creator's Calendar Year 1871

Nathan Sandar looked on in a mixture of disbelief and expectation as the man who was his father in name only emerged from yet another would be coffin, this time seemingly restored to his vaunted title and position of Brother of Angels, complete with enough power to pose more than a few seconds challenge to his progeny. However, while the re-elevation of Gwydeon Sandar may have been a shock to some, it was an eventuality that Emries had prepared Nathan for. Men like Gwydeon Sandar and Logan Ranthall had a troubling knack for defying expectations and becoming incredible nuisances when it was most problematic. Victory assured, one of them would likely emerge at the last possible second to save the day. However, this was not some fairy tale told to a stupid child to make them believe that the hero always saved the day and that anything was possible. This was reality, and reality said that no matter what, the strongest would ensure that their will would dictate the course of the future. Once upon a time, Gwydeon and Logan could have been considered the strongest. Their convictions and their faith had carried them through times so dark that most mortals would have crawled into a hole and waited for death to take them. But now their convictions had been shaken, and their faith had been eroded to nothing. Believing in the rightness of their cause would not be enough against Emries and those that he trained. There was enough doubt in the future to drown thousands of the most pious men, and Nathan would strike the first blow for the future by ripping the wings off the Brother of Angels and casting him down to the fires that should have claimed him long ago.

Gwydeon to his credit did not seem as though he was eager for the confrontation, nor did he seem to be worried about the others who had been the victims of Nathan's aggression. Though his wife lay broken and bleeding in a crater only a few feet from where he stood, he did not rush to her aid like some long lost puppy. He held his ground, his eyes never leaving Nathan. Nathan kept his eyes on Gwydeon as well as he slowly floated back to the ground, a blade of pure light energy forming in his hand. He had been waiting for this opportunity for millennia, and it was far beyond his hopes that he would get the chance for revenge against his father so soon. But here it was, and Nathan would make sure to make the most of the opportunity. But Nathan was also not stupid. There were too many plans in motion and too many tasks yet to be accomplished for his patron to be removed from the game so soon after it had begun. This errand to Rashaleb was to inflict pain, nothing more. It was a great warning shot from Emries to remind the so-called Dark Gods that they were not invincible.

"The black wings are a nice touch," Nathan said coldly, "but cunning fashion statements will not make you more of a match for me. Let's see how you fare."

Nathan hesitated for only a moment before charging forward. As Gwydeon prepared himself for the strike that would come, he saw that within the pulsing light of the blade of energy that the younger man held in his hands was the tell-tale crystalline structure of a blade like the one Emries constantly favored in combat. The clear pulsing blade arced downward, and Gwydeon raised his own blade to meet the powerful strike. Seconds stretched on as the two combatants leaned into the fulcrum created by their blades, neither one able to gain an advantage on the other. Nathan's features twisted into a hard sneer, hatred etched into every wrinkle. Despite himself Gwydeon did his best to keep his features calm, letting the emotion of the moment pass through him like mist across the face of a calm lake. The contest of wills continued, beads of perspiration budding onto Nathan and Gwydeon's foreheads. The ground beneath Gwydeon's feet was shaky from his crash to the ground, and he could feel the instability begin to weaken his stance. Gwydeon's balance unintentionally shifted, drawing Nathan's blade closer, shifting the balance so that the crossed blades were only inches from Gwydeon's throat. Gwydeon felt Nathan's lunge a moment before it happened, and had he been a second slower, the blades would have ripped into his neck and probably ended his life. At the last possible second, Gwydeon turned his left foot and leg, changing the point of leverage and sending Nathan and his blade sliding off past its intended prey. However, Nathan recovered quickly and brought his blade back around in a vicious slash intended to separate Gwydeon's head from the rest of his body. Gwydeon was quick enough to block the blow and prevent the end of the combat, but had not set his feet firmly enough to prevent being thrown backwards. Nathan did not follow up on the assault and waited as he watched Gwydeon recover his feet. He knew that his erstwhile father was more than a competent opponent and many of his opponents had met their end rushing in when patience was the proper tactic. Once perhaps Nathan would have been rash and out of control, but time with Emries had honed his patience and practicality to a vicious edge. The father and son began to circle each other, waiting for the tiny opening that would have been missed by most of lesser skill. Gwydeon was the first to strike, letting a long lazy slash out at his opponent. Nathan easily parried the blow and returned with one of his own, a deep thrust at Gwydeon's heart. The taller man flapped his black wings once and pulled himself back away from the tip of the blade, giving enough of an opening that the strike found nothing but air. Setting his feet again, Nathan wheeled the blade of his sword over his head in a mockery of his father's practiced defensive posture.

"If I wanted to, I could have had you there, father. You're much slower than I remember, and weaker. If this is too much for you, I can always take your head now and spare you the embarrassment of being out-fought. There is no shame in letting the superior man win, father. You should know, you have made a legend of proving your superiority. But that ends now. Lie down and die like a good dog should."

Gwydeon responded by beating his wings once again, this time initiating a charge that Nathan only half expected. The slash was much more precise than the last, but the result was no different. Nathan parried the blow and let the block once again flow into a quick controlled thrust. This time however, Gwydeon was not content to fall back in retreat. He lowered his shoulder and ducked under the attack, letting the flat of the blade pass just fractions of an inch over the back of his head. Wings pulled tight against his back, Gwydeon continued forward until his shoulder struck true in the center of Nathan's chest, forcing all of the air out of his lungs and throwing him backwards. However, the strike was not enough to force the young man off of his feet. The two men locked eyes, and it was Gwydeon's voice who found the silence next.

"The blade is not the only weapon in battle, Nathan. From your toes to your head, every part of you must act in unison if you are going to defeat a superior opponent. The longer it takes you to realize that, the less chance you have of actually beating me. No matter what skill and power Emries may have imparted in you, there is one truth that you cannot refute. I have more skill, more experience, and now…"

A bright green aura burst into being around Gwydeon, the power of the Blaze wreathing him in bright fire.

"I have more power than you or your patron can resist."

Nathan sneered.

"Emries was the greatest of all of the Children of the Creator, and his brother was a coward who hid behind the rules of the Creator. Emries is a visionary who will reshape this cosmos for the betterment of all, and not even the mythical hero Gwydeon Sandar can stand in the way, no matter his delusions of grandeur. But come father; let us see how well you wield your new parlor tricks."

Nathan charged the next moment, and Gwydeon countered with a charge of his own. The two collided with a sound like thunder and the force of their collision radiated in all directions, triggering avalanches high up in the surrounding mountains. The escalation was extreme, both pushing every ounce of power they had at their disposal into the series of strikes, blocks, counters, and feints. The two moved in a deadly dance at incredible speed, leaving streaks of white and green in their wake, ghostly trails of the deadly accuracy of the combatants. The blades of pure energy struck each other in small explosions that sent more shock waves battering the surrounding area like tidal waves against a pristine shore. Strike after strike flowed between the two, highlighted with bursts of flame and huge gusts of wind. Faster and faster the two moved until suddenly a plume of red erupted into the space between the two men. The tip of Gwydeon's blade had struck true to the center of Nathan's chest, leaving a deep jagged scar. The young man formerly known as the Ram of the prophecies fell back, his chest rising and falling quickly from the exertion, the evil smile still sitting on his lips. Without a word he ran his free hand over the scar, and as he wiped away the blood, so too did he wipe away the wound itself. He cocked his head to one side, regarding Gwydeon.

"You Dark Gods never had the knack for healing, but Emries has taken a long time to perfect the art. So, unless you give me no chance to even touch a wound, then there is no way you can defeat me. And don't think about just cutting my hands off. I can regenerate a limb with a thought. Face it father, you are outmatched in every way possible, and I'm only humoring you by resorting to mundane weapons like swords. Emries taught that you had to give your opponent hope before ripping it away. It was a hard lesson to learn I must admit, but in the end I think it was worth it. Especially when I get to see the look on your face after I've beaten you."

Gwydeon didn't see the strike that followed until it was too late. Nathan extended both of his hands toward Gwydeon and a portal appeared inches from Nathan's extended fingers. The beam of pure divine energy flooded into the portal and emerged from the portal that winked into existence behind Gwydeon. The beam struck true in Gwydeon's back making him stumble forward. The portal behind him closed and then opened in front of him at his feet. The next strike was a fist constructed of solid steel and rock that connected to Gwydeon's chin sending him sprawling backwards. When the portal opened a third time, the blast of ice struck the Brother of Angels firmly in the chest and sent him to the ground. Above where he lay, the portal opened again, and this time it was Nathan's hands that emerged from the portal, wrapping around Gwydeon's throat and squeezing tightly. Blood pounded in Gwydeon's ears so loudly that he could barely hear Nathan's taunting voice above the din.

"You see father? This is just a sample of the new abilities that Emries has been honing in his time away from the world of mortals. You Dark Gods have been complacent in your superiority, knowing that nothing could touch you in your Dark Citadel. Emries has had millennia to learn how he was beaten and to make sure that it never happens again. There are a thousand ways that I could flay the flesh from your bones right now, and there is nothing that you would be able to do to stop me. It's almost not worth it to kill you now. Perhaps I should just let you wallow in your failure while I gut my poor mother. But no, I think it would be far better to watch her cry over your dismembered body before I rip the still beating heart from her chest. Goodbye father. This has been…disappointing."

Gwydeon felt Nathan's hands squeeze tighter around his throat, and above the pounding blood he could hear the bones in his neck begin to crack under the pressure. It would only be a matter of seconds before Nathan made good on his threat of ending Gwydeon's life, and unless the Dark God could quickly come up with a tactic that would buy him more than a few seconds of breathing room, the fight would be over with lethal consequences. Reaching into his new reserves of power, Gwydeon took hold of the edges of the portal in his mind and tried to will the swirling blue construct closed. However, no matter how much force and will he exerted, he could not wrest control of the portal away from Nathan. Changing his focus, Gwydeon remembered a trick from his time fighting against Nightwing. He channeled flows of earth and water into the feathers of his wings and solidified them into razor-sharp daggers. In as fast a motion as he could manage as the darkness was beginning to encroach on his vision, Gwydeon brought the wings up around him like a shield, severing Nathan's arms at the wrist. There was a cry of pain from where Nathan stood, and the portal snapped shut. As much as Gwydeon wanted to bounce back to his feet, all he could manage was a slow rise, getting to one knee and locking his focus back on his opponent. Though blood flowed freely from the severed appendages, Nathan's countenance was not one of concern. The flow of blood ceased after only a few moments, and the severed hands simply reconstituted themselves out of the nothingness.

"You see father, there is nothing that you can do that can hurt me, and my skills have progressed far past your meager understanding of power. I'm sure in your day the little tricks that you know were enough to give you the upper hand against the likes of the pathetic phasia, but now, against those trained in the application of real power, you are hopelessly overmatched. Now, as much as I would like to continue teaching you the folly of your arrogance, it is time to end your pathetic existence once and for all."

Nathan raised one hand over his head and light energy began to collect in such quantity and brilliance that in a matter of seconds it was hotter and brighter than the twin suns. The next moment a group of arrows struck Nathan in the back and exploded in unison sending pieces of the young man flying in all directions. The victory was short lived, as mere seconds after detonation the pieces of the servant of Emries pulled themselves back together. Once reconstituted, Nathan whirled on his heels and let loose a brutal assault of wind, fire and rock that struck Midarin full in the chest and sent her flying backwards. When she finally stuck the ground, blood flooded from her mouth and nose and a huge gash had been carved in her side. Several of her ribs were exposed under the ruptured skin, and the pool of blood that she lay in grew as the seconds passed. When Nathan whirled back around to face Gwydeon, he found that his father had quickly closed the distance between them and launched in with a renewed assault of his own. The first blow took the form of a hundred small feather-shaped daggers of ice and stone that whipped from Gwydeon's wings in Nathan's direction. Most of the assault missed, but it served the purpose that Gwydeon intended, it shifted Nathan's focus long enough for Gwydeon to close the distance and land several pummeling strikes to the young man's midsection with Blaze-wrapped fists. Blood spurted from Nathan's mouth and nose and Gwydeon continued to connect with blow after blow to Nathan's unprotected midsection. Reaching deep into himself, Gwydeon focused his power on increasing not only the strength of his blows but the speed at which they connected to Nathan's stomach and ribs. One last hard palm strike to the sternum sent Nathan flying backwards. However, moments before Nathan struck the ground a portal opened beneath him, and he fell through. The other side of the portal winked into existence behind Gwydeon and allowed Nathan to launch into a brutal counterattack. Twin blasts of fire and ice erupted from Nathan's fingers, but just before they struck, Gwydeon felt the blow coming and wrapped his wings around his body creating an almost impregnable shield. The fire and ice stuck to Gwydeon's wings like oil, and when Gwydeon thrust his wings backward he flung pods of fire and ice back at their source. Several struck Nathan in the chest before he was able to move clear of the line of assault. When Gwydeon turned to face his son, the young man was several hundred feet away, blood smeared across his face and bare chest, and hate smoldered in his eyes hotter and brighter than the closest stars. Each hand was wreathed with brilliant white energy and Gwydeon knew that the only thought in Nathan's mind was the hatred for his father and his desire to end the man's life quickly and as violently as possible. Whatever happened in the next few moments, it was clear that the battle would be decided in the next collision.

"Emries may have taught you good use of your powers, Nathan, but he obviously never corrected that arrogant nature of yours. As long as you're so sure you're always going to win, you'll continue to lose."

The words felt hollow as they passed from Gwydeon's lips, but he hoped they would have enough of an effect on Nathan's psyche that his next attack would not be as focused or controlled. Any advantage that Gwydeon could create across the next few moments could mean the difference between life and death. Nathan growled and let a blast of pure energy erupt from his hands before charging. The blast went wide and Gwydeon took the opportunity to use one of Nathan's own tactics against him. Gwydeon opened a portal at Nathan's feet, and as expected the young man changed his focus for a fraction of a second to avoid the obvious assault. However, Gwydeon never intended for Nathan to fall into the portal, instead Gwydeon reached through the end of the portal that winked into existence in front of him and grabbed Nathan's ankle. The attack caught Nathan completely by surprise and Gwydeon pulled as hard as he could at Nathan's ankle, pulling his leg through the portal and then closing it. The portal severed Nathan's left leg at the knee and sent the young man sprawling to the ground. His recklessness however did not give Nathan the opportunity to let the energy in his hands dissipate as he fell, and when he struck the ground, the twin balls of energy in his hands detonated. Blood splattered in all directions, and the young man was slow to pull himself back together. Taking another page out of the young man's book, Gwydeon wasted no time in following up on his attack. Gwydeon's wings made it easy to cross the distance between himself and Nathan before the young man had an opportunity to recover. Gwydeon's next attack was more in line with something that Pike would have done. He allowed twin blades of fire to form and brought them down over and over again on the prone body of his son, severing both arms and the remaining leg from Nathan's torso. Channeling flows of dark energy, Gwydeon wrapped each of the limbs in cocoons of chaotic power, and then did the same with Nathan's torso. Portals appeared under each of the cocoons, and after they dropped through, the portals winked out of existence. Though Nathan had the uncanny ability to pull himself together and heal wounds rapidly, it would take him some time with his body and limbs scattered to different places in the cosmos.

The extreme exertion of power had pushed Gwydeon to his limits, and left him totally exhausted. He fell to his knees and tried to take a deep breath but his chest seized. The cough that followed expelled blood onto the ground, and led to several more coughs that produced more and more blood from Gwydeon's aching chest. It took a few long moments for Gwydeon to get back to his feet, and though he was standing again, the rumbling in his chest and stomach would not subside. No matter the pains and illness that filled his body, Gwydeon's only thoughts were for his wife who lay in a crater hundreds of yards away. His wings hung limp at his back, and his right arm ached with such ferocity that Gwydeon didn't know if he could lift it. Gwydeon turned to make his way to where Midarin lay, but when he raised his eyes to try to locate her, he saw a robed person standing half way between where he stood and where Midarin lay. At first, Gwydeon though that his eyes were playing tricks on him, a side-effect of the damage to his head and the loss of blood. It was then that the brilliant white wings extended from behind the robed figure. Power radiated from the being in ways that could not be mistaken for anyone that had been in the presence of the Creator. There was only one possibility for the identity of the being that stood before Gwydeon.

"I was wondering how long it would take before the Creator would send one of the Servants to find me. I should have known you would have waited until I wasn't at my best."

The robed figure made no movements, but when it spoke, Gwydeon's ears could make out both male and female voices intertwined speaking in dozens of languages and in dozens of dialects all at the same time.

"You must understand, Gwydeon that you were never far from the Creator's sight. The Creator has always found your actions to be noble and with proper intentions, even though they have been shaped by a misguided understanding of the politics of the universe. You have fought against the Children of the Creator, and you led a rebellion against the Throne, and while any of those actions have warranted your destruction, it is your purity of purpose that has saved you from a purge. However, your alliances with the Phoenix and the Abomination have threatened your position as the Brother of Angels, and have led the Creator to order your termination. We know the goals of the Abomination, and though he may have different motivations than Dorovar and the Children, it is his arrogance and his single-mindedness that make his pursuit of this blasphemous fallacy troubling and worthy of the Creator's attention. Thusly, your termination has been mandated by the Throne and given to me to accomplish."

Gwydeon wasted no time in allowing a sword of crystalline energy to form in his hand.

"So the Creator sent the Spirit to destroy me, and of course you waited until after I expended most of my strength in a fight before you took your shot. I guess I shouldn't be surprised."

The pure white wings of the Spirit fluttered for a moment and then radiated with brilliant white light. The light flashed and Gwydeon suddenly felt as though all of the injuries in his body and all of the exhaustion that held him dissipated.

"Your physical condition should no longer be your concern. But I'm sure you are quite well aware Gwydeon that there will be nothing fair about this fight. I am the embodiment of the Creator's power on the mortal plain, and no amount of power that you have inherited from Halicon will give you an advantage against me. Nathan may have pushed you with his sheer ferocity and unabashed brutality in the application of his powers, but no amount of guile or tactical proficiency will avail you against me."

Gwydeon pulled his shoulders back.

"Did Evan give Aerith the same speech before Aerith cut him down?"

The Spirit seemed to hesitate for a moment.

"Do not delude yourself Gwydeon. Comparing the Voice or any of the other Servants to me is a mistake. Their powers are finite, mine are infinite. But I make you an offer for the sake of the Creator's historical fondness for you. I will restrict the use of my powers to those granted the other Servants, and we shall duel one another using conventional weapons only. No direct applications of power for offensive purposes, short of enhancing your own physical strength or agility."

Gwydeon set his jaw and tried hard to hide the grimace.

"So, a duel then."

The Spirit nodded.

"You have a deal."

The Spirit nodded once more, and let a sword of pure crystalline energy form in its hand as well. With its other hand, it pulled back the hood of its cloak, revealing a woman's features and short blond hair.

"You've never beaten me before, Gwydeon," Eldar Merin said with cold determination that hid an undertone of remorse, "and I think we both know that you can't beat me now."

CHAPTER 74

Chapter LXXV

The Climb Will Kill You
Long Before the Fall

Year Four of the Just Emperor Kaitain "Dragonsbane" Lorien, Creator's Calendar Year 1871

Pike's skin crawled as he looked up at the abomination wearing the name Dorovar. Despite all of their years on Espre, Pike had not sought much more information about the creature other than he was a criminal so vile that the Creator had mobilized all of his Servants and angels in an effort to capture him. The effort had caused the death of Evan Sinn's wife, Meredith Heron, as well as hundreds of angels and others that directly served the will of the Creator. Though Dorovar had been captured, his deeds had not gone unnoticed by all who could see past terrestrial constraints. Many of the Creator's worlds had been shattered by Dorovar. Every world that he set foot on was instantly embroiled in wars so terrible that either the planet itself would shudder and shatter from the weight of the destruction, or the inhabitants would simply fight themselves into complete and total extinction, leaving only Dorovar standing atop and mountain of corpses. It was said that he made a deal with the dragons that granted him terrible power and immortality. But as Pike forced himself back to his feet and called Fury back to his hand, thoughts ran through his mind of all of the other immortal foes that he had faced. He had not been afraid of any of them, and this Dorovar would certainly not be the first to cause Pike Rhuiden to lose his nerve. Seeing the sparks of defiance in Pike's eyes, Dorovar sighed audibly. However, instead of taking steps back away from his foe, Dorovar blinked back through the space, moving through his own will rather than through physical exertion. To Pike's eyes, it was no different than the frantic beating of a hummingbird's wings.

Pike Rhuiden had never been considered a tactical genius. In fact, were anyone to say that Pike employed tactics at all would have been gravely misinformed. Pike was very much a straight-forward warrior. He knew only what was in front of his face, and as long as he had his weapon in hand, he wouldn't stop until he had torn his way through his opposition. The beginning of this battle with the immortal Dorovar would be no different than any other. Pike screamed in rage and charged forward, the head of his ancient axe crashing down on the man in the dark gray robe with silver accents. Fury found nothing with this strike, as Dorovar was simply gone as the gleaming blade passed through the air where he had been only moments earlier. Pike was not deterred as the axe flashed out again, this time aiming for where Dorovar now stood. Again, the blade passed harmlessly through nothing. Pike feinted toward Dorovar's new location and then struck in a wide arch that was intended to land where Dorovar would be next. But instead of striking something as Pike had expected Dorovar had vanished completely as though he had anticipated the strike and reappeared several paces away from where Pike stood fuming. Rage was building in Pike. It was obvious that the creature was either playing with Pike or testing him. But this was no different than what Halicon or Emries had done once upon a time. They were always supremely confident in their abilities right up until the moment that a sword was buried in their guts. Pike had picked up enough tricks over the centuries to turn that arrogance against even the most powerful opponent.

He couldn't help the fact that one half of his mouth cocked into a smile as he formulated his next strike. Pike held several flows of power in the back of his mind and kept them just below the surface so that they could not be sensed, a technique that Aryx had taught him long ago. In a single deft motion, Pike reared back and let Fury fly from his hands toward Dorovar. At the same time, Pike let the flows of power break the surface, first forming a portal to Pike's left whose exit opened a split-second later behind Dorovar. It took only another heartbeat for Pike to channel the flows of ice through the portal. Nearly instantly the ice enveloped Dorovar, holding him immobile and freezing him solid. The next moment, Fury struck the frozen form, and a sickening shattering sound could be heard resounding through the countryside. Frozen pieces of the creature flew in all direction, leaving the legs standing upright, one broken at the knee, the other at the hip. Dorovar's head rolled around on the ground for a long moment before coming to a rest near a large rock several feet away from Pike.

It took little effort for Pike to call Fury back to his hand. The two had been joined together for far too long, and the axe was almost like a third arm at this point. Power flowed through both of them equally, and Fury was often the conduit through which Pike's anger and hatred flowed. There were even times that it seemed like the axe knew what Pike wanted it to do long before Pike knew himself. At this moment, there was no question about the next course of action. It was one that would satisfy both the weapon's bloodlust, and the growing sense of justice and retribution in Pike's heart. Pike nudged Dorovar's frozen head with his left foot, rolling it into position by the rock, with his face pointing upward. Pike took a long moment to look down at the creature's face. It struck Pike that Dorovar at one time must have been human, much like Pike and the other Dark Gods had been. But instead of following the light, Dorovar had been compelled to know only darkness. He chose his path, and this was the place that his threat would end. Taking Fury in both hands, Pike raised the ancient weapon high and then brought the gleaming blade crashing down, splitting Dorovar's head in two like a ripe melon. Pulling Fury from where it had buried itself in the ground, Pike let the weapon rest on his shoulder before turning his attention back to the shattered inn where his original quarry had been. Emperor Kaitain Lorien had not escaped Pike's notice, and Pike would have his wife back no matter how many fell before him, even if he had to spill a river of blood.

Pike had taken only a handful of steps toward the inn before he heard the low laughter begin behind him.

* * * * * * * * * * * *

Korin Melcab looked around bewildered. Only moments ago he had been on the verge of crushing the life out of the leader of the Dark Gods.

Then the robed man had appeared and Korin was sent elsewhere in the blink of an eye. Instinctively Korin knew the identity of the robed man, and though it filled him with annoyance that he had been pushed out of the fight, he would not dare question the will of Dorovar. It had been Dorovar's servant Jerah that had found him all those years ago. For the first few years, Jerah had taught Korin everything he wanted to know. He could speak a dozen languages, knew the identities of every person with power that had walked the Heavens, and knew over a hundred ways to kill a mortal. It took ten years before Korin was made aware of his parentage.

Looking around his surroundings, it was somehow fitting that the memory of the first meeting with his family would come to his mind. Korin stood in the middle of a massive field of snow and ice, the wind whipping around him like scythe blades of cold. However because of Korin's nature, elements could not break through his tough hide. That he had his father to thank for. Which brought Korin back to memories of the day Jerah had imparted to him what would be coming. Two women simply appeared one day at the door of the small cottage in the Pritan Islands, the only home Korin had ever known. The first and older of the two had a cold wrapped around her that rivaled even Jerah's icy disposition. She called herself Talisia Masile, and said that she was Korin's mother. The other woman, looking as though she had just broken into her twenties, had small black horns emerging from her head and broad black wings that spread from just below her shoulder blades. The wings were not bat-like or angelic with feathers. They looked more like they were constructed from black lace or at the very least a conglomeration of spider webs. The younger woman had identified herself as Seraphina Masile, Korin's half-sister. Seraphina did not stay for long, and seemed irritated by the fact she had to be there at all. Talisia though seemed to take great interest in Korin, wanting to know everything about his upbringing. Korin was evasive as he was trained to be, and never breathed a word about the woman he had known as his mother for almost ten years. Talisia would not know about Jerah from his mouth. He would not flaunt Dorovar's will, no matter what the Child of the Creator tried to make Korin believe.

However, Talisia was quite clear that Korin had a purpose in what was coming. He was a member of something called the Hand of Chaos, and he would help Talisia bring an end to all of the indignities that she had suffered at the hands of the Creator and her siblings. She also told Korin that he was bred for one purpose and one purpose only.

In the Rebellion in the Heavens that had earned Talisia her banishment to the world of Espre, Talisia had made several deals in order to secure the complicity of the factions of the armies of the dragons and angels that would follow her into battle. One bargain was made with the angels, an easy enough deal. All it cost her was the creation of her daughter Seraphina. She was half angel and half demon, a creature that would not owe allegiance to anyone but Talisia, but whose blood allowed those angels who drank it to disobey the call of the Creator. The second deal was far more costly. In order to secure the assistance of the dragons, Talisia made a blood pact with Shadowweaver, the most powerful opponent of the Creator in the ancient race. This coupling would result in Korin's birth. Korin was the first of his kind, a melding of dragon and Child of the Creator, a vessel that could be filled with nearly limitless power. Talisia made it clear that Korin's power could even surpass that held by Seraphina because she was not a being of flesh and blood, and had constraints based on the fact that she was a construct of power, not a living creature. Talisia hinted at a third deal, but would not give any details on it. It seemed almost as though she was ashamed of what she had to do to fuel that part of her rebellion. Regardless, Korin was quickly pressed into service, and he found himself on the fast-track within the Cadarian military, his patron and benefactor the Court Sorceress, Irene Drage, the unwitting and sometime unwilling host for his mother's spirit. He would be within striking range of the Emperor of Cadaria for when it was necessary, but the true purpose of his life still haunted his mind. It was like a constant hum that never went away. Shadowweaver's price for his forces had been high. He wanted a weapon. A weapon that would eventually be aimed at one target.

Out of the corner of his eye, Korin caught a small pillar of smoke in the distance. It could have been coming for no other source than a chimney. Somewhere in this frozen wasteland there was at least a shred of civilization. Perhaps there he could find out where he was and exactly why Dorovar had sent him. As the snow crunched under his feet, the drone in the back of his mind got louder and louder, as though the voice was being carried on the wind itself.

"You have but one purpose," Talisia had said, "to kill my brother Emries."

* * * * * * * * * * * *

Pike watched in horror as the scattered pieces of Dorovar began to pull themselves back together, reconstituting the frozen form of the creature exactly as he had been before Fury impacted his body. The laughter seemed to roll in from all directions and was deep and full of malice. As soon as the last piece of Dorovar was back into place, light returned to the man's deep-set eyes, and the sheen of ice disappeared completely.

"I have to say, Pike, I was expecting more from you. You are renowned for your ferocity and guile. Parlor tricks do not become you. Who knew that Evan Sinn would prove to be a more competent warrior than you."

The bait was obvious, but Pike swallowed it whole. He took half a step toward Dorovar, planting his right foot and then pushing off with all of the force that he could muster. This time before bringing his axe crashing down on his opponent, Pike reached for the power inside of him and let a portal form just in front of him. When he emerged from the other side, he was behind Dorovar, and the blade of Fury slashed downward. Again, the ancient axe struck nothing but air as Dorovar was simply not there. The creature had appeared behind Pike, mimicking the Dark God's attack, and slammed his open hand into Pike's back. Fire and ice shot through Pike's body at the same time, and he felt as though he was going to explode. But the pain only ignited his anger further. Pike swung in a full circle madly, all of his self-control lost. The blade passed just short of striking Dorovar's chest, but that did not deter Pike. He slashed again and again, each time coming up short, all form abandoned for pure power. After the tenth errant strike, Dorovar stepped into Pike, another hard palm strike landing this time in the middle of Pike's chest. This time lightning flashed through his body, burning him from the inside out. The force of the strike caused Pike's hands to spasm, and he lost control of the haft of Fury. A second strike hit Pike in the same place, sending him sailing backward through the air until he struck a tree. The force of the collision broke the trunk of the tree at the point of impact, sending the top half of the massive tree toppling away from the Dark God's broken body. Pike's chest was crushed, and blood poured from his mouth and nose. His right arm also hung limp at his side, bones protruding from the skin. Tears and blood streamed from his eyes so he could not see clearly, but he could make out the form of his opponent approaching slowly, the familiar form of Fury clutched in the creature's hands.

"You endure such pain for this deluded fantasy that you are so strong and so righteous. For centuries you have sustained yourself on righteous indignation, knowing in your heart that no matter what you were doing, that you were a champion. Whether you were a champion of the light, or a champion for vengeance, or just a champion who could not do anything but stand in the way of an unstoppable evil force. You had conviction once, Pike Rhuiden of Onea. You had purpose once. But what do you have now? Look what you have been reduced to."

Pike listened to the creature's voice, but it was faint and muffled because of the pounding of blood in Pike's ears. Something in Dorovar's attacks had made it difficult for Pike to concentrate on the flows of power in the back of his mind. The more he reached for them, the more they seemed to retreat. If he could not channel some of his powers to knit the broken bones, he would be choking on his own blood soon and would lose consciousness. He wasn't sure if it would kill him or not, but certainly losing consciousness at the feet of an enemy was not conducive to survival. Finally he was able to create a tickle of healing energy, and prioritized knitting the bones in his chest.

"A fallen hero, a fallen idol, a fallen god. The Creator tempted you with a life far beyond the one you were fated to live, and you grasped at it like a greedy child who did not know when to be content with what he had."

Dorovar knelt now, balancing Fury on his knee while looking Pike in the eye. Pike could see nothing but blackness in the deep-set wells that served as Dorovar's eyes, but as the man continued to speak, a sparkle began to appear. Something like starlight, emitting a gravity that pulled the soul toward it. Looking at the cosmic light, Pike forgot the pain that wracked his body and the attempts he was making to heal his batted and broken form. Fighting was no longer a priority. Nothing was a priority except listening to Dorovar's hypnotic words.

"You know what the Creator is," Dorovar continued. "He is nothing more than a pretty lie that is just true enough to be believed by the masses. And his children are the conduit through which that lie manifests. You know this first hand, Pike. You have heard the lie with your own ears. First from the tongue of Emries, and then from Halicon. Finally you heard it from the slattern himself, the Creator. I have never heard the voice of the Creator. I have never stood in His presence, but I am sure that it is nothing short of impressive and empty."

Little shocks were erupting through Pike. He didn't know where they were coming from, or what exactly they were. The words that dripped from Dorovar's tongue were familiar, and Pike felt as though he had heard them before, but he couldn't place them. They were tugging at the back of his mind, taking him back to a place in his past. A past soaked in drunkenness, pain, and loss.

"You were a man. You had the goals of a man, the desires of a man, the will of a man. You had a wife. You wanted a family. Friends around you, people you loved. Then the Creator's children came, wielding the lies and the half-truths they breathe like air. They twisted you, all of you, all of the mortals that walked your world, into shadows of themselves. You became the lies that the Creator wanted you to be. Puppets just waiting to have your strings cut. And you stood by, you watched, as the generation before you, your generation, and the generation that followed was swallowed by the arrogant game. In the end, you could have died. You should have died and been allowed to leave the painful and pointless game once and for all. A freedom you denied yourself. The same freedom that was stolen from me. And you found yourself in the Heavens, still at the mercy of those you hated. Learning more and more about the pain and the torment that was inflicted upon your world for little more than bragging rights and the love of a father that would never be given."

Warmth began to spread through Pike's body. Suddenly he realized that Dorovar had reached out a hand, and laid it gently on Pike's knee. All of the injuries caused by their brief encounter were starting to heal, but there was a burning that was left behind, a burning that Pike could not explain.

"And what was waiting for you in the Heavens, Pike? What was your grand reward for all of the sacrifice and all of the pain? What did all of the loss create for you in the womb of the Creator's love? You were a second-class citizen in the Heavens. The other gods looked down upon you. The angels saw you as interlopers. The Children of the Creator despised you. The Servants of the Creator saw you as a plague, and the Creator ignored you. At least until you were needed. When Pyrrus was threatened by his own sister, when the Heavens threated to rip themselves apart, and be stained forever with angelic blood, it was time for Pike Rhuiden and his fellows to be heroes again. You stood against the tide of madness once again, feeling that righteous fury. Feeling that need to defend the weak against the tide of the strong and the evil. You held the line and watched as thousands died, died in ways that no mortal should have been able to lay eyes upon. And when it was over, when all the blood had been spilt, when the pillars of Heaven had stopped shaking, what was left for Pike Rhuiden and the other so-called heroes? In a word, nothing."

Bile began to rise in the back of Pike's throat. Though he hated to admit it to himself, Dorovar's words had the sickening ring of truth, not the hollow ring of the manipulated reality that Emries and others had tried to make Pike believe all of his life. From the first moment that he sat at the table with Logan and the others, listening to Aryx Terian, hearing the call of the old heroes to a war that didn't need to be fought, Pike's life began to spin out of control. It had brought him to this point, where everything around him was a lie, and everything before him was nothing but destruction and misery.

"They still hated you. They still looked down upon you. They still wanted to see you fail at every opportunity. So what did that righteous fury demand of you, Pike? What were you forced to do? You rebelled. You fought against those you tried to save. You killed angels and dragons by the hundreds. You made them pay for the hatred they showed you. Right until you stood at the foot of the Creator's throne. And then what happened, Pike. Did you finish what you started? Did you take this glorious weapon and cut your way through Evan Sinn and all of the other servants of the

Creator? Did you try to bury this shining blade into the heart of the Creator and stop the madness that you were fighting against? Did you?"

Pike's stomach churned. His heart pounded. Hate, pain, loathing, sorrow; every powerful negative emotion he had ever felt in his life boiled under his skin.

"DID YOU?"

Dorovar's voice rolled like thunder through the countryside, and crashed against Pike like a breaker against the shore. It shook Pike to the very core, but at the same time, caused strength to leap up within him that he had not felt since the days fighting against the forces of the phasia in the Dark Mirror reality. When everything was hopeless, and every day could mean death for thousands, Pike stood oftentimes alone against the onslaught. He destroyed those that stood against him, and what he knew to be right.

"No."

Pike's voice was weak, robbed of its power, robbed of its fury.

"No. You were restrained. You were held at bay by the will of the one you called your friend. The one who was loved by the Creator. The one who had been called the Brother of Angels. He kept your hand from doing its work. He kept you from visiting your fury upon those who deserved it for what they had done. And then, upon this world, he had kept you on a leash, keeping his promises and not doing what you knew to be right. You were restrained, you were lied to again, this time by the man you thought was your friend. The man who this very day still walks Espre and furthers his own agendas at the expense of all those you have lost."

Pike could not keep his eyes from going wide. Gwydeon was alive? Gwydeon had lied to him all these centuries? How could he have been so wrong? How could he have been so completely betrayed by the man who he thought of as a brother? Dorovar saw the pain and the confusion in Pike's eyes, but saw something more. Something deeper. He saw the righteous fury bubbling back to the surface. The very thing that gave Pike his true strength. Dorovar rose back to his feet. He extended his hand and after a moment, Pike reached out and accepted the gesture, allowing the robed man to help him up. Standing together, Dorovar held Fury out between them.

"This has been an instrument of your will, your wrath, your anger, and your judgment of the wicked for thousands of years. This weapon is feared in every corner of reality that knows of its existence, and it has tasted rivers of blood. Your enemies have fallen to its immortal steel. However, you allowed this to be touched by the corruption of the Heavens. You allowed it to do the Creator's work; you allowed it to be tainted by the will of those manipulators and unclean wretches. Filth leaks from this haft like the sweat of the profane. This is no longer a weapon of the righteous. It is Fury no longer, for it breeds nothing but restraint and the need for permission."

In a single motion, Dorovar brought the haft of Fury down upon his knee, snapping it in half. At that moment Pike felt as though his heart had broken in half. But in a strange way, he also felt free. Dorovar tossed the broken weapon to the ground, and with a single move of his fingers, impossibly hot flames sprung up around the axe. Pike watched as the carefully forged steel began to ripple from the heat, beads of steel dropping like tears from the glistening blade.

"You are unfettered now, Pike Rhuiden," Dorovar said coolly. "You are now free to visit your righteous fury upon this world and every other that knows the corrupted touch of the Creator and his Children. Bring Judgment to this world. Ride among my heralds and visit true righteousness upon those who will hear you, and judgment upon those who will not. Fill my chorus with the souls of the wicked, and bring my love to the souls of the redeemed."

Dorovar placed his hand on Pike's shoulder, and suddenly they were both gone, wind whipping through the ruined branches of the fallen tree, and the sound of fire consuming the forgotten soul of a hero.

The Lost Children of a Lesser God

*Year Four of the Just Emperor Kaitain "Dragonsbane" Lorien,
Creator's Calendar Year 1871*

Tolon felt a certain level of absurdity setting in as he sat in a plush chair in front of a fireplace. The Frozen Wastes were supposed to be a barren wasteland where nothing should have been able to survive for long. Not even wildlife called that place home, and yet, sitting in the chair, Tolon was faced with improbability manifest. Not only was there a speck of civilization carved into the wasteland, but it seemed that this refugee for lost children had thrived in the inhospitable climate. Stranger still, these refugees as they called themselves were not completely cut off from the rest of civilization, and proved to be amazingly informed. They were so informed in fact that they were able to recognize one of the Maldovrin Triplets on sight, something that few people in the whole of the world should have been able to do. Though there was an air of peace that seemed to permeate the place, the same could not be said for its inhabitants. Tolon's survival early in his adult life had been dependent on being able to size up at a moment's notice the person standing in front of him. Every person that he had come across in the refuge had worn danger about them like a cloak. It seemed to be a part of their very essence, none more clearly than the man who had introduced himself as Gideon. Before any further words could be spoken, the woman who had greeted them at the door of Glacier's Rift returned with a tray full of food and drink. After placing the tray on the table before them, the woman excused herself, leaving Tolon and Jerrica with Gideon and Jared. Jared had chosen to perch on the edge of a table in the corner of the room, the light from the fireplace giving an ominous glow to his face. Gideon opened his mouth to speak again, but Jared cut him off.

"Please Gideon," Jared said putting his fingers to his brow and rubbing slowly, "spare us the accent. Those of us who have known you all these years can barely understand you so our guests stand little chance."

Gideon glowered in Jared's direction and then flashed a roguish smile in Jerrica's direction followed by a subtle laugh.

"You'll have to forgive me," Gideon said in an accent that was closer to common Cadarian, "I fall back into old habits sometimes."

Jerrica returned the smile, but Tolon kept his expression neutral. The change in accent and tone did nothing to alleviate the uneasy feeling in the pit of Tolon's stomach.

"I'm sure you'd like to know why we're all up here in the middle of nowhere surrounded by nothing but snow and ice."

Jerrica nodded, but Tolon gave voice to his thoughts.

"Because you're hiding out from something and don't want to be easily found. What other reason could you have for being in the Frozen Wastes?"

Jerrica's face betrayed her horror at Tolon's bluntness, and Gideon could only laugh.

"I see that your role as a Knight of the Flashing Blade has not introduced civility into your gladiator's tongue, Tolon," Jared teased.

"Blunt is good," Gideon added. "We have far too little blunt around here these days. We all know each other far too well, and if we can't have polite conversation, we choose not to talk at all."

"I'm sure it has nothing to do with the old grudges," Jared offered.

"Or the fact that I killed half the people in this house," Gideon returned.

Jared frowned.

"Ok," Gideon retreated. "Maybe I didn't do it, but I was certainly there for most of them."

Tolon couldn't keep his neutral expression any longer, and the confusion caused his mouth to drop open slightly. Jerrica's eyes sparkled with fascination. When she spoke again, her words began to make connections for Tolon.

"You're all Dark Gods."

Jared frowned, Gideon smirked, and Tolon gritted his teeth. It was Jared that let his voice rise to meet the verbal bait.

"Technically you have to be an ascended being before being considered a god. No one here ever ascended to the Heavens, and so none of us ever fell. So, at least for the way you understand it, we aren't Dark Gods. But we aren't from this world and were brought here, largely against our will through divine providence."

Gideon glared in Jared's direction.

"Jared truly has his mother's way with words."

It seemed for a moment that Jared was going to retort, but it was Tolon who let his voice intercede.

"So if you aren't Dark Gods, what are you?"

The bluntness of the question caused Jerrica to pale slightly, but Gideon's smile and calm expression allayed some of her fears that Tolon's indelicacy was going to offend their hosts.

"I've been trying to figure out who you remind me of, Tolon, and I just put my finger on it. I knew a man once who spent all of his nights singing and carousing in bars, and all of his days wading into enemies by the dozens. He didn't have much tact either, and come to think of it, he doesn't have much tact now. But if I could get used to it from a drunkard like Pike Rhuiden, I'm sure that a gladiator's niceties will easily be adapted to."

Tolon wasn't sure, but at that moment he felt as though he had been insulted.

* * * * * * * * * * *

Korin Melcab continued to trudge through the snow toward the column of black smoke in the distance. He wasn't sure why Dorovar had dropped him into the middle of nowhere, but the implication was clear that there was something here of interest, and something that needed to be taken care of. Neither Talisia nor Dorovar liked loose strings. No matter how the cold and the wind batted at his exposed skin, Korin forced himself to continue moving forward, toward what, he knew not.

* * * * * * * * * * *

As a seer, Jerrica Maldovrin had many influences that she constantly needed to both be aware of and block out from her consciousness. She saw the world much like normal mortals did, but at times she could also see images and colors floating around those people that she looked at. The colors and patterns were easy enough to ignore when she wanted to, but almost as easy to incorporate. Colors typically conveyed emotions being felt by the person, and took very little effort to understand. The patterns within the color took a little a little more concentration. Where the colors were emotions, the patterns were more like the emotional thoughts of the person. For example, Tolon had a haze of red and white circling him. Those colors normally meant a mixture of anger and confusion. However, within the colors was a pattern looked like rain. That normally meant that in his mind Tolon was trying to make sense of what he was seeing and hearing, but there was so much that he felt like he was in danger of being overwhelmed by it all. He felt as though he was drenched in the uncertainty, like standing out in the rain. It had taken Jerrica many years to understand the vocabulary of the colors and patterns that she saw. However, even after all the years of practice, the visions were still difficult to understand. Most of the images were disjointed and seemed to have no context. She could be looking at a wounded warrior and see a dog or a set of carpenter's tools. Looking at Gideon, she was more confused than ever. There were no colors or patterns around him, so either he was feeling nothing, or he was in so much control of his emotions that she could not see them. However floating around Gideon's head were a roaring fire and small rocks that seemed to bob and move with his breath. But there was something else, something even more confusing. Green thread seemed to be winding itself all around his body from his feet to his shoulders.

Gideon waited a long time after playfully chiding Tolon for his manners and Jerrica was relieved that Tolon did not have a visceral reaction to the teasing. Tolon was not a tender man, though he did have a good heart. At times though, Tolon was torn between the more sensitive and caring nature of his heart, and the seasoned reflexes of the warrior that had been beaten into him since the day he could hold a weapon. There was something about Gideon that reminded Jerrica of Tolon. His casual almost uncaring posture belied something deeper. The man was a fighter to be sure, and one that was not to be trifled with, especially with the casual manner in which he joked about death. Men such as that personified danger in a way that few could find palatable.

"You have to understand, Tolon," Jared said after a long moment, "there is far more to this war of yours than anyone in your position is privy to. As long as you are leashed to the side of that pathetic boy that you serve, then you will just end up the same way that all of his loyal servants will. Dead."

Gideon frowned.

"And we know a lot about dying."

"You keep talking about death," Jerrica said with a hint of frustration in her voice. "How can we believe that you have died before? How can we believe any of this? I've known since the moment of my birth that there was more to this world than most people can see, and even with all of my abilities I can only see shadows of what is to come, and without context enough for me to know for certain until it's almost too late."

Tolon reached out and touched Jerrica's hand.

"You mean like with the brothers?"

Tolon saw Gideon and Jared exchange glances for a long moment before turning their attention back to Jerrica.

"Yes. When I was near them, I didn't understand what I was seeing. But once I saw them both together, it was like I was hit by a huge tidal wave of strength and power. I still don't understand what it all means. I just know that them being in the same place together at this point in time is extremely hazardous to all of us."

Jared moved from where he was perched and sat in a chair across from Jerrica.

"Would you be able to describe these brothers?"

Jerrica paled slightly, but Tolon came to her defense.

"I can do better than describe them. One was the General and leader of the Army of Fire, Arin Chandara, and the other was the wanted criminal and heretic Dane Rhuiden."

Gideon chuckled slightly.

"A heretic. That's funny. I've heard him called a lot of things, but never that. I could introduce you to some people here that would call him stubborn, bull-headed, single-minded, naïve, and consistently outclassed by all of his opponents. But much to their annoyance, he always survives, and he has outlived almost all of the people who have ever taken up arms against him. People have fought and died at his side, and they would gladly do it all over again if given the choice. He may be calling himself Dane Rhuiden now, but when I knew him and fought with him, he was Logan Ranthall, and the man calling himself Arin Chandara is his older brother Korrd Ranthall."

Gideon let his words hang in the air for several seconds before speaking again.

"And I am sorry to say that you are very right, Jerrica. If Logan and Korrd are together, then it is almost assured that something bad is going to happen. Two Ranthalls in the same place at the same time can only lead to death and destruction. Hopefully this world survives."

Jared spoke again before Gideon's fatalistic words sank too deeply into the minds of their guests.

"Glacier's Rift is more than just a home for lost children, and it is far more than just an orphanage out on the frontier of society. There are only seven of us here now, but there were and should be more of us. We are all refugees from another world, a world called Onea. It is one of the many worlds that the Creator gave to his children to shepherd. But unfortunately it became a world where the conflict between two of the Children of the Creator boiled over to such a degree that everything was ripped apart by the battle. It marked the first time that servants of one of the Children of the Creator took up arms against another of the Children. Of course for millennia they had worked behind the scenes against one another, waging campaigns of subversion and sedition. But on our world, Emries and Halicon became directly opposed, and not totally because of their own interests."

Tolon's expression was blank. He was far passed the point of disbelief. Now all he could do was sit and listen and try to make as much sense as he could of what he was hearing. He hoped that Jerrica was more connected to the information and would be able to ask questions intelligent enough to be worth the time they were being given.

"Do you know how it all started?"

Jerrica's question may not have been the most elegant, but it struck to the heart of the information that would have been most beneficial.

"The short version is all you probably need to hear," Gideon said in a manner that told Tolon it wasn't supposed to be as crass as it came across. "Onea was supposed to be a neutral world, as far as we are aware of. Of all the worlds under the control of the Creator, only a small few are given to the Children. The rest simply exist as the Creator intended. Life is put there in one form or another, and one of the Children or one of the Servants is tasked with bringing that life the Creator's laws. They are taught what is expected of them, and taught respect for the Creator, and left to their own devices. Some of the worlds fail, and some simply continue. However, something went wrong when Emries was given the task of bringing the Creator's laws to our world. Instead of acting as a shepherd and instilling in the mortals of Onea a love and respect for the Creator, Emries added his own chapters to the Book of the Creator, making himself the mortal embodiment of the Creator, the true genesis of the mortals that roamed Onea."

Jared added his voice to the tale.

"Emries saw what was happening on other worlds, and thought that the Creator was not giving his children a chance to succeed on their worlds. That perhaps they were being given inferior tools to work with. It never crossed Emries' mind that it was the fault of the Children themselves that their worlds were failing. So he thought that by taking Onea for his own, that he would have an advantage over his siblings in their ideological war that could not be overcome. Unfortunately for our world, and unfortunately for the people of this world, Emries underestimated the Creator's reprisal for his slight. To combat Emries influence, the Creator sent Halicon to Onea, with the stated goal of erasing Emries blasphemous influence, even if it meant killing every last mortal on the planet."

Horror lit up Jerrica's face. Gideon thought he could see tears welling up in the corners of her eyes. From the far side of the room, another figure entered, Tolon saw the motion out of the corner of his eye, but when he saw that neither of his hosts tensed, he assumed that the new addition to the conversation was resident of the refuge.

"Jared is always so melodramatic," a woman's voice said with almost a maliciously intelligent tone. "The Creator simply could have purged the world Himself if He so chose. But he gave the mortals a fighting chance, not only against Halicon, but also against Emries' manipulations."

Jared smirked in the new arrival's direction while Gideon didn't look up to regard her at all.

"Tolon Morr, Jerrica Maldovrin, let me introduce you to Natalie Yetre. In a manner of speaking, my cousin."

"A fact that makes Gideon's blood boil every moment of every day, I can assure you," Natalie offered. "But regardless of how ashamed Gideon is of his extended family, it does not change the fact that our commonality of blood is what has made us victims of this circumstance."

Jared leaned back in his chair.

"Never fails. Every time I hear her talk it makes my ears bleed."

Natalie's ice cold expression curled into a mocking frown.

"It's clear you get your intellect and tact from your father, my dear brother."

Jared's eyes narrowed.

"Half-brother."

Natalie nodded.

"Fortunately enough for me. Now, as I was saying before I was interrupted by old grudges. Emries bent the rules through his arrogant machinations, and Halicon was bound by his role as the nightmare of men. But it was the mortals caught in the middle that not only became the fulcrum for the war between the brothers, but also proved to be the template for the battle that is being waged here. Mortals like the brothers that your seer is so afraid of are the ones who made everything far too complicated. And it was mortals like the damnable Gwydeon Sandar and Midarin Rice that cursed us all. We are here because of the folly of our birth, no more. It is our blood that may force us to fight as it forced some of our compatriots. Ultimately it may prove to be our blood that makes us an enemy to your people."

Tolon's composure against his frustration snapped.

"How can your blood compel you to do anything? You're not Dark Gods, but you may have to become my enemy? What is this? What is all this?"

Jerrica reached out and laid her hand on Tolon's arm trying her best to console him. She could feel the muscles in his forearms tensed so tightly from gripping the arms of the chair. Gideon too seemed to be impacted by Tolon's outburst, standing straight and seeming to take on a more serious air rather than his casual lean against the mantle of the fireplace. Jared simply closed his eyes and took a deep breath. Only Natalie seemed to be completely unaffected by Tolon's irritation.

"Your reaction is something I would expect from a mundane. You mortals are so limited in your ability to grasp the true nature of the universe. I weep that there are so few here of loftier stock that can follow the patterns. What I wouldn't give to be able to speak with my mother for a few hours. This would all seem like less of a waste of my time and talents."

Gideon glowered.

"Has anyone ever told you that you are an arrogant bitch, Natalie?"

Natalie kept her eyes focused on Jerrica.

"As though it mattered, Gideon, but you and Jared tend to do so on a regular basis when you have nothing more intelligent to say. To think that your mother is perhaps the second most intelligent of all of Halicon's children, and that your father is a prodigy makes me weep for their other children. And you Jared, the fact that we share the same mother is far more depressing than it is a source of hope for any possibility that you will eventually match the intelligence of a garden snake."

Natalie sighed and shook her head.

"You see, Jerrica, in his war against his brother, Halicon created children that he called the phasia. They were a mix of his own divine essence and the distilled power and natural destructive drives of the humans. A hybrid if you will. The phasia were under strict command not to have children of their own, but unsurprisingly, the part of them that was tainted by mortal drives made them less obedient than Halicon would have intended. Aryx was the first to disobey, but to his credit he had already left the fold by that time. And his child was with a mortal. Gideon is one quarter mortal because of this fact. Jared's father was a mortal as well, making him half. As for me, both of my parents were phasia. My blood and my power are completely derived from the divine. However, as I said, it is this connection to divine power that made us ripe for the Creator's goal of bringing all of those touched by the hand of his children to this rock. This is where the battle of ideologies will be fought. This is where the

Children of the Creator and their followers will kill each other until only one side is left standing. But of course, that is the great trick."

Jerrica felt as though there was a great veil that had been lifted from her eyes. Suddenly everything was so clear. The reason that the brothers could not meet so soon. The reason they had been drawn to this place. It was as though all of the pieces were beginning to fit together.

"Because the Creator doesn't want any of the Children to win."

Gideon's head dropped, Jared let out a huge sigh, and Tolon's eyes widened. Whatever had prompted Jerrica to make the statement had been lost on Tolon, but the fact that it had come from her did not immediately draw his ire.

"Finally one with a little intelligence."

Natalie's statement fell largely on deaf ears. However, Jerrica's next words were ingested by everyone with a mixture of revulsion, fear, and unavoidable acceptance.

"If the Creator brought all of his Children here, and all of their servants, and all of their children, and the dragons, and Dorovar and his Heralds, that would not only allow the Creator to get rid of his children, but also remove any threat to Him. He would give them hope of some resolution in order to thin the herd, and then when the Creator learns whatever He wishes to learn from this experiment, he wipes the slate clean and starts over."

Natalie nodded her agreement.

"It's an exceedingly elegant trap," Natalie said softly. "One fitting of betrayal of this scale. If only the Creator had been able to keep the truth from being discovered. Perhaps He would have succeeded in his plan. But the Creator has proven over the millennia that He is not infallible. He has shown a level of arrogance that was unexpected, and it has extended the game longer than would be tenable given the risk involved. Which my dear Seer is why you are beginning to perceive cracks in the veil, and why you were drawn here."

Natalie brought her left hand to her chin and closed her eyes in thought for a long moment before turning to look at Gideon.

"I think perhaps it's time that our seer here met our patron."

Gideon looked to Jared who took only a moment before nodding. Gideon in turn nodded to Natalie. Before Natalie could make a move, the door in the far wall of the room, the one that Tolon and Jerrica had entered before the strange conversation began, flew open admitting a heavily armed and armored man who looked as though he could have been Natalie's twin.

"We have company," the man said with anger thick in his voice. "I think it's one of Talisia's."

Gideon produced daggers from some unseen pouch on his belt and started toward the door. Jared was only a pace behind.

"Keep our guests out of harm's way, Natalie. As you're so fond of reminding us, you're the most powerful of us, so make sure the party crasher doesn't get by you."

For the first time in his life Tolon felt helpless and that if he were to join the battle that was about to take place that he would be hopelessly overmatched. It was not a feeling he relished, and deep inside himself he vowed that he would never feel that way again.

All the King's Horses

The ground was still shaking when the Emperor's Guard finally assembled on the far side of the inn that was serving as the makeshift capital of the Cadarian Empire. Kaitain Lorien, dressed from head to toe in the finest black silk shirt and riding pants, with equally fine riding boots stood looking off into the distance where Korin Melcab, the Captain of the Imperial Guard and the creature that could have only been one of the Dark Gods had been engaged in combat mere minutes before. Even now the sky was still darkened from the expended energy, and lightning flashed in all directions, radiating out from the center of the conflict. Kaitain's expression was hidden by the silver streaked ebony mask that he wore, a mask that struck fear into his soldiers as he turned his attention back to the inn. The Dark God had destroyed most of the eastern wall of the inn, and the supports that held the second floor in place had been badly damaged. Creaking and straining wood could be heard even above the distant thunder. From what Kaitain could see it looked as though a strong wind would topple the structure. Ivan Quicksilver was just emerging from the structure with their hostage, the so-called Queen of the Dark Gods, Sadrina Annis in tow. A dozen of the Emperor's Guard took possession of the hostage and pulled her in the direction of a small group of figures dressed in black cloaks that obscured all of their features. Once he was sure that the hostage was well tended to, Ivan reported to his Emperor.

"The scouts have found no sign of Korin Melcab, nor the Dark God. From your description of the man, I have no doubt that it was Pike Annis, the leader of the Dark Gods, and the husband of your hostage. It seems that you have successfully stirred the hornet's nest my Emperor, if they are making brazen moves like this against you here in Aldere."

Kaitain looked past Ivan, over his shoulder to Sadrina.

"He would have never gotten that close to me if the Imperial Palace were still standing and we had a decently defensible position. Though I detest the thought of leaving Aldere, even temporarily, I believe we have no choice in the matter. Lordhill would be the ideal choice, but there are too many concerns with Peregrim and his connection to my brother. The Imperial Guard is already massed on the Zevarit border, poised to take direct control over the kingdom, even if it means eliminating the royal families. I will take direct command of the invasion. Yaron and his cabal will join the army. I intend to make an example of Zevarit and prove to the rest of Cadaria that I am still very much in charge of the Empire. You, Ivan will be responsible for our hostage. I will have nothing happen to her, and she must stay with the army. If she dies, your life will be forfeit."

Kaitain turned toward the ranks of soldiers without waiting for a replay or even finding Ivan's eyes with his own. Ivan lingered. Something wasn't right. His eyes scanned the distance, and he thought on the far side of the inn he had seen something move. Kaitain stopped in his tracks and turned his head back in Ivan's direction.

"Send a squad to eliminate the innkeeper and his staff. They could have been privy to too much information and cannot be trusted. Hang them as heretics."

Kaitain did not wait for a response before turning to walk away. Ivan was only half paying attention to the Emperor's words. His eyes were locked on the place that he saw movement. The feeling started to fill him that there were insurgents on the other side of the inn, ones that were adept at not being noticed, and posed a far bigger threat than anything the

Emperor would find in Zevarit. Ivan drew his blade and set his feet. He looked in the direction of two of the Emperor's Guard who were nearby.

"Sound the advance, and keep a close watch. The Dark Gods have already made one attempt on the Emperor's life today, and I have a feeling that it won't be the last we see for quite some time."

One of the guards nodded and the two fell into step behind the Emperor. Whatever the danger that had appeared, Ivan had to make sure that the Emperor was protected. He heard the orders being passed through the ranks and the sounds of trumpets signaling the march. In a matter of minutes the soldiers would be out of sight, and in a matter of hours they would meet the main force at the border of Zevarit. If the Emperor had his way, the invasion would begin the next day, and in less than a week the Emperor would go from the Imperial Palace of Aldere to the Palace of Blood in Zevarit.

* * * * * * * * * * * *

The portal closed behind Warron Ysamaran and Arin Ranthall, the ruins of the Imperial Palace of Aldere in the distance, and the nearly ruined temporary Imperial Palace creating a barrier between their position and the ranks of the Imperial Guard that were preparing for their march. For the last hour Arin and Warron had been watching the Imperial Guard assemble, and both of them had felt the disturbance to the area. There had been a battle with great power waged nearby, and no doubt it had been that battle that had caused the Emperor of Cadaria to abandon his makeshift palace. Though Warron had been against it, Arin wanted to try to get closer to the Imperial Guard, with the possibility of finding out where they were marching to and who they intended to ply their force against. If possible, Arin and Warron could warn the prospective target and deal a powerful blow to Kaitain's destructive goals.

"This was a bad idea," Warron said gruffly.

"My son gets the girl, and I get the bitter old man," Arin muttered as he found a place to look at the movements of the troops without being observed.

Warron joined Arin at the corner of the inn. He could not help but allow his lips to curl into a smile. It had been a long time since Warron had presided over an army of any size. The last time had been during the War of Ascension when he served as a general working for Grawn Aplee. Grawn and Warron shared many qualities. They were both ruthless, vicious, and had no problem sending thousands of troops to their death to gain even a moment's advantage. Soldiers were expendable. That was a lesson that Warron learned early on in his time as a member of the phasia. Warron put his hand on Arin's shoulder.

"Between the two of us, we could rip that army to shreds. It wouldn't take much just to open up the ground beneath their feet and then bury them all alive. You know it'd feel good."

Arin frowned, but didn't let his expression find Warron's eye. Though he was new to the understanding of the kind of power that Warron had had the possession of his entire life, Arin began to see how everything looked as though it could be solved by the application of that immense power. To Warron, swallowing an entire army under the ground and burying them alive was a simple solution to a simple problem. Such a thought would never have occurred to Arin. Arin was a farmer that was pressed into military service because of his sense of justice. The whole world was at stake, and the lord of the land called for all able bodied men to take up arms to protect what needed to be protected.

Arin was in his late twenties when Cedric Binosear became the lord of Marcwell. By that time, Arin had been in Aradon for five years, and had built a farm and farmhouse with his own hands. He had just begun to be accepted by the locals as a member of the community. Aradon was an insular community and did not accept outsiders well, but Arin had proved that he had skills that would benefit the community after a series of particularly devastating storms. Most of Arin's formative years had been spent in Illimar. As the son of a fisherman, Arin spent the majority of his days on the sea, moving from one port to another to purchase supplies or to offload their catch. Illimar was populated with many men and women who made their living on the sea in one form or another, and the local fishing industry was flush with large crews that brought in enough fish to supply the whole of Illimar. However, few crews were brave enough to fish the deeper waters away from Illimar, and even fewer chanced the high seas to bring their catch to other cities and kingdoms of the world. Just as Arin spent most of his formative years on a boat of some kind or another, Arin's father Korrd had spent his entire life on the high seas as a pirate. This history of piracy removed all fear from the dangers of the seas, and created a lucrative future for the Ranthall family. But when a storm capsized the family fishing vessel many miles from Illimar, the entire crew was lost, including Arin's father. Arin eventually was able to make his way back to shore, but the experience made it difficult for him to see his life continuing on the water. His future was as a farmer, hoping that the land would be kinder to him and his family than the water had been.

In Aradon there were challenges far more daunting than learning how to make the land bend to his will. For the first time in his life, Arin felt the pangs of love in his heart. She wasn't the most beautiful woman in the village, nor was she the most feminine. She was the blacksmith's daughter, and she was as gruff and hard as many of the goods that came out of her father's shop. Lady-like things were alien to her, and she was as much at home in the taverns drinking and singing as she was in the sewing circles that her mother tended to frequent. Most of her suitors didn't end up with polite rejections, and more than a few ended up with bloodied lips and broken noses. But Arin was salty and persistent, and more importantly could take a punch. Their final collision would have been legendary if anyone had dared to tell the tale. Arin had become tired of her arrogance and tedious denial of affection, so he cornered her behind the blacksmith shop one evening. They argued for many minutes before Arin finally grabbed her by the collar of her shirt, pulled her to him, and kissed her. His presumption was met with a right cross to his chin. The only response Arin could muster was to slap the woman in retaliation. For a long minute the shocked expression was the only communication between them until Victoria Rhuiden pulled Arin to her and kissed him. That was the end of the courtship and they were married several weeks later. Just in time for war to break out in Lakestone.

The barely eighteen year old Cedric Binosear had inherited a fractured kingdom just before the invasion of Lakestone took place. The army had been disbanded due to corruption and laws had been passed that prevented the Lord of Marcwell from raising another one. With no army to muster a defense of one of their longest standing allies, Cedric had to hire mercenaries as well as call on all of Marcwell's allies to field a force large enough to rescue the citizens of Lakestone from the danger that threatened their lives. Aradon was a vassal of the Kingdom of Trelon, and Trelon had a mutual defense pact with Marcwell that went back generations. So it was largely Trelon's vassals that met Cedric Binosear's request for troops, though most came from the city of Askronilka that had been part of the Kingdom of Alimidar before being ceded to Trelon as part of a settlement following an ugly war. When Arin began to pack his things to travel to Marcwell, his wife would not let him leave without her. So, the husband and wife joined the Lion's Mane under the command of Arathorn Geoffry and waded deep into the nightmare of a war against the forces of Shau-ling and the phasia. That was where Arin first met Jeroch and Warron. They were the enemy generals during the last battle of Lakestone before Cedric's victory over Shau-ling. That was the battle where Cedric defeated Jeroch in personal combat, which broke the spirit of the Jeresei that made up the bulk of the enemy army, causing them to flee. Warron stayed and fought before being dispatched by Diana Terian. Arin and Victoria had been in the deepest parts of the fighting, constantly surrounded by enemies. Both were wounded during the fighting, and it was the wounds suffered in that battle combined with Ellis' intervention years later that would lead to Victoria's death during the birth of their second child, Logan.

Being a father, soldier, fisherman, and farmer however had not prepared Arin for the new life that he would find on Espre. One minute he was laying in his bed in the house he had built with his own hands, the last embers of life fading, and the next he was standing on the shore of an island looking at one of the most beautiful waterfalls he had ever seen. His old friend was waiting there for him, though Cedric Binosear looked so much older than he had been when the two had fought together. The months that followed were filled with Cedric giving Arin a crash course in all of the things that Arin wished he didn't have to know. But he knew the importance of the task ahead, and together with Cedric, Arin hunted down the members of the phasia that had been brought to Espre, as well as his mentor Arathorn Geoffry, and Mailock, the member of the Moridon who helped to uncover the Prophecies of the *Coromor* that led Cedric to his ultimate fate. And while there were never any good ways to kill a friend, Cedric tried his best to be merciful in the execution of his plans. When

Arin and Cedric parted ways, the light had gone out of Cedric's eyes, and all he wanted to do was find the last few members of the phasia and then just find a place to let the sins of his life catch up with him. And while Cedric's journey was at its end, Cedric was clear with Arin that his path was just beginning. All of those touched by Aerith's power had a destiny, and no matter what that proved to be, Cedric made sure that Arin met it with his eyes open. At the moment, that led him to looking over the ranks of an enemy army with a former adversary turned ally.

"It's not the army I'm worried about," Arin said looking over the ranks. "See those black robes? Rumors have been going around for a while now that Kaitain has been recruiting disgruntled and disgraced members of the Academy of Arcane Arts to create a group that would not follow the same rules in the use of their abilities that the Academy held them to. They could be an offensive force that could be mobilized against the dragons or the Dark Gods."

Warron scoffed.

"Wizards. I hate wizards. You never know what they're capable of."

"Is that why the Moridon always got the better of you?"

Warron growled again and started to move toward the other side of the inn wall.

"Those pathetic excuses for sages were more hazardous to themselves than they were the phasia. Just because two of them were competent enough to latch themselves on to marginally bothersome military minds doesn't fill me with fear. This Academy though; they're organized. They're disciplined. If someone like Kaitain cracks that non-aggression mandate of theirs, they could cause some real damage. The world-shattering kind."

From off in the distance Warron and Arin could hear shouts and trumpet blasts. The soldiers were beginning to mobilize. The two men watched for a long time, and when the soldiers started to disappear over a ridge, Arin's attention was drawn to the lone figure that lingered.

"You can come out now," Ivan Quicksilver called. "We won't be disturbed, of that I can assure you. The Emperor has taken the bulk of his forces to Zevarit. Even if you get through me, you would have to wade through the entire Imperial Guard and the Black Shroud to get to him. You missed your best chance to strike in the confusion after the last attack. Now he will be more vigilant and he will never be without members of the Black Shroud to protect him. The Emperor is beyond your grasp."

Warron stepped out from behind the inn first, revealing himself to the former member of the Knights of the Flashing Blade. When Warron saw that the taller man had his weapon drawn, Warron allowed an axe made of ice to form in his hand. It was not the most elegant weapon that Warron could have conjured, but Warron was not one who engaged in elegant combat. For lack of a better term, Warron was a brawler, and he enjoyed the more brutal aspects of personal combat, and had been known for killing with his bare hands as often as any other form of weapon. Some thought he did it to gain the respect of the other members of the phasia, but the truth was that Warron simply enjoyed the personal nature of the kills. He liked watching the light go out of his enemy's eyes as they died. It was something that he had begun to miss in his millennia of retirement from the rigors of war. Warron covertly motioned in Arin's direction, an effort to keep the man hidden.

"So, a disgraced traitor has returned home to the nest?"

Warron continued to walk toward Ivan as he spoke.

"First you get sent to the Dark Continent to eliminate a Dark God. You like it there so much that you end up staying for several years as a loyal subject of the Queen of the Dark Gods. Then when you see an opportunity to cozy back up to the Emperor you turn your back on the people who took you in, and kidnap the boss's wife. You're an obedient little lap dog now. But how long until you decide you want to bite the hand that feeds you again?"

Ivan smiled.

"And what do you know about it? I don't remember you from my time at the Citadel, so you must not be in good standing with Pike or his people. Either you hate them, or they hate you. Either way, you can't matter much."

Warron returned the smile with a malicious one of his own.

"You'd be surprised."

Warron took hold of the haft of his axe with both hands and started into a slow jog toward Ivan. Within a matter of seconds he began to push some of his powers into his legs, increasing his normally plodding speed into something more combat-ready. The greater measure of his power he channeled into the muscles of his arms and chest. Ivan braced himself for the charge of his opponent, however, he couldn't have been prepared for what was about to happen. In his time in the Dark Citadel, Ivan had sparred with some of the best and brightest of the Dark Gods, but none of them had the savagery that struck Ivan when the first downward blow of Warron's ice axe came crashing down on his blade. The force of the downward strike forced Ivan back several steps, and he barely recovered his balance before another hard blow pounded his guard. This strike sent Ivan sprawling backwards where he landed on his back. Fortunately his blade landed right beside him. Warron was content with the display of power and waited several feet away, twirling the ax in his hands.

"Still convinced that I don't matter?"

Ivan got back to his feet again, but gingerly. His right leg ached. There had been a large rock on the ground that the back of his right knee struck when he hit the ground, and it felt as though something had been seriously damaged. Ivan knew that his mobility and speed had been compromised. The sole advantage that he had over the smaller man had been removed, and now only tactics would prove to be Ivan's salvation, since it was painfully obvious that he could not match him power for power. Warron watch Ivan move and knew he had been hurt. Smirking to himself, Warron let the ax disappear from his hands.

"Why don't we make this more interesting? No weapons."

Ivan regarded Warron for a long moment before letting his sword clatter back to the ground. In a purely hand to hand fight, the smaller man had the advantage. But Ivan would not be deterred by bravado alone. Testing his damaged leg for a moment, Ivan kept his eyes focused on his opponent and then balled his fists and charged. The first blow was more of a range finder than anything else, checking how much distance he could keep between himself and Warron without closing into the smaller man's obvious power. The blow glanced off Warron's right cheek, causing no damage and seeming less annoying than a mosquito bite. The second strike had more power behind it, but it never had a chance to connect. Warron ducked under the long right handed punch and took hold of Ivan's arm at the elbow. The phase pulled the taller man down, bringing up his knee at the same time so it connected with Ivan's stomach. The force of the blow knocked all of the breath out of Ivan, and the former Knight of the Flashing Blade could feel the force of the impact all the way to his spine. However, Warron was not finished, as he planted his leg used in the knee strike, foot just inside Ivan's stance, the smaller man turned his body thrusting his left shoulder into Ivan's chest and pulling hard at the captured arm. Ivan felt the snap before he heard it. The torque on Ivan's arm was incredible and the limb was broken at the elbow, but Warron was not content with disabling one of the man's arms. Warron used his shoulder as a fulcrum and propelled Ivan into the air, throwing him by his now dislocated elbow to the ground. It was only Ivan's trained reflexes that allowed him to avoid the hard stomp that followed the throw that would have shattered the skull of a lesser man. Ivan rolled away from Warron, the pain in his arm excruciating, but not enough to take all of the fight out of him. Coming back to his feet, Ivan was aware that his arm was hanging obscenely limp from the elbow, the hand and forearm completely disabled. Ivan feinted in as though he were going to throw another ranging punch, but instead ducked his shoulder and tried to ram the shorter man. Warron seemed prepared for the tactic and lowered his own shoulder. The two men met like bucking rams, shoulders and heads colliding with a sickening thud. Ivan was far more impacted by the collision, stumbling backwards, his vision briefly stolen by explosions of light in his brain. Warron wasted no time in following up his attack, closing the distance with a hard palm strike to the side of Ivan's head and then a series of rapid punches to the ribs and sternum, each blow fracturing the bones it connected with. Blood spewed from Ivan's mouth and nose with every ragged breath. As Ivan staggered backward from his opponent, Warron sensed that the end of the conflict was upon them.

From where he watched the battle, Arin saw what was about to happen, but he was not fast enough to stop it. Had he been more practiced with his abilities, he might have been able to create a portal under either Warron or Ivan, or at the very least done something to stop the collision between the two men. The best he could do though was draw his weapon and hope that Warron could defend himself long enough to allow Arin to cross the distance. In what must have seemed like an act of futility, Ivan threw his damaged arm out at Warron, swinging the useless appendage like a club. But what looked like the last act of a desperate man was actually a distraction that allowed Ivan to retrieve the dagger hidden at the small of his back with his good hand. Warron didn't see the strike happen, but felt the scorching heat of the thin blade knife as it ripped through his stomach. As it pierced his flesh, Warron knew something was wrong. All of the power flooded out of his body, and the strings of power that had been with him since the moment of his birth were suddenly stolen from his perception. It was as if the dagger had stolen all of his power the moment it pierced his skin. The confusion was more than enough time for Ivan to capitalize upon, spinning past where Warron stood, bringing the dagger back around to bury deep in his back between the shorter man's shoulder blades. Barely a whimper passed through Warron's lips, but the man fell all the same. For a long moment, Ivan stood over Warron's fallen form, breathing heavily and wiping the blood away from his mouth and nose with his good arm. Gore dripped from the blade of the dagger, and it seemed to glow with ominous energy. Ivan sneered down at his fallen opponent before putting his boot to Warron's side, flipping him over onto his back. Warron's face was frozen into a look of pain and horror, and Ivan wasted no time in plunging the dagger into Warron's chest, piercing his heart and ending the man's life. When Ivan stood straight, he smiled and admired his handiwork. It wasn't until Arin's hand took firm hold of his shoulder and spun him around that Ivan realized he was not alone. The former Knight of the Flashing Blade barely had time to gasp and feel his eyes widen before the blade of the Sacred Weapon Balance came streaking up from the ground. The scythe blade struck true at the joint between Ivan's left leg and his groin. The force of Arin's blow combined with the otherworldly strength of the weapon sent the blade ripping through flesh and bone until the scythe blade emerged from Ivan's right shoulder. The halved body of Ivan Quicksilver fell to the ground, spewing blood in all directions.

Arin knelt at the side of his fallen ally, pulling the hideous dagger from his chest and tossing the foul thing to the ground. There would be time enough to understand what the weapon had done to the immortal Lord Boar later, but for now, Arin had to bury another former member of the phasia. Once upon a time, he would have taken pride in the act, but now, on Espre, with the whole of creation seemingly speeding toward oblivion, Arin found himself weeping over yet another fallen friend.

The Only Safe Move

Year One of the Divine Empress and Child of the Creator Marlae Tamerlane, Creator's Calendar Year 1871

Isabella Relivin was used to not being noticed as she walked down the halls of the Royal Palace of Hedorah. She had lived in the walls of the palace since her mother was employed as a seamstress and chambermaid by one of the royal families fifteen years ago. Guards ignored her, and she could wander wherever she wished in the palace, so long as she did not approach the rooms of the royals themselves. However, now that the Divine Empress called the royal palace home, things had changed a great deal. It always felt as though eyes were on her, and the angels that roamed the halls took long moments examining her with their piercing eyes before continuing upon whatever errand they were on. Of course, they had good reason to examine anyone moving through the palace ground, as people with power could hide well in plain sight according to the stories. Anyone could have been a Dark God in disguise trying to get to the Divine Empress. Isabella had heard about angels since she was a little girl, and in her mind, they were beautiful and radiated such light and purity that to be in the presence of one would fill you with such peace and contentment that you would know your life had reached the purest moment the soul could experience. However, these angels did not live up to her dreams. They were gruff, and seemed to be constantly angry and waiting for an opportunity to kill. Their armor gleamed, but not as brightly as their constantly burning weapons. Instead of filling Isabella with a sense of peace, they filled her with a sense of fear, and she kept her eyes down when their eyes were upon her for fear of drawing unnecessary notice. Now, even though she was on a mission for the Divine Empress, she did not chance meeting their gaze.

Isabella's thoughts turned to the Divine Empress. The moment that she had been in the woman's presence she had felt something akin to resentment. It didn't make sense, but she did not like Marlae Tamerlane when she first set eyes upon her. But then, upon returning to the Divine Empress's chambers after fetching the things for her bath, the woman had seemed to change. She stood straighter, and there was a kindness and understanding in her eyes that Isabella knew had not been there the hour before. Whatever had come over the woman suited her. And perhaps that is what Isabella saw. When Isabella first beheld Marlae, she held herself like a girl; mature in body but not in attitude. When Isabella was in her presence the second time, she saw and felt the aura of a woman. Attitude was something that people wore like clothing, and just like clothing, some attitudes fit, and others didn't. And just like clothing, attitude was a compilation of many pieces, both the conscious and unconscious. The set that Marlae wore fit like a glove.

Slipping quietly from the confines of the royal palace, Isabella moved through the dark streets of Hedorah. Ordinarily she would have feared for her life walking at this late hour, but since the Divine Empress had made Hedorah her home, the normal pervasive criminal element had been all but eradicated. The threat of reprisal for the harming of one of the Divine Empress's servants would be swift and brutal, that much was clear, and no one would dare be the first to see how true the threat was. All the same, Isabella did not tarry. Just because the danger had not presented itself, did not mean it would not. There was a chill in the night air, and Isabella pulled her cloak tightly around her as she crossed from the royal district into the port district. As Hedorah was a kingdom situated on an island that lay in the bay between the kingdoms of Zevarit and Iltorp, most of its landscape was devoted to some kind of seafaring enterprise. Hedorah boasted the largest shipyards in the whole of Cadaria, and more than half of them were devoted to building, repairing, and resupplying the Imperial Navy. The morning that the Divine Empress took power, angels swept through the ports, eliminating all of the members of the Imperial Guard stationed there and took control of the ports as well as the vessels docked there. It was theorized that in a matter of minutes, the Divine Empress had taken control of almost a quarter of the Imperial Navy.

Taking a deep breath, Isabella crossed the invisible line into the southern half of Hedorah. The very center of the port distract was the home to a large open air market, as well as the largest concentration of merchant's homes. Shaking slightly from the cold, Isabella withdrew the small piece of parchment that she had scrawled the directions that the Divine Empress had given her. Not looking at the directions, Isabella easily found the well-appointed house seemingly hidden deep in the residential area. There was a single candle burning in one of the windows, and Isabella hesitated at the door before knocking. In the old Hedorah, she would have already been dead or worse, and knocking on the door of someone you didn't know in the middle of the night was asking for something bad to happen. But these were different times, and she felt the protection of the Divine Empress upon her. It took several long moments before the door opened, but when it did, Isabella smiled at what waited on the other side. She was happy to see the woman dressed in a fine dress, one that would have been reserved for royalty, her dark hair properly done, and her eyes bright and awake.

"I was beginning to wonder when you would come," the woman said in a smooth and calm voice. "You have a message for me?"

Isabella bowed slightly, adhering to well-practiced protocol.

"The Divine Empress, Marlae Tamerlane graciously requests your presence at the Royal Palace at your earliest convenience."

The woman frowned at the name slightly, but the expression did not linger.

"Very well. Let us go."

* * * * * * * * * * * *

The angels flanking the door of the Divine Empress's quarters tensed as Terrance Aldora approached. It was highly irregular that any kind of meeting would take place at this late hour, and it felt even stranger that Terrance was making his way to a young woman's room under the cover of night. His brother had all the experience with such things, and all it left Terrance with was a feeling of anxiety and uncertainty. He knew that courtly matters were all that were to be discussed, but the once Marlae Lorien did have a reputation, and Terrance did not know what awaited him on the other side of the door. Several paces from the door, it opened and an older woman that Terrance knew as the court seamstress emerged carrying a basket of supplies. Sweat beaded on her brow, and the woman looked as though she had been working at a feverish pace for quite some time. Whatever Terrance had been expecting when he walked through the door, it certainly wasn't what awaited him. The Divine Empress Marlae Tamerlane stood with her back to a full-length mirror facing the door. She wore a full length gown that looked to be either black or a very deep blue, but sewn through the fabric were dark red and platinum flecks that shimmered in familiar but ambiguous patterns. The shimmer was subtle, and the light had to catch the dress just so to make the effect more than unconsciously noticeable. The dress covered Marlae from her feet all the way to her neck, and the high neckline stopped just short of coming to her jawline, but gave the impression of a very long and elegant neck. There were triangular slits in the neck of the gown that exposed areas of her throat and neck but none of the openings plunged lower that the level of her collarbone. Covering the shoulders of the gown were very ornate pieces that looked as though they might have been recovered from an ancient suit of armor, but they were light and looked as though they would not have been cumbersome in the slightest. The shoulder places were triangular and extended just past the plane of her shoulder from the neckline, and then plunged down in front and in back coming to a point at would have been the bottom of her sternum. Delicate golden chains held the pieces together and crossed her chest at the level of her breasts. Most of the dresses that Terrance had seen Marlae wear would have accentuated and drawn focus to that area, however, this dress downplayed her femininity in all but the most subtle ways. Gold and silver filigree decorated the shoulder plates, with no distinct pattern with the exception of what looked like feathered wings stretching across the plunging portions of the plate, and the body of a bird across the top. Marlae's hair was beautifully done, with the majority of her hair pulled to the left side of her face, and hanging down in front, while a generous bough of hair draped down the right side of her forehead, stopping just above the level of her eye. She wore little makeup, short of a dark shade of red on her full lips. An ornate bow held her hair in the back, looking like segmented black butterfly wings, only half of which was visible when looking straight at the Empress. It took Terrance a long moment to remember his manners, and he fell to one knee as soon as his mind could process what he should have done immediately. He bowed his head and waited to be acknowledged.

"Welcome, Terrance," Marlae's voice came like a soft evening wind, "I apologize for the lateness of the hour, but I understand you have been in consultation with the Captain of the Flying Guard so it is not as though you were abed."

Terrance kept his head down.

"Even if I were, your Grace, I would have come as soon as you needed me."

Terrance thought he could feel Marlae's smile.

"Please Terrance, sit with me. We have much to discuss."

Terrance got back to his feet and found a chair on the far side of the room. He waited until the Divine Empress sat a few feet away from him before sitting himself. The Divine Empress folded her hands in her lap and looked Terrance in the eye, her expression serious but not grave.

"You seem to disagree with Azure as to the way we should be handling this war. Do you not agree that the Dark Gods are a threat that needs to be dealt with? Do you not agree that their very existence is an affront to my role as the designated heir to rule this world as decreed by the Creator Himself?"

For a moment Terrance was worried until he realized that there was no malice or accusation in the Empress's tone. The questions were just that, questions.

"You Grace," Terrance began, keeping his tone as respectful as he could, "I agree that the Dark Gods are a powerful force that if they wanted could destabilize the whole of Cadaria. But I think that if they had wanted to move against your father, or any of the Lorien Emperors that have sat on the throne in violation of the treaty that ended the Shadow War, they could and would have, and I don't think that the whole of the Cadarian military could have stopped them. The fact that your father still lives despite everything that has happened both here, in Albitonin, and Aldere, indicates to me that the Dark Gods are serious only about their own goals, and those do not include us at the moment. I believe Azure wants to move against the Dark Gods to fulfill his own ego, and to settle a millennia long grudge. His interests I believe are not your Grace's."

Marlae considered the words for a long moment.

"And Ayden?"

Terrance paled a bit.

"I believe that Ayden is completely and totally dedicated to you, your Grace, but I believe he is conflicted because of the goals of the Creator and the Will. He will serve you loyally, and will never betray you, your Grace, but I believe that his duty as the Will will always come before his duty as your servant and protector."

Marlae smiled.

"In a matter of moments, Terrance, you have questioned the motives of a god, and one of the Servants of the Creator. Are all members of the Aldora family as unable to control themselves as you and your brother have proven to be, or are you simply so misunderstood that the only way you can be seen is as traitors?"

If the Divine Empress had not been smiling, Terrance though the next words out of her mouth would have been to call for the guards to come and take his head. But there was something in her calm and regal eyes that told him that he had nothing to worry about. Perhaps she was testing him, wondering if she could trust him to do what she needed him to do in the days to come. Rather than waiting for an answer, Marlae continued speaking.

"But you are right, of course, on both counts. Azure is a man who is trying to punish a bully for what was done to him, and my darling Ayden is trapped between duty to me, duty to his father, and duty to the Creator. Ayden doesn't think that I am aware of his parentage, but there is little now that I do not know about what is truly going on."

Terrance couldn't help himself.

"What is going on?"

Marlae's smile widened.

"Another discussion for another time," she said with a hint of comedy in her voice. "But one I promise we will get to have. So tell me, what is the prevailing thought as to our next actions?"

Terrance slumped back in his seat, but did not intend to look as defeated as he did.

"Unfortunately, your Grace, there is no prevailing thought. Azure is still pushing for a direct strike against Mythryn, especially with the facets of the Imperial Navy that have been seized. He believes that with the support of the angels and his fellow gods that have arrived, that the Dark Gods would not be able to muster enough of a defense. A quick strike at the heart of their power would give a victory that everyone would have to notice."

Marlae nodded.

"His victory. One that restores his reputation and does nothing to enhance mine. It will take place on a battlefield that no living person on Cadaria has seen and without any trophy to make it real to them. It quickly becomes as dismissed as the victories my father trumpets over the dragons. His men did the fighting and dying while he sat in the safety of the Imperial Palace. Still the people suffer and his stunning victories are nothing more than tales ghosts can tell one another."

"Ayden's plan is bolder, but problematic. There have been rumors for quite some time that the attempt on your father's life was carried out by Seraph Kore under the direction of the Dark Gods. Whether this is true or not, there are many among the people who believe it. The fact that your step-mother…"

Terrance's voice trailed off. Marlae sensed Terrance's hesitation.

"It's alright Terrance. As much as I tried to hate Dominique, there is nothing to hate. She was placed in an impossible situation and did her best to try to make the best of it. I think if she would have had a choice in the matter, the last thing she would have wanted to be was the Empress in that place and in that time, and she would never have chosen to be the wife of a monster, and step-mother of a spoiled princess. Dominique should be lauded for the successes that she had, and if it were in my power I would pardon her for the things that she did under duress. Perhaps I will have that opportunity in time. But I must save that for a time when it benefits us both. Now it would seem disingenuous and manipulative. She would see it as an act the old Marlae would take, and she would be right. She must believe that it comes from an honest place, and I have not done anything to prove that. I cannot run from the reputation that I put so much effort in creating, but I will make sure that it is not my legacy. So please, do not feel afraid to say her name."

Terrance nodded and continued.

"The fact that Dominique condemned Seraph and made him the most wanted criminal in Cadaria helped to create the illusion that something more had to have been behind his actions. Ayden believes if we move against Thorigald directly, it could be seen as a victory against the elements that sought to corrupt one of the Knights of the Flashing Blade, and destabilize the Empire. It then puts us in striking distance of Saldarine, which would remove one of the military strongholds loyal to your father, and it would also give us access to Albitonin which has already sworn fealty to your rule. And as the center of the Church of the Creator, it would be a clear message to everyone of your position as the Chosen of the Creator, and would fly in the face of your father's decree that made worship of the Creator a crime punishable by death."

Marlae nodded slightly.

"And the problem?"

Terrance sighed.

"It would be a military incursion, your Grace, and one on the scale that has not been seen in Cadaria since the War for Ascension. It would require the entire military of Hedorah to be mobilized, as well as all of the forces from the Heavens that could be mustered. Hedorah would be completely undefended, and if we were to fail to gain a foothold in Thorigald, there might not be anywhere to retreat to."

Marlae considered for a moment, but the look on Terrance's face said there was more. She nodded and waited for the rest.

"And then," Terrance continued, "if we were victorious, there are more problems waiting for us. If we don't eliminate Seraph Kore, there will be elements within the Army of Water that will continue to oppose us, either in collected military fashion or as cells of insurgents who will commence hit and run attacks designed to inflict the most damage with limited losses. Those we don't convert or induce to our side will have to be eliminated, and that could be considered an act as ruthless as your father might commit, which would invalidate the reason for the invasion. Further, if we incur too many losses in the invasion, it may embolden Saldarine to launch a strike of their own to not only wipe out their ancient enemy but also to end your rule before it becomes established."

Marlae's features darkened slightly.

"Did Ayden give any chances on the possibility of getting reinforcements or even a second invasion force from Albitonin or Galateria?"

Terrance grimaced.

"The risk would be too great hoping for reinforcement from Galateria. Their long common border with Saldarine would be another frontier of battle, and that is the largest common border once you take the fight to the Kingdom of Fire. There might be a chance to get soldiers from Albitonin, but since Hannah Ironheart's disappearance, the Army of Stone is in disarray. Much of the assets in Albitonin have been dedicated to repairing the Heart of Stone, and the army took a great deal of losses in the Heretic's escape from captivity. As I understand, you also nearly lost your life in that incident."

Marlae's features were unreadable.

"There was much that happened that day, and a great deal of it could be put in the category of massive misunderstanding. Too many decisions were made that day without enough information to be making them, and I am just as guilty for what happened at the Heart of Stone that day as Aerith Seth. I think that if Gabriel Shadowfall and I switched places, I would have made the same choice he made. I hold out hope that I will be able to tell him that, but I don't hold out much hope that he is still alive."

Terrance waited for several moments before continuing to answer Marlae's question.

"The other danger Empress is that if we were to send a missive to Albitonin asking for their assistance, that we might alert Thorigald to the possibility of invasion. If they are ready for us, it will greatly increase our loses, and the potential for counterattack by Saldarine."

For several long moments, silence held between the two. It was then that Marlae focused her eyes intently on Terrance.

"You have a third option."

It was not a question. Marlae knew that Terrance was holding something back. He was not comfortable it was clear with voicing all of his thoughts, but he also was not adept at hiding the fact that he had more to offer.

"Yes, your Grace," Terrance said shifting in his seat, "but it does not accomplish the goal of scoring a victory against the Dark Gods, or against your father's forces."

"Perhaps the best way to win the game against Azure's interests is not to play in the first place."

Terrance could not hide the smile that tried to curl his lips.

"While we could conceivably win a fight against Thorigald, there is almost no chance for us to hold it, and immediately fight another war against Saldarine. The Kingdom of Fire and the Kingdom of Water have been trying to wipe each other out for generations and it's foolish of us to think that with a military the size of what Hedorah can muster is going to conquer both of those kingdoms just because they are under your command, your Grace. No offence meant of course."

Marlae smiled once again.

"None taken, Terrance. Please continue."

"When you proclaimed yourself the rightful ruler of Cadaria, and started the rebellion, Iltorp was one of the kingdoms that recognized your rule. They didn't commit any forces to your command, but they did acknowledge you. If we were to take an expeditionary force into Iltorp, gauge where they stood in the whole conflict, perhaps we could firm up their commitment to your rule and double the size of your army without losing what you already have or leaving Hedorah without the ability to defend itself. Iltorp also has a direct path to Albitonin, which puts both Albitonin and Galateria in play for a move against either Saldarine or Thorigald. Iltorp also shares a border with Aldere, and the Imperial Guard would have to protect your father's interests which would hurt his ability to consolidate his power in any of the other kingdoms whose allegiance may be in question. This plan may not impact the Dark Gods, but it certainly will damage your father, and put you one step closer to reunited Cadaria under a single banner."

"And it seems to offer the least amount of risk of the available plans."

Terrance nodded in response.

"Congratulations, Terrance," Marlae said getting to her feet. "I believe you have crafted our course of action. You have also shown that you will be invaluable to me in the days to come as an advisor. We will have to find someone else to oversee the day to day operations of Hedorah, and I expect you to have some names for me tomorrow."

Terrance fell to one knee immediately. He was sure that he needed to say something, but no words would come to his mind. What was there for him to say? In a matter of hours he had gone from a minor functionary with no real power, to the head of a kingdom, to an advisor to the Empress of Cadaria. The absurdity of it made his head spin. Terrance's fumbling was interrupted by a knock at the door.

"Come."

The Empress's command was quickly followed by the creek of the door. Marlae tapped Terrance lightly on the shoulder, and he quickly found his way back to his feet and turned to face the door. After a short moment a girl entered with a more mature woman following behind her. The girl was obviously a servant whose name Terrance was trying hard to recall, but the woman was dressed in regal finery, and Terrance wondered if he should bow again. Out of the corner of his eye, Terrance could see Marlae's lips curl into a wide satisfied smile. The servant girl fell to one knee immediately after closing the door, but the woman remained standing.

"Thank you Isabella. Please rise."

The servant girl, Isabella, got back to her feet, and waited for another command.

"Terrance, let me introduce you to a very important person whom I am hoping will join you as one of my advisors. Terrance Aldora, this is the Lady Anabel Binosear, the Lioness of Trelon."

Patience and Wrath

Year Four of the Just Emperor Kaitain "Dragonsbane" Lorien, Creator's Calendar Year 1871

Aerith Seth's hands tensed, and in the deepest parts of his mind he was already preparing for the contingencies that were about to play out. The Wrath was impressive, wreathed with angelic fire, four wings batting in gentle opposition, glowing sword and shield poised for a quick strike. As a Servant of the Creator, the Wrath would be one of the fastest opponents that Aerith had ever faced, and he had stared down both the Voice and the Will. But the Wrath was different. The Voice was designed to be nothing more than a politician, the vessel of the Creator's words throughout the whole of creation. The Will was a warrior, but was primarily a defender of the Throne. His bulk and his temperament were more suited to large scale combat with ranks of angels at his back, performing some grand last stand to defend a prized artifact or beloved worshipper of the Creator. The Wrath on the other hand was different. The Wrath was created in a time when many of the worlds under the control of the Creator experienced problems accepting the Creator's rule. The Wrath was a creature that lived on death. He loved the death, he loved the slaughter, and every one of his divine abilities was tailored to the destruction of hundreds of people at a time. Those careless or stupid enough to think they could engage the Wrath in single combat were quickly cut down, or immolated on the spot for their mistake, paid quickly for their arrogance. If Aerith weren't a cagy opponent battle would have already been joined. It was careless to produce a weapon against one of the Servants until it was absolutely certain that there was a fight to be had.

"The Heretic," Wrath said coldly, its modulating voice echoing in the still air. "Somehow I expected more from the man who killed the Voice and has the Children of the Creator shaking in their boots. I thought you would be some larger than life giant or perhaps all scarred and disfigured from your generations of war. But here you are, another pretty boy who thinks he can topple the universe. I've killed thousands like you. I've made whole worlds burn because of prideful mortals like you. But the Children fear you, and the Creator respected you enough to accept your bargain. However, it's time for you to pay your end. You've lost."

Aerith could not keep the self-satisfied smile from coming to his face.

"The deal is far from concluded, and you know it. We're still standing, and the Dark Gods are still fighting. And I know for a fact that at least two of the Dark Gods are responsible for running and protecting a whole kingdom. The people who live under their rule love them. And I know for certain that there are elements in the Cadarian hierarchy that are looking to ally themselves with the Dark Gods. This Emperor Lorien will fall, and the world will shift again. Then all that will be left is Dorovar, and you know that Dorovar will fall if it takes every last drop of blood in my body."

The Wrath laughed a deep bellowing laugh.

"Blinded by your own arrogance again, Heretic. So much in your vision, and yet so much out of your grasp. So you believe that this whole continent is going to swing to the Dark Gods, and that magically all of your sins will be erased. But the Creator understands all the terms of your wager, and has exercised a contingency of His own. These new pieces on the board make the wager fall in the Creator's favor, and as such, you are now expendable. Halicon has rendered you impotent and tainted. Now, I promise you that you will see your own beating heart before you die."

The Wrath landed several feet from Aerith and raised his sword into a dueling position, shield held low, waiting for his opponent's coming strike.

"I was you once," the Wrath said, a sudden deadly seriousness filling his voice. "Idealistic, careless, stupid. There were opportunities for me to be something other than this, something other than a Servant of the Creator, something other than a martyr. But Emries changed all that. He came into my life the same as he came into Azure's. Gave me a choice, with no choice. If I had not become what he wanted, when he wanted, he would have killed me. I would have been yet another pointless martyr to a pointless cause."

The Wrath paused, the wings at his back slumping slightly.

"Emries came to my world, came to Onea. He brought with him the Creator's laws, and yet he said that he was the one that gave life to the humans of Onea. He stood by the book, in the middle of the field near my village and demanded that we build a church in his honor. Some flocked to his call willingly, and those who didn't were either guilted into service, or burned as heretics. Death followed his footsteps. Those who did not fall at his feet died on their knees. People feared him more than they loved him, and gave him the name that would echo through history. *Coromor.* The One Who Brings Destruction. The wars that followed his coming were brutal and bloody. The heretics against the believers. But the believers were more brutal than the heretics expected, and too great in number. Then the nightmare came. Halicon descended upon our world like a great shadow, ending all of the wars between mortals and uniting them against beasts of such horror and ferocity that people cowered in their homes and begged the one who brought war and death to their world to save them from the real demons."

Somewhere deep inside himself Aerith shuddered. He had never imagined that there was someone from the beginning of Onea still drawing breath, let alone one who had served Emries in the first war against Shauling. But here was this man, this brutalized and broken man, filled with divine power to bring retribution on the Creator's enemies, who had seen it with his own eyes.

"And so the mortals fought, emboldened by the One Who Brings Change. They threw themselves like waves against the unyielding rock. Men, women and children died by the thousands, and still they fought. Monsters continued to slaughter, but then the true monsters appeared.

They had human sounding names, they looked like us, but as they waded onto the battlefield, they struck with such ferocity that they broke the will of whole kingdoms. The worst of the lot was Aryx Terian. I remember the battle where he earned the name that was a curse for the first half of his existence and a badge of honor for the rest. An army under the command of one of Emries' greatest generals, the man you now know as Azure broke through the lines of Jeresei and Kalbraks with most of their number still intact. Aryx stood on a hilltop alone, watching his enemy advance on him; thousands were armed and ready to taste his blood. But the man reached a hand into the sky and called down lightning from the heavens. It was the first time most mortals had seen the true power of what they were fighting against. Dozens died with the first strike, but the frenzy of battle had blinded most to fear. They charged up the hillside, screaming the name of their god. Aryx did not relent one footstep. Bolt after bolt of lightning struck the ground all around, raining down from the sky an endless torrent of death and destruction. Broken and burning bodies of men flew in all directions. Those that weren't killed instantly were wounded in ways that would never heal."

The Wrath reached up and pulled the faceplate up so that it sat on the top of his head. Aerith had never set eyes upon the man before, but it was obvious that the man had seen a lot of battle. His face was a canvas of scars and half-healed wounds. One of his eyes had been damaged to such a degree that it had turned white, while the other was blood red. The right corner of the man's mouth was down-turned into a permanent frown by a scar, and the jagged scar in his forehead caused his right brow to dip lower than the left. When he spoke again, the modulated voice had eased to a more common man's voice, but there was a slight impediment to the man's voice as though his tongue and throat had been damaged as well.

"This is what the life of a willing servant gains you, Aerith. I was there that day, on the outskirts of Lakestone, trying to take a hill that after that day no longer existed out in the middle of a wasteland that no one dwelled upon again except for the man who created the stench of death that permeated that place for the rest of Onea's existence. These scars on my face, I earned them that day. I stood on the hillside, sword in my hand. I stared into his cold dead eyes. He knew that I was no real threat to him, and yet he leveled his hand, pointing it in my direction and called down another bolt of lightning. The fires passed through me, burning me from the inside out, and sent me flying through the air. For a long time I felt that moment that I died. That as I floated through the air, my soul was being freed from the hell that I lived and I would be standing in the heavens. But then I hit the ground, and lay there in a pool of blood. I don't know how long I lay there, how long I listened to my friends, my brothers, my family die. How long I heard their screams of terror. And yet, when my eyes finally closed, death did not welcome me. My breath did not stop. The horror did not end. My soul was lifted up, but not by the Creator, and not to some great rest that had been earned through service to His laws."

Horror filled Wolf's face and heart as the realization filled him.

"You were one of the first *Erieal*."

The Wrath's broken face twisted into a hate-filled frown.

"That is my legacy. My name lost to time, and only the mantle remains. Emries pulled me back from the brink of death and said that I had more work to do. That he saw the way to take the fight to the phasia, to get revenge for all of the people I lost that day. To pay back death with more death. But there was no choice given by his words. There was no other option. I became his vessel. The fires that burned and twisted my body became mine to wield, to level destruction and death upon all those who stood against me. For years that is exactly what I did. I lost count of how many Jeresei and Kalbraks I killed. Then when the violence of the war and the senselessness of the killing set in so deeply that there was no difference between the monsters that served the phasia and the mortals who willingly lived under their rule, I killed them by the thousands as well. But the greatest horror of my life came when I was brought to my patron and he gave me a task. He gave me the means to get my revenge, and the means to strike a blow for the cause. Emries had learned that Aryx had left the service of Shau-ling, that he was trying to live a life outside of the war. That he had a wife, and a child. Emries learned where they lived. Learned where they could be struck. Knew when they would be at their most vulnerable."

Aerith's blood began to boil and the churning in his stomach went from pity from what the man had suffered to pure, unadulterated rage. All he wanted was to make the man suffer more. He balled his fists and began to slowly draw on the power that was available to him, listening as more of the poisonous words dripped from the Wrath's mouth.

"Emries insured that Aryx was informed of a threat that was approaching him. He invented a story about one of the new members of the phasia that were trying to get revenge for Aryx's traitorous ways. I lay in wait as Aryx left to investigate. Night fell and I crept into the home. For a long time I stood and watched his wife sleep. She had no idea of the danger that was around her, no idea that she would never see another sunrise. She tuned over on her back, and I reached down with both hands and put them around her throat. Her eyes went wide and she tried to scream, but she didn't realize that she was already dead. I let some of the fire inside of me flow through my fingers and slowly seep into her body. The same way that Aryx tortured me years earlier and brought me to the edge of death, I brought his love to the edge of death before finally snuffing out her last breath. Then I moved across the room where you lay, Aerith. Little baby Aerith, asleep in his crib, oblivious to the fate that awaited him. I held you in my hands, Aerith. I was seconds away from snapping your neck and ending all of this before it began. But you were saved. Something came from behind me and prevented me from ending you. Now I have another chance to finish the job I once began. I will wrap these hands around your throat just as I did your mother and I will watch the light go out of your eyes. I will be your end as I should have been all those years ago on Onea."

The scream of rage that came from Aerith was like nothing that Wolf had heard before. It was a primal guttural exhalation of such emotion that Wolf felt it at the very core of his being. Aerith charged the Wrath, the twin blades of light and darkness formed in Aerith's hands only a moment before he struck the first time. Wrath seemed to be ready for the attack, raising his shield to block the first blow, and then falling back slightly to avoid the long sweep of the follow-up strike. Aerith continued into another set of wild slashes, very unlike his typically cocky and restrained fighting style. Again and again Aerith struck, each blade either finding the Wrath's glowing shield, or being blocked harmlessly aside by the flaming blade. After several fruitless exchanges, the Wrath struck with his own blade, a single hard downward slash that seemed to catch Aerith by surprise. Aerith was able to get his blade of light up at the last moment to prevent the flaming blade from doing any damage, but the total committal to attack had left Aerith open to the hard shield strike that caught him on the side of his head. The sickening thud of metal striking skull turned Wolf's stomach and sent Aerith flying through the air and coming to a crashing halt in a puddle of mud hundreds of feet from the Wrath. Rather than following up on the vicious strike, the Wrath stood in place and waited. Aerith pushed himself back onto his hands and knees, a stream of blood flowing from a gaping wound on the side of his head. Sinking back onto his knees, Aerith took a deep breath but refused to wipe the blood that streamed down his face. When he finally got back to his feet, he drew the long blade from the sheathe on his back, and held the Sacred Weapon Valor ready to strike. The Wrath held back for a long moment before floating forward. As he passed Wolf, the Wrath pointed his blade in the man's direction.

"You know the law. You may not be Pyrrus, but by accepting his power, you accepted the oaths he took as a Child of the Creator."

Wolf put his hands in the air and took a step away from the Wrath. Holding his shield ready for Aerith's next attack, the Wrath darted in. Bringing his blade into a long sweeping blow aimed for Aerith's throat. Taking a page out of his opponent's book, Aerith skipped backwards, just outside of the range of his opponent, and lashed out with Valor, letting the longer weapon's range give a tactical advantage. A quick hard slash found the Wrath's shield, but with enough ferocity that it interrupted the Wrath's next attack. Aerith charged in again, and again, the Wrath met the blade with his own. But Aerith was not content with a stalemate, and he had recovered his wits enough that his tactical prowess was returning. Aerith charged in again, lowering his shoulder into the glowing shield. The Wrath took the bait, bringing his glowing sword down onto where the back of Aerith's neck should have been. But Aerith was not there. He dropped Valor from his grasp, spun off the shield toward the Wrath's shield side, and drew Discipline from the sheathe on his hip. The upward strike found the gap between the Wrath's arm and the shield, severing the strap that held it in place and cutting deeply into the Wrath's wrist. A howl of pain came from behind the Wrath's mask, and he fell back, the shield dropping to the ground. Despite the severity of the wound, no blood erupted from the Wrath's injured hand, but rays of light instantly sealed the ruptured flesh and brought the Wrath back to full strength. In the repaired hand, another flaming blade appeared, and the Wrath stood defiant.

"You see, Heretic, none of your skill or your bravado will avail you. I know all of your moves, all of your tactics, and there is nothing that you can do to change the advantage I have over you. Lay down and die."

In answer, Aerith bent down and recovered the Wrath's shield. As soon as Aerith's hand touched the shield, it ceased glowing. For a long moment, Aerith took his eyes off the Wrath, looking down at the shield, judging its weight with gentle movements. Finally Aerith pulled the shield into a defensive position. He brought his eyes back up to look at the Wrath's face, and for the first time in the battle a small smile curled the corners of Aerith's mouth.

"Never was one to fight with a shield," he said, calmly, "but I'll wager that my skill with a shield is better than yours with two swords."

The Wrath answered by lunging in, a hard slash coming at the level of Aerith's head, while the true attack was a thrust whose target was the center of Aerith's chest. Aerith was a step ahead of his opponent, using Discipline to deflect the lazy slash, while he charged forward, letting the nearly immortal metal of the Wrath's shield intercept the point of the flaming blade. There was a flash of brilliant light, and instead of Aerith being thrown backwards by the force of the Servant's blow, the Wrath's attack was turned to one side, and Aerith extended his arms, thrusting the shield into the Servant's chest, forcing him backwards. Again the Wrath charged, and again Aerith deflected the attack and pushed away his opponent. From where he was standing, Wolf could see something happening. Aerith was collecting energy, drawing deeply on the power around him, and touching deeply the power of the Blaze. Through his connection to both Basille and Draven, Wolf could feel what was happening, even if he could not divine the reason. However, Wolf did not have to wait long before he saw the truth of the maneuver. Aerith's defensive tactics had made the Wrath sloppy in its movements. The strikes were not precise and left small openings for counterattack. So far all Aerith had done was push the man away, and time and time again he passed up opportunities that could have been used to strike. But every small window that Aerith passed up created future opportunities as the Wrath became more and more focused on offense and ending the battle. Finally, the last set of strikes came from the Wrath, and Aerith finally let a counter attack fly. Discipline darted through the Wrath's guard, the tip of the blade burying into the Wrath's stomach. Aerith pushed forward, pushing the blade deeper and then pushing the Servant away. However, he was not finished with the prey. Aerith channeled all of the power that he had been gathering over the last few moments into the shield, and Wolf could see lightning dancing over the surface of the metal. The Wrath managed a weak slash with one of this blades before Aerith struck again, slamming the shield into the Sacred Weapon that was still embedded in the Servant's stomach. Lightning flashed and rocketed through the Servant's body, and the smell of burning flesh filled the air. The blades of fire disappeared from the Wrath's hands and he fell back to the ground, still twitching. Aerith let the shield fall to the ground.

"That was for my father."

Aerith picked Valor up from where it lay on the ground and walked slowly over to the fallen body of the Servant. He towered over the fallen man, blade poised for the last strike.

"And this is for my mother."

Aerith was primed to bring the blade crashing down on the neck of the Wrath, but Wolf's hand stayed his strike. For a long time Aerith stood, staring down at the Wrath, wanting so much to let the blade in his hands finish what he began. But deeply inside himself, Aerith knew that Wolf would not have intervened had there not been a good reason.

"I know you want to kill him, Aerith. But there may be more that we can accomplish here. We may be able to save our friend."

Wolf knelt down at the Wrath's side and put his hand on the man's mask. For a long moment he stayed there, his eyes closed, barely breathing. Finally Wolf nodded slightly and opened his eyes before taking hold of the Wrath at his shoulders and then pulling the Servant back to his feet. Upon pulling the Wrath up, Aerith watched with a bit of horror and a bit of puzzlement as Discipline snapped in two, and the hilt and half of the blade clattered to the ground. Holding the Wrath up, Wolf snaked one hand around the Wrath's body and put it on the Servant's chest. Aerith couldn't see what was happening, but there was a soft white light that started to radiate from Wolf's hand.

"Put your hand on the Wrath's faceplate. Channel as much of the Blaze into it as you can."

Aerith didn't question and placed his hand on the cool metal and reached deeply into the flows of power that resided inside of him and opened himself to the roaring green flame at the back of his mind. When finally the power flooded through him, instead of putting it to active use, he simply allowed it to travel through his body, down his arm and into his hand. In the back of his mind, Aerith could see the green flames licking at the smooth metal of the faceplate, as if searching for a way inside. There was another power that joined the Blaze, a gentle blue glow that radiated up from the Wrath's chest. The two powers met in the center of the faceplate, and there was a powerful flash of white light that caused Aerith to pull away and cover his eyes. When Aerith was able to look back again, the body of the Wrath was gone, and all that remained was the faceplate. Aerith first looked down at the gleaming piece of metal on the ground, and then back up at Wolf.

"You heard the Wrath," Wolf said after a moment. "I had to obey the law. The Creator set forth laws concerning how the Servants could interact with other divine beings. The one the Wrath referred to was that no Child of the Creator could take direct action that led to the death of a Servant."

Aerith nodded absently.

"I'm sure that fact grated on Emries and Talisia terribly."

"After Evan's elevation to the position of Voice, and Talisia's ultimate failure in her rebellion, Emries spent a long time pondering how to act against the Servants should it ever become necessary. Eventually he came up with a way to circumvent the laws, and also prevent the Servants from just popping back up in new bodies. The secret was that it took the powers of two of the Children to pull it off. Thankfully for us, because of the way that Halicon invested his powers, the Blaze is available in full strength to anyone who can touch it. Your connection to Sabrina bridged the gap."

A sudden understanding shown on Aerith's face.

"So that was why Emries recruited Draven. Not just to mess with our minds, but he was also planning his eventual move against the Servants and the Creator. Very shrewd. I guess he was counting on the fact he would have to eliminate Talisia at some point, or that she would betray him. He certainly has kept his eyes open for all possibilities."

Wolf cocked his head.

"I doubt he counted on Pyrrus or Halicon doing what they did."

Aerith nodded, and bent down to retrieve the faceplate. For a long moment he just stared at it, feeling a strange power resonating from it. It wasn't purely the touch of the Creator, but it was certainly divine. Wolf reached out the next moment and took the faceplate from Aerith's hands. Holding it in both of his hands, Wolf pushed gently on the edges of the faceplate, collapsing it down into a small diamond shaped pendant with a glowing chain that emerged from the top. He held it out to Aerith with a bit of a smile tugging at the corner of his mouth.

"If I'm right," Wolf said lightly, "Sabrina might be able to find a use for this. But tell her that if she's not careful, the power is still going to eat her alive."

Aerith took the pendant and reached into his pocket for one of his stones.

"Thank you Wolf."

The younger man nodded.

"What will you do now?" Aerith asked as he threw the stone into the air and let the portal form.

Wolf looked off in the direction of the Dark Citadel and lifted a hand, and a moment later a series of explosions triggered deep in the structure causing it to shatter into thousands of pieces. A moment later he turned back to face Aerith.

"The Dark Gods time here is done. Mythryn is no longer a safe haven, and I have a feeling that there is more than even I know that is happening. I need to check out some of the memories that Draven and Basille have. I have a sinking suspicion that we have all been betrayed, and that I am at the center of it all. I can't take an active role in this conflict until I know for sure. And you?"

Aerith clutched the pendant tightly.

"Sabrina, and then Dorovar. Have to strip away his defenses before I take the fight to him."

Wolf reached out and took Aerith by the arm.

"Be careful old man," Wolf said with genuine concern in his voice. "Dorovar isn't like anything you've faced before, and he has more tricks up his sleeve than any of us know. And no matter what, do not move against Jerah. Leave that to my father."

Aerith considered for a long moment before nodding and stepping through the portal, leaving Wolf alone to watch the final destruction of the place that was equally his home and his tomb.

Chapter LXXVI

The Afters and Befores

What was left of the receiving hall of the Palace of Celidar seemed to shudder with anticipation as Bryn Aplee, the Lady Fox of the Brotherhood of the Phasia and Logan Ranthall, the second *Chosen One* of the prophecies of the *Coromor* and the erstwhile Lord Phoenix, lastborn of the Brotherhood of Phasia stood nearly nose to nose, eyes burning invisible holes into one another. There were so many things in Logan Ranthall that Bryn hated, and most of them were not the man's fault, but there were many things that she hated that were every bit as a result of his conscious efforts. He was a member of the phasia, and even though he had not come into that distinction in the same way that any of the other members of the Brotherhood had, it did not change what he was. The distinction made him totally untrustworthy, vindictive, malicious, and capable of killing her with a thought. And he was also an inheritor of the mantle of her husband's power. This fact also made him untrustworthy, treacherous, and more than anything an annoyance. No one should know that much about her and her capabilities, and Bryn knew from experience that Logan was in possession of some of the more personal and private memories of her relationship with Aerith. Bryn was not one to be considered modest in the least, but the moments that she had chosen to show vulnerability were for her husband only, not some backwards farm boy who knew how to control his tongue about as well as Aerith did. Elwyne Tamerlane's influence had not bettered Logan Ranthall, and Bryn had wondered if the recklessness in the boy was more a hindrance to his progress than to his elevation into the role of a hero. And that was what grated on Bryn the most when she looked at Logan. He should not have survived this long. He should not have become the hero that he was in any lifetime, let alone this one. Everything that Bryn knew told her that Logan Ranthall lived on an ocean of borrowed time, but it didn't look like he was going to be running out of it any time soon. Were she anyone else, she might have admired the boy, but there was too much there that would not allow her to see him as anything other than a younger version of Aerith Seth, and that could never under any context be considered a compliment.

Jillian Corven was about to step between the two, coming to the aid of the man that had quickly become very important in her life. She wasn't sure exactly what he was to her, and she wasn't sure what she wanted him to be, but it was clear he was more than just someone she had come across during her travels that had pulled her from danger time and time again. But as she began to make a move toward the pair, the blond haired woman that stood beside her that she had heard called Taya put her hand on Jillian's shoulder.

"I wouldn't do that," she said with a sliver of concern, "those are two people you don't want to get between under any circumstances. Besides, Logan can take care of himself."

Jillian bristled, but held her ground. Bryn tapped her foot impatiently but would not break her stare.

"I'm waiting, lastborn."

The insult did nothing but bring a smile to Logan's face.

"You forget, Bryn, I know more about you than anyone in this room, and more than just about anyone alive. And I know as much as you want to kill me right now, you won't. And you also know that I'm going to tell you everything you want to know without your threats and insults. So why don't we skip the part where we act like immature siblings and get right to the part where we start helping each other and making the best of this situation."

Bryn exhaled sharply, in annoyance, flipped her hair back away from her face and gave a curt nod. As soon as Logan returned the gesture of the nod, Bryn backhanded Logan across the face, sending him sprawling to the ground. She had only used a little bit of the power at her disposal, but it was enough to get her point across. Logan sat up laughing and rubbing his cheek.

"I love you too, Bryn."

Bryn moved to Sabrina's side to try to help her to her feet.

"Don't try my patience, Ranthall. Erika, we should probably move Sabrina to a place where she can rest, and we can talk more privately and comfortably."

Erika nodded, leading Bryn, Rhain, and Sabrina out of the receiving hall. By that time Logan had made his way back to his feet and was surveying the damage to the room. Jillian had returned to his side.

"What a mess."

Logan nodded but didn't look back at her.

"Believe it or not, I've seen worse."

When Logan did change his focus, instead of looking at Jillian, he looked past her to where Jerrard and Taya stood.

"Any appointments for today?"

There was a hint of comedy in Logan's voice, but Jerrard's expression did not change. Jerrard took his position as the head of the government in Celidar very seriously, and he had always considered the receiving hall to be the place where people both of his kingdom and other kingdoms were the safest. Once they were in his presence or the presence of his wife Erika, there was no danger that could touch them. If any of his subjects saw the receiving hall in this state, it would shatter that illusion and set back a great deal of the progress that Jerrard had made in his time in power.

"With Emperor Lorien's newest set of decrees, there are naturally going to be a great deal of concerned and fearful citizens. Many of them are going to be looking to me for whether I will back the Emperor, or if I will join one of the rebellious groups. So far I have been able to keep Celidar out of the squabble between Kaitain and Marlae, but I fear that I won't be able to do so for much longer."

Logan nodded and the smile faded from his face. He reached into his pocket and took out a coin and flipped it to Jerrard. Jerrard caught it out of the air and held it in his hand looking at it for a long moment. Several expressions passed over Jerrard's face for the next few seconds; confusion, annoyance, surprise, disbelief, and sudden understanding. However, before he could say anything, Logan interrupted by looking back at the damage.

"We can talk about that in a minute. First we have to deal with this. Taya, would you give me a hand?"

There was no confirmation from the blond-haired woman, and Jillian watched in amazement as the two began to repair the damage to the receiving hall. Beams mended themselves, and massive blocks of stone lifted from the floor and returned to their proper places. Where the pieces were too broken to be mended, new blocks of stone and beams of wood seemed to just spring into being from the ground below, forming into the proper shapes and then levitating into place. The only pieces that the pair was not able to fix seemed to be the tapestries that had been ripped and burned during the battle. However, within a matter of minutes, the receiving hall was back in one piece, and the two didn't seem to have even broken a sweat. Logan looked around nodding and then set his eyes on Taya.

"Not bad. Your control has gotten a lot better. Your father would be proud."

A little color came to the woman's face, but faded quickly. Whatever vulnerability shown through for that brief second was instantly hidden behind the emotional armor she constantly wore.

"It was the only way I could keep my ships in the water. Gave me an advantage over the Cadarians since I could repair my ships and the ones I'd captured quicker than they could build new ones. I'm going to go check on Sabrina."

She turned and left the room quickly, bringing another shake of the head from Logan.

"Just like her father," Logan said in a barely audible voice. "He couldn't take a compliment either. But then that's what happens when your parents are killers."

Logan turned to face Jerrard and walked to where Gabriel knelt over Devlin's remains. Logan put his hand on Gabriel's shoulder.

"Don't worry Gabriel," Logan said in his best comforting voice. "We'll make sure he gets a proper burial. He had a lot to live for, I know, but I don't think he could have wanted to die any other way than protecting someone. What he did was heroic, and the lives that he saved by protecting Sabrina will number in the thousands."

It took a moment, but Gabriel got to his feet and pulled his shoulders back hard.

"Everyone here seems to know you, but I don't. But somehow you seem to know who I am and who Devlin is."

Logan looked over to Jerrard who shrugged.

"You have to admit, Logan," Jerrard said crossing his arms, "sometimes your memories do you a disservice. And I know how much you enjoy explaining how you know things and frustrating the mortals."

Logan grimaced and turned his attention back to Gabriel.

"The short version is that Aerith and I are very close, and I know a lot about you. If Aerith thinks highly of you, then you can be sure…"

Logan's voice trailed off, and a sword of pure energy appeared in his right hand. With his left he pulled Jillian behind him and spun toward a spot in the middle of the room. Just as Logan's sword started through the air, a swirling blue portal opened, and a man stepped out. He had short blond hair, and piercing blue eyes, but the first thing that Jillian noticed was that he was missing his right arm past the elbow. The glowing blade stopped just under the man's chin, ready to slice through his exposed throat, and Jillian knew that Logan had stopped the strike short. The blond man didn't make a move and put his hand up. Whoever the newcomer was, Jillian thought that he was a very controlled and disciplined man to be faced with that kind of threat and simply and calmly react.

"That's a pretty good trick, Alderin," Logan said, keeping the weapon where it was, "I bet if I hadn't been standing right here, I never would have felt the portal forming. Guess you just picked the wrong spot if you were trying to sneak up on us."

Alderin's face held just as much surprise as confusion. But before he could say anything, Jerrard added his voice.

"Logan, can't you feel it? Alderin didn't do this. He doesn't have any abilities. They've been taken from him."

Logan took a long hard look at the man, and then let the sword disappear from his hand. He reached out and put a hand on Alderin's shoulder.

"I take it you had a run in with Tess."

Alderin's eyes went wide.

"Tess was here? Where did she go? Was Darrien with her?"

Logan wanted to comfort the man, but it was Jerrard who spoke first.

"Tess caused quite a lot of damage, Alderin, and no, Darrien was not with her. We're not sure where Tess has gone, but I can assure you that will be a topic of great conversation. But first, we must attend to our fallen friend and to those who have been injured. I think then we should find some food and perhaps some drink. Then I am sure there will be much in the way of talking about not only Tess, but how we all found our way here."

* * * * * * * * * * * *

Hours had passed since the battle in the receiving hall in the Royal Palace of Celidar, and the passage of time had not done much to ease the nerves of those in the palace. There had been enough time to share news from different parts of the world, and everyone listened with interest as Logan and Jillian gave news from the Plains of Steam and Alderin filled everyone in on what had happened in the Citadel of the Dark Gods as well as the Heart of Stone. Bryn added some detail about the short battle in Iltorp, while Gabriel added his own details about Albitonin. There was so much happening in all parts of Cadaria, and when Jerrard added the information about the decrees from Emperor Lorien and the apparent fractures in the Cadarian ruling family, the picture didn't get much better. When they had adjourned together to the former war room of the palace, Erika Mystic chose not to join them. Instead, she felt it was important that she try her best to explain the situation to Feyd Lorien, and break him gently into the morass of politics that he had unwittingly stepped back into. Logan kept his eyes on Sabrina as she entered the room, looking pale and weak, barely able to support herself without the help of either Rhain or Taya. The three women sat together while Jillian sat with Logan on the other side of the table. Alderin chose not to join the others at the table, preferring to lean against the wall near where Logan sat. Bryn and Jerrard sat opposite each other at the head and foot of the table. Gabriel stood near the door, unsure what role he would have in the conversation that was about to take place. Once everyone was seated, as expected, it was Bryn that fired the first salvo.

"All I care about right now is what my dim-witted husband has planned," she said gruffly. "The rest of you can play politics with the mortals, but none of that will matter if the troublemaker keeps making it up as he goes along."

Logan was ready to speak up, but it was Sabrina's weak voice that answered Bryn's annoyance. Though Sabrina and Logan shared many memories from Aerith, and new facets of the plan, Sabrina had an angle on the genesis of the plan that no one but Aerith could. Sometimes Sabrina wondered if she had a fuller understanding of everything than Aerith had, and then she would scold herself that it didn't truly matter. Aerith was smart and connected enough to grasp everything that Sabrina did, he just chose not to. There was a large part of Aerith that didn't want to know and understand all of the things that he did, and at times he simply chose to be more naïve than he truly was. It was a tactic that had served him well all of his life, even if one of the side effects proved to be his death from time to time. Sabrina's voice was raspy, but there was power enough to convey the important things she needed to convey.

"I know you want to be mad at him, Bryn, but we all owe Aerith a debt. We would all be dead by now if it wasn't for him."

Bryn couldn't suppress the laugh.

"Sabrina, dear," Bryn said in her best mocking tone, "I know that you love Aerith, but even I have a hard time believing that."

"You may not want to believe it Bryn," Sabrina said, sitting forward and leaning both of her forearms on the table, "but it's true. It all goes back to Talisia's rebellion. Things were so far gone then. Open warfare in the heavens, the Children at each other's throats to the point that the silent machinations had exploded into wanton destruction on each other's worlds. Angels and dragons choosing up sides, and the other ascended beings trapped in the middle of it all, most owing their lives or their allegiances to one of the Children. Then Talisia struck openly against Pyrrus. Halicon was in seclusion, Emries was missing and brooding over his defeat, Raenera was still recovering from her own losses, and the Servants were all off hunting the threat we would come to know as Dorovar. All of them except for the Spirit. Which proved to be both advantageous and dangerous. Once Pyrrus had died, and Talisia had been banished to Espre, I was offered the position of the Spirit, because it was felt that I would bring a calming voice to the reconciliation of the heavens. What it did however was make me privy to the Creator's secrets, and what I knew, Aerith knew."

Logan took the opportunity to take up the story.

"And what Sabrina uncovered was as terrifying as it was unbelievable. The Creator was deeply hurt by the death of Pyrrus, but it seemed to create in Him this feeling that He had failed. His Children were no longer trying to prove their thoughts and theories through deeds, but instead were bent on winning through attrition. If only one of them were left standing, then only one of them could be right. It was the nightmare scenario for a father who wanted nothing but to see his Children work together as they built the Cosmos in His image. Pyrrus' death was the final evidence that the experiment had failed. The Creator began to enact a plan that would eliminate the Children."

Jerrard stared at Logan, his mouth hanging open.

"But Espre was supposed to be the last battleground. So that one of them could prove they were right. The mortals were the test. Whoever could sway them; that was why the Dark Gods were sent down, like another faction in the game. A foil to the Children."

Sabrina shook her head.

"Gwydeon's rebellion was a result of what I knew, not a plan of the Creator's. I went to Aerith and to Gwydeon and laid out the plan that led to the rebellion. Aerith made a bet with the Creator that the mortals who fought against the Children on Onea could not only defeat the Children on Espre, but could also lead the mortals on a path that took them out of the Creator's shadow. If Aerith won the bet, the Creator would let all that remained on Espre live out natural lives if they wanted, removed from their ascended status and left to die like mortals. If the Creator won the bet, Aerith and his conspirators, namely Gwydeon, Logan, and myself, would serve the Creator until the end of time, and never raise arms against him or any of His servants ever again."

Bryn cursed.

"The bastard did it for me."

Taya scoffed.

"Everything is always about you, Bryn."

Logan cocked his head to one side and fixed a withering gaze on Taya.

"That's exactly why he did it. Aerith and Bryn have been alive longer than anyone should be made to live. And as much as they love each other, and as much as they love their children and their friends, they cannot and do not want to go on forever. And as long as these battles continued,

Aerith knew that he and Bryn would be at the heart of them. He wanted out. And he wanted to stick it to Emries one more time. This was his way. He will get his revenge for everyone who has suffered and died because of him. He will pay Emries and the Creator back for every soul on Onea, and he will make sure it can never happen again. Because as much as this is about ending the game once and for all. It's about making sure the game can't ever be played again."

Jillian, though she had no idea who some of the people being discussed were, was trying her best to keep up with the concepts. But there was something that kept disjointing her understanding.

"So the Creator made this bet, and this Aerith wanted to make the bet. But I don't understand why it needed to be made. So the Creator was going to wipe out these Children. What does that have to do with us?"

"Spoken like a pathetic mortal," Bryn chided. "You have no understanding of anything past your own immature infatuations. If you could live even double your lifespan you would understand how truly insignificant you are."

Jillian balled her fist, but Logan reached out and held her hand.

"Mortals annoy Bryn. She never was one, and it offends her that those who were have had such an important role in all of this."

Rhain, though slightly embarrassed at her mother's behavior tried her best to answer Jillian's question.

"It's not just about the Children. The Creator could kill the Children whenever He wanted. But the Children represent ideas, and those ideas have spread down into their followers, the ones chosen to wield their power, and has also seemingly corrupted the angels and the dragons. Even if the Creator were to kill the Children now, it would not kill their ideas or their influence. So the Creator would have to get them all into one place at one time."

The shock on Jerrard's face faded to sobering understanding.

"And what better way to convince the Children that they all needed to be in the same place but to give them the opportunity to do what they most want. Kill each other."

Sabrina nodded.

"Then it was a simple matter to get the dragons here. All the players are on the board, except for perhaps the angels and some of the remaining gods, but I'm sure it won't be long before they are here too."

Silence filled the room. It was Gabriel who broke it.

"What's Aerith's plan? If I learned anything from the man it's that while it may seem like he is reckless and foolish and doesn't think about anything before he does it, the truth is that he doesn't do anything without thinking out every possible way that it can play out."

Logan smiled.

"Took Bryn a few hundred years to get that."

Bryn ignored the jibe and looked to Sabrina.

"It's simple," Sabrina answered. "Simple even for Aerith. Eliminate the Children, Eliminate the Servants, and then kill the Creator and replace Him."

Gabriel sputtered and most just stared, with the exception of Bryn and Logan. After a moment for it to all sink in, Logan began speaking.

"Aerith had the few of us who have held his mantle, and a couple of other allies, but our numbers are small and spread out. Halicon is already out of the game, but as Korrd has shown us, we have to topple the remaining vessels too. Anyone who was a servant to Emries is compromised. That means the former *Coromors* and the former *Erieal*. The only ones I know that are still out there are Lissa and Taya. But because Taya also has phasia blood and Aerith's blood, I don't know how much pull Emries is going to have over her. Either way, we have to find a way to strip the *Erieal* influence from both of them before they can be trusted completely."

Sabrina put her hand on Taya's shoulder.

"Through Halicon I know the process. It should be fairly painless."

Taya nodded.

"Good. Didn't want it anyway."

"The hard part will be tracking down Talisia's kids, and the *Coromors*. Arin went to keep tabs on Kaitain because he has one of Talisia's kids working for him. Hannah went to Jelan to check in on the Academy there and to look for Ayden who has gone missing, and I drew the short straw for rallying the troops. Well, that and to talk to Jerrard about ways that we can stall Kaitain's advance. You have to know he's going to be coming here soon."

Jerrard nodded.

"With Prince Feyd here, we have some legitimacy for a while. But that won't stop Kaitain, in fact it may speed him up. I'm not sure how we're going to fight him off. Celidar's army is fractured and with our Knight of the Flashing Blade, Tolon Morr off who knows where with one of the Maldovrins, things don't look as though they are going to get brighter any time soon."

Logan smirked.

"Don't worry about Tolon, Aerith sent him to gather some reinforcements for us. But in answer to your question, Jerrard, I think it's long past time for you to reclaim your birthright."

Jerrard pulled the coin out of his pocket that Logan had given him. On one side was the image of a raven and on the other was the crest of the phoenix.

"Fly your father's banner, and proclaim that you are a Dark God and that you have been and will keep protecting this kingdom. And then introduce Prince Feyd as the regent from the Lorien family. It will be the first time that a Dark God and a Lorien worked together and it will give a lot of people pause, and it should buy you time."

Jerrard frowned.

"And are you going to stay here and fight off the scared rebels?"

Gabriel stepped up at that moment.

"No. I will. I still have a reputation from my time in the Knights of the Flashing Blade. And with the might of Taya's navy, I think we can hold without any losses, and without it becoming a police state. Logan is right, it's the smart move, if Prince Feyd is with us."

"In the meantime," Logan said, "Jillian and I are off to Galateria. We have some allies there that Aerith wants us to check in on, and try to get some support in the coming battles. Then we're going dragon hunting."

Bryn's nose wrinkled.

"I'm going to find Jeroch and Saurn. My other family has a lot to answer for. Jeroch thinks he has always been clever, but I will find him."

Sabrina's eyes sparkled.

"I can help you with that," she said weakly. "Now that I have Halicon's power, I can find any of the phasia. Taya, Rhain, and I have business of our own far from here. We will be heading to Oradrim as soon as I am strong enough to travel."

Alderin was the last to speak.

"If Sabrina can help me, I need to find Darrien. Once I know what happened to her, we'll go after Tess."

The meeting simply broke up at that point. There was too much to do, and no time to do it, and everyone around the table realized that more talking would not get them closer to their goals. Bryn and Rhain spoke briefly before Rhain returned to Sabrina's side. Taya excused herself to speak with Jerrard and when Alderin attempted to take her place, Sabrina waved him off.

"I need some time to rest, Alderin," she said quietly, "but I can help you. Help Jerrard and the others, and Rhain will come and get you when I am ready."

As soon as Alderin was out of earshot, Sabrina locked a sobering gaze on Rhain.

"I have a favor to ask of you, my dear friend."

Hungry No More

Year Four of the Just Emperor Kaitain "Dragonsbane" Lorien,
Creator's Calendar Year 1871

The fields outside the Academy of Arcane Arts in Jelan were already soaked with more blood than had been seen in the last three Cadarian civil wars combined. Three ancient dragons had met their end, contingents from two of the great armies of the Kingdoms of Cadaria had been decimated, as had an army of beasts that served the Dark Gods. Now another army took the field, this one bloodless, but no less willing to add their number to the growing body count. While at her core, Hannah Ironheart regretted all of the killing, she knew that the stakes were too high. Many believed, whether rightly or wrongly, that the students of the Academy of Arcane Arts in Jelan could become the pivotal force in a war that ignited the whole of Espre. Kaitain Lorien wanted to use the Academy for a purpose that their oaths expressly forbid, as a weapon against his enemies. Naturally, traditionalists and those who saw Kaitain for the madman that he was wanted to keep the Academy out of his hands at all costs. Marlae Lorien had sided with the traditionalists, not because she believed that the Academy should be protected, but because it put her in direct opposition to her father, and thus gained her the support of his opponents. The Dark Gods did not want to use the Academy, nor did they find their abilities to be a threat, but also they wanted to keep such a weapon out of anyone's hands to prevent needless suffering. Dorovar wanted to either use or eliminate the Academy, it mattered little to him. Somewhere in the back of her mind, Hannah found it both ludicrous and galling that it was the Dark Gods that seemed to have the best interests of both the Academy and the innocents they could hurt at heart. But as Hannah looked sidelong at her unexpected ally, she began to wonder what stake the dragons had in the fate of the Academy. Or, had the huge winged beast not come for the Academy at all? Perhaps Mariti's true purpose was to attack Hannah, and a more appealing target just happened to present itself. Whatever the ancient creature's true motivations, for the moment she and Hannah found themselves on the same side of an engagement, and the beast was not going to wait for her opportunity to taste the flesh of one of Dorovar's sadistic Heralds.

Mariti charged in with a roar, gliding across the distance with incredible speed, landing in the very center of the ranks of skeletal troops, crushing dozens of them with the sickening sound of breaking bones. Hannah was ready to charge in as well, but it seemed that Seraphina Masile had other ideas. With her bat-like wings she lifted from the ground and charged, her gleaming spear pointed at Hannah's heart. Hannah was sure that Seraphina was not expecting the Knight of the Flashing Blade to hold her ground, but hold Hannah did, and when the point of the spear flashed in, Hannah reached out with one hand and caught the spear on the haft, just past the glowing head. The momentum of the strike suddenly halted, Seraphina collided with the butt of the spear, the hard metal catching her in the breastbone and sending her crumpling to the ground like a dead bird. Macero and Orchid scattered as Seraphina got back to her feet, the spear lying discarded on the ground where she fell. The creature possessed of divine power screamed an unintelligible slur and let twin beams of fire and ice erupt from her hands in Hannah's direction. Hannah dropped to the ground, letting the beams pass over her head and then got up to a crouch and charged the taller woman. Channeling all of the flows of earth she could manage into her smaller frame, Hannah turned herself into a speeding chunk of iron and collided solidly with the self-titled Fallen Angel. Unbeknownst to Hannah, Seraphina had also filled herself with the flows of stone, and when the two women collided, it was as though two mountains had suddenly been thrust into one another. Neither budged, but Seraphina was the first to follow up the collision with an attack. As Hannah struck,

Seraphina pivoted her body to the left slightly, and when she swung her right arm back again, she connected with a hard elbow strike to the side of Hannah's face. When Hannah reeled back from the blow, Seraphina allowed the momentum of the pivot continue and she followed up the elbow strike with a rising palm strike to Hannah's chin. The force of the blow sent Hannah flying backwards, landing in a heap on the ground a dozen paces away from Seraphina. Dazed slightly, Hannah got to her feet as quickly as she could and prepared herself for the inevitable flurry of attacks from her opponent. She could feel blood trickling from the corners of her mouth and her nose, but there wasn't even time to wipe the blood away as Seraphina flashed in. She fainted to the left, and Hannah overcommitted, leaving her left side open for the brutal knee strike that followed. Hannah felt and heard several ribs crack and she could not stop the cough that rattled her lungs and produced a plume of blood from her mouth. But the Fallen Angel was not finished, as a clubbing two-fisted blow caught Hannah on the back of the head and forced her into the bloody ground at her feet face first. Seraphina brought her right foot down hard on Hannah's back between her shoulder blades and pushed the Knight of the Flashing Blade farther into the mud.

"It's no use, pretender," Seraphina mocked. "I know all of your moves. My servants have been watching you and your patron for some time. I have stood toe to toe with Dark Gods, and you are nothing compared to me. I will do this world a favor and squeeze every last drop of blood from your body before I blow you into so many pieces that it would take the Creator a millennia to put you back together again. The only thing you will know for these last few seconds of your life, will be pain."

* * * * * * * * * * * *

The mindless skeletal troops fell by the dozen with every one Mariti's movements. Strikes with her glowing talons scattered ten at a time, while a single sweep of her tail sent fifty or more flying, or shattered them into nothing. After no more than five sets of attacks, Mariti beat her wings hard and lifted off the ground, forcing many of the troops to fall to the ground as they could not stand against the force of the winds. Floating fifty feet off the ground, Mariti opened her massive jaw and let a beam of white death fly from her mouth and engulf the army below. At that range, the beam cut through not only the ranks of troops, but also through the hillside, digging long furrows that destabilized the landscape. Many soldiers that were not struck directly by Mariti's attack found the ground beneath their feet failing and collapsed into quickly expanding sink holes that swallowed troops by the hundreds in a fruitless attempt to quench its voracious appetite. The land itself had become an efficient killer at Mariti's hand, and when she touched back down to the ground, over three quarters of the army had been reduced to dust or swallowed whole by the land. Though the rest did not run, they ceased their advance, leaving Famine alone to face her massive opponent. Despite the carnage that Mariti had just wrought upon her troops, Famine seemed unimpressed.

"Somehow I expected more," the twisted feminine voice intoned. "Whatever you think you are going to accomplish here, you overgrown lizard, know that my master has had lifetimes to learn how to destroy you."

Mariti's claws flashed brilliantly as she swiped in Famine's direction, the tip of her claws passing a hair's breadth from the creature's abdomen.

"Dorovar is a thing, a thing that the dragons created. What we make, we can destroy."

Famine smiled.

"Dorovar may once have been that lost lamb in search of salvation, but he has been listening and learning to the Cosmos cry out for change. The souls of this world will be freed from their servitude to the perverse whims of the Creator and His Children, and they shall sing their praises to the one who delivered them from their bondage. Their song will lift Dorovar from this mortal shell and raise him to the heavens, where he shall use the bloated decaying husks of every last member of the dragon race as a staircase to the throne of the Creator. He shall strike down the Father, leaving him low and cast his broken corpse down to the bonfire that this world shall become in Dorovar's honor. Dorovar shall sit upon the throne and free every world from the touch of the Creator. Every last world shall burn in an effigy to their fallen maker, and then Dorovar will be free to craft a new Cosmos. One where the people shall truly be free to pursue their lives, and they shall never have to worry about the interference of those who think themselves better. No angels, no gods, no dragons, no servants. Just the simple people who have always been preyed upon by the strong. Dorovar shall save the Cosmos from itself, even if he must destroy it to do so."

Mariti stood firm in the whirlwind of madness, feeling a wave of revulsion pass over her. Whatever became of the people of Espre, it was clearer now than ever that Dorovar was the greatest threat that roamed the world. He had to be stopped at all costs, and it started with the Herald that stood before Mariti. Letting another roar hit the air, Mariti spread her jaws and belched forth another beam of burning hot energy that sped toward Famine. The Herald raised her hand and the beam of energy split and passed harmlessly to either side of Famine. The dragon stared in disbelief for a moment but charged in with a long hard claw strike intended to rip Famine into pieces. From the frail appearance of the Herald, it was obvious that if but one of Mariti's gleaming claws struck true, that the battle would be over. But as the dragon's attack sped in, the Herald made no attempt to dodge it, and again simply raised a hand and intercepted one of the claws with her palm. Famine smiled a wicked smile as the strike was halted, impotent. With a single push, Famine sent Mariti hurtling through the air. It took several long moments before the dragon was able to right herself in mid-air, but once she did, she stayed hovering, a disbelieving stare burning holes in the Herald of Dorovar. Famine's eyes met the dragon's and the evil smile widened even further.

"How foolish do you think we are, dragon?" Famine mocked. "Do you think that after all this time Dorovar would not have studied the foul creatures that are responsible for his very existence on this backwards rock of a world? You and the rest of your kind brought unparalleled destruction to Dorovar's world. You took a society predicated on the ordered and restrained life taught by Raenera and turned it into a chaotic morass where those with power craved more and more of it. Though they believed their actions to be justified in the protection of the lives of innocents, that lust for power did nothing but destroy. This destruction would not have been possible or necessary if it were not for you."

Mariti growled.

"You would condemn a whole race for the misguided actions of two of our number? You and your master have already taken our leader, the greatest of our race to have ever lived. Would you murder all of us? All of our children? All of our unborn?"

The smile disappeared from Famine's face.

"You condemned a whole world," Famine thundered. "You killed hundreds of thousands because you were afraid of your own mortality. How many other worlds have burned because of your interference? How many races have you condemned to flame because of your arrogance? You weep for Tarot, but he was the leader of your Council, and is responsible for the deeds of all that belong to that Council. The deaths from Dorovar's world are on his head. The death of every world the dragons have ever called home are on his head. And now his head lay in pieces on the ground that once was the chamber where decisions for the whole of your race were made. Dorovar bathed in his blood, stole his power, and now he will stand upon the corpses of the whole of your race. So come Mariti Brightblade, slayer of angels, bring your outrage, bring your hate. Let me taste your blood and add your power to the might of the great Dorovar."

* * * * * * * * * * * *

The pressure on Hannah's back felt as though it would snap her spine at any moment. Already the tactical part of her mind, which had been largely infiltrated by Aerith's consciousness, was cataloging the damage that Seraphina's attacks had inflicted upon her body. Even with the additional defenses erected through the use of the flows of stone, many bones had been broken by the stinging blows. At least a half-dozen ribs and one collar bone were broken. Her jaw and one of her cheekbones had also been fractured by the vicious blows. She was bleeding internally, and one of her lungs had been badly damaged making it difficult to draw breath. But she was still breathing and her heart was still beating, and so she was still able to fight. It would have been too risky to try to heal any of the damage that Seraphina had inflicted because it meant releasing the flows of stone. Doing so would have weakened her body, and the force of the boot between her shoulders would break her spine in two and end her life before she could take any action. It was time for some of Aerith's famous guile. Though she was not practiced with her abilities, Hannah had at her disposal the memories of a man and woman who had plenty of time to practice with theirs. She found a risky tactic in the memories of Logan Ranthall, one that he had never tried, but one that seemed to be the only way out of her current predicament. It called for perfect timing and perfect execution, and if Seraphina so much as felt what she was trying to do before she did it, Hannah would be dead in a matter of heartbeats.

Filling herself with the roaring green flames of the Blaze she prepared herself for the strike from Seraphina. Hannah knew that the Fallen Angel would feel the increase in her opponent's power and stomp down hard to dissuade her from continuing. That brief opening would be all Hannah would have to work with, and if she timed it wrong, she wouldn't get another chance. As expected, Seraphina lifted her boot and was about to bring it down in another hard stomp. Hannah took the moment to open a portal parallel to her back. Hannah knew that Seraphina would see the portal and quickly close it, but that portal was only a feint. At the same time Seraphina was closing the portal above Hannah, Hannah was opening a portal beneath her. The Knight of the Flashing Blade fell through the portal and braced herself for emergence on the other side. Escaping was only the first part of her plan. The other end of the portal opened behind where Famine stood, and the moment Hannah set one foot out the other side, Hannah opened another portal in front of Famine. The Herald of Dorovar was shocked by the action and had no time to respond before Hannah kicked out with one foot and struck Famine in the small of her back, sending her through the portal. The portal opened in the exact same place where Hannah had previously departed, and Famine fell into Seraphina's rapidly descending boot. The Fallen Angel's blow struck true in the center of Famine's chest, and the Herald cried out in pain. However the assault triggered some kind of automatic defense inside the Herald, and a wave of dark energy exploded in all directions, sending Seraphina flying through the air, her wings hanging limp behind her.

Hannah wanted to fall to her knees, but she knew that she couldn't. The fight was far from over, and she took the few moments of respite to channel all of the power that she could into mending her bones and healing the injuries from Seraphina's first assault. She didn't have long to act, as Famine was already back on her feet and speeding across the distance with purpose. Seeming to take her queue from Hannah's attack, Mariti changed the target of her strike, swooping down in a dive at incredible speed toward where Seraphina was just making it back to her feet. One extended clawed foot connected with the Fallen Angel, talons wrapping around her body and crushing her. The Fallen Angel tried to resist the strength of the grasp, but it mattered less when Mariti touched back off and soared high into the air. At the height of the climb, just above the cloud tops, Mariti released Seraphina, but instantly grasped one of her wings with a talon laden claw, ripping through it like paper. Mariti's other claw struck, ripping the other wing clean from Seraphina's back and the dragon watched as Talisia's daughter tumbled from the great height and hurtled toward the ground, picking up speed with every second. The creature struck the ground with such force that she created a massive crater. That threat dealt with, Mariti turned her attention to where Hannah and Famine were locked in combat.

* * * * * * * * * * * *

Hannah braced, and the lithe woman did not disappoint with the strength of her blow. If Hannah had not filled herself with the flows of stone once more, she would have been knocked clear off her feet. As it was, Hannah was pushed back at least three feet, but Hannah bent her knees and sprang back at her attacker. A foot from Famine, Hannah let twin blades of fire form in her hands. Famine reached out to grab hold of Hannah, but the knight spun away from Famine's reach and propelled herself faster toward the Herald's back, completing the spin and bringing one of the flaming blades like a scythe toward the back of Famine's neck. The blow stuck nothing but air as one moment Famine was there, and the next, she was gone. The Herald reappeared a dozen feet away, standing in the middle of a series of fissures that Mariti's flaming attack had created only moments earlier.

"Impressive," Famine said coldly. "But ultimately futile. Your patron has taught you well, Hannah Ironheart of the Knights of the Flashing Blade. But you are not Aerith Seth. He thinks that he can kill my lord and master. He thinks that he can get revenge for the death of Evan Sinn's woman. But there is no vengeance that burns brighter than that which burns in Dorovar. There is no hate that is stronger than the hate that fuels my master. Dorovar is eternal. Dorovar will be the fire that burns the entire Cosmos to the ground, and no Heretic or his whore will stop it. You followed the Creator once, you feel the betrayal. Abandon all hope now.

Abandon your new patron. Join Dorovar. Lay down your arms and embrace eternity."

Hannah's attention was on Famine, but she saw the vicious attack that Mariti had launched on Seraphina, and watched the woman's body plummet to the ground below. Keeping her eyes locked on Famine, Hannah tried to push her thoughts to the dragon high above. She tried to impress upon the dragon the desire for her to breath once again, a strike so powerful that it would reduce the whole area to ash, centered right on the space between where Hannah and Famine stood. Hannah felt the wave of disbelief come in answer and knew that her message had been received loud and clear. A moment later, Hannah released the weapons from her hands and put her hands out at her sides in an indication that she was finished fighting.

"Aerith has tried to turn me into something I'm not," Hannah said calmly. "He needs a killer to fulfill his purpose, but Dorovar wants the same thing, killers who will do nothing but murder in his name. I have always worked to save those who were not strong enough to save themselves. I cannot stand by and watch as you and your fellow Heralds kill for the purpose of injuring the Creator. Fight him directly. Fight his children. Fight the Dark Gods, but leave the innocent alone."

Famine frowned.

"There are no innocents, Hannah. There are no innocent souls on this world. Their very lives show that they carry the corruption of the Creator within them. In order for the Creator's lies to be purged from the Cosmos, so must every being he has ever crafted. You are doing them a favor by ending their miserable existences. They are puppets whose strings must be cut to save them from the horrors that their lives will continue to bring."

Hannah felt the confirmation from Mariti that the attack she wanted was on the way. Again, Hannah's timing would have to be perfect if this was going to work. If her timing was off, or the execution of the trick that Sabrina had developed didn't manifest the way it was supposed to, Hannah was going to be a victim of her own cleverness.

"Then perhaps you should burn too," Hannah said her eyes going cold, "since you too were made by the Creator."

Famine was aware of the strike from the heavens that next moment, the wide beam of fire speeding down. Predictably, Famine leapt backward almost fifty yards, and Hannah's eyes never left the twisted woman's form. Mere feet from where Hannah stood, close enough that she could feel the searing heat bearing down on her, Hannah opened the largest portal she could manage, and at the same time opened a dozen portals in a ring around Famine, and one more directly above her head. The instant that the stream of white flame rushed through the portal above Hannah, it emerged from all of the portals surrounding Famine. The dozen separate blasts all collided in the center, igniting Famine's body. Hannah could hear the tortured screams coming from the Herald, and no matter what protection the woman was trying to weave around herself, the flames burned hotter and hotter, dissolving any defenses right along with Famine's skin and bones. Hannah could feel Famine trying to open a portal of some kind in an attempt to flee, but the flows were so weakened that the Knight of the Flashing Blade was able to prevent the portal from forming. The moments of agony passed slowly not only for Famine, but for Hannah as she could almost feel the woman's pain. Then there was an explosion of energy. The wave of darkness expanded in all directions, blowing the ring of portals shut. One of the waves of energy cut like a scythe through the air, right toward Hannah. There was no time to defend as Hannah had poured all of her energy into controlling the portals. But at the last moment, Mariti landed in front of Hannah and used her great wing to shield them both from the strike. When it was over, Hannah and Mariti walked wordlessly over to the remains of Famine. All that was left was a desiccated skeleton whose jaw was twisted into a permanent tortured scream.

"This is the first blow against Dorovar and his servants," Mariti said calmly. "He will step up his attacks now. The retribution for this attack will be severe."

Hannah nodded.

"But this is also proof that we can work together Mariti, and that we don't have to be enemies. Dorovar is the true threat, and so are the Children of the Creator. They have manipulated all of us for too long. Do you think that Shadowweaver and Stormbane would have done what they did if it hadn't been for Emries and Talisia? Go to your fellow dragons. They supported Pyrrus once in the civil war, so they are accustomed to fighting angels and gods."

Mariti glowered.

"You would have us fight for your Aerith Seth? The man who has been responsible for so much death that even he cannot stomach it?"

Hannah turned to Mariti.

"Aerith became a killer because that is what his world needed. He continued to be a killer because it is what the Cosmos needed. The fact that he cannot stomach what he has been forced to do should prove to you that he is worthy of following. Will you continue to be led by the nose by the Creator and his Servants? Will you continue to be arrogant animals that the Children can manipulate? If so, we should settle our business now. We either leave this field as allies, or one of us doesn't leave this field at all."

Mariti looked away in the direction of the crater that had been made by Seraphina's fall. There was no body at the bottom of the crater, but Mariti never expected the creature to have been killed by a simple fall. She would be licking her wounds somewhere, plotting her next move with her demonic mother.

"I don't trust your Aerith Seth," Mariti said finally. "Or the Heretic that serves at his right hand. But you, Hannah Ironheart, I have seen your true quality in battle. If the dragons fight for anyone, they will fight for you."

Slipping the Noose

*Year Four of the Just Emperor Kaitain "Dragonsbane" Lorien,
Creator's Calendar Year 1871*

Jeroch woke with a start, for a long moment not knowing exactly where he was. Both he and the luxurious silk sheets that covered him were drenched in sweat, and as he tried to sit up, the ache in his side warned him to not move too quickly or abruptly. That was when the memory of the past day flooded back to his mind. Life though eventful had largely been quiet in Iltorp, and though often Jeroch was called away to perform the duties of his alter ego Vallic Ultiv, he spent much of his time in his quiet keep in the middle of nowhere. In the early days of his time on Espre, he had found the alliance with Ellis to have been one of convenience and nothing more. However, over time they began to understand each other, and their respect for one another blossomed into something more. If pressed, Jeroch would not be sure if he would use the word love, but there was certainly a fondness for one another that made separation and distance difficult, even for beings that had lived as long as they had and under the circumstance they had lived. Life had slowed to a steady dull pace, but the arrival of Logan Ranthall on their doorstep was the mark of impending strife. But hadn't that always been the way? The phasia were created to perform a task, a task that they were quite successful at, even in the days of Cedric Binosear and his band of heroes. For all of the lore and the myth that rose up about the man, he was a flawed hero, one that Jeroch respected more with years of distance, but one that he also understood had been largely carried by Aryx Terian. After the defeat of Shau-ling though, Cedric had become something else entirely, more than just bitter and tortured, but it was as though he came into full understanding of what he was.

Logan Ranthall and his band were something different entirely. They were heroes in every disgusting sense of the word. They thrived on impossible situations and insurmountable odds. Naturally they were afraid, but they did not let fear own them; and together they were stronger than they ever would have been apart, with two exceptions. Gwydeon Sandar would have stood against Shau-ling unarmed and never batted an eye if the opportunity presented itself. Jeroch had been impressed with the man from the second he laid eyes on him, though the respect had been grudgingly earned after the death of Jeroch's son. Hawk had not been careless as Jeroch had initially thought. His tactics had been stellar, and his proficiency was not to be brought into question. The fact of the matter was that Gwydeon Sandar was a superior opponent, plain and simple. Jeroch learned that himself, the hard way, with Gwydeon Sandar's blade ending his life at the Hall of Terrors. But Jeroch had also dealt Gwydeon a fatal blow, and the two men ended the second generation linked in death.

But while Jeroch was assured to return for the battles of the third generation of the prophecies, the Creator had seen fit to twist matters for everyone thanks to the interference of one of Jeroch's brothers in the phasia. Basille's misplaced affection for his son had sparked the creation of the woefully dubbed Dark Mirror reality, a place where the forces of Shau-ling enjoyed the same prosperity that Emries' heroes enjoyed in the other version of history. In the Dark Mirror, Gwydeon Sandar still lived, and he continued to be a thorn in the side of all who crossed his path, none more than Jeroch. But just as Aerith Seth had taught Jeroch that the path of destruction that he walked upon was not the way to escape the hell that everyone was being condemned to, it was Gwydeon Sandar who taught Jeroch that fighting for the sake of fighting was never going to lead to anything other than death, and that fighting the good fight, as nauseating as those words were to a member of the phasia was the better path. Those lessons more than anything is what led Jeroch to turn against not only his master Shau-ling, but also against his brethren in the phasia. But if

Gwydeon Sandar was a thorn, Logan Ranthall was a flaming spike that continually found the soft flesh of every member of the phasia and now every creature that served the Creator.

Those who knew Logan Ranthall from the beginning saw the man as nothing more than a farm boy who wanted to be a hero, but consistently fell short because of his own insecurities and inability to commit to anything past his own dreams. Perhaps that was because the young man didn't realize the type of people that his father and mother had been. What Jeroch would learn later in Logan's life is that Jeroch knew much more about Arin Ranthall than Logan did. But despite whatever insecurities Logan tried his best to conceal; it was when he was thrust into the ill-fitting role of savior that he truly began to shine. Where Cedric was coddled and carried by his companions partially because of his own failings and partially because of his position, Logan consistently thrust himself into the heart of danger, uplifting his companions to become more than they ever believed they could be. Pike Rhuiden went from a failed blacksmith who was fated to spend the rest of his days drinking and carousing in bars across the countryside to one of the most feared warriors and eventually a man who would shake the very foundation of the heavens. Midarin Rice, a spoiled, ego-centric exile who couldn't keep her legs shut as a princess, became the most formidable woman and the driving force behind two generations of heroes and now a rebellion against the architecture of the Cosmos. These were just two examples of dozens that flooded to Jeroch's mind. All had the same common denominator. Logan Ranthall. But the man was not content with sparking revolutions in those that were to serve Emries. In the Dark Mirror reality he seized an opportunity that should have been impossible for a mortal to seize. He crossed the line from mortal to immortal by embracing the life force of Shau-ling, the Blaze, and becoming a member of that order which he had dedicated his life to destroying, the phasia. As a member of the Brotherhood of Phasia, Logan turned the hearts and wills of some of the most powerful members of the order, leading them down a heroic path. Forever altering the balance between what all on Onea believed were light and shadow. Because of Logan's interference, Rael and Trece Starlin would walk away from the Brotherhood, and the cold and vicious killer Caris Vale would find her humanity.

Now Logan Ranthall was in the center of another conflict, continually challenging and changing the landscape of conflicts across Espre and the Heavens, and had been for nearly two millennia. And in the strangest turn of fate, Jeroch now found himself having more in common with Logan Ranthall than he did with his own brother Saurn whom he now found himself in the company of. In fact, Jeroch had taken an active role in hunting down members of his own extended family as soon as he arrived on Espre, eliminating them from a game that they would no doubt end up on the wrong side of.

Jeroch twisted, pulling his feet from under the covers and bringing himself to sit on the edge of the bed. His right hand immediately went to the wound at his side while his left wiped some of the sweat from his brow. Saurn had warned that the antidote to the poison that had been ravaging his body could cause some side effects, and the fact that his body temperature was fluctuating wildly must have been one of those side effects. Trying his best to stretch his aching muscles, even though the poison had only been in his system a few minutes, it seemed as though he had been lying in bed for several months. Weakness gripped every muscle and every joint. The first thought that came to Jeroch's mind as he hunched over was that he wished Ellis was there with him. But she was gone, and Jeroch was on his own again. It took several attempts for Jeroch to get his legs to cooperate and support his weight.

Pulling on his shirt, Jeroch stumbled slightly out of the elegant bedroom. Saurn had spared no expense in outfitting the headquarters of the Shadow Guild, and the accommodations rivaled anything that would have been found in the finest suites in the royal palaces across Espre. The hallways were dimly lit, and though Jeroch could not see anyone, there was certainly a feeling as though every moment he was being watched. Jeroch was sure that was the case, knowing Saurn's paranoia. Surely enough, only a few moments after emerging from his room, Jeroch saw Saurn walking in his direction from the central hallway. Saurn made sure that Jeroch saw him before quickening his pace. Though the two had a long relationship there was still an incredible amount of distrust between the two men. They had tried to kill each other on several occasions, and were the situation different on Espre, they would have tried to kill one another yet again.

Saurn stopped several feet away from Jeroch, though being in arms reach did not change the amount of danger that held between the two men.

"Difficulty sleeping, Shadow?"

Saurn's tone would have been considered calming to most, but Jeroch could not hear anything other than manipulation and the constant probing for an angle to attack.

"Perhaps I've been asleep too long, Saurn," Jeroch said finally. "I have been embedded like a tick on a bloated dog, serving the mortals as one of the Knights of the Flashing Blade while Logan and the others have been working behind the scenes. Emries has not sat idly by. Talisia has not sat idly by. However, I feel like I could have done more."

Saurn put his hands behind his back and looked down to the floor. He understood Jeroch's sentiment and despite himself, there were parts of him that agreed.

"We are men of action, Jeroch. Time has shown that we cannot rise above our natures in the same way that the mortals have been able to. That is why they have consistently defeated us and our schemes. That is why I could not see the danger that Aerith Seth posed, or the viper that I allowed into my home with Korrd Ranthall. Why you were vexed by Cedric Binosear and Logan Ranthall. Why Bryn stands against us. Why Caris serves Dorovar. Why Rael and Trece abandoned us. But those examples have given me hope that what Halicon made us, is not all we can be. We were imbued with the worst of mortal failings as our driving spark. But if we can be exemplars of the worst, then we can grasp at the best."

For a long moment Jeroch stayed silent. Finally he shook his head.

"Your speeches have not improved over the centuries, Saurn. You still sound as though you are only speaking half the truth, and the truth that you are speaking is so wrapped up in evasions and obfuscation that it's not even recognizable as truth."

Saurn looked up, and though his violet eyes flashed, a smile came to his lips.

"And I am still amused by your lack of vision."

Saurn turned to face the hall leading off to the west, deeper into the complex, but away from the rooms that Jeroch had been in when he first arrived. Several steps down the hall, Saurn stopped and twisted slightly back toward Jeroch as an invitation to join him. Jeroch silently accepted the invitation and fell in step behind his brother.

It took several moments and several turns down blind hallways before Saurn stopped in front of a wall. When Saurn placed his hand on the wall, Jeroch could perceive the use of a subtle flow of the Blaze to reach through the wall and trigger some kind of device either within the wall itself or just on the other side. A segment of the wall slid away, revealing a large room on the other side. Upon entering the room, Jeroch felt a pang of loss and regret. On the floor of the large room was the form of a stylized dragon surrounding by concentric circles that had smaller emblems around the perimeter. It was a smaller representation of the room that the Brotherhood of Phasia had used to meet for generations, and here in this secluded room, it was as though a piece of Onea had followed them. Lining the walls were large shelves filled with books, no doubt the true histories of everything that had occurred on Espre since the world's creation. After giving Jeroch a moment to soak in the surroundings, Saurn stood in the center of the room and channeled more flows of the Blaze into the art below his feet. After several moments, light filled the emblems on the floor, some filled with bright green flames, while others were filled with white. Saurn looked on as Jeroch moved around the room, taking in the information that had just appeared. After seemingly aimlessly wandering, Jeroch stopped in front of one of the emblems and looked down for a long time. That was the emblem that had been the representation of his life and service for the entirety of his life, and it glowed with the bright green flames of the Blaze.

"So, are you going to tell me what it is that this represents, or would you like me to guess?"

Saurn said nothing, he simply motioned in Jeroch's direction.

"It wouldn't take long for someone with your intelligence, Saurn, to realize that all of the Phasia would have been brought to this world. And

I'm sure once Grawn got his hands on a little bit of power and started trying to take control of Cadaria, that you took a great interest in our brothers and sisters. The only question I would have for you is whether or not this representation is based on information you have gathered, or if you have some other means to track the life force of the members of our Brotherhood on this world."

Saurn moved to stand atop the glowing green emblem of the viper that was the representation of his life force. He kept his hands behind his back and instead of meeting Jeroch's gaze kept his eyes fixed on the dragon emblem in the center of the floor. After several long moments, bright green flames began to stretch up from the floor, and eventually became like a bonfire. The Blaze filled the room with incredible warmth, but more than that, filled both Jeroch and Saurn with a familiar feeling of home.

"I have had a long time to study the different uses of the Blaze. Just as Shau-ling used it to keep us tied to him, and tied to each other, I can use it to monitor whether or not we are still alive. I have experimented over and over again with trying to use it to actually track the locations of our brothers and sisters, but no matter how hard I try, I have never been able to replicate the level of control that our father had. I'm sure that I am missing something that connected Halicon's divine power to the Blaze."

Jeroch smiled despite himself.

"Always the schemer, Saurn. But this information is enlightening."

Jeroch looked around the floor once more and in his mind ran down the names that were connected with the emblems on the floor. It didn't take long to realize that the emblems bathed in white were the members of the Brotherhood that had fallen. Grawn Aplee, the Lord Shark, killed by Logan Ranthall and Warron Ysamaran. Jeroch had not been there for the battle, but he had been part of the plan. Erdric Yarrow, the Scorpion had also fallen in that conflict. Ellis Chandara, the Leopard, killed by one of Emperor Kaitain Lorien's assassins. Jeroch saw the emblems of Rane 'Falcon' Larion, Stryfe 'Python' Cadre, Grimm 'Bear' Salde, and Cash 'Lynx' Griffon, four members of the phasia that he and Ellis had tracked down and killed after the end of the War of Ascension, after the first Cadarian Emperor took the throne. They were all members of the phasia that could not be trusted to wait until the time was right to make a move. They would not have patience, and they would have eventually followed the path that Grawn took. So though Jeroch took no pride in it, he hunted down every last one of them and destroyed them. As the leader of the Brotherhood of Phasia, it fell to him; it was his responsibility to either bring the members into the fold, into the plan, or to make sure they could not threaten it. But there were names among the fallen that Jeroch didn't expect. They had been integral parts of the plan, or at least part of ensuring that the plan would continue to move forward. As if sensing Jeroch's question, Saurn let his answer flow unsolicited.

"While you were doing your duty and bringing the rebellious young members of our Brotherhood in line, your echo, Cedric was doing his best to track down and eliminate as many of our number as he could. Naturally he wasn't as educated on your schemes or the schemes of Gwydeon and his band, so he cared little for the ripples that the rocks he was throwing were making. He had only one goal. Eliminate the phasia. No different than his days on Onea and no different than the hatred he showed there. Aldridge, his old enemy was the first to fall. Zarsi and Farax came not too long after. However, then he seemed to mellow, as though his thirst for blood had been sated. He disappeared from everyone's sight until you tracked him down and eliminated him."

Jeroch shook his head.

"Cedric let me kill him," Jeroch said finally. "He saw what was coming. He saw what was going to happen, and he didn't want to be a part of it. So he fell."

Saurn fell silent, but Jeroch did not let the silence hold for long.

"What about Warron, Taron, Basille, and Draven."

Saurn shook his head.

"They are all recent additions. My spies have been able to uncover that Taron fell in Albitonin at the hands of Aerith Seth and his newest protégé, Hannah Ironheart."

Jeroch's lips turned into a frown.

"Aerith recruited Hannah? I've known Hannah for years. She's not one of those people who would easily fall under Aerith's sway. She's too devoted to the Creator and to doing good in all cases to follow the fatalistic dogma that constantly spews from Aerith's big mouth."

Saurn ignored Jeroch's character assessment and continued to answer the first question.

"As far as Warron, Draven, and Basille, your guess is as good as mine. These have literally changed within the last few hours, and I as of yet have been able to get spies into the areas needed to gather information. Hopefully tomorrow morning or the next day will clear away some of the fog. But regardless of the fate of those members of our order, that leaves six of us. Bryn in lock step with Aerith, Caris serving Dorovar, Rael and Trece serving some mysterious agenda that I can't help to think is somehow related to our half-brother Logan, and then you and me. The last survivors."

Jeroch looked around the floor nodding absently to himself almost as though he was trying to remember something. As though suddenly figuring out what he was trying to remember, Jeroch looked up.

"Do you see what you've overlooked here, Saurn? Do you see who is missing?"

The first instinct that Saurn had was to defend the thoroughness of his work. But then when he saw the look in Jeroch's eyes, Saurn knew that his brother was not trying to show Saurn up. There was genuinely something that Jeroch saw that needed to be addressed. Taking another long look at the room he had looked at every day for years, the suddenly obvious oversight practically slapped Saurn in the face.

"Kamen."

Jeroch nodded. The first member of the Brotherhood of Phasia that had been created by Shau-ling was Kamen. After the defection of Aryx from the ranks of the phasia, Kamen took a new position as the Flame, the guardian of Shau-ling's throne room and the enforcer of his will. But at his core, Kamen was still a member of the phasia, and needed to be considered as one of the beings that could have been brought to Espre. It took only a moment for Saurn to channel more flows of the Blaze to create an emblem for Kamen among the rest of the Brotherhood. Jeroch waited nearly breathlessly as the color beneath the emblem changed to bright green. Frustration was thick in Saurn's voice when he finally spoke.

"Kamen is still alive? Where could he be? Who could he be working for? Now more than ever I need to be able to track our movements, I need to be able to feel the members of the phasia the way that our father did."

Jeroch sighed.

"Then perhaps you need to come out of hiding. Halicon has invested his power in the girl Sabrina. If there is anyone who can teach you how to use power that way, or perhaps can do it herself, then we must be less insular. We must find out Kamen's fate. With the amount of power he had at his disposal when he lived, the danger he could pose if he were doing the Creator's will or Dorovar's is too much to overlook."

Saurn stood silent looking at the ground, and then clicked his tongue. Jeroch initially though that Saurn was dismissing the idea, but when the man moved toward a pair of bookcases on the far side of the room, Jeroch realized that Saurn had more to show. A simple wave of the hand and the bookcases sunk into the floor below revealing a wall that contained renderings and plates that featured the names of individuals. Represented on the wall were the names of everyone who had worn a mantle as a servant of Emries, or of Aerith Seth, but also the names of all of the children of the phasia. Jeroch's mind raced at the new complexity of the problem.

"I wish Kamen were the only problem, Shadow. You have here a nightmare that has been plaguing me for far too long. There are too many names here that I have not been able to determine the fate of through my spies or through the details I have pieced together from the first day I woke on this world. With Emries here, we can ensure that any who ever held his power could be turned to his will. Look. Names like Talon Aielin, Arin Domae, Gwillim Crill, the Mystic children. I cannot account for their deaths. That does not mean that they were brought to this world, but we would be fools if we did not attempt to account for them. And here…."

Saurn pointed to another series of names, several of which caused Jeroch's stomach to turn.

"I can't account for the children that you and our less controlled brothers and sisters gave birth to. They can touch the Blaze, they have our blood, and so again, they would be ripe to be brought to this world. We know that Jerrard is here, so why would I think for one moment that Hawk or Natalie would not be here as well?"

Suddenly light began to dawn in Jeroch's mind.

"That is why your spies have been scouring Espre. You're looking for clues."

Saurn nodded.

"And the fact that I haven't found any have begun to fill me with much more uncertainty and fear. Who could they be working for? Where could they be hiding? How have then not been seen yet? And of highest concern to me, is that if the Creator has held them back why did He do so, and for what ultimate purpose? Reckless men are hanged by the ropes created with such loose ends, Jeroch, and right now the noose if firmly about all our necks."

The two men stood silent, looking at the nightmare in all its glory. The first thought to come to Jeroch's mind was what more did they not know. Were there servants of the other Children of the Creator that had not been accounted for? Were there any like Kamen that had been overlooked? Whatever the case, there was only one plausible course of action left open.

"It seems, Saurn, that we have little choice but to go hunting as we did in the days of the War of Ascension. But to that end, you must go to see Sabrina and learn all you can about finding our brother Kamen, and also perhaps the children of the phasia that could be on this world. I expect that it will be several days before your Natalia returns from securing the help we need, so I will begin my own hunt. But I will not stray long. It is important that we get the information out of your Irene Drage's head so that we can learn all that we can about Talisia and her plans."

Saurn sighed.

"Rest for a few days, Jeroch. The poison in you still has work to do before it works its way out of your system. If in a week, Natalia has not returned, then we will need to be more proactive. In the mean time I will send missives to Celidar. Jerrard must be made aware of what we know, and through Jerrard we will inform your old friend Logan. Just promise me Jeroch that you will keep Logan from killing me long enough that I can bring him here."

Jeroch nodded.

"I will do my best. But after, Saurn, you are on your own."

Frozen Flame, Icy Heart

Year Four of the Just Emperor Kaitain "Dragonsbane" Lorien, Creator's Calendar Year 1871

Gideon felt the first collision with the reinforced doors of Glacier's Rift as he emerged from the small meeting room with Jared and Natalie trailing close behind. Tolon and Jerrica were also following, interested in what was about to happen, but at the same time waiting to be spirited away by Natalie to a more secure part of the refuge. As the group entered the receiving hall, Tolon was slightly surprised to see four other residents of the refuge standing there waiting. One of the residents was the woman that had originally welcomed them to the Rift. Gideon immediately took a quick look around the room and started barking orders. First he motioned to the woman with long dark hair that had welcomed them who now wore a long flowing sheer maroon dress with black accents.

"Jessica, we're going to need you and Natalie up top. If it is one of Talisia's, then you know it's going to be packing a punch. You two have the best range of all of us, and the most control. Get up to the parapets and try to keep him outside the walls. We'll delay our intruder long enough for you to get into position. Then rain down everything you've got."

Jessica and Natalie both nodded quickly and hurried up the twin staircases at the back of the room. Tolon found himself impressed that though Natalie and Gideon seemed to have long standing grudges that threatened to pull them apart in casual conversation, once a threat was presented, they pulled together and worked like a team. Perhaps it was the familial aspect that they had alluded to, or perhaps it had just been forged by time. Gideon then turned his attention to a short haired younger looking man with bright eyes and flawless features. He had the look of one who had never worked a day in his life, and could easily have been confused for royalty anywhere in Cadaria.

"Michael," Gideon said calmly. "You're not exactly the most proficient combatant of the group, but you know how to use your abilities to keep our guests protected. Take them to the back room and lock it down. Use all the defenses you can muster. No one gets to them, no matter what. If you have to, you know where to go."

Michael gave a half bow and moved to Jerrica's side, taking her by the arm and indicating in the direction of one of the doors in the far side of the room. Tolon wanted to linger, wanted to see how the battle would progress, but he knew from the gravity in Gideon's voice and the growing pounding against the door that he would perhaps be considerably outclassed. All he could see on the other side of the door was the monster that had called itself War, and he knew that he had as much business fighting that battle as a gnat did fighting a dragon. While Tolon had never doubted his abilities as a warrior before, now he began to feel that there were enemies that he could not defeat no matter his skill or guile. However he comforted himself by understanding his role. No longer was he a Knight of the Flashing Blade, tasked with protecting an Emperor and an Empire. Whatever he had stumbled on with Jerrica at his side, it was more important now that he see that through and dedicate all the strength in his body to protecting her. Answers were not going to be found blindly charging into every battle, no matter what his instincts demanded of him.

Once Michael had led Jerrica and Tolon from the room, it left Gideon and Jared with a blond woman in what could have been a military uniform and a middle-aged man with closely cropped dark hair and deep set eyes. Both had looked as though they had seen a great deal of combat, and both had already produced weapons. The blond woman held a crystalline blade that was flawless from its hilt to the tip of its blade and glistened like diamond. The man wielded twin blades that seemed to be made of a black material that oozed and crawled as the second passed, reconstituting itself constantly. Jared had produced a golden scepter with a large ruby at its top that pulsed like a beating heart.

"Hawk," Gideon began, "you and Leane are going to have to take the fight to our guest. I'm not sure what kind of abilities are going to be available to the intruder, but assume the worst. Whatever it takes, don't let the door get breeched. If the battle comes in here, we lose the advantage. Jared and I will do our best to keep the thing off balance, but keep it tight and controlled."

The four exchanged quick nods, and then four portals opened simultaneously.

* * * * * * * * * * * *

Standing at the large double doors that lead into the building that should not have been standing out in the middle of an ice field, Korin Melcab pounded his fists once more at the unrelenting wood. For whatever reason, Dorovar had sent him here, and whatever was on the other side of the door was a threat that needed to be neutralized. Filling himself with as much power as he dared, he pounded his fists once more, the door shivering under his assault but still refusing to relent. Korin took a step back and wiped the sweat from his brow. Once more he let the power flood through his body, and instead of assaulting the stubborn wood once more, he channeled all of the power into his own body, increasing his size and strength ten-fold. In a matter of moments he went from standing just over six feet in height to standing nearly double that. His shoulders were now as broad as the width of the double doors themselves, and his fists when balled could have filled the gap of one of the large stone blocks that served as the foundation for the building. Korin raised one of his massive fists and was ready to swing at the door, but suddenly felt the flows of power behind him. When he spun slowly around, he saw four people, all of whom were brandishing weapons and looked ready for a fight. Laughter boomed from Korin's barrel chest, his voice dropping a full octave with his increase in size.

"So these are the little bugs that I was sent to squash. Know that you now face Korin Melcab, the Captain of the Imperial Guard and son of Talisia Masile, the true power of the Cosmos."

The lone woman of the group was the first to charge in, her gleaming diamond blade slicing at Korin's thigh. However, Korin, while slowed by his increased size, was still more than a match for the woman who was obviously unpracticed with her abilities. Against a mortal warrior she might have been a match, but against someone like Korin, she was an irritant at best. The attack was straight-forward with very little hint of skill, and rather than attempting to dodge the attack, Korin let the blade strike, the diamond blade cutting a jagged wound into his leg, but Korin's counterattack was far more vicious. With the foot of the leg that Leane Torne had attacked, Korin kicked out, catching her square in the chest and sending her sprawling backwards, her ribs broken and her sternum cracked. She landed in the snow a broken mess, blood spewing from her open mouth and nose, her breathing labored and barely dragging through her tortured lungs. One of the other men, the one holding the golden scepter raced to her side, using his abilities in an effort to heal her extensive wounds. Korin made no effort to stop the healing. The woman was no threat, and he turned his attention to the other two men who seemed as though they might be able to put up a decent fight.

It was the smaller of the two men wielding nothing but a pair of daggers that was the first to attack. He darted in, obviously depending on his speed to save him from Korin's superior strength. But at the last moment, right before he would have been able to strike at Korin's legs, the man leapt into the air and propelled himself with uncanny grace over Korin's head in a twisting somersault. At the highest arc of the leap, the small man let fly two of his daggers. Korin swept his arm to bat them out of the air, but the blades split into a dozen smaller projectiles, and rather than being deflected, most of the splinters embedded themselves in Korin's arm. The huge man felt no pain from the attack, but the splinters of steel managed to draw several trickles of blood. However, the smaller man was not content with scoring a few annoying strikes. As soon as he touched down on the ground, he spun and loosed another volley of the small blades. Korin was able to bring his arms in, shielding his body before the majority of the blades struck, but he realized too late that the assault was merely a diversion. From behind, the man with the twin blades charged, and he leapt and stabbed both of the blades deep into Korin's back. Using all of his body weight, Hawk pulled downward on the blades, cutting long bloody furrows in Korin's back. The huge man roared in pain and reached back in time to grab Hawk's leg before he was able to leap free. Helpless, Hawk tried to brace himself for what was about to happen, but he was unable to prepare himself for the velocity and force that Korin exerted in whipping the helpless man toward the wall of Glacier's Rift. Gideon's reflexes were good, but they were not good enough to stop the sickening impact. Hawk slid down the wall leaving a gruesome and obscene blood trail smeared behind him. Gideon could see that Hawk was still breathing, but the damage done to his body was extensive, and without medical attention he would not live much longer. Jared could mend the wounds, but it would be too much of a risk to cross the distance between where Leane lay and where Hawk now rested. Gideon knew that his distraction tactic would not work again, and any move that Jared would make likely would end with him joining Hawk in a state of debilitation. Gideon's only hope was to try to stall.

"There's no need for this, Korin," Gideon said, trying hard to make the larger man believe his words. "Your mother is just using you, no different than my mother and father used me. None of us are here by choice, and we're just trying to make our lives as quiet as possible while the Children try their best to kill each other. We've done our bit for our parents and their schemes. All we want is peace."

Korin scoffed.

"I was sent here to dispose of pacifists and weaklings? What a waste of my talent. Obviously Dorovar thinks far more of your than you think of yourselves. No matter. In a few moments you will all be dead and I will take great pleasure in tearing this place down to its foundation with my bare hands. Already I have injured two of your number, and no matter the healing ability of your friend back there, there is nothing he will be able to do to recuse all of you in time. I will ground you into nothing and leave this white plain stained red with your blood. Pray to whatever gods you choose, little man, for you will not have your tongue much longer."

Gideon held his ground and waited as the larger man raised both of his massive fists in to the air and started the blow that would reduce Gideon to nothing more than a smear on the landscape. However before the fists began their downward trajectory, twin blasts of energy struck the huge man squarely in the chest, forcing him to take a step backwards. Inwardly Gideon thanked Natalie and Jessica for their timing and for their accuracy, but praise would wait until they were all out of danger. Gideon needed to buy Jared some time to get to Hawk, and the only way he could do that was to press the moment of advantage that the assault from on high had given them. Gideon feinted in to get Korin's attention before leaping backwards and channeling his abilities into the ground beneath Korin's feet. Columns of stone erupted from the ground under Korin's feet and Gideon tried his best to tip the larger man off balance further. However, it seemed that Korin's weight was keeping him from being toppled by such rudimentary tactics, and though Jessica and Natalie were doing their best to keep the pressure on, it was obvious that they too were nothing but an annoyance. However, what happened next shocked Gideon.

Over the next few seconds, instead of using his powers to strike directly at the women who were raining down streams of fire upon him, Korin channeled all of his power inside of himself once more and doubled in size again. Now, Gideon stood barely tall enough to reach Korin's knee, and with a single stomp, Gideon was sure that the giant could end his life. But Korin's eyes were not focused on the ants that scurried around under his feet. No, his eyes were fixed firmly on the parapet above the double doors, the place where Jessica and Natalie stood. Korin brought one of his massive hands crashing down on the roof of the structure, sending stone and wood flying in all directions, and Jessica diving to escape the assault. When Korin withdrew the hand, he swiped at Natalie with the other, sending one of the chimneys flying through the air, and Natalie along with it. The force of the impact had done no direct damage to the woman, but the force had propelled her several hundred yards away from Glacier's Rift, where she slammed into the ground. Her head struck a rock with enough force that her vision clouded and blackness encroached, stealing consciousness from her. Jessica did not fare much better. As she tried to get back to her feet, the structure beneath her gave way, and she fell through the roof into the receiving hall below along with roofing beams, stone and other debris. Most of it struck her body as she lay defenseless, and what didn't strike her directly buried her under such weight that were she conscious she would have had difficulty extracting herself. Gideon felt the wave of hopelessness grip him as he stared up in disbelief at his huge opponent. No matter what tactic ran through his mind, it was quickly discarded. Nothing in any of the battles he had ever fought had prepared him for something like this. Jared however seemed to be unfazed by the giant, as he had scurried across the battlefield to where Hawk lay and did his best to stabilize the man's condition. At least one of them was having success in something they were doing. Korin took a step away from the structure and beamed a hateful stare down at the miniscule Gideon who stood below.

"Now, watch as I destroy this home of yours. It will crack like an egg for me now, and if you are lucky you'll be crushed by wood and stone long before I have time to rip you apart."

Korin raised both of his fists above his head, and looked up as he was about to strike Glacier's Rift directly. However, when his eyes returned to the roof of the building, a diminutive woman stood at the very edge of the roof amid the debris and destruction. She could not have stood much taller than five feet, and she wore a shimmering green dress with inlays that could have been either pink or peach depending upon how the light hit it. The dress left her shoulders and her upper chest completely exposed, but despite the cold and whipping wind it did not appear that the woman was affected by the cold in the slightest. Her features were sharp, almost as though they had been chiseled from the most unrelenting of stone, and there was no compassion or caring in her features at all. She looked as cold and unyielding as the snow and ice that coated the area. Even her skin seemed to radiate cold, tinged with a purple hue more akin to one who had frozen to death. However the skin color was in stark contrast to the bright and fiery red hair that was neatly braided upon the top of her head. One long thick braided strand fell down over her left shoulder. The strange woman's eyes met Korin's, and despite himself, the giant hesitated. To cover his hesitation, he let another jibe hit the air.

"Another weakling has crawled out of the rubble to try to stop me. You should run back to whatever hole you climbed out of, and pray I forget about you. I've already incapacitated the rest of your petty little band, and you wouldn't be worth my time. But if you choose to stand there and be destroyed, perhaps it is better than living out the rest of your life in fear and cowardice."

The woman gave no reaction at all, and Korin wondered if she even understood the amount of danger that she was in. In the end however, it didn't matter if she understood or not. She would be just as dead as the rest of them soon, and death required no great understanding. Death found all, no matter how smart, stupid, proud, or foolish one was. And Korin at this moment brought that swift death. The next moment one of Korin's massive hands came crashing down upon the spot where the strange woman stood. At the last moment, the woman put one hand up and met Korin's, blocking the blow and preventing any damage to herself. Korin did not feel the force that was resisting him, it was simply a matter that all of the strength and momentum of the blow had been stolen from his arm, and the fist stopped in its tracks. Korin withdrew the hand and punched with the other, but again the strange woman intercepted the strike and stole all of the strength from Korin. This time when the giant pulled back his fist he realized that blood poured from the palm of his hand, however there was no visible wound. It seemed that blood simply oozed from his pores. The streaming blood forced Korin to take a step back and shrink away from the strange woman. Whatever power she was wielding, it was something that Korin had never seen before, even during his fight with the leader of the Dark Gods, and it was only akin to the kind of power that Dorovar had brought to bear in the last moments of his battle with Pike.

The woman watched and waited as Korin took another step away, mesmerized by the hot viscous liquid that squeezed from his palm. After a moment of watching, the woman raised her right hand but kept her eyes locked on Korin. Over the next few seconds, a form began to appear above the woman's fingers. At first the form was nothing more than a small smoldering ember, but as the moments passed the ember grew into a roaring flame. The flame started to take shape, the center coalescing into the torso of a creature. The form became more solid and recognizable as two wings stretched from the central mass, followed by a definite fan of fiery feathers that formed a tail. The head and beak came into being last, completing the bird's form. For a few heartbeats, the bird rested on the woman's fingers as though it were resting comfortably on a familiar perch.

The fire-wreathed bird was no larger than a sparrow, and it looked about familiarizing itself with its environment before beating its wings several times and taking flight. It hovered in front of the woman and then moved toward Korin. The closer that the bird approached to Korin the larger the bird began to grow. A pace away from Korin, the bird had tripled in size, nearly six feet from tail to head and double that from wing tip to wing tip. The giant Korin staggered backward another two paces, but the bird did not relent in its pursuit. When the bird reached three quarters of Korin's size, it charged the giant man and sunk the talons of its great feet into the larger monster's chest. Korin howled in pain but could not escape the repeated blows and the tearing of his flesh by the fires. With its talons fully engaged in the flesh of Korin's chest, the bird launched a serious of blows to Korin's head and shoulders with its powerful beak. For the first time, the giant cried out in pain, but the fiery bird did not relent. It continued to peck away mercilessly until Korin began to fall backwards. With one beat of its powerful wings, the bird was able to arrest the giant's fall, and then it wrapped its wings around Korin's body. The next instant, both were enveloped in bright unquenchable flames, burning as brilliantly as stars. A moment later, the bird had disappeared, and the now normal sized body of Korin Melcab lay bleeding just feet from the doors to Glacier's Rift.

Jared was helping Hawk back to his feet, and Leane had just staggered over to the doors when the doors opened and the woman in the green dress emerged. She strode past the carnage without even looking in the direction of Gideon or the others, her eyes were locked on the fallen form of Korin Melcab who was just beginning to stir. Three strides from Korin, the woman in the green dress stopped and just stood with her hands on her hips watching the powerful man struggle. It took a few moments, but Korin finally made it back to his feet. Before the Captain of the Imperial Guard could make any moves, the woman moved in and wrapped a single firm hard around Korin's throat. Her cold eyes burned into Korin's and when she finally spoke, there was no compassion and no emotion of any kind in her voice.

"Who sent you here?"

Korin made no attempt to answer the question, and despite the pain he was in, his eyes were filled with nothing but hate and contempt.

"You misunderstand me," the woman said, her voice radiating an unimaginable chill. "You are going to answer my questions. There is no version of this reality or any other that you will escape here without telling me exactly what I want to know. The only thing that could change is the amount of pain you inflict upon yourself before telling me. I ask you once more. Who sent you here?"

Korin did nothing but stare. There was no sign of frustration, and the woman simply closed her hand tighter around Korin's throat. Lightning flared all around Korin's body, causing him to spasm uncontrollably and cry out in pain. The lightning stopped and it gave Korin a moment to breathe, but the respite did not last. Another set of lightning bolts raced through Korin's body and finally when the second assault stopped, the woman spoke again.

"This can continue; it matters little to me. You will not outlast me. You will not die before telling me what I want. All that will change is how much you suffer. Tell me who sent you."

Finally sound cracked through Korin's throat.

"Dorovar."

There was no reaction on the woman's face. She held firm onto Korin.

"Does your mother know you are here?"

Korin hesitated and the delay was met with another merciless assault of lightning.

"Does Talisia know you are here?"

The woman's voice bored into Korin's body no differently than the lightning had.

"No."

Korin's voice was labored and filled with intense pain.

"Do you know who I am?"

Korin's eyes widened, but he quickly answered.

"No."

The next assault of lightning wracked Korin's body, burning him from the inside out. The smell of burning hair and flesh filled the crisp cold air, but the lightning did not relent. In a matter of moments the impossibly strong man had been reduced to a deflated bag of skin hanging off a scorched skeleton. The woman let the body fall to the ground and turned back toward the open doors to Glacier's Rift. She passed by where Gideon and Jared stood without looking in their direction, but finally before crossing the threshold looked off into the distance where Natalie lay.

"Bring everyone to my chambers, Gideon. Including our guests."

Gideon bowed slightly, and let his voice hit the air just as the woman disappeared into the refuge.

"Yes, Lady Raenera."

Chapter LXXVII

Interludes for Peace

Following the confrontation with the woman who called herself Serrina, Dominique Lorien and her newly constituted entourage travelled slowly toward the border of Rashaleb where reinforcements from Lordhill waited. At normal speed, the litter would have been able to cross the distance in a matter of hours. However, with Chelsea recovering from a near fatal wound, the litter had to move slower. Liara had healed the physical damage but the shock to Chelsea's system was of such a profound degree that she would need several days before she would be back to full strength. It would be nightfall before the entourage would make it to Rashaleb, and Rhionna, who was controlling the speed of the litter, pushed as much as she could to prevent having to stop before the rendezvous. Inside the litter, Chelsea lay on one seat, her head in Dominique's lap. The bench seat on the opposite side of the litter door was occupied by Quyhn, and on the other large seat sat the sisters Liara and Mirana. For a long time silence held between the five women, but with Chelsea fading in and out of consciousness, and not wanting to lose herself in the worry about her friend, Dominique spoke up.

"It's amazing to me," she said in her best diplomatic voice. "If I hadn't seen what you had done, I would never have believed that you were Dark Gods."

Mirana smiled.

"Well, most of the Dark Gods were people just like you. There aren't very many of us that were born as divine beings. Serrina was born here, but is a divine being. Liara and I were actually born in the Heavens. The only other Dark God who can say that is Camille, our good friend."

Liara nudged her sister.

"You're bragging, Mir."

"I'm not sure I wouldn't brag too, if I were born in the Heavens," Quyhn chimed in.

Dominique ran her hand through Chelsea's hair once before speaking again.

"I'm not sure if you're aware, but I met another of the Dark Gods. Her name was Midarin, and I believed from the moment I set eyes on her that she was a Dark God. She had that presence about her. She was quite intimidating."

Liara laughed softly.

"Midarin has been fighting for a long time, so it makes being a Dark God come more naturally to her than any of the rest, except for those who had powers before they were Dark Gods, I guess. You have to understand, that most of the Dark Gods were born to common circumstances. And really, you and Midarin have more in common than you might think."

Mirana looked at her sister with confusion in her eyes.

"Lee, what are you doing?"

Liara smiled her best smile, but didn't let her eyes leave Dominique.

"Mir, we're in the presence of the Empress of Cadaria. We saved her life. Some people might take advantage of that, but all I want to do is talk. We have the opportunity to finally tell the truth and let the Cadarian leadership know what the Dark Gods are really all about. The covenants have already been broken and with Dorovar and the rest of the nightmares running wild, it would make sense for us to find allies of our own. It's what father would do. It's what both of our grandfathers would do. So maybe we should show a little more of our Ranthall blood and talk for once."

Mirana looked at her sister with exasperation and finally nodded her ascent. However, it was Dominique that had a strained look on her face.

"I'm not sure how versed in Cadarian politics the Dark Gods are, but recent events may have taken me out of favor with my husband, and I could be days away from being branded a traitor. So as much as I would relish the opportunity to speak with you and deepen the understanding of the Dark Gods among my people, my bargaining position is highly dubious."

"But mine isn't," Quyhn interjected. "As the Imperial Heir and Voice of the Emperor, I am empowered to negotiate on behalf of the Cadarian Empire. And my adoptive mother, as the Empress of Cadaria, has all the legitimacy to act as my councilor in those negotiations."

Dominique was shocked by Quyhn's words, but she could not help but let the smile turn up the corners of her mouth. For all that the young woman had lost, she was starting to come into her own, and it seemed that whatever had met her in the halls of the palace of Lordhill had suited her, and filled her with a new strength. Liara was generally pleased with what Quyhn had said, and also seemed as though she were relieved. It suddenly occurred to Dominique just how much of a chance the sisters had taken in protecting them from Serrina, and what it may cost them in the future. Perhaps in time it would be Dominique and Quyhn who were extending their protection to Liara and Mirana.

"Good," Mirana answered. "There isn't time for the whole story, but there is time enough for now to make you understand what is important, and what must be done if we are going to live through the weeks and months to come."

There was a sudden gravity and near fatalism in Mirana's voice that Dominique found shocking, but wasn't melodramatic in the least. With all of the events that Dominique had witnessed in the past few months, the world could very well have been trying to come to an end, and her husband and her former lover were doing everything in their power to hasten that coming. If anything in the conversations with Mirana and Liara could reveal a path that would prevent that horrible fate for any of her subjects or any of her loved ones, Dominique had a responsibility to try to see it through. It was her duty to her people and to her conscience.

"As Mir is fond of reminding me," Liara began, "what we know about our family is limited to the lessons that we learned from our mother and from one set of our grandparents. The rest of our information we've put together from stories and I have to admit that a lot of them seem like tall tales, even when you consider that we're divine beings."

"We're closer to divine beings than our parents are, or any of the Dark Gods for that matter," Mirana continued.

"Except for Camille."

"Of course Camille," Mirana answered her sister's statement.

The two women spoke so fast that Dominique was having trouble following, and the conversation was more between the two of them than it was with Dominique and Quyhn. As if suddenly remembering that there were other people there, Liara's face colored, and she put her hand to her mouth in embarrassment.

"I'm so sorry, Empress, we spend so much time together, we sometimes forget there are other people listening."

Dominique smiled and nodded.

"It's alright. And please, call me Dominique."

Liara closed her eyes and smiled widely, nodding her head.

"Well," Liara said, smoothing her dress and exhaling slowly, "before we got embroiled in our own little back and forth, I was going to tell you about Onea. That is where we are all from. It's another one of the Creator's worlds, like Espre."

Mirana stopped Liara with a raised hand.

"How much do you know about the Creator and his Children?"

Quyhn answered.

"Dominique and I had a tutor at the palace when she became Empress. They taught us about the Creator and the Servants, and there were hints to the fact that the Creator had children and that they were off doing His work throughout his domain."

Mirana could not contain her laughter.

"I'm sorry, Quyhn. It just that having been in the Heavens, and having heard the lies told to the people of this world for so many years, it's just so hard to take. The Church of the Creator knows so little about what is really going on in the Heavens, and that's because the Creator wants it that way. If people knew the truth, no one would ever want to worship Him."

Liara shot her sister a serious look.

"Mir, we're not here to talk about faith. We're here to talk about the Dark Gods."

"Can't talk about one without the other, Lee."

"There is a time and a place, Mir."

Again, Liara blushed.

"I'm so sorry. We sometimes just can't help ourselves."

Dominique put on her best understanding smile, but the two sisters were starting to make her feel small and stupid. There was so much that the two women knew, and they could probably travel together the length of Cadaria and back and not have exhausted their knowledge. As an Empress, Dominique felt embarrassed. As a person, she felt tiny.

"Anyway," Mirana continued. "Two of the Children of the Creator, Emries and Halicon were bitter rivals. Emries set up these prophecies so that he could give the mortals on Onea enough power to kill Halicon. But Halicon created servants of his own to counter those mortals with power. So this war raged on for several generations before it all came to a head and there was the big confrontation between Emries, Halicon, and all of those people who were touched with power. Unfortunately, Onea couldn't survive the battle, and was destroyed. The Creator spared all of the innocents, wiped their memories and put them here on Espre so that they could live out their lives in peace. The heroes from Onea who fought against forces that they had little hope of defeating impressed the Creator and proved that they deserved places in the Heavens as Ascended Beings. Our mother and father were two of those heroes that were elevated after Onea."

Dominique was fascinated. She knew that she wasn't getting the whole story, and that the abridged versions barely covered what she needed to know, but it was still engrossing.

"So we were born in the Heavens after the elevation and right before the first rebellion."

Quyhn's face betrayed her thoughts.

"Rebellion? Who rebelled? What was it about?"

Liara was the one to answer the question.

"That is complicated, but the gist of it is this. One of the Children of the Creator, Talisia, hated that the heroes of Onea became ascended beings, and she used that excuse to start a rebellion in the Heavens. Her real target though was to kill her brother Pyrrus. Well, she succeeded, and Talisia was cast down, but nothing else really happened, to her or to her followers. Of those heroes from Onea that had become gods, the leader, Gwydeon Sandar, was very upset with the whole situation and decided that the Creator was wrong in the way things had been handled."

"Gwydeon petitioned for months to get an audience with the Creator," Mirana continued, "but he was refused time and time again. Finally, since he wasn't getting answers through the channels open to him, he took matters in his own hands, gathered the rest of the survivors from Onea, and launched a rebellion of their own."

Understanding dawned in Dominique's head.

"And when they were defeated, they got cast down, which turned them into the Dark Gods."

Mirana smiled.

"Half right. They didn't lose. They made it all the way to the throne, and instead of continuing the fight, they chose to be cast from the Heavens so they could be free of the politics and try to live peacefully with the mortals here. But of course the Creator had other plans and sent his Servants here to insure that the Church of the Creator taught that the Dark Gods were evil and they only wanted to kill and destroy the Cadarians. That they were all blood-thirsty monsters bent on ruling the world. It was a betrayal of the highest order, and it started the Shadow War."

Dominique was equal parts crest-fallen and sickened. To think that all this time all of the teachings about the Dark Gods and their history had been nothing more than propaganda perpetuated by a vengeful Creator was laughable and bizarre.

"But Gwydeon didn't want to fight," Liara continued. "And he didn't want any of us to fight, though there were some of the Dark Gods that wanted to. Any one of the Dark Gods could have stood against the whole of the Cadarian army and defeated them all and killed the emperor and sat on the throne. But that wasn't what the Dark Gods wanted. They just wanted to be left alone. So Gwydeon did the one thing that he knew he could do to stop the war."

Liara and Mirana both fell silent here. Dominique and Quyhn knew what must have come next, the duel between the first Emperor of Cadaria, Terrik Lorien and the leader of the Dark Gods. The epic duel that lasted for days and led to Terrik severing the head of the leader of the Dark Gods, and then Terrik issuing the proclamation that the war was over and the Dark Gods had vowed to never set foot on Cadarian soil again.

"Gwydeon didn't want to do what he did, and he agonized over it for a long time," Mirana said softly and with deep emotion in her voice. "I remember the day that he left the Citadel. Camille cried so much because she knew she would never see her father again. And Midarin, she tried so hard to be strong, but even a woman as strong as Midarin couldn't keep the tears from leaking out of the corners of her eyes."

"Gwydeon knew that the Cadarians would never accept a truce, and that surrender would only delay the inevitable," Liara said, tears coming to her eyes. "The Cadarians had to have a victory that wouldn't be questioned by anyone. So Gwydeon sacrificed himself to Terrik Lorien to seal the bargain that the war would end and the Cadarians would take no action against the Dark Gods ever again."

Quyhn could not keep the horror from her face.

"So all the stories about the valiant Terrik Lorien, the Godslayer, they're all lies?"

Mirana frowned.

"I wish it were that simple. The Cadarians needed to believe that the Dark Gods weren't a threat. That they were safe and could go on with their lives. And if the only way that could be achieved was to sacrifice one of our own, then so be it."

Dominique frowned.

"No wonder Midarin was so hostile when I met her. She lost her husband to try to keep the peace, and then had to deal with my husband trying to kill all of the Dark Gods. Kaitain has been obsessed with the Dark Gods, and he doesn't care about tradition or deals or bargains or sacrifice. He wants everything to be his legacy. Kaitain is reckless and violent, and I'm not sure what made him that way, but the attack on him on our wedding day certainly didn't improve him."

Mirana frowned.

"Have they found out who did it?"

Quyhn looked at Dominique and wondered how she was going to answer the question.

"It was blamed on my former lover, Seraph Kore," Dominique said. "And just like all of the lies you are exposing here, there are just as many if not more lies in the circles of power of Cadaria. I know that while Seraph wanted Kaitain dead, he didn't have access to the kind of poison that put Kaitain into his long sleep. Whoever was behind it wanted Kaitain out of the way, but not dead. We thought it was the Dark Gods, but when Midarin showed up, it was obvious to me that there was nothing for the Dark Gods to gain. Whoever did that to Kaitain wanted to sew discord and chaos. And they succeeded. If it weren't for Chelsea and Quyhn, the whole of the Empire probably would have fallen apart worse than it did. Hannah and Marlae complicated things, but that would have happened even if there hadn't been an attack on Kaitain."

Quyhn was the next to add her voice.

"So Kaitain has broken the truce, the Dark Gods have already told Dominique that they are on the move. Dorovar and his nightmares are wandering the countryside. Members of the Knights of the Flashing Blade are in open rebellion, and Marlae Lorien is somewhere still trying to be the voice that leads Cadaria. Kaitain has alienated the entire Church of the Creator, and is doing his best to turn the whole of Cadaria into a military state. What do we do?"

Everyone was silent for a long time. It was an unexpected voice that gave the possible direction.

"We kill Kaitain."

Chelsea's voice shook everyone, and Dominique did her best to help the Knight of the Flashing Blade to a sitting position. It was obvious that Chelsea had been listening to every word, and she had the bravery to say the thing that all of them were thinking. Chelsea looked across the faces and knew that there was an agreement amongst them all.

"He is the thorn in everyone's side," Chelsea said. "I know that the Dark Gods have much larger concerns, and have to deal with Dorovar and the dragons and everything else. Kaitain is our mess to clean up. If the wars in Cadaria stop, then everyone can unite against the larger problems."

Chelsea's eyes then fell to Quyhn.

"How many troops did you mobilize out of Lordhill?"

Quyhn thought briefly before answering.

"We have a small force for escort," she said softly, feeling slightly unsure, "no more than a thousand soldiers. Most of them are Connor's trusted troops that have been with him since his posting in Rashaleb. The rest of the troops in Lordhill can't number more than ten to fifteen thousand. Kaitain made sure that Lordhill never had more than a token defense force that would delay any invaders long enough for the Imperial Army to arrive. But Connor has said that he has friends in Rashaleb that could help him raise as many as two hundred and fifty thousand troops."

Mirana perked up.

"You're headed for Rashaleb?"

Dominique nodded.

"That is where I was to be exiled to. But Chelsea and I thought that I could establish myself there as the true Empress of Cadaria and forge a strong enough power base to challenge Kaitain and take back Cadaria for the people. With Quyhn's help and the forces from Lordhill, it gives us a better chance if there is open conflict with Kaitain."

Chelsea leaned back.

"It would be enough to defend ourselves," she said finally. "Rashaleb has some natural defensive characteristics that make it hard to assault. But if Kaitain threw everything he had at us, the Imperial Guard would eventually wear down any defenses that Rashaleb has. That amount of troops certainly wouldn't be enough to launch any kind of meaningful assault. The only chance we would have is if Saldarine joins us, and we could use the Army of Fire as the assault force and divide the elements of the Army of Ice as home-guard in both Saldarine and Rashaleb."

Liara looked at Mirana and then smiled.

"We actually have allies of our own in Rashaleb. We would be happy to introduce you to them."

Dominique wasn't sure if she was hearing Liara correctly. She traded looks with Quyhn and then with Chelsea, and the three women were obviously having the same thought at the same time.

"Are you suggesting an alliance between Dominique and the Dark Gods with the goal of overthrowing Emperor Lorien?"

Quyhn's question brought a quick nod from Liara.

"As you said," Mirana answered, "Kaitain is a threat that needs to be eliminated. He has shown that he wants the Dark Gods destroyed, and if we have a common enemy, then we should band together to remove the threat. Of course, there would be a condition."

Dominique leaned forward.

"I assume the condition would be that once Kaitain is eliminated that we would then assist you in taking up arms against Dorovar and his followers."

Liara shook her head.

"Men and swords and armor will mean nothing but death against Dorovar. We would never ask you to throw away your soldiers' lives meaninglessly. We are not cold and cruel. If we made an agreement like that, we would be no different from your Kaitain. No, the only condition that we would have would be the reinstatement of the terms of the original agreement between Terrik Lorien and Gwydeon Sandar. The Cadarians leave us alone."

Before Dominique could answer, Chelsea spoke up.

"Do you have the authority to make this deal?"

Mirana smiled.

"If we bring the terms to Midarin, she will agree. Once we meet up with your allies at the border, Liara will go ahead to our friends in Rashaleb and bring them to meet you. Then you can negotiate the deal and come up with a plan."

Finally, Dominique nodded.

"I would like the opportunity to speak with Midarin again, this time under much better circumstances. And I think if those are the only terms for our alliance against Kaitain, then I would quickly and gladly agree. Who would have thought that in escaping from my husband that I would find allies like you waiting for me."

The small window that led to the drivers perch opened, and Rhionna's voice chimed in.

"We should be at the border within an hour, but I'm getting concerned. There are fires off in the distance, closer to the Zevarit border. I think the Imperial Army is on the march, and the Emperor is starting his push to consolidate his power."

Chelsea sighed.

"Zevarit is a smart target. They are in disarray. Those still loyal to Gregor are fighting against those that are loyal to Gabriel. It looks like we did too good of a job keeping them loyal."

Quyhn interjected.

"We can't worry about Zevarit. Rashaleb, and then Saldarine, and then we can worry about what is next. Hopefully this new alliance will be the push we need. Thank you Mirana. Thank you Liara. I think this may be the turning point for Cadaria, and it's all thanks to two gods, a soldier, an orphan, and a commoner."

Dominique smiled.

"Thank you Quyhn," she said suppressing a laugh. "You could have used a few different words to describe my origins. Commoner is probably the nicest of them."

There were smiles all around, and it wasn't until Dominique felt Chelsea squeeze her hand that she thought they had a chance to set things right.

How Outrage Becomes Normality

*Year Four of the Just Emperor Kaitain "Dragonsbane" Lorien,
Creator's Calendar Year 1871*

Deep in the darkest recesses of the Kingdom of Night Galateria, there were pockets of resistance to the rule of the Cadarian Emperors. The stronghold, known as the Hand of Chaos, was also the name of the band of malcontents and terrorists that the stronghold produced. They chose to become a cabal, a cabal that was dedicated to overthrowing the rule of the emperors of the Lorien Family, and to put the rule of the whole of Cadaria back in the hands of the people where it belonged. At the heart of the Hand of Chaos was a man by the name of Xavier Cormea. Xavier had been known for many years as the man with the golden voice. It was said that his words were like honey in the ear and could change the mind of even the most fervent detractor. Dozens flocked to his call, and for every ten that entered the shadow stronghold, one vicious and wholly dedicated member of the Hand of Chaos emerged. Though some were less human than they were when they first passed through the gates. Yaron Telsin, the mad wizard who had turned his sights on crafting a black order was one of those members of the Hand of Chaos. But the Hand of Chaos was not an invention of Xavier Cormea or any other mortal. Nor were Xavier's abilities to influence the wills of others wholly natural. The Hand of Chaos was the invention of the sometime goddess Talisia Masile and her daughter the Fallen Angel Seraphina. They were dedicated to preparing forces that would not only take control of Cadaria, but also be ready to stand against whatever foe Talisia saw fit to loose them against. In time that set of threats included the dragons. However, it was the appearance of the Dark Gods that caused Talisia to make her devil's bargain. She reached out to Dorovar through an intermediary. Syren Belloch arrived several days later, and before long, her Blood Moon group bolstered the Hand of Chaos. The alliance with Dorovar held. Until it was strained by the arrival of the first Herald.

Now, the stronghold of the Hand of Chaos stood all but empty, with only a few indentured servants left to insure that the fires would remain burning for when the structure was needed once more. So no one was watching when the swirling blue portal winked open and a red-haired woman in brilliant armor stepped through. She looked around for a long moment before drawing one of the two swords that hung at her hips and began to carefully creep through the halls of the stronghold. After several creeping footsteps Lissa Terian found herself in a larger receiving hall, and immediately knew that she was no longer alone. Sitting on a small throne in the far corner of the room, was a woman with dark hair and flawless skin. But her body was riddled with small cuts that she was slowly knitting with the gentlest application of power. Talisia Masile looked up from where she sat, regarded the visitor for a long moment, and then pointed to the ground at her feet. Lissa stood defiant, sword in hand, and then finally let the blade return to its scabbard, and then she approached Talisia Masile and fell to her knees.

* * * * * * * * * * * *

Time Immemorial, the Heavens

The Heavens were a place whose features and configuration were largely at the whim of those who dwelled within it. Pieces of the landscape were granted to those who were ascended beings to alter and design as they saw fit. Wolf and Lissa Terian had turned their home into a copy of the farmhouse that Wolf had grown up in. Lissa had grown up without a real family, an orphan given up to the whims and charity of the Binosear family.

She found a sometime sister and sometime rival in Sabrina Binosear, and eventually found love in the arms of Wolf. But the man who formed her view of the world had been a gruff and somewhat broken version of Pike Rhuiden. He was a man who trusted no one other than himself and saw danger behind every tree. He drank too much, slept with anything that moved, and spent most of his days incoherent. But Lissa had learned to wait for the moments of clarity in her adoptive father. In those times she was able to wrest from him pearls of wisdom and tactical prowess that was far above the level of what could have been considered a common drunk. Pike may have been a drunk, but there was nothing common about him. It was the drink and the unpredictability however that alienated Pike from his fellow heroes of the second generation of the prophecies. Lissa learned powerful lessons over the years, but the most important thing that she ever learned was loyalty to family and dedication to doing what is right, no matter the cost. Together Lissa and Wolf had built a life and a family in the Heavens, and there was nothing that Lissa wouldn't do to protect them.

Lissa sat in a small chair looking out the window at a vista that nearly defied description. Stars and lights of all shapes and sizes dotted the sky, clouds floated through the air deflecting light in all direction and created bands of multi-colored radiance. In the next room her infant children slept, and they were just a few days old. Wolf was so proud, and tried his best to ensure that his children had everything and every opportunity. Just like his father, all Wolf wanted was a quiet place that he and his wife could settle down to raise their children together, and to that end, Wolf had left the house that day to petition the Creator for a place on one of his worlds. Wolf didn't want to be in a position of authority, but if the Creator would grant his request, it would get them out of the politics of the Heavens and put them in a place where they could simply live. When the door to the home opened, Lissa felt her heart drop. If Wolf was already back from his meeting with the Creator and the Servants, then it likely did not go well. However, when Lissa looked up, a woman walked through the door.

Talisia Masile was one of the Children of the Creator, and there was a great deal of tension when she was around. It was no secret that Talisia was a close ally of Emries, the great threat that eventually destroyed their world of Onea. She also seemed to have nothing but contempt for the heroes of Onea who had ascended to the Heavens on the back of their deeds. It took several months before Talisia would even openly acknowledge their existence. Now the woman was walking through the door as though she and Lissa had been friends for years. Lissa started to rise from her seat, but Talisia extended a hand and indicated for her to keep her chair. Talisia sat in a chair across from Lissa, and leaned back with her legs crossed, and her bright eyes fixed on Lissa.

"So you are the daughter of Aryx Terian. I can see what all the fuss is about."

Though most would have taken the statement as a compliment, Lissa could not help but feel that she had just been insulted.

"To what do I owe the honor of a visit from one of the Children of the Creator? Are you here to lend your support to Wolf's petition? If so, I'm sure that he would appreciate you speaking in his defense at the Throne. He should still be there now."

Talisia relaxed back in her chair.

"Oh, I know where he is. I thought I would come and keep you company. It would be unfortunate if you were to collapse or something equally terrible while he was off trying to secure your future. After all, having just given birth to twins, you must not be in the best of health, nor must you have much energy to deal with challenges."

Lissa leveled her gaze on Talisia.

"Are you threatening me?"

Talisia uncrossed her legs, put both feet on the floor and leaned forward, her delicate and thin fingers coming together under her chin. The wide smile came to her lips, parting them just enough that her perfect white teeth were visible.

"Yes."

Lissa was taken aback by the abruptness and forthrightness of the statement, but then Talisia had a reputation for her vicious honesty. She was a Child of the Creator and in her mind was unrivaled in the Cosmos.

Lissa kept her face as calm as possible, but her insides were starting to twist. If Talisia wanted to, she could easily have destroyed Lissa; the fact that the Child of the Creator was giving her warning meant that there was something that she wanted.

"You see Lissa, I hope that your Wolf succeeds in his quest to get you removed from the Heavens. I don't want any of you here. All you are doing is cluttering up my home. You're an interloper, nothing more, and the fact that you have earned your place here on the back of trying to kill my brother makes me like you even less. Soon however it won't matter. I will ensure that your entire band of would be gods are expelled from the Heavens. Every last one of you will fall before I am finished with you."

Talisia's words shot through Lissa like a dozen arrows. But the Child of the Creator was not finished. She sat back once more, crossing her legs and letting the evil smile come back to her face. Her pale skin seemed to glow with malice, and her bright eyes burned with unrepressed hate.

"I give you a choice, here and now, Lissa. How much are you willing to do to protect your family? If I were to sit here, in this chair, right now, and tell you that I can guarantee the safety of yourself and your children if you do as I tell you, would you be willing to do what I tell you? You will not have to kill anyone. All you need do is follow my instructions."

Lissa opened her mouth and began to speak, but Talisia cut her off with a single raised finger.

"Now understand, Lissa, I do not come here to have my proposal rejected. Let me tell you what will happen if you say no. First, before the word is finished passing your lips, I will be up from this chair, cross the space between us, and snap your neck. Make no mistake, it will not kill you, it will just insure that you are unable to do anything but watch. I will bring your daughters out one by one, and let you watch as I strangle them. There will be no way for you to save yourself from those moments. If you try to run, I am faster. If you try to fight, I am stronger. If you lie and agree to my proposal and then try to wiggle out of it by not holding up your end of the bargain, your fate, and the fate of your children will be the same. If you tell anyone about our deal, the result will be the same. So carefully consider your next words. Shall we become partners in this endeavor of mine? Or shall I start dismantling your family piece by piece?"

Lissa realized finally that she was holding her breath. The horror that had just been laid out for her was almost too much for her to bear. In the end, when she exhaled, the only thing she could do was hang her head and subtly nod. Her heart was broken and tears streamed down her face.

"Good."

* * * * * * * * * * *

Time Immemorial, Talisia's Rebellion, the Heavens

Lissa could hear the fighting raging outside of the house, and she gripped her sword tightly, waiting for Wolf to return. Talisia's forces had struck without warning, angels and dragons tearing into their counterparts with a fury that the Heavens had never seen. The smell of smoke was everywhere, and corpses burned in the streets. The Creator's forces were already mobilizing to try to stem the assault, but Lissa knew that they did not have the experience for the kind of war that would be fought. That was why Wolf was trying to get word to Gwydeon and the others. If anyone was able to fight off Talisia's forces, then it would be the heroes from Onea. Wolf insisted that Lissa stay with their still young twins to protect them from whatever came. There was a sound from the twins' room, and Lissa feared the worst. She moved as fast as she could through the house, nearly knocking chairs over in the process. The moment she walked through the door, fear gripped her heart. In a small chair in the corner of the room, Talisia Masile sat, bouncing Mirana on her knee and waving at a giggling Liara. The girls were nearly eleven now, but they had all the vigor and fire in them of girls years younger. Seeing Lissa, Mirana wanted to get down off of Talisia's knee, but the Child of the Creator pulled her in tighter and locked her eyes on Lissa.

"You never told me how scrumptious these little girls were, Lissa," Talisia said in a warm voice that belied her evil intent. "I could just squeeze them until they pop."

The girls laughed at the statement, but Lissa knew it was full of malice.

"Girls," Lissa said softly. "Why don't you go play in the other room, and let mommy and her friend talk."

Talisia finally let Mirana off her knee and the two girls skipped arm in arm out of the room but paused at the door for just a moment to turn back and wave at Talisia. Talisia waved back and as soon as the girls were out of the room, Talisia locked a deadly serious gaze on Lissa.

"So, you've obviously heard about my little rebellion."

Lissa tried her best to keep her anger in check.

"There are people dying out there by the dozens. And you're calling it a little rebellion and sitting here threatening my children?"

Talisia chuckled.

"The deaths have not even begun yet, and just wait until you see my ultimate goal come to fruition. There is nothing that can stop me from achieving my ends, and even if I fail in toppling the Creator, I will make sure that the Heavens burn before I am cast down. But that is not why I am here. You have no role in this battle Lissa, and you will be relegated to the back lines. Wolf would never risk you. And now, my dear little puppet, it is time for you to fulfill part of your agreement with me."

After letting the words sink in for a moment, Talisia produced a small black box.

"In this box is a treasure that I am entrusting to you. Hide it well and make sure that no one sees it until the time is right. In the days to come, your heroes will start to become disillusioned with the response to my rebellion. My spies have been planting the seeds of discord for long enough to ensure their reaction. It will be your Gwydeon that sparks the next wave of unrest. When they begin the talk of rebellion, you will recover this little black box, and you will open it. Inside you will find a small stone that pulses with blue light. Wait until your husband sleeps and then rest the stone on his chest above his heart. Make sure he is sleeping soundly, because the stone needs a few minutes to complete its work. The stone will be destroyed by the process."

"And Wolf?"

Talisia shook her head.

"You needn't worry about your precious Wolf. He will not be permanently harmed by what you will do. I can't predict the exact reaction, but he will not die. If you refuse now to do this, I can ensure the death of both you and your children during this rebellion, and if you get any ideas, believe that my agents will still be watching you, and they will not hesitate to eliminate you and your children. I will not allow you to derail my plans now."

Talisia stood and cross the distance to Lissa and extended the box to her. Lissa hesitated, but took the box. As Talisia walked past Lissa, she hesitated at the door and looked back over her shoulder and smiled an evil smile.

"Sit back and enjoy the show, Lissa. This is something that has never been seen in the history of the Heavens. Today you will see a Child of the Creator die."

* * * * * * * * * * * *

*Year Ten of the Just Emperor Terrik Lorien I,
the Creator's Calendar Year 50*

Lissa's body hurt from her toes to her hair. Her clothing was torn and blood squirted from wounds all over her chest and arms. She vaguely remembered stepping off the platform and into the swirling void below. The next thing she knew, she was hurtling to the ground at incredible speed. Impact with the ground shook every part of her and made her hurt in ways she didn't even know were possible. Her next thought were her children. Liara and Mirana were in their teens but had not known anything like the kind of strife they had seen over the past few days and weeks. Her eyes hurt to look around, but she finally found Mirana, helping her sister up over the lip of the crater that their impact had created. Wolf still lay at the bottom of the crater, unmoving and unresponsive. As Lissa lowered herself down to where Wolf lay, she saw a trail of blue smoke emerge from his chest and leap to the wall of the crater. Try though she might, Lissa could not rouse Wolf from his sleep. Finally, she had no choice but to pick her husband up, put him over her shoulder, and pull herself out of the crater.

* * * * * * * * * * * *

Year Twenty of the Just Emperor Terrik "Godslayer" Lorien I,
Creator's Calendar Year 70

Arturious Demascious carefully made his way down the crater wall of the Endless Crater. Even though he was in his declining years, Arturious felt as though he would be able to make enough progress to get the samples of stone he needed for his work. No one had ever been this far down in the Endless Crater since the Day the Heavens Fell, and it was largely virgin territory for people who wanted to understand the nature of things. Finally, after many hours and many disappointments, Arturious descended to the lowest level of the Endless Crater. There was a vein of pure obsidian that would be perfect for his research. Arturious knelt down at the edge of the vein and started to extract a sample when a blue glow radiated from the stone and flowed through Arturious' tools and into his body. The rush overwhelmed the weapon smith, and his body seize. Darkness blurred the edges of his vision and consciousness fled from his mind. When he finally awoke, he could see a green glow coming from a path at the bottom of the chasm. He was sure that the path hadn't been there before, but he could feel as though he were being drawn there. As if propelled by a will not his own, Arturious walked down the path that would lead to an unimaginable fate.

* * * * * * * * * * * *

Year Four of the Just Emperor Kaitain "Dragonsbane" Lorien,
Creator's Calendar Year 1871

Talisia looked down at Lissa Terian and bared her teeth in anger. After a moment, the Child of the Creator kicked out with a foot and hit Lissa on the shoulder forcing her backwards. Talisia was on her feet the next moment.

"You arrogant bitch! How dare you come here after failing to live up to your end of the bargain. You were to keep me informed of anything and everything that happened in the Citadel of the Dark Gods, and anything that had to do with Dorovar. But instead of knowing what I was going into when I moved on Jelan, I was intercepted by that dead woman Jerah. I should have known that she was on the move. You should have known that she was on the move. And then you let your husband's waking slip your mind? Not only that, but that he inherits my brother Pyrrus' powers? You should have crawled to me on your hands and knees, but instead you walk into this stronghold like you were going to strike against me, sneak up and stick and knife in my back."

Talisia towered over Lissa, power filling both of her hands.

"Give me one reason that I shouldn't tear you apart right now and then set about tearing apart your children. Tell me what use you are to me."

Lissa managed to get back to her knees and raised her hands.

"Wolf has Pyrrus' powers, and he still trusts me. I can keep him out of the thick of the fight, and I can keep him from interrupting your plans. My daughters are taking a more active role, but I can control them. No one has ever suspected what I did for you. No one has figured out yet what Wolf brought to Espre. And no one will figure out. Not even Aerith Seth, no matter how much he tries to dig. Not only that, I know what you have been looking for, and I know where it is, and I know how you can control it."

Talisia opened her hands and let the energy dissipate.

"You found the Dragon's Tear?"

Lissa nodded.

"You know who it is, and you know how to control it?"

Lissa nodded again. Talisia regarded the kneeling woman for a long time before stepping back. She found her seat once more and stared holes into Lissa's chest.

"I'm listening."

Before Lissa could begin her tale, a portal opened on the far side of the room, and a battered and broken Seraphina Masile fell through with Orchid Strages and Macero Furiae close behind. The Fallen Angel's wings trailed behind her in tatters and blood poured from dozens of wounds. Talisia was on her feet and at her daughter's side the next moment.

"The dragons have turned on us," Seraphina croaked out. "Famine is gone, and Dorovar will move against us soon. That bitch protégé of Aerith Seth's is coming into her powers."

Macero chimed in next.

"Lexa, Kyrie, and Lucian are gone. Fell at the hands of Hannah Ironheart."

Talisia balled her fists and turned back to Lissa. With a single motion of her hand, the Dark God was thrown against the wall and pinned in place. Talisia approached slowly, her eyes smoldering and hatred creasing lines into her face.

"Now you will tell me everything you know, and if you leave anything out, I promise you that you will suffer pain and agony unlike you have ever dreamed. Creation has been my teacher, and I have burned worlds, so do not think for a moment that I will hesitate to wring every drop of life from you and then breathe on the embers just so I can do it again."

A First Stroke

Year Four of the Just Emperor Kaitain "Dragonsbane" Lorien, Creator's Calendar Year 1871

Gwydeon stood dumbfounded, though he tried his best to keep his jaw firmly set. He had not set eyes on Eldar Merin in over two thousand years, and he had done his best to put her memory to rest. There was too much history between them, too much that had been lost and could never be replaced. Gwydeon still clearly remembered the day that Eldar died. The day that Taron Steen stood with his massive hand around her throat. Her death meant nothing to Taron, meant nothing in the larger scheme of things. But in the end, her death fueled those who were left behind, those who were still there to fight. Pike was impacted the most, at least as far as everyone knew. He wore his hatred and his hurt on his sleeve. But Gwydeon felt the loss as deeply as Pike had. He and Eldar had been close friends since the moment her family came to Aradon. At first she had wanted nothing to do with the children of the town, seeing herself as more of a match for adults and so much better than those her own age. But in time, the walls broke down, and Eldar found herself chained to the hip of Elwyne Tamerlane. Gwydeon was the next to be included into the circle, and while Elwyne gave Eldar a place to channel her dreams of nobility, and Gwydeon gave Eldar the opportunity to be more than her upbringing had allowed her to be. Together they learned the art of swordplay, and they spent a dozen years pushing each other to be the best. And they were the best. But no matter what Gwydeon learned, Eldar was just a bit faster, just a bit more agile. Gwydeon eventually would have the edge in strength and perhaps technique, but Eldar was more nimble and always seemed to be one step ahead of Gwydeon's tactics. How different would things be now when their blades crossed? Gwydeon was possessed with some of the powers of a divine being, but also had touched the powers of the Blaze. Eldar had been possessed by the power of the Spirit, the right hand of the Creator, and the vessel of His power. The Spirit was the only Servant that the Creator could take direct control over. And were the Creator to invest such power in the Spirit, there was no creature on any world that could stand against the Spirit's might.

"I wish I could say I was happy to see you, Eldar."

He tried to keep the emotion out of his voice, but he could feel it wavering slightly. Gwydeon folded his wings back and squeezed hard the hilt of the crystalline sword.

"I'm afraid the sentiment is shared, Gwydeon. Though we all knew you were too stubborn to stay dead. The Creator has been impressed with how much you have accomplished on your own over these past two millennia. You never lost sight of your goal, and that garners respect."

Gwydeon's mouth went dry, and he ground his teeth.

"You'll excuse me if I don't take that as a compliment. Why are you here?"

Eldar released the sword from her hand and crossed her arms across her chest.

"You know why I'm here Gwydeon. The Creator was happy to humor Aerith's little wager for a while, but now it has lost its novelty. Once Sabrina stepped down from her position in the Heavens, I was the logical choice. The Creator has created contingencies for all of you, but you and Logan specifically were addressed. Aerith will self-destruct in time, it has already been arranged. Your friend Sabrina has seen to that. But now, the end game has begun, and you are a thorn that must be excised. So that is why I am here."

Gwydeon sighed and shook his head.

"So the Creator has begun dismantling everything. I should have known. But you know as well as I do, Eldar, that the Creator has been nothing but overconfident, and the worst thing He ever did was make the deal with Aerith and Sabrina. It's going to cost Him, and even if you defeat me now, not you, the Servants, or the Children of the Creator are going to stop Aerith and Logan from saving these people and preventing all this from ever happening again."

Eldar let the sword form in her hand once again and took a defensive stance.

"Your faith in your friends has always been your weakness."

Gwydeon knew that the sentiment did not come from Eldar, but instead were the words of the Spirit. Perhaps that would be his only advantage in the fight to come. The Spirit inhabited Eldar, but had a will of its own. If there was any hesitation in Eldar's technique, any flaw in her movements, it could mean the difference between life and death. Gwydeon could not be conservative; he had to take every opportunity afforded to him and exploit any opening. He slid his foot back and fell into the practiced defensive position that was as natural to him as breathing, and the moment before the first strike descended between the two. Tension filled the air, and inside it was as though they were two wild animals clawing at the doors of their cages, waiting for the opportunity to tear each other to pieces. However, on the outside they were pictures of calm. Knowing that he was facing a superior opponent, Gwydeon chose a cautious opening, moving slowly forward, edging closer and closer to Eldar until their blades touched. There was a moment of hesitation from both, a last exhalation of doubt before battle between the two old friends was joined. But the touch of the blades was the spark that ignited the fire of battle, and the two moved in unison, drawing back their blades and extending their arms into a full swing. The slashing perfect crystalline blades struck, sending a shower of brilliant white sparks in all directions.

The two combatants leaned into one another, feeling each other out, and Gwydeon was trying his best to determine how much of an advantage the Spirit had over him. He was surprised to find that they seemed to be nearly equal in strength, and as he pushed off and pulled away to disengaged from the test of strength, he felt slightly emboldened. He charged in, feinting with a hard downward slash, and when Eldar committed to the high block, Gwydeon dropped all his weight down and brought his blade in hard at the woman's knees. Eldar's wings flared and she pulled herself out of the range of the sweeping strike. Gwydeon countered with a burst from his own wings, pulling himself back to his feet and using his practiced long lunging strike with the tip of his blade aiming at Eldar's right shoulder. The lunge was foiled as Eldar spun away, her weapon spinning in like a scythe whose only goal was to separate Gwydeon's head from his body. Gwydeon felt the strike rather than seeing it, and he fell forward, Eldar's crystalline blade passing just a hair's breadth from the back of Gwydeon's head. Gwydeon continued into a roll, twisting to one side and lashing out with his blade just to keep distance from his opponent. Eldar waited well outside of Gwydeon's effective range as the man slowly came back to his feet. Instead of returning to his practiced defensive posture, Gwydeon kept his blade extended, pointed in Eldar's direction and started to circle the smaller woman. Eldar kept her blade tight, her eyes scanning for any opportunity to strike. Finally Eldar darted in, ducking under the extended blade, the razor-sharp blade targeting Gwydeon's exposed ribs. Gwydeon felt the strike coming, and barely had time to get his own blade in place to block. The flare of sparks lasted only a second, and Eldar rose up, bringing the hilt of her sword under Gwydeon's chin and delivered a blow that rattled his teeth. Gwydeon fell back, and Eldar let her sword follow in a long arc again aiming at his ribs. The tip grazed Gwydeon's armor, and he could hear the tip of the sword scrape against the metal. The two combatants separated, Eldar lowered her blade and her lips twisted into a knowing smile.

"I've seen every duel you've ever had, Gwydeon. I know the tactics you favor when you are overmatched. Your fight with Rael on the Island of Mist was particularly interesting. I see that you have tightened your internal defense over these past centuries. Not that it will avail you much."

Gwydeon grimaced.

"The Eldar that I knew, the one who was my friend and my equal was never that arrogant. Whatever the Creator has turned you in to, you are not

Eldar Merin. You are just a thing that is wearing her face. That means you can be beaten. You're not better than me, and by wagging your tongue you've shown me the truth."

The Spirit charged the next moment, the gleaming crystalline blade coming down in an unrestrained downward slash. Gwydeon brought his blade up to parry, and when the two blades met, the sound of breaking glass echoed through the still cold air. The Brother of Angels felt the power of the blow, and his knees buckled slightly. Apparently his jabs at the character of the Spirit had sparked an escalation. If that was what the Spirit wanted, Gwydeon would be glad to oblige. With their blades still connected, Gwydeon reached down inside himself and filled his body with as much power as he could manage. The roaring green flames of the Blaze crawled across his skin and all of his muscles practically tingled with enhanced strength. Gwydeon flexed his arms to bring the crossed blades closer into his body and then pushed with all of the might he could manage. The Spirit was thrown clear, and landed several dozen feet away. By the time that Eldar got back to her feet, Gwydeon had eased back into a defense stance again, and waited for Eldar's next strategy. The longer the fight raged, the more comfortable Gwydeon began to feel with his new powers. Gwydeon held his ground, standing as still as he could manage, despite the fact that he felt his whole body was vibrating. Eldar brought her sword up and watched for any hint as to what direction Gwydeon would move, if he favored one side or another. But from where she stood it appeared that his weight was evenly distributed and he was ready to defend any attack from any angle. His technique had improved greatly since the last time they had crossed blades. She took several long careful strides before she finally darted in and lashed out with a quick hard slash. Gwydeon, rather than blocking the blow with his blade chose instead to sidestep the attack. But Eldar was not finished with her assault. The long slash was followed with an attack with the flat of the blade aimed toward the side of Gwydeon's head. The crystal struck him on the side of the head at the level of the brow, instantly splitting open the flesh and drawing a flow of blood. The Brother of Angels however had not missed the attack, he knew it was coming, and chose to let it strike to bring his opponent closer to him. In response, Gwydeon struck out with a tight thrust of his own, that grazed Eldar under her sword arm, connecting with the flesh beneath and cutting a near eight inch furrow across her side. Blood streamed down her side, and when she leapt backwards, her entire side was drenched in blood.

"You've improved," Eldar said quietly. "More than I thought you would. But I have not even begun yet. Do you have enough left in you to keep up with me?"

The words were followed with two quick thrusts, the point of Eldar's weapon focused on striking Gwydeon directly in the heart. Gwydeon's warrior reflexes allowed him to parry away each of the blows with little effort. The next set of blows came in much faster this time, and Gwydeon's parries flowed into strikes. Those strikes were then turned aside with another set of parries. Strike to parry, parry to strike, feint to spin and sidestep, the two combatants moved through and around each other in a deadly dance that accelerated as the moments passed. After several minutes of balanced combat, Eldar and Gwydeon swung at each other at precisely the same moment, the two blades colliding and creating a fulcrum that each of the two leaned into with all the force they could manage. The stalemate held for several moments before Gwydeon relented and fell backwards with Eldar's momentum. He fell back to one knee and spun away from the suddenly on-rushing Eldar. The maneuver caught Eldar completely off balance, and she had no chance to adjust before her momentum carried her past where Gwydeon knelt. Gwydeon let his blade fly nearly blindly, and it luckily struck the back of Eldar's right leg just below the hip. More blood flowed, but instead of being disabled by the blow, Eldar dove forward, tumbled through, and popped up on a knee herself. She let her blade flash out, and it was just in range to scrape across Gwydeon's sword shoulder. For a long moment the two just stared at one another, blood flowing from open wounds, both breathing hard. Physically they were pouring everything they had into the conflict, but the true strain was on the mental and tactical aspects of the duel.

"It doesn't have to be this way, Gwydeon," Eldar said getting back to her feet with sword extended in Gwydeon's direction. "You stand on the precipice of the abyss, and only you are the one who will determine whether you go over the edge or you can be pulled back. You are a hero, an asset, and one who can marshal forces to your banner. That is a great talent that could be put to so many constructive uses on this world. Already the

Creator has extended His hand. The girl you knew as Marlae Lorien has a new name, a new purpose, and a new mandate. The Creator stands behind her with everything at His disposal. The Will stands at her side, and angels flock to her beck and call. When she marches into battle, her troops will wield blades of holy fire. This Divine Empress needs a general to lead her troops into battle against the forces of the Children of the Creator. With you at her side, she can resurrect the rotting corpse of this world and revitalize it for the Creator."

Gwydeon remained on a knee, trying to use the momentary respite to catch his breath and restore his expended energy.

"Why should I believe any offer from the Creator? What incentive do I have to go back on everything I believe in and turn a blind-eye to the horrors that the Creator has perpetrated? How do you and the Creator intend to buy my conscience?"

Eldar lowered her blade.

"The Creator has decreed that were you to accept the position as the general of the Divine Empress's army, you, your wife, and your daughter would have all of your sins expunged, and when the fate of this world is decided, you would be welcomed back into the Heavens with positions befitting your sacrifice. All you must do, right now, is lay down your weapon. You need say nothing else. The less we compromise your precious honor."

Finally Gwydeon pushed his way back to his feet, but left his sword at his side.

"I'll burn for the rest of eternity before I serve the Creator again. There is nothing you can offer, nothing you can say that will change that."

Eldar didn't hesitate to launch another salvo of brutal attacks. Blow after blow rained down on Gwydeon and each one was parried in turn. Gwydeon retuned several of the strikes, but largely was defensive. Another hard set of strikes came from the Spirit, but Gwydeon turned up the pressure himself and parries became counters which became unfettered strikes. Eldar suddenly was shifted to the defensive, having to block more blows than she was able to deliver. In a matter of seconds, Eldar was totally on the defensive and found herself choosing her footfalls carefully as the seconds passed. She was not going to let the battle end because of a stumble. As the moments passed, Gwydeon's strikes became more savage and more unfocused, but their strength was such that Eldar had no opportunity to do anything other than parry and dodge. A hard downward crushing blow struck Eldar's blade and forced her to take a step backwards. When the second blow came crashing down, it forced her to one knee. The third blow took the woman down to both knees. Over and over again Gwydeon brought his blade crashing down on Eldar. In a matter of moments the battle would be over, and Gwydeon would break through Eldar's defenses and end the battle. The vessel of the Spirit however was not going to fall, not to a backwards farm boy from an insignificant town on a world that no longer existed. The Creator's will would not be thwarted by an accident of fate. Brilliant white light manifested around Eldar's body, glowing brighter and brighter as the seconds passed. Gwydeon could feel the heat radiating from the woman, and a moment later the light flashed brighter and Gwydeon had no choice but to close his eyes. The Spirit's wings flashed open and with a single flap the Spirit was pulled away from Gwydeon's assault, and stood strong against her blinded opponent. But the Spirit was not content to be safe. She darted in, sword slashing with wicked precision, opening dozens of broad cuts across Gwydeon's chest.

"You will suffer for your sins. You will repent your blaspheme. I will make you kneel, and I will make you beg your Creator for forgiveness."

The Spirit extended her free hand, and Gwydeon's body was seized by an invisible force gripping him at the ankles and the wrists. The force pulled him up off the ground and suspended him in the air several feet above the ground. Gwydeon cried out in pain as the force pulled his limbs taut. Blood flowed from the open wounds on Gwydeon's chest and shoulder, and his muscles flexed in rebellion. He tried his best to concentrate, to channel the powers deep within him in an attempt to either escape or to strengthen his body to resist Eldar's attack. However, as the pain ravaged his body, it robbed any attempt at concentration or focus. As the seconds passed, Gwydeon felt more and more that he was going to be pulled apart, and nothing he could do would prevent it. The next moment, a burst of lightning shot through Gwydeon's body. It was not meant to kill, it was merely meant to torture. Pushing through the pain, Gwydeon pulled the sparks of lightning back into his body rather than letting them dissipate. As the Spirit kept up the torturous assault, Gwydeon continued to absorb strike after strike. Then, just when he could not take any more of the pain, he released all of the energy that he had acquired along with all of the energy he had been able to store up within himself. However, instead of striking directly at Eldar, he left the energy to release in an unfocused burst, spreading out in all directions. Gwydeon could feel his skin crawling, as though it were going to liquefy and drip off his bones. He was at the heart of an inferno, and had no energy left to defend himself against the ripples of power that folded back in on himself. Several of the ripples of power collided and exploded with such force that Gwydeon was blown free of the confinement that held him, and he landed hard on his back. His ears rang, and his brain felt like it was three sizes too large for his head. After a moment, he tried to force his eyes open but they felt swollen and unresponsive. Finally a sliver of light broke through the stubborn lids, and Gwydeon could barely see the snow-filled sky. With great effort Gwydeon's eyes opened, and the sight made his heart sink. Standing above him with her foot on his chest, and the tip of her sword pointed at his throat was the Spirit.

"An impressive tactic," Eldar said with venom dripping from her tongue, "but ultimately pointless. You may have talent, and you may have power, Gwydeon, but you had to know you were never going to be a match for me."

Reflexively Gwydeon swallowed, and felt the tip of the Spirit's blade dig deeper into his flesh. His whole body hurt. There was little he was in a position to do if he needed to defend himself, and if he tried to do anything, Eldar would feel it immediately and the battle would end badly.

"This is your last chance, Gwydeon. Repent now. Accept the bargain that the Creator has offered you. Let go of your foolish pride and accept the fact that no matter what you do, no matter how you struggle, you will fail. You have seen the power that rests in the hands of the Creator's Chosen. You have seen that even at your best, even at your most powerful, you cannot stand against me. What hope would you have against the legions of angels that will flock to His call? What hope would you have to stand at the foot of the Throne and try to shout down the Creator Himself? Abandon this foolish quest. Abandon this fallacy. Embrace the only hope you have to live past this moment."

Before Gwydeon could even breathe, he saw Eldar's eyes go wide and her head spin around. The next thing he knew, a beam of brilliant white energy came in from nowhere and slammed hard into Eldar's chest. The woman was thrown clear of where she towered over Gwydeon, and by the time Gwydeon was able to sit up, Eldar too was getting back to her feet. A pair of angelic wings flashed past Gwydeon and a woman stood firm in front of where Gwydeon sat. The woman looked as though she had already fought a war, but Camille was a welcome sight to Gwydeon's eyes. Without a word, Camille lashed out again, both hands pointed at Eldar, and twin streams of white hot fire taking the Spirit full in the chest. But the Spirit was not going to be felled so easily. She put one hand on the ground, and extended one hand into the torrent that was desperately trying to consume her. The effort was able to push back the assault and give the Spirit some room to breathe and maneuver. It took only another moment for the woman to get to her feet, but Camille was not deterred. She continued to pour on the assault, hoping that she would be able to overwhelm her opponent. Just as Eldar made it back to her feet, another blast of energy rocketed in, this one claiming the Spirit in the side. Camille hadn't expected the blow either, so it took her a moment to adjust to her target being thrown several feet. But after she made the adjustment, Camille's strike found Eldar again. Gwydeon looked to his left, trying to find the source of the second attack, and was pleasantly surprised to see that Felicia had survived her encounter and was back in the fight. With the armor of Nightwing wrapping her body, her jaws were open wide and the broad beam of energy continued its unrelenting assault. Struggling to get back to his feet, Gwydeon again pushed past the pain that was wracking his body and channeled all of the might of the Blaze that he could manage into a focused burst aimed at the Spirit.

"Keep up the pressure," he called out. "Don't let her have enough time to get her defenses back up."

There were no answers from Camille or Felicia, but the streams of power continued to batter their opponent. The Spirit was down on one knee, arms crossed in front of her face, trying her best to deflect as much of the combined assault as she could. The white aura around her flared, and her wings wrapped around her body creating an impervious shell. When the divine light flared brightly once more, the Spirit was gone. Each of the attackers in turn let their powers go silent, and Gwydeon fell to his knees, all strength fleeing from his muscles. Camille was at his side the next moment, her arms wrapped around him.

"It's good to see you too," Gwydeon said, kissing Camille lightly on the arm. "Though it looks like you've seen some combat too."

Camille looked up into her father's eyes and did her best to smile.

"We have a lot to talk about."

Gwydeon nodded, and Camille helped him back to his feet. By that time Felicia, who had let the Nightwing armor retract beneath her skin had made her way to Gwydeon's side.

"Felicia," Gwydeon said exhaling, "you did well for your first real battle. I'd like you to meet my daughter Camille."

The two women nodded to each other.

"Now, let's go see how many of our allies are still breathing. And figure out what we're going to do next."

The White Horse and the Crown

Year Four of the Just Emperor Kaitain "Dragonsbane" Lorien, Creator's Calendar Year 1871

The Kingdom of the Soul, Menoris, had been one of the few Kingdoms of Cadaria that had known peace since the establishment of the Cadarian Empire. They were great friends with their neighboring kingdom Oradrim on their island, and at times it felt like the rest of Cadaria lay somewhere across a vast ocean, and the politics of Emperors and soldiers did not touch them. Unlike the rest of the kingdoms, Oradrim was not ruled by a spoiled and petty family of royals. Instead the monks of the Brotherhood of the Flickering Flame made up the ruling council for the kingdom. They made all of the decisions for the people, and the Tiger's Eye Knight of the Flashing Blade had always been a member of their order. The Brotherhood looked at their role as a stewardship, their only true responsibility to protect all those who entered the borders of Menoris. There was no greater calling than to serve the needs of the people, and those who were suffering had the most needs of all. On the battlefields of Cadaria, the monks were considered non-combatants, moving through the ranks to pull injured soldiers away from the fighting and back to those who could save their lives. Unlike the Church of the Creator, the Brotherhood did not consider itself a religious order. They understood the existence of the Creator and found that the Creator drove them to useful and needed ends, but the purpose of the Brotherhood was to elevate man. The Brotherhood long ago had a different name, a name that was their identity through the madness of the War for Ascension. A man calling himself the Lord Phoenix built his order from the fragmented members of fallen armies, rallying them together under a banner whose only goal was to protect the innocent and to champion the mortal cause. The Brothers of the Phoenix were a proud order whose deeds saved the lives of thousands, and their actions were held in such regard by Terrik Lorien that the brothers were given control of the newly formed Kingdom of Menoris. Sometime during the madness of the founding of the Cadarian Empire, the order's founder, the Lord Phoenix, disappeared. He left behind him final words, a version of which had been spoken by every member of the brotherhood on the occasion of their joining.

The Phoenix returns to flames when its life is ended, only to be reborn once more to continue its work. My life before was the Phoenix. Now I am but the flickering flame waiting to be reborn. Only though my deeds on this world may I become the majestic Phoenix once more. I shall walk this world, the flickering flame, to raise up those who cannot rise by themselves. I shall use this flickering flame to bring comfort to those who have none, and to shelter those who know only the ravages of the world around them. I am the flickering flame, and yet I am so much more.

From the day of their patron's disappearance, the brotherhood adopted the name the Brotherhood of the Flickering Flame. They served in the tradition set by their founder, and made their home in the capital city of Menoris in the shadow the Peak of Patience. It was said that the highest peak was where the Lord Phoenix's words were found, which began the tradition that every prospective member of the Brotherhood had to make their way to the highest peak on a pilgrimage before they could become full members of the order. Now with the whole of Cadaria once again embroiled in wars that would determine who would control the Empire, the Brotherhood of the Flickering Flame prepared to fulfill their ancient charter. There were battlefields a plenty that their services would be needed at, and there would be no shortage of the fallen and the hungry for the Brotherhood to care for. Since the members of the Church of the Creator were now considered traitors to the Throne and were to be arrested or killed on sight, the Brotherhood of the Flickering Flame were the only ones who could bring comfort to the injured or save the innocents from becoming collateral damage. Never were the order's services needed more.

Standing on a plateau overlooking the valley that Menoris stretch across, Pike Rhuiden looked down at the people preparing for their journey. The docks that held Menoris' small fleet of ships were bustling with activity, and the caravans of supplies were being loaded and readied for the several hour journey to the coast of the larger continent of Cadaria. Though there were many pirates and other undesirables that patrolled the channel between the island that housed two of the Kingdoms of Cadaria and the larger portion of Cadaria itself, none would have dared to pray on the ships of the Brotherhood. There were some things that even pirates and criminals would not do, no matter the potential profits. Pike's eyes next went to the majestic Peak of Patience, the very tips of which scraped the sky and stabbed through the clouds like a dagger. There were chains of light moving through unseen paths from the peaks, as the leadership of the Brotherhood made a pilgrimage to the highest peak before their departure in order to reaffirm their commitment to their role in the world. In a matter of hours the Brotherhood would be scattering themselves to the corners of Cadaria, trying, Pike knew, in vain to bring some kind of meaning to the madness that gripped the Empire. However, things were spinning wildly out of control in Cadaria, and it was only a matter of time before even the Brotherhood would not be able to save even one soul from the fires that were waiting to claim them. It was sad really, but Pike understood it. How many times had he himself charged headlong into a hopeless situation that he had no chance to change? Hopelessness didn't touch these Brotherhood members.

But Pike was not alone overlooking the city of Menoris, and Pike was sure that his companion did not feel the same about the people below. Dorovar stood a half pace behind Pike, looking not at the city below, but looking at the mountain.

"They don't know what is ahead of them," Dorovar said coldly. "I have seen this march to war on dozens of worlds. And every time it was met with some level of success, but ultimately fruitless. Battles are won or lost, wars ebb and flow. But on those worlds, in the end, the results were the same. People died by the tens of thousands. Homes burned. Rulers rose and fell. Blood flowed like water. I have watched worlds burn, consumed by the fires set in the name of freedom. I have watched the rising tide of blood consume everything in its path, the last two inhabitants of the world passing into nothingness with their hands around each other's throats. This world will share that fate. Unless we do something to prevent it. The Creator and his Children care nothing for these people. But they will be wiped from existence nonetheless because they are corrupted."

Pike finally looked back at Dorovar and saw the faraway look in the monster's eyes.

"This Brotherhood of the Flickering Flame bears a stain upon its soul. It is touched both by the foul pride of Emries, and the indecisive coddling of Halicon. Your would-be brother, Logan Ranthall is responsible for these people, and he is the genesis of this order. Because of that, when the purge comes to this world, they will all fall. Not because of something they did consciously, but because two thousand years ago, people who they may not have any relation to made the decision to follow the words of a man who wanted to do nothing more but escape the madness he had seen as his own world burned. No matter if Logan was right or wrong in what he did; these people will suffer for it. They will choke and die. They will be swept away like so many fallen leaves. Would you not spare them from that fate? Would you not rescue them from an eternity of suffering?"

Pike felt an odd emotion rising for Dorovar. It was something like pity, but not as intense. Whether or not he genuinely cared for the fate of these people was still in doubt, but his argument was compelling.

"All of these people will die. Every single one of them has no future past this world. Espre is lost, and so is everyone who walks upon it who is mortal. Either old age, or natural disaster, or dragon attack, or war, or famine, or senseless murder; they will all die. Would you not rather their deaths mean something? Would you not rather that their deaths serve a greater good than simply passing into the beyond, lost for all eternity? If so, you are every bit as cruel as I have been accused of being."

Finally Dorovar's eyes met Pike's. Though a shudder passed through the one-time mortal hero, Pike kept the reaction from showing. Something rose up within him, something that he had not felt in a long time.

"What about their lives?" Pike said with a righteous indignation he didn't know was still within him. "Every day that they are alive they can strive to make this world a better place. They can save lives that can in turn save more lives. Why do only their deaths matter?"

Dorovar reached out and laid both of his hands on Pike's shoulders.

"If all of their lives are going to end, how can they save anyone? If death is inevitable, why does it matter if they ease the suffering of millions, when those millions will meet the same fate, just an hour, or a day, or a week, or a month, or a year, or ten years later? Better that their souls be freed from their servitude to the Creator now, and their voices be added to the growing chorus that will see the end of the Creator's bloody reign. Isn't that a far better purpose than postponing the inevitable? The sooner the Creator falls, the sooner that all of the suffering on every world is ended. Do you not think that these people, who are so dedicated to sacrificing their time and their belongings to the cause of saving others would not leap at the chance to give their lives to end the suffering of millions? If they could be made to understand, I would give them that choice. But the Creator has twisted their minds, has made it impossible for them to see the veil of lies that has been pulled over their eyes for what it is. So the only path open is to save them from themselves. Remove the veil of lies by freeing them from the prison of the flesh. Let their souls sing. Give them the freedom they deserve."

Dorovar's words shook Pike to the core and though his mind tried to fight against the horrors that the words lay bare, he could not. He could feel Dorovar's power rushing through him, spreading like spider webs through his insides. The touch of the monster invaded Pike's heart, and a cold radiated through him unlike any he had ever known. Then suddenly there was an explosion of light in the deepest part of Pike's core. It was searing light and heat that burned away all doubt. The surface of Dorovar's words were peeled away, revealing the profound truth beneath. Not only was Dorovar truly trying to save these people from a fate worse than meaningless death, but his path was the only true way to accomplish it. Yes. The people had to be saved from their invisible bondage. They had to be delivered from the Creator's lies. Death was the only release. Death was the only possible salvation. Pike's path was now clear.

Pike pulled away from Dorovar's reassuring grasp and turned to face Menoris once again. He walked to the very edge of the plateau, allowing the toes of his well-worn boots to hang over the edge. Reaching down into the very depths of his being, Pike found the flows of divine power that slumbered inside of him. For so long, Pike had ignored their existence, using only the barest fraction of what he could have called upon. Even in the fights with Korin and Dorovar he had only touched the surface of that power. To pull upon any more would be to acknowledge the Creator's influence upon his life, and rarely did Pike require any more than a fraction of his full capabilities. His body hummed with power, and he could hear the small pebbles being shaken loose from the ledge beneath his feet. His eyes immediately found the focus for his power's release. Pike reached out with both hands, his eyes locked on the Peaks of Patience, and in his field of vision he placed one hand in the middle of the far side of the mountain, and the other at the peak on the side that faced Menoris. From Pike's perspective it looked as though he held the whole of the mountain in his hands, and with the power that filled him, he felt as though he was doing exactly that. With an exertion unlike any he had undertaken before, Pike pushed with his right hand, and the exertion was matched by the vision of the mountain beginning a slow move toward Menoris. Like a massive tree being pulled up by the root, the Peaks of Patience creaked and rumbled. The amount of power that Pike held allowed him to hear the tumult coming from below him, the screams of terror and the disbelieving cries. The mountain that had been their shelter, their spiritual center was suddenly going to be the instrument of their demise. In a heartbeat it would be too late. Inertia and gravity would take over, and the fall of the mighty mountain would be unable to be arrested by any force. Even Pike did not know if he could have stopped it in time. He held it there, at the point of no return, an inner war raging in his heart and mind. It was still not too late to stop this. To walk away, to fight against Dorovar's influence. To fight the good fight as he always had. But Dorovar spoke with such conviction, and Pike knew that none of this would matter so long as the Creator still lived. The Creator and his Children would need to be crushed, and to do that, the leverage of the mortals of Espre had to be eliminated. The game had to be broken from its inside out. But no matter the conviction of his new cause, the itch in the back of his mind would not relent. What he was doing was mass murder on the scale that even the phasia had not been able.

Only Dorovar, the monster who stood behind him had been the architect of such devastation.

"Do not torture them, Pike," Dorovar said coldly. "That is not your way, and it is not my way. That is the Creator's way. End this. Take your place at my side and help me to topple the Creator."

Pike's left hand moved away from his field of vision before he really understood the ramifications of what he was doing. Uncontrolled, the Peaks of Patience fell. Though he wanted to watch with detachment, the amount of power that still radiated within Pike would not allow him. The massive slabs of rock crashed down, crushing houses and people alike. The death toll was immense, and the impact sent debris flying in all directions for miles. Several large pieces of the mountain flew into the sea creating tidal waves of such size and force that they enveloped the small fleet that rested impotent in their docks. The city and infrastructure that had existed for almost two millennia had been wiped from the face of the world in a matter of minutes without a single survivor. They were all dead. But as Pike stood and watched, his eyes widened in shock. From the devastation below he began to see a kind of movement. Light green wispy shadows stirred from the rubble, raising from the death below into the sky. Pike thought that he could make out faces, but it was the sound that they were making that shook him to the core. First it was one voice, a single low note that rumbled like thunder. Then another joined, a delicate high note at least two octaves above. Then two more, then a dozen more, a hundred more. Finally the entirety of the population of Menoris floated like a cloud into the sky, their sorrowful song filling the air. Behind Pike, Dorovar reached his hands into the air, and the wispy mass began to glow.

"Aren't they beautiful, Pike? Don't you see the great gift you have given them?"

The song intensified, the mournful dirge changing to something more hopeful, as though a light had been shown upon a room that had known only darkness. The cloud glowed even brighter, all the voices locking into a single chord, growing louder and louder until Pike felt it would make him go deaf. Then, just as it had begun, the voices began to go quiet one by one, and then in groups until only the first voice remain, low and somber. Then it too was silenced. When Pike turned back to face Dorovar, he glowed with a power that only those who knew true power could see. Pike had stood at the foot of the Creator, he had seen that glow before. It was divine power, the power of Creation, and through absorbing those souls, Dorovar had infused himself with a measure of the power that should only have been wielded by the one who shaped the Cosmos. However, the next moment it was a different power that drew Pike's attention.

Several feet from where Dorovar stood, a blue portal winked open. As soon as Dorovar saw the portal, he wrapped the light of the sun around himself, essentially hiding himself from view to anyone who wasn't standing right on top of him. A moment later a blond haired woman in a black dress stepped through the portal. Pike recognized Serrina Mistic immediately and felt as though a dagger was twisting in his stomach. Serrina's eyes were wide when she saw Pike, but quickly ran to him.

"I came as quickly as I could Lord Pike," she said with a mixture of pain and longing in her eyes. "Everything within the Citadel has gone crazy. Sabrina and Taya have gone to support Jerrard, Midarin is in Rashaleb, and it seems like Aryx and Diana have just disappeared."

Pike put her hands on Serrina's shoulders.

"Calm down, Serrina," he said in his best calming voice. "Just breathe and tell me what you want to tell me."

She took a long deep breath and refocused herself.

"Midarin and Camille are in Rashaleb, and there are rumors that Gwydeon is alive and there with them. Maybe the three of them have plotted against you and are going to take control of the Council. With Diana and Aryx missing, it seems that Wolf and Lissa have gone rogue too. Wolf as far as I can tell is still at the Citadel, but Lissa has disappeared too, and I'm not sure where. What I am sure about are their two daughters. Mirana and Liara actually fought against me. I was trying to get revenge for us. I was trying to kidnap Kaitain's wife. But they stopped me. I'm so sorry, Pike."

Tears came to her eyes, and despite himself, Pike pulled her in to him and held her tightly. Serrina surrendered to the embrace, her arms going limp for a long moment before wrapping around him. This was what she had wanted for as long as she could remember. She had dutifully followed every order he had ever given, and in return all she wanted was his attention and affection. Perhaps now that Sadrina was out of the way, his eyes would fall to her where they belonged.

"It's alright Serrina, we should have seen the betrayal coming. What about Alderin? What about Darrien? Or Tess? Any word about them?"

He felt Serrina's grip tighten around him.

"Darrien is in the wilds where the Dragon Council once was. I don't know how she got there, but that is where she is. Alderin is in Celidar with Jerrard and Sabrina. It seems that they could be another pocket of rebellion. But we know that Jerrard is part of the Cadarians, so maybe Sabrina and the others have gone to the other side. They never believed in what we were doing anyway. As for Tess, I've never been able to follow her movements very well. Bryn is also there, but I can't imagine that she would work for the Cadarians. Has to be something to do with her husband. Aerith is all over the place, and as usual he is interfering where he is not wanted."

Pike's hand gently rubbed Serrina's back.

"You've done so well Serrina. Your parents would be so proud."

Serrina pulled back from Pike, and there were tears in her eyes. Pike's hands went to the side of her face, and with one thumb he wiped the tear from her cheek. Her eyes were filled with love and devotion.

"I'm proud of you."

Pike leaned in and gently kissed her forehead. When he pulled back, the smile faded from his lips and sorrow was the only emotion in his eyes.

"But where I am going, my little lamb, you cannot follow."

Serrina's end was violent but quick. Pike's hands pressed in on the side of her head and twisted hard. The sound of her neck snapping came to his ears quickly, and the light went out of her eyes as though a candle had been blown out by a violent wind. He did not let her fall, but gently laid her upon the ground and knelt beside her for a long time. Dorovar reappeared from his pocket of seclusion and walked slowly to where Pike knelt. He put his hand on Pike's shoulder and joined his new ally in looking down at Serrina's body.

"She was a good girl," Pike said, "but she would not have understood what I did here, or what comes next. There are so many that must be purged in the days to come, and all must bend their knees to the rightful ruler of this world. Only together can we topple the Creator. But I must take the fight to the Children of the Creator. I must hold their lives in my hand no differently than I held Serrina's. I must look into their eyes and watch the light drain from them. Only then, once we have stripped away the Children and the Servants will we be able to assault the Throne. We must attack the Creator the same way he has attacked us. Take that which we love, take that which we value. We must topple him from the inside out."

Dorovar smiled wickedly.

"The rest of my servants will continue the fight against the dragons, but before you take your righteous fury to the Children of the Creator, you must secure two of the great treasures entrusted to the dragons. Mortis will allow you to steal the power and strength from the Children as you fight them, and Avaril will protect you from their most treacherous abilities. It will shield you from death itself. After that, you can do as you see fit, and bring my enemies to their knees. You shall be the herald of my conquest of all that oppose me. You shall stand atop the highest peaks on this world and bring them crashing down upon my enemies. You will lay them low and add voices to my choir."

A moment later an iron crown appeared in Dorovar's hands. It appeared to be no more than a collection of iron plates arrayed in a circle, and together it gave the appearance of a chain of mountains that had been cobbled together. Dorovar wasted no time in placing the crown atop Pike's head. From the moment it contacted his brown, the crown glowed with golden power.

"This crown, my new servant, allows you to hear the voices of my choir, and to feed upon their power. The Creator thrived on the energy of their love and devotion, the love that was not given freely but in their indentured servitude. Now freed from their invisible prison they impart their power to me, and through this crown to you. Use this power as you will, my servant, for they will sing louder and produce as much as needed. Their vengeance is a righteous one, and so it is limitless."

Dorovar took a step back.

"Arise, my servant. Rise into your new life. Arise Conquest; the bringer of righteous fury upon those who have wronged us."

When Pike rose, he was physically no different, but in his hands he felt he had the power to remake the world.

"When you have finished with the two dragons that make their home in Galateria," Dorovar said with a sly smile, "then you will set your sights on the Frozen Wastes, and a place called Glacier's Rift."

Epilogue

The Children of the Creator

"**A**re you out of your mind?"

Rhain Seth sat in a chair across from where Sabrina sat on the bed in her small room in the Royal Palace of Celidar. Sabrina looked as though she hadn't slept in weeks, and her color was so pale. However her eyes were so bright, a sparkling golden color ringed with green. Rhain had been listening for several minutes before she could not hear any more. Sabrina had said something about needing a favor, and now that Rhain understood the depth of what was being asked for, Rhain knew there was no way she could accept. Sabrina hung her head for a long moment before looking up again and meeting Rhain's shocked gaze.

"It's the only way, and you can try to look as shocked as you want, but you and I both know that deep down, somewhere inside of you, this is the only way."

Sabrina's head turned slightly, and her ear was cocked toward a shadow in the corner of the room. She smiled weakly and let a small chuckle pass through her lips.

"You can come out of there, Aerith. I know keeping your mouth shut has to be killing you."

Rhain watched as her father emerged from the deep shadow, and the look on his face showed his annoyance with Sabrina uncovering his deception.

"I taught you too well."

Rhain was up from her chair the next moment, and the father and daughter shared a quick but meaningful embrace. When Rhain returned to her chair, Aerith moved to Sabrina's side, but instead of sitting with her on the bed, he knelt beside her and put one hand on her hip.

"And you never knew when you were supposed to stay away. What if Emries or Talisia found out that you and Logan and I were in the same place? I'm in no condition to fight, and there are too many innocents. This is reckless, even for you."

Aerith reached into his pocket and produced the charm that had been so valiantly won from the Wrath.

"Wolf and I figured you could use a little bolstering."

Rhain craned her neck to get a better look.

"What is that?"

It was Sabrina's voice and not Aerith's that gave rise to the answer.

"The faceplate of the Wrath. Wolf and Aerith worked together to kill a Servant of the Creator, and they were able to do it for good. The Creator won't be able to easily resurrect that Servant, and it would take more time than will matter to forge another one. Pyrrus was always clever."

Aerith nodded.

"And when you mix it with some Ranthall resolve and a little bit of phasia cunning, it's quite impressive. It's unfortunate that I never really got a chance to know Pyrrus. I think I would have liked him."

Rhain leaned back in her chair.

"Alright, I'll play. What does the faceplate of the Wrath do?"

Again, it was Sabrina who answered, and her tone made it seem that this was something she had known for quite some time. It was that tone, and not the information itself that shook Rhain's resolve. When Sabrina had asked for her favor, she had already taken all of this into account.

"It's a vessel of divine power. Aerith and Wolf believe that if I were to wear it that it would slow the rate at which Halicon's powers are killing me. It may even give me time to see the end of this war. But unfortunately, it's too late for all that. Tess's little outburst and the shield that I had to erect to protect everyone put too much of a strain on my body. Even with the faceplate, I doubt I will live another month."

Rhain saw the look in Sabrina's eyes, and knew that she was not exaggerating. Her gaze immediately fell to her father, and she saw something she had only seen on very rare occasions, and never openly in front of people. There were tears in Aerith's eyes. That next moment, Rhain thought Aerith was going to argue, to raise his voice, to try to convince Sabrina that there was another choice, another path, and something more that could be done. There were still so many things they didn't know about the nature of the Children of the Creator. There had to be hope. They could not have come this far without hope. But instead Aerith got to his feet, tears barely restrained from flowing down his cheeks, and then pulled Sabrina into his arms. She meekly snaked her arms around his waist and together they stood like that for a long time, not moving. There was so much that was passing between the two, so many emotions, so many thoughts. Rhain saw Aerith kiss Sabrina lightly on the forehead and then pull away.

"You've been like a daughter to me for so long, I don't know what I'm going to do with you gone, kid."

Sabrina smiled.

"This is the only way, Aerith, and you know it. As long as I have connection to Halicon's power, and still have some remnant of your mantle inside me, it leaves you and the whole plan vulnerable. We don't know how much the Creator can look into the minds of his Children or influence the use of their powers. I'm not as much worried about Him manipulating me as I am about Him reaching through me down your mantle to hurt you, or Logan, or Hannah. We have to stem the tide and protect those we can. Everything is spinning so madly out of control, if we can't start winning some of these engagements, then I don't know that we have much chance of getting out of this, wager or not."

Aerith pulled Sabrina to him again. He knew it would be the last time that he would lay eyes on the woman. Steeling himself, Aerith turned to face his daughter.

"You have to do as Sabrina asked," he said finally. "We can't lose Halicon's abilities, and with the faceplate, it should give you more control than even Wolf has with the help of Draven and Basille's knowledge. It also means that you are going to be the force behind the phasia, all of them, and you're going to be the one to help eliminate Emries' influence from those who still can't save themselves. Korrd and Nathan are lost, but maybe we can save the *Erieal* that are still out there. I know you'll do your best. I can't think of anyone else I would want to have the job."

Aerith leaned in and gave his daughter a long hug before turning and walking toward the door. There was so much emotion churning in his heart and in his soul, and he wasn't sure what to do with it all. He wasn't sure where he was going to go next, nor was he really sure if he should go to see his wife. He could feel her close by, but he had learned long ago how to block her perception of him. Putting his hand on the door handle, part of him wanted to look back. He wanted to see Sabrina's face one more time before the end. But what good would it do? How many other deaths would he carry in his heart before it was all over? Maybe he couldn't take any more. Maybe his heart would give out before he reached the end. No. He would keep pushing. He would keep fighting. He would not betray the memories of those that were sacrificed in his name. He would endure because they could not.

After Aerith left the room, Rhain saw the tears stream down Sabrina's face. She sat back down on the edge of the bed, and did her best to regain her composure. She knew that the moments that remained in her life were slipping away, and there was no time to wallow. There was still so much to do, and so many things left to accomplish in the short time remaining. She hoped she had the strength to do it all, but as long as Rhain was beside her, she knew that she would be able to endure. Finally the tears stopped, and Sabrina looked up into the flushed and tear-streaked face of the woman that was somewhat her sister, and somewhat her aunt. No matter what lineage one used to try to explain the connection between the two women, there was one truth that was unavoidable. The bond between them was more than blood, more than time, more than one of common interest or goal. That bond, that unquantifiable bond was what they were fighting for. That connection that words could never describe was at the heart of everything, and it was something that the Children of the Creator would never understand, the Servants could never see, and the Creator could never break. That bond was why the mortals and those that fought for them would win the war.

Sabrina forced a smile onto her face.

"You should get Logan and Alderin. I'll leave you to deal with Taya once I'm gone. She won't understand and will try to talk me out of it. Better that she hear it from you."

Rhain put on her best wry smile.

"Thanks. And now I'm never going to be able to get you back."

Once Rhain had left the room, Sabrina's resolved cracked. She collapsed back on the edge of the bed and just stared at the wall, tears streaming down her face.

* * * * * * * * * * * *

Stepping out of a swirling white portal, Tess had to blink her eyes several times before they adjusted to the dim light. It took her only a few moments to recognize the landscape. She was standing on the southern frontier of the continent of Mythryn. To the north, almost a hundred miles away stood the Citadel of the Dark Gods. Very few came down this far, and aside from the small port that served as a southern defense garrison, the forces of the Dark Gods had no presence here. After a few moments of surveying the landscape, Tess felt a hand on her shoulder. The man who had called himself Emries, the man who had been so kind to her since he had found her sitting alone in that dark forest, had brought her here because he said he wanted to show her something. He knew about her abilities; knew that she had been struggling to control them, and thought he knew the way to make it all make sense. He brought her to the very edge of the plateau they stood upon and pointed to a broad space in the center of the valley below. It was a wasteland, desolate, and looked as though people had never dwelled there, even before the Dark Gods chose to make the continent their home.

"See that void there, Tess? See how it just aches to have life upon it? But life has never blossomed here. Isn't that sad? Would you like to grant the land's wish? Would you like to make life upon it?"

Tess's face lit up. To think that she could actually fulfill a wish like that. To create life where it had never been able to take root. She knew it would make the land happy, and more importantly it would make her feel as though she had done something right. Maybe, maybe if she did these things, maybe if she fulfilled these wishes, she could make Camille understand. Devlin was dead, and if Camille didn't understand why it had to be done, then she might hate Tess for doing it. And Tess couldn't live with the thought that Camille hated her. So Tess had to prove to Camille that what she did had purpose, and that her purpose could only bring good things to pass.

"Now," Emries said kneeling down so that he was nearly the same height as his smaller companion. "What does life need to take root? What is missing here that would make life blossom?"

Tess tried to think, but her mind was so foggy. She had been alive long enough and had learned at the feet of some of the smartest people to walk the face of Espre, but so much had happened, and now it seemed as though she were just a little girl again learning to lace her own boots. Having the nice man Emries at her side made her feel better; made her feel confident. Finally the thought came to her mind that she had been searching for.

"Water."

Emries smiled and his blue eyes lit up.

"Very good. Now, look at that ugly empty patch of ground. We need water, so what do you think we should do?"

Tess bit her lower lip and then as though of its own volition, her right hand reached out in the direction of the empty space, and the tips of her fingers glowed with a golden energy. For several seconds nothing happened, and then, there came a golden glow from the center of the lifeless area. The glow spread slowly, feet at a time, until suddenly it engulfed nearly the whole area. When the golden glow receded, the barren land was gone, replaced by a wide and sprawling lake. The waters were pristine, and as the gentle wind brushed across its surface, small waves formed. Emries smiled and put his hand on the girl's shoulder.

"Very good Tess. We have our water. But do you think the lake is too big? Where are we going to put houses and farms? Can you make it smaller?"

Tess frowned. She hadn't thought about all that. She had just thought about making the water. Maybe that was what Emries was trying to teach her. It wasn't enough just to be able to do a thing, you had to think about what happened after you did a thing. What were the next steps? If she had thought about houses and crops and all of that, she would have known the size to make the lake. She reached out again with her right hand, only this time it did not feel like the hand was doing the work on its own. She was in control now. She knew what she wanted to do, and she was going to do it. The whole of the lake was enveloped once more in the shimmering golden light, and when the light receded again, the lake had been reduced by almost half its original size. Tess smiled to herself for being able to do it and looked at Emries.

"Better?"

Emries could not suppress the smile.

"Very very good, Tess. You are a good student and a quick one too. Now, what should we do next? Maybe some grass and some trees?"

Confidence filled Tess, and without giving a verbal answer to the question, she turned and extended both of her hands toward the remaining barren land. The golden light covered everything, and as though it were some great net that covered the land, in a matter of moments bright green blades of grass began to poke through. In some places saplings emerged, and over the following seconds they grew and expanded into mighty trees that looked as though they had stood in that spot for generations. When the golden glow finally faded once more, a living breathing glade sat in the valley below where only moments before had been nothing but dead infertile ground. Before Emries could say anything else, Tess turned to him with an excited look in her eyes.

"We need animals now. Some deer and some rabbits, birds, and oh, some fish for the lake. This is going to be so much fun. It's like painting. I tried painting a long time ago, but I wasn't very good at it. Liara was always the painter, and she tried to teach me, but it didn't go like this. Can I try to make animals now, can I?"

The girl's enthusiasm was infectious, and as soon as Emries nodded his ascent, the girl turned and went to work populating her little glade. Each experiment increased her control and her power, and as Emries watched in partial astonishment, the schemes began to churn through his mind. How long would it take her to reshape the whole of the continent of Mythryn? How long until she filled it with life? Could she create mortals that would be obedient to her will? Could she create other things, like dragons, or angels, or even things that had never walked any world anywhere in the Cosmos. The limitation was her imagination, and she needed to put that imagination to the test. Finally, Tess wiped sweat from her brow and turned to face Emries. She was so happy with what she had done, and she could hear the chirping of the birds and the splashing of the fish below. She hadn't created too many, and she stopped once she thought she had the balance just right. Midarin had always tried to teach her about trying to do too much, reaching too far without being able to see what it meant. And making the lake had taught her a lesson about considering all of her actions before she committed to anything. Emries face beamed with pride. It was time to test the girl and to see just how far he could push her.

"So, what should we do next? Do you want to try another barren part of Mythryn? Do you want to try making some houses or some people, or do you want to try something more challenging."

Tess grinned.

"I like a challenge."

Emries smiled a sly smile.

"Good. There is something that I want you to make for me. But you're going to have to listen very carefully to get it right."

* * * * * * * * * * * *

Talisia Masile sat in the darkness of the stronghold of the Hand of Chaos and brooded. So many things had gone wrong over the last few hours. The Academy of Arcane Arts had been denied to her. Korin was missing, the truce with Dorovar was clearly over, and the information source that she had buried deep within the Dark Gods had proven to be worthless. Emries would sense her weakness soon enough and make a move on her, and she had not martialed enough troops to turn away his advances if they were of any substance. It seemed as though the whole war had turned on her, and there would be nothing she could do to prevent her life from ending on this ball of dust. She still had one contingency plan left open to her, but the time had not come for that drastic measure. Somewhere on Espre, the weak and pathetic girl that called herself the Ethereal Sorceress still lived, though she was protected and shrouded from Talisia's vision. It had been an easy thought to dispatch Seraphina and Syren to recover the woman. If she could be introduced back into the court of Kaitain Lorien, perhaps the mad man could still be bent to her purposes. If not, Talisia would simply have to accelerate her plans for the arrogant pig of a man. She felt a presence enter the room a moment later, one that was familiar to her, but in this case familiarity had not bred tolerance. The dragon that called itself Shadowweaver may have been able to take mortal form to walk about on two legs and fit into places his normal girth would not allow, but that did not make him any more welcome in Talisia's stronghold.

"Stay where you are dragon," the Child of the Creator said coldly. "You were not invited, and I would be well within my right to tear you apart. It might be pleasurable to see how long you can hold that human form as I am pulling organs from your chest."

Shadowweaver stopped, but kept a wide smile on his lips.

"Your threats are misplaced, Talisia. I did not come here for a quarrel. I came here to negotiate."

Talisia knew that the dragon's words were dubious at best, but she motioned with one hand for him to continue.

"With Dorovar's incursions and his blatant hatred for every one of my brothers and sisters, a rift has formed in the dragon race. Those that were blindly loyal to Lord Tarot now cast their allegiance behind Mariti Brightblade who quests to wipe out our ancient enemy. But we both know that though Dorovar thinks himself the star of this little drama, he is only a bit player at best. The rest of the right thinking members of the dragon breeds have given me their will, and as such I have come to honor the terms of our agreement during your rebellion. In return for killing your brothers and sisters and helping you to overthrow the Creator, you will give us the freedom to go where we want, do what we want, and kill what we want without sanction from the Throne, so long as we do not support any move against you."

Talisia could not help the smile that came to her lips.

"How many are loyal to you, Shadowweaver?"

The dragon's face went cold and the look in his eyes deadly serious.

"Enough to blacken the sky."

* * * * * * * * * * * *

Darrien Annis felt as though there was danger pressing in all around her. Without powers at her disposal she had trusted the woman who called herself Faelara to bring her where she needed to be. However, she had not counted on the mysterious woman depositing her on the edge of the Endless Crater. Darrien had lived her entire life with the powers of a Dark God, so the enterprise of scaling down a several mile deep crater with her bare hands did not fill her with a sense of joy. But, no matter the trial, she would have to endure. That is what her father had taught her, and he had accomplished so much more as a mortal than she ever had as a Dark God.

The deeper she got into the Crater, the harder it was for her to see, and the minutes seemed to pass like hours. Several times during her descent, her hand holds had given way, and she ended up showered by sharp volcanic glass that sliced through her skin like the sharpest razors. But in the end, bloody, hungry, and exhausted, she reached the bottom of the Crater, the place where her father and all of the members of the Dark Gods had crashed down on the surface of Espre after their failed rebellion in the Heavens. Almost immediately the green glow appeared, beckoning her down the long and winding path that Faelara had told her would lead her to the Vault of Terrors, the prison from which Dorovar had only recently escaped, but that also held some of the most dangerous weapons to ever darken the Cosmos. The huge iron door was open and Darrien could feel the deep foreboding and dread that filled the Vault. But there was something else. There was another presence, one that didn't belong there any more than she did. She wanted to call out, but the fear gripped her throat so tightly that no sound would emerge. Suddenly she saw the fire of a torch emerge from deeper in the Vault, and as soon as the light was cast upon the person's face, the fear that held her tongue was broken.

"Wolf? What are you doing here?"

Wolf continued to approach, but there was no lightness to his features.

"Darrien? I should be asking you the same thing. How did you even get here? Did Alderin find you? He's been worried."

Darrien felt the blush color her cheeks, and hoped in the dim light that it didn't show.

"Tess did something to me, and I've lost all my abilities."

Wolf frowned.

"The same thing happened to Alderin. He said that you started to open a portal and were thrown through but he didn't know where you ended up. Did it bring you here?"

Darrien shook her head.

"No. It took me to the home of the dragons where their leader's corpse lay. Dorovar killed Tarot, and now he's working his way through the rest of them. There were a woman named Faelara there, she said that she was from Dorovar's world and wanted to help us stop him. She thought that there might be a weapon here that we could use against him, something that he overlooked."

Wolf smiled his best smile, though it made his face ache.

"I hoped to find something too, but not a weapon. Information. But whatever we're going to find, it will be easier with two sets of eyes. Let's get to work."

Wolf handed Darrien his torch and picked up a discarded piece of wood and created another one. There was a lot of ground to cover, and Wolf had no idea how much time they actually had to find something that would prevent the catastrophe that was looming.

* * * * * * * * * * * *

Raenera knew that she was keeping everyone waiting, but she needed the moment to clear her head. The time was finally upon her, the time that she had been dreading for so long. Deep in the darkest corners of Glacier's Rift was a secret armory. Raenera knew that it would take an army to accomplish her goals. She had hoped that the lost children she had gathered would be up to leading that army, but having seen them in combat with one of Talisia's children she had begun to have doubts. Entering the armory, as expected she saw the Maker hard at work. The Maker's work was legendary across Cadaria, and no one knew who he really was. A number of different names had surfaced, but it seemed that the most exotic one had stuck. They called him Fu'Isharic Bar'lohn. But Raenera had only ever known him by his true name. She crossed the distance to him and saw the pile of swords and armor that lay completed on the table beside him. He pounded at the piece of steel on the forge, mumbling to himself as he always did. When Raenera put her hand on the Maker's arm, he stopped. His tired eyes found hers, and he mumbled to her.

"Can't sleep, can't stop. Must work. He's coming."

Raenera ran her fingers through his sweat and oil laden hair. She cooed to him and tried her best to give him comfort.

"It's alright Arturious. Soon you'll be able to sleep as much as you want. The work is almost done. I promise, you will sleep more peacefully than anyone ever has. You've earned that and more."

Arturious Demascious, the great weapon maker of legend smiled a weak smile before bringing his hammer down on the forge once more, the mumbling rising against the sound of metal striking metal.

Appendicies

Dramatis Personae

The Imperial Court

Terrik 'Godslayer' Lorien
Emperor Lorien I

Liette Lorien
Wife of Terrik Lorien
Empress of Cadaria
Seer

Kaldawyn Lorien
Emperor Lorien X
Father of Ender Lorien

Ender 'Justhand' Lorien
Emperor Lorien XI
Father of Feyd and Kaitain Lorien

Meara Lorien
Wife of Ender Lorien
Mother of Kaitain and Feyd Lorien

Kaitain Lorien
Emperor Lorien XII
Father of Marlae Lorien
Adoptive Father of Quyhn Lorien
Twin Brother of Feyd Lorien

Dominique Arais Lorien
Wife of Kaitain Lorien
Former Mistress of Seraph Kore

Marlae Lorien
The Celestial Princess
Crown Princess of Cadaria
Daughter of Kaitain Lorien

Korin Melcab
Captain of the Imperial Guard

Feyd Lorien
Prince of Cadaria
Brother of Kaitain Lorien
Overseer of Lordhill Province
Father of Felicia Lorien

Felicia Lorien
Princess of Cadaria
Daughter of Feyd Lorien

Galen White
Member of the Imperial Guard
Personal Guard of Felicia Lorien

Gabriel Shadowfall
Member of the Imperial Guard
Personal Guard of Marlae Lorien

Geoffry Aramour
Imperial Historian and Bard
Master of the Shadow Guild

Quyhn Ravenheart Lorien
Sorceress
Ward of the Empire
Daughter of Alistair and Estelle
Ravenheart

Rhain Seth
Personal Guard of Marlae Lorien
Daughter of Aerith Seth and Bryn
Aplee

Irene Drage
The Ethereal Sorceress
Court Sorceress
Protégé of Alistair Ravenheart

The Knights of the Flashing Blade
Bernhardt Yeoman
The Moonstone Knight
Kingdom of Iron, Pellatori
Wielder of the Hammer Gravity

Chelsea Zarova
The Garnet Knight
Kingdom of Fire, Saldarine
"The Wolf of Saldarine"
Wife of Seraph Kore
Wielder of the Katars Tenacity

Devlin Rannoch
The Onyx Knight
Kingdom of Night, Galateria
Half-Dragon
Wielder of the Kopesh Discipline

Gregor Quicksilver
The Ruby Knight
Kingdom of Blood, Zevarit
Husband of Hannah Ironheart
Paladin of the Church of the Creator
Son of Ivan Quicksilver
Wielder of the Greatsword Valor

Hannah Ironheart
The Celestine Knight
Kingdom of Stone, Albitonin
High Priestess of the Church of the
Creator
Wife of Gregor Quicksilver
Wielder of the Mace Spirit

Jaccob Aldora
The Topaz Knight
The Flying Kingdom, Hedora
Former Member of the Academy of
Arcane Arts
Wielder of the Double Sword
Temperance

Leonora Wastri
The Jade Knight
Kingdom of Soul, Oradrim
Wielder of the Naginata Wisdom

Natalia Pressen
The Sunstone Knight
Kingdom of Gold, Bellnoc
Master of the Shadow Guild
Wielder of the Rapier Perseverance

Orren Eldrath
The Sapphire Knight
Kingdom of Ice, Rashaleb
Former Member of the Academy of
Arcane Arts
Wielder of the Long Sword Courage

Seraph Kore
The Emerald Knight
Kingdom of Water, Thorigald
Husband of Chelsea Zarova
Wielder of Twin Sword Patience

Tolon Morr
The Amethyst Knight
Kingdom of Steel, Celidar
Former Gladiator
Wielder of Battle Axe Strength

Vallic Ultiv
The Serpentine Knight
Kingdom of Steam, Iltorp
Wielder of Scythe Harmony
Alias of Jeroch Yetre

Xaran Firesoul
The Tiger's Eye Knight
Kingdom of Knowledge, Menoris
Blind Since Birth
Wielder of Staff Faith

Ivan Quicksilver
Former Ruby Knight
Father of Gregor Quicksilver
Advisor to the Dark Court

Tutio Illik
Former Onyx Knight

Heremon Tal
Former Amethyst Knight

The Seers
Jehna Feris
The Dark Seer

Jania Maldovrin
Oldest of the Maldovrin Triplets

Jerrica Maldovrin
Youngest of the Maldovrin Triplets

Jordyne Maldovrin
Middle of the Maldovrin Triplets

The Academy of Arcane Arts
Alistair Ravenheart
Grandmaster of the Academy of
Arcane Arts
Master of Water
Imperial Sorcerer
Husband of Estelle Ravenheart
Father of Quyhn Ravenheart

Estelle Ravenheart
Sorceress
Wife of Alistair Ravenheart
Mother of Quyhn Ravenheart

Fiona Ebonsight
Master of Fire
Mother of Aris Ebonsight

Aris Ebonsight
Master of Air
Daughter of Fiona Ebonsight

Jastra Mythryn
Master of Energy

Ashinica Maupin
Master of Stone
Member of the Imperial Family

Ayden Seth
Son of Aerith Seth and Bryn Aplee

DRAMATIS PERSONAE

The Dragon Hunters

Jillian Corven
Self-Titled Lady of Cadaria
Wielder of Scaleripper
Leader of the Dragon Hunters

Kiara Aren
Dragon Hunter
Former Priestess of the Creator

Angelina Lynn Sydor
Dragon Hunter

Jacqueline Escandi
Dragon Hunter
Former Member of the Iron Legion

The Chorus

Dorovar
The Destroyer of Worlds

Pestilence
The Grey Man
Carrier of the Crawling Plague

Famine
Formerly Isabel Relin
Carrier of the Wasting Disease

Death
Formerly Ardis Franel
The Collector of Souls

Jerah
The Woman in White

The Hand of Chaos

Dimitri Sulano
The Voice of the Lost

Syren Belloch
The Priestess of Blood

Torda Safrick
The Master of Secrets

Xavier Cormea
The Corruptor of Souls

Erik Relcan
Pursuer of Lost Love
Former Personal Assistant of Hannah
Ironheart

Seraphina Masile
Second in Command of the Hand of
Chaos

The Children of the Creator

Emries
The First *Coromor*
Creator of the *Erieal*

Halicon
Formerly known as Shau-ling
Father of the Phasia

Talisia Masile
The Dark Goddess

Pyrrus

Raenera

The Court of the Dark Gods

Sadrina Annis
Queen of Mythryn
Wife of Pike Rhuiden

Darrien Annis
Half-Dark Goddess
Daughter of Pike Rhuiden

Tess Annis
Half-Dark Goddess
Daughter of Pike Rhuiden

Alderin Parran
Dark God
Son of Aryx and Diana Terian
Protector of Darrien Annis

Camille Renar
Dark Goddess
Daughter of Gwydeon and Midarin
Sandar
Protector of Tess Annis

Serrina Mistic
Dark Goddess
Voice of the Dark Council
Daughter of Jerrard and Erika Mystic

The Dark Gods

Aryx Terian
White Lightning
Fire *Erieal* of the First Generation of
the Prophecies
Husband of Diana Geoffry Terian
Father of Lissa Terian
Father of Alderin Parran
Former Host of Nightwing

Diana Terian Geoffry
Wind *Erieal* of the First Generation of
the Prophecies
Sister of Arathorn Geoffry
Wife of Aryx Terian
Mother of Lissa Terian
Mother of Alderin Parran

Pike Rhuiden
Water *Erieal* of the Second
Generation of the Prophecies
Refugee from the Dark Mirror
First Cousin of Logan Ranthall
Eldar Merin's Former Husband
Husband of Sadrina Annis
Father of Darrien and Tess Annis

Gwydeon Sandar
Brother of Angels
Husband of Midarin Rice Sandar
Father of Nathaniel Sandar
Father of Camille Renar
Also Known as Wynne

Midarin Rice
Wife of Gwydeon Sandar
Mother of Nathaniel Sandar
Mother of Camille Renar

Lissa Terian
Fire *Erieal* of the Third Generation of
the Prophecies
Daughter of Aryx and Diana Terian
Wife of Wolf Ranthall

Sabrina Binosear
Third *Chosen One* of the Prophecies
Refugee from the Dark Mirror
Daughter of Cairyn Binosear

Wolf Ranthall
Son of Logan Ranthall and Elwyne
Tamerlane Ranthall

The Forgotten
Aerith Seth
The First *Chosen One*
Husband of Bryn Aplee
Father of Ayden Seth, Cedric
Binosear, Anabel Binosear, Gideon
Viruci

Bryn Aplee
The Lady Fox
Member of the Brotherhood of Phasia
Wife of Aerith Seth
Mother of Gideon Viruci
Mother of Ayden Seth

Taya Viruci
Daughter of Gideon Viruci and Erika
Belnosian
Refugee from the Dark Mirror

Logan Ranthall
AKA Dane Rhuiden
Second *Chosen One* of the Prophecies
Brother of Korrd Ranthall
First Cousin of Pike Rhuiden
Father of Wolf Ranthall
Leader of the Order of the Flickering
Flame
Refugee from the Dark Mirror

Jerrard Mystic
Son of Basille Mystic
Husband of Erika Belnosian
Father of Serrina Mistic

Erika Belnosian Mystic
Wife of Jerrard Mystic
Mother of Serrina Mystic

Other Cast
Cole Breon
Freelance Assassin
The Living Shadow

Liandra Nightshade
Freelance Assassin
Death Blossom

Alise Modrall
Assassin

Dane Rhuiden
Monk
Leader of the Order of the Flickering
Flame

Blade
Merchant
Purveyor of Oddities

Isa Shar
Companion of Vallic Ultiv
Alias of Ellis Chandara

Evan Sinn
Inheritor of Aerith Seth's power
The Voice of the Creator
Husband of Meredith Heron

Meredith Heron
Emissary of the Creator
Wife of Evan Sinn
Murdered by Dorovar

Tera Dawnrunner
Guardian of the Council of the Winds
Guardian of the East
Last of the Tigrelle

Jander Eveningstar
Guardian of the Council of the Winds

Eldar Merin
Best Friend of Elwyne Tamerlane
Wife of Pike Rhuiden
Killed by Taron Steen at the Battle of
Taren

Heralds of the Creator
The Voice
Formerly embodied by Evan Sinn

The Will

The Wrath

The Spirit
Formerly embodied by Sabrina
Binosear

The Council of Winds
The Elder Dragon Tarot
Leader of the Council

Mariti Brightblade
Second in Command of the Council
Companion of Tarot

Khalas Skydancer
Friend of Xaran Firesoul

The Demon Dragon Shadowweaver
Chief Opposition to Tarot

Krangoth Granitewill

The Arcane Dragon Serentis

Brux Mightytide

Charnada Ivorytooth
Ally of Shadowweaver

Stormbane the Traitor
Ally of Shadowweaver

Sheyruushk Bottomdweller
Ally of Khalas Skydancer

About the Author

Brian Kershner is a life-long dreamer, writer, and problem-solver. He grew up absorbing anything and everything he could get his hands on, and as a child of the Star Wars era he constantly wanted to see the worlds beyond the little Indiana town he grew up in. There was no adventure too far, and no problem too big.

Emboldened by parents who always supported his curiosity and his thoughtfulness, Brian found himself bounding from Space Camp to Laser Summer Camp to Athletic Training Camp to Piano Lessons to Football Practice to Basketball Practice to Choir Practice and back again. Despite all of the roaming and traveling, his family remained close-knit and supportive.

Though he flirted with the idea of becoming a doctor, Brian's attentions always fell back to the computer world. He got his first computer when he was six, and not long after found his way into a word processing program and began crafting his own fantastic worlds and even more fantastic characters.

As he has grown and changed and experienced life, so too have his characters. He continues to write, craft, and create; whether it is websites for his customers, or characters and worlds for his audience.

www.ingramcontent.com/pod-product-compliance
Lightning Source LLC
Chambersburg PA
CBHW021122260626
47169CB00005B/1398